RAVES

"If you like twists and turns, you're going to LOVE Joseph Pittman's CALIFORNIA SCHEMING. The title is, for a change in crime novels, a fair description of the plot, as the reader is directed into a maze, then scales a wall of hedges only to be transported to a roller-coaster. Protagonist Todd Gleason is an imperfect, but reasonable and likable 'fixer,' who, despite his better judgment, can't refuse to help two 'best friends' from his college days a decade earlier. Great dialogue, credible supporting characters, and enough of a 'mystery-within-the-mystery' to keep you guessing through the last page of the final chapter. Highly recommended."

—**Jeremiah Healy, author of SPIRAL and TURNABOUT**

"Joseph Pittman's CALIFORNIA SCHEMING is fast, fun and wacky, with enough crooks, cheats and cons to satisfy all caper fans looking for that one big score."

—**Chris Ewan, author of**
The Good Thief's Guide to Venice

...AND LONDON FROG

"Will have readers groaning, laughing, and scratching their heads—all at the same time. Plot twists and coincidences will keep mystery lovers amused all the way to the chase's delightful end. This sassy, sexy, funny tale will please and entertain."

—**Mystery Scene magazine**

"Some people are just asking for conning. "London Frog" follows Todd Gleason, confidence man who, appalled that a filthy rich couple wins the lottery, sets out to gain a piece of the pie himself. With a strong dose of humor and a tale that spans the Atlantic, Todd's adventures bring in plenty of characters, both human and amphibian. "London Frog" is a choice pick for anyone who loves a good crime novel, highly recommended."

—**Midwest Book Review**

"Joseph Pittman's LONDON FROG is a wry, witty, page-turning caper. Grab a pint (or a martini) and settle in for a fun, fast-paced read."

—**Jeff Abbot, Edgar-nominated author of ADRENALINE**

"Fast and furious action. A final stunning climax. An extremely well done example of the genre, one that I enjoyed as I raced through it."

—**I Love a Mystery**

"LONDON FROG is a wild crime caper starring a rogue who finds his latest caper totally out of control from the moment he steps inside his temporary lodging and spins further into chaos. The support cast enhances the zaniness as they take Todd on quite a rowdy ride. Fans who appreciate something offbeat in their thrillers will enjoy Todd's tale as he struggles with who is conning whom."

—**The Mystery Gazette**

"Clever word-play and engaging characters make LONDON FROG a terrific treat. And Todd Gleason can certainly steal from me…starting with my heart. A funny, twisting plot that culminates in an Agatha Christie-like ending on helium."

—Tamar Myers, author of
THE HEADHUNTER'S DAUGHTER

"If you enjoy a crime novel with a sense of humor, you'll love Joseph Pittman's LONDON FROG. You can't help but love (Todd Gleason). A great read."

—ReviewCentre.com

"LONDON FROG is a lively romp across New York and London with a dimpled con man and his wacky cohorts. Lots of fun in the Westlake spirit and full of surprises until the final page."

—JoAnna Carl, author of
THE CHOCOLATE CASTLE CLUE

CALIFORNIA SCHEMING

ALSO BY JOSEPH PITTMAN

Tilting at Windmills

When the World was Small

Legend's End

A Christmas Wish

London Frog: A Todd Gleason Crime Novel

CALIFORNIA SCHEMING

A TODD GLEASON CRIME NOVEL

JOSEPH PITTMAN

This is a work of fiction. Names, characters, places and incidents are the product of the author's imagination or are used fictitiously. Any resemblance to actual events, locales, or persons, living or dead, is coincidental.

Vantage Point Books and the Vantage Point Books colophon are registered trademarks of Vantage Press, Inc.

FIRST EDITION: February 2012

Copyright © Joseph Pittman, 2012
All rights reserved, including the right of reproduction in whole or in part in any form.

PUBLISHED BY Vantage Point Books
Vantage Press, Inc.
419 Park Avenue South
New York, NY 10016
www.vantagepointbooks.com

Manufactured in the United States of America
ISBN: 978-1-936467-15-0

Library of Congress Cataloging-in-Publication data are on file.

0 9 8 7 6 5 4 3 2 1

COVER DESIGN BY Victor Mingovits

This one's for...

Michael Cravotta and Joey Isidro.
Thanks for showing me around town.

PROLOGUE

123

PART ONE: BERMUDA SHORTS

123

PART TWO: CITY OF ANGLES

123

PART THREE: MAMAS AND PAPAS

123

EPILOGUE

123

PROLOGUE

Fantasies live here, on the streets and in the mansions and in the star-crossed eyes of ambitious youth who seek to make this town their own. We call this place Hollywood. In reality, though, the city that bears such an idealized moniker is not much more than an old haunt for pimps and hookers and some lost, lingering hope at redemption.

And here, now, is the block that defines both the good and bad, the real and the imagined, the famed, and some say the infamous, a corner known as Hollywood and Vine. A lofty sounding address that falls trippingly off the tongue, full of beautifully bronzed names embedded in cement casing, that represents the pinnacle of a lifetime of dreams played out against screens silver and small.

What wouldn't one do for such a stake at immortality? Feel it—the applause, the adoration, the gilded gazes when you get your star on the Walk of Fame. You smile for the cameras, while inwardly you shudder at the thought of pudgy Midwesterners traveling thousands of miles to be able to say, "I just walked over Tom Cruise." All of it fans the flame of fame and the truth of the matter is this:

everyone here desires it. Because that's life in LaLa Land, where bad publicity is considered a good career move. Where modesty is always booked on an outbound flight.

This is the twenty-first century idea of the American Dream.

Unless your name is Fast Cash.

Fast Cash was a media creation. They didn't know his true identity, so they got cheeky and created a nickname that described him to a T. Fast Cash—it was a name that came too close for comfort for the city's mysterious money marauder. It was simple, an ideal thing for L.A. and even dallied on the romantic. Our own D. B. Cooper. The papers loved it too—the name was short enough to fit across front-page headlines. Moguls, movers, movie stars, even when it came to reading the newspapers they just liked to see the treatment. Not that our Fast Cash wanted the publicity; he'd rather everyone forget he even existed. Just let him go about his business, illegal as it was. Of course the same laid-back approach couldn't be said for those bank managers and tellers and those retired cops now cast as security guards, all of them like extras on the lot. These folks were his real victims, not to mention the unlucky patrons who happened to need something beyond an ATM cash-by on the day Fast Cash showed his face.

If you're not from L.A., chances are good you never heard a thing about Fast Cash. But for Angelinos who held a fascination with the darker side of human nature, whenever you saw his name in the paper or being talked about by seasoned anchor Morgan Logan of "Daily LA," it was reason to sit up and take notice. Because even though your money was FDIC insured, there was something heady about hearing that the local branch of your financial institution had been hit, that your hard-earned money from that poorly-grossing film had been hijacked. It was enough to put fear into the hearts of any B-list actor and his waiting-to-be-paid agent slash manager slash pool boy.

You see, Fast Cash had struck twenty-three banks in a twenty-three month period and had reportedly accumulated upwards of two and half million dollars. Not a dime of it had been recovered and Fast Cash remained as elusive to the cops as a celebrity conviction. The only lingering questions? "When and where would Fast Cash strike next?"

Turned out, he struck next (and last) on the final day of March, just shy of the second anniversary of his first score. And it was right here, on that faded corner of Hollywood and Vine that fate awaited him. Unlike the previous twenty-three robberies, the twenty-fourth attempt wouldn't go so smoothly and some sepia-toned legend from yesteryear would find her oft-walked-upon star suddenly, awfully, violently smeared with blood.

Here's how it probably went down, more improvised than directed.

His car was as nondescript as you get in L.A.: a silver Porsche Boxster convertible, top-down, gleaming in the day's abundant sunshine. Leave the roof up on a sunny day, you're begging for suspicion, and truth be told there was no one Fast Cash wished to attract. In this city, it was always good to be conspicuously inconspicuous. The right car, the right agent, the right job. Oh, and the right reputation, you can't forget that.

This day also seemed to come with a change in his modus operandi. Fast Cash wasn't alone, and his companion was nervously tapping four fingertips against the sleek dashboard. Something was not right. And on the 101 at this hour, there were any number of folks who could peer in and watch those fingers tapping out a tuneless song; traffic was that backed up, even in the fast lane.

"Please stop that," said the driver.

"Stop what?" asked his oblivious passenger.

Annoyed eyes stared daggers at nervous fingers. The driver shuddered. How he hated seeing that partial middle finger, the tip missing so it couldn't happily tap along with the others. But his withering glance worked. The tapping stopped.

"Sorry."

"Listen, you said you'd be okay. Your nerves wouldn't interfere with our plan."

"Yeah, I'll make sure," the four-fingered tapper replied, his voice shaking from a clear lack of confidence. Still, he made an effort. He stuffed his hands into his pockets. But then they emerged, and in one hand was a small metal flask. The man unscrewed the top, took one quick swig.

Then he smiled as he showed off his newly steadied hands.

"How comforting," the driver dryly replied.

You see, the driver was the brilliant mastermind, the passenger a mere henchman. To be successful in a town like this, you needed people. And usually these people, the so-called entourage, would never find any level of success without their leader, without their bread, their butter.

"Hey, Jack?" asked the finger-tapper.

"Yeah?"

"Are we really going through with this?"

"Christ, Marty, if you've got cold feet, you better tell me now. Because so help me..."

"No, no, sorry. I'll be fine. I need this, you of all people know how much. Can't exactly afford to lose another finger, what if I ever need to type something? Or what if my nose itches?" He showed off his damaged digit before taking another flip from the flask. Then he offered it to Jack.

"Never touch the stuff."

"Right, sorry. No more doubts. No more questions."

Now, you might be a bit confused here. The police sure would be—but only after the fact, after the robbery had been executed. In all of Fast Cash's previous withdrawals, never was there mention of an accomplice, either inside the bank or waiting in the getaway Porsche. So, why now, on this twenty-fourth and final robbery did he bring along Flaky the Four-Fingered Fiend, and why was he allowing him to knock back a few hits of hooch? Some mysteries, they are not so easily solved. Some motives, they are not so easily deciphered.

The man we now know named Jack zoomed across

three lanes of mid-morning traffic, receiving back angry blasts from fellow Freewayers. He was too busy driving to give any of them a finger in return; Marty, well, he just couldn't. Just part of the everyday in LA, just part of the routine. Jack fit in, he played it the way it should be played. In seconds, the Porsche curved around the exit ramp before being dropped into the stop-and-go motion of La Cienaga Boulevard. At the stoplight, a bottle-blonde in a BMW slid in next to them. Jack smiled her way, receiving back a look of disgust. His smile widened. To her, he was probably just another middle-aged guy jerking himself off with a fancy sports car. The illusion was perfect, because if truth be known, if she really knew who he was—how famous he was—she wouldn't be peeling rubber to get away from his leer.

"Ya gotta love this town," said the man called Marty.

"Beauty as deep as your plastic surgeon's knife."

They drove quietly for a couple more blocks before turning onto Sunset, each of them concentrating on their thoughts, their plan, and in Jack's case, his ulterior motives.

"Hey, Jack?"

"Yeah, Marty, now what is it?"

"The guilt. I'm just wondering. How do you—well, how do you rationalize it?"

"Easy, Marty, I'm guilt free. Think about it. You really think these people will miss any of their money? The amount I score in one take would be considered a huge disappointment at the box office. Anything less than a ten million dollar opening and you're done for in this town. I'm small potatoes, worse than cable television. I'm like a VH-1 reality show. So, no, there's no guilt."

Marty slumped in his seat. "Okay, sorry, no more questions. Let's just get on with it."

"Swallow your worries, Marty. Thirty minutes from now it will all be over. And you'll be that much closer to solving your problems. Now, put your gloves on and for now keep your hands in your pockets. We don't want to leave any fingerprints behind, now, do we? The only thing dirty we want to be touching is the cash."

And indeed, there was truth to that statement, they didn't need any piece of them left at the bank. But was there more to this preventative action than sheer protection? Did the man named Jack know something his friend Marty did not? Could it be this robbery was just slightly different from his other successful schemes, like a rerun cut for syndication? If this had been a script, no amount of studying his lines could have helped poor, suckered Marty.

Because Jack had rewritten the scene.

What happened next is based on surveillance video and eyewitness accounts.

Fast Cash entered the Hollywood and Vine branch of California Fidelity Trust at 10:06 a.m. He joined the line, five people back. To get to a teller took ten minutes (and there was no free toaster for the long wait), and that's when, simply, ridiculously, brazenly, Jack walked up to a teller and, in front of bullet-proof plastic shielding, insisted the woman hand over all the money from all the stations. It still wasn't his turn you see, there was someone else already at the stand, and Jack just snuck in behind him. Jack had a gun in his pocket, pointed right at the bank patron, and he claimed to the shocked teller he was not afraid to use it. The teller, a young woman who was only three weeks on the job, actually froze in her place. She didn't know what to do, she was too scared. "Actually, I was peeing my pants. But then I did as he asked," she said on the news that night, watching her performance in front of her proud parents. Yes, she did as instructed, because she could see the fear written all over the innocent patron's face. She went to each of her co-workers' stations and just started taking their money. They all gave her strange looks but no one stopped her. The rest of them were seasoned tellers and they knew what was going on. They also had been on alert that Fast Cast might be targeting them at some point during his criminal campaign. But they were all powerless to stop it, despite having those handy triggers at their desks to alert security, the police, Superman, Jerry Bruckheimer, whoever else might come to their rescue. That could come later, once the innocent patron was safe from possible injury... or worse. And so, Jack got his desired cash, lots of it in this take, and started to make his way out of the branch and back into the blazing sunlight of an L.A. morning.

That's when all hell broke loose.

The newbie teller started to scream the moment Jack hit the door. That of course alerted a couple of sloppy, somnolent-minded security guards, who sprang to action far too quickly for anyone's comfort level. Really, a yawn should not precede the drawing of a weapon. The first guard, achy knees and all, chased after Jack while wildly waving his weapon. Locals in their cars just kept driving; tourists strolling along the Walk of Fame applauded, thinking they were witnessing the making of a movie. Someone even asked, "Where's Brad Pitt? Are they filming Oceans Nineteen?" Such were their hopes. And in truth, they sort of got what they wanted, because the whole scene unfolded just like a movie, complete with realistic visual effects.

The sequence of events that followed was confusing—and certainly not consistent based on the several eyewitness accounts. But here's the gist: a man identified as Fast Cash hopped into his waiting convertible silver/gray/maroon Porsche and gunned the engine. A second man was following behind him shouting, "Wait for me." Our gun-wielding guard took aim and fired directly at the Porsche. That's when the car took a sudden swerve, as though the driver had been hit. A second bullet went wide and ended up hitting the man who'd been chasing after the car. He went down, hard, the blood from his chest wound leaking out of his body and onto the sidewalk, staining the star of a film legend that hadn't been thought of in decades. It was the most recognition she would receive in years.

Sirens could be heard all over town. People scattered, some clapped, most just stood there waiting for the director to yell cut. That's not what happened, though, because the action continued with the wounded man somehow managing to get to his feet and start off down the street. The guard couldn't keep up, not with those balky knees that had cost him the last couple years of his pension on the LAPD. But he was at least able to provide a good description of the man he shot. The bank teller added her own description. And finally, after all the confusion had died down, after the police had had a moment to break down all the facts, all the supposition and all the rumor, they admitted to being more baffled than before.

The man who was shot matched the description of the bank robber.

The man who drove away matched the description of the innocent bystander.

No one knew which man had the satchel of cash.

"In truth, we know this was Fast Cash," said an LAPD detective. "What we don't know at this point was whether that second man was operating in conjunction with Fast Cash, or was in fact, a victim. In either case, both men have disappeared and we have no leads at this point."

What the police would soon come to realize, and this realization came only through time, was that Fast Cash's reign as the notorious L.A. bank robber had come to an end. There would be no more attempts, there would be no further word from the man the press had dubbed Fast Cash. In fact, the night of that fateful, final robbery Fast Cash ended up being the lead item on the 6 and 11 o'clock news, and if you think about it, if that's not success in Hollywood then what is?

———

So what really happened? The blood found on the fabled star's star was matched with that of a gentleman from Palos Verdes Estates ironically named Jack Cashman.

When police went to his known home, his squirrelly wife, with the unlikely name of Lottie, stated she was just as surprised as anyone; why would Jack steal money when they lived in such a beautiful home and did not seem to lack for anything? And as for the man who drove that getaway car, the cops had reason to believe he was a small-time thief named Marty Beam, who has since disappeared. Again, the wife had no idea about her husband's plans. All the police had been able to surmise was that the two men had been partners in crime. But the question begged, why, after twenty-three successful, solo steals had Fast Cash brought along a partner?

"They were working together," spoke a fresh-faced detective named Ernest Dalrymple. "At least until they had all that cash in hand. That's when each other's agenda took over. There's nothing worse when partners in crime turn on each other. But really, what else can you expect from crooks." And then, Dalrymple followed up with the perfect sound bite: "If you're listening, Fast Cash, I'll get you. If not tomorrow, then someday."

And so ends the story of Jack "Fast Cash" Cashman, right?

Of course not.

Fast Cash would be back. Hollywood loves a sequel.

(Reprinted with permission from the *Los Angeles Daily News*; reported, imagined, and written by Pulitzer Prize-winning reporter Carl Beaufort; first appeared in his weekly "Carl's Column.")

PART ONE
BERMUDA SHORTS

CHAPTER 1

GO AHEAD, picture this scene and convince yourself there's any other life. An island paradise, endless stretches of sun-bleached sandy beach, blistering temperatures during the day and cool, comfortable breezes during the night. At your tanned fingertips a fruity drink, the alcohol relaxing your muscles and relieving your mind, the stresses of the real world long gone, faded into memories as hazy as the effects of that last rum swizzle. There too lies the promise of romance with each and every plane that touches down, the commitment lasting for the duration of the vacation, maybe not even that long. Just fun in the sun, love under the stars. Like it? Good, hop the next flight and money be damned, get yourself a beach towel for the day, a bar stool for the evening, a cabana that looks out over the crashing waves for the long night. Oh, and a certain someone to share it all with.

In the throes of just this kind of life, Todd Gleason was at the moment in the throes of something else. He lay on his back, elbows propping him up slightly, eyes closed to the waning sun—which was just as well, he wasn't exactly focused on his tan lines at the moment. Her head bobbed up and down, up and down again, energetically and enthusiastically, driving him wild with ecstasy. She'd been at this for days—not literally, they'd stopped to do other things, walks along the beach and eating some fine, fresh seafood, dancing to music that made their bodies sway like fronds on a palm tree, sharing stiff drinks under the moonlight. But now they were alone, and they were indulging their forbidden passions.

When they finished, the lovely lady snuggled up beside his body, almost challenging the warm temperatures to keep her from his touch. Her naked, perky breasts pressed against him while her fingers grazed through the dark hair that blanketed his chest. Todd inhaled and then exhaled, his dimpled-cheeks creasing as he sought to catch his breath. Their torrid relationship had been this way ever since she'd walked into the bar three nights ago. The lovely Lana had easily ditched the two blonde-haired friends at her side, claiming she "needed a little distraction." Todd had proved to be an enticing one.

"Don't your friends miss you?" Todd now asked.

"Oh, them. They're used to this—just like college all over again," Lana answered.

"Gee, I wish I'd gone to your college," was his easy reply.

"I've gotten better with age."

"A perfect vintage."

Lana stretched her lithe body on the big blanket. "Speaking of, I could use a drink. What do you say, Toddly, let's head on back to the Factory."

Toddly. He liked that. "I'm a bit thirsty myself. But again with the Factory? Don't get me wrong, I should pay rent on the place given the amount of time I spend there. But you and me…for us my cottage has a nice fridge, stocked with beer… and privacy?"

"Your fridge is stocked with privacy?"

"What, we're in paradise and you're giving me a grammar lesson?"

She kissed him sweetly. "Oh, but I love the Factory. I like Buzz. He's a character."

"For a grizzled old guy, yeah, Buzz rocks for sure. Okay, fine, we'll go to the Factory. What are we drinking? No more Rum Swizzles, you're making me feel like a tourist."

Lana smiled. "How about a Sex on the Beach?"

"Sounds like a drink made for two," he remarked.

Lana gave him a big smoochy kiss. "Great, a last toast at the Factory awaits us."

A last toast because Lana was soon scheduled to leave this lush island called Bermuda. To the Factory because it was where they'd met. The Factory's official name was the Buzz Factory and it was one of several watering holes in the port city of Hamilton, a place Todd had come to call his home away from a temporary home, including that serendipitous night when Lana had strolled in, an auburn-haired beauty flanked by two dark-rooted blondes. And while the other boys in the bar beamed beady eyes at the bottle-blondes, Todd's eyes had zeroed in on the rust-haired vision. Good thing too, since hers were gazing directly at him…almost through him. Buzz, standing directly behind Todd, had seen it too, that…*look*. She was a lady on a mission. So while the dozen or so guys in the bar had to fight over the two sultry friends, Todd had their luscious leader all to himself. For that moment, for five minutes later when he bought her that first drink, later that night, and ever since. Now their brief time together was coming to an end. August had given way to September, summer was winding down, the hurricanes were coming, and Lana was returning home to, as she would put it, "my so-boring life." As for Todd Gleason, he wasn't all that inclined to return home. This life suited him just fine.

"Ol' Buzz is probably blending up some dangerous concoction right now," Todd said, flashing that set of dimples which so often got him into trouble, both good and bad. "My lady?"

So they prepared to leave their secret enclave, Lana tying her bikini top back on, Todd pulling up his shorts, tossing on a T-shirt. He took Lana into his arms and gave her a passionate kiss. She kissed him back, smiling as she did.

"They should call this place Club Met," he said.

She pressed against him. "Or maybe Club Meat."

"Don't get me started—now."

She laughed. "Toddly."

Todd grabbed the blanket they'd brought with them and, hand in hand, the two of them started back down the empty stretch of beach. The crystal blue water lapped against the shore, momentarily washing their feet of residual sandy entrails. Todd thought about tomorrow, alone except for the wonderful memories. He'd met several women in the six months he'd been lounging in Bermuda, but none had captured his attention so vividly or so quickly as had Lana. She had a delicious laugh and a handy habit of touching his arm whenever that laugh rose up from her throat. Todd made sure to keep her amused; he liked her touch.

Ten minutes later they'd made their way from the beach to

Lana's hotel, the intimate and quiet White Sands, located on the southern beach known as Grape Bay. They'd spent a fine night and subsequent morning there just…was it only hours ago? Todd smiled at the thought, tossing that smile over Lana's way. She caught it, kept it.

"You know, Todd Gleason, a girl could get quite taken with you."

"Luckily for you, Bermuda means 'transient.'"

"You're bad," she said, slapping him lightly against his scruffy cheek. "Seriously, Todd, I didn't come to Bermuda to meet a guy."

"You make your vacation sound…premeditated."

"Well, I did have some things to accomplish. But you've proved to be a nice—no, make that a very nice—surprise."

"Come on," he said. "That drink—and the oncoming night—await us."

It all just seemed perfect. Which of course means it was all destined to end.

Badly…for Toddly.

TODD HAD rented one of those motor scooters that help folks more easily navigate the island's narrow, take-your-life-into-your-hands streets and so-called highways. Lana admitted to being scared to death riding one of those, but with her arms secured around Todd's hard body, she also admitted to enjoying the comfort factor. So, with their helmets on, they took off down the road, gliding their way around curves until they hit the main drag. From there, it was only about an eight-minute ride into the city of Hamilton, where cruise ships docked daily and where revelers could indulge their vacation pay on any number of tourist trappings.

Todd parked the scooter in a lot filled with others right across the street from the Buzz Factory. A small, harbor-front establishment that catered mainly to the local clientele, the Factory occasionally saw the brave tourist enter its dark, dank quarters and enjoy a taste of Bermudian intoxication. Such was the case at this hour, just past five in the afternoon with happy hour in full swing. Crass, loud-mouthed young men were playing darts, watching English football on three flat screen TVs, and drinking down the cheapest brew in town; men and women in golf shirts and khaki shorts watched these locals, no doubt envisioning what they would write on their homebound postcards: "I was the only one wearing Bermuda shorts."

As unwelcoming as the locals were, the man behind the bar—one Buzz Smith, a white-haired, thick-bearded, salt-of-the-earth-kind-of-guy—was always ready with a welcoming grin and a drink for whoever held cold hard cash in their ready hands. With his faint Irish accent and bent smile, Buzz was as much a selling point as the variety of beers he kept on tap, as rich in character as a stout was in murky colors. And at that moment, his smile widened at the sight of Todd and Lana.

"Ah, yes, the young lovers. What'll it be, champagne?"

"You only carry the cheap stuff, so no thanks, Buzz," Todd said. "Why not just make it a rum and coke for the lady, a Jameson for me."

As Lana settled into a spare stool at the bar, Todd paid for the drinks. They took hold of their glasses and raised them in that long-discussed toast. With tempting images in their minds of the afternoon just spent, of the night still to come, they clinked glasses and drank. Their moods couldn't have been better. Electricity sizzled between them, lighting up the dim bar.

So of course the moment had to end.

"Uh, Todd, my friend—I hate to spoil your little celebration…" Buzz said, his voice unceremoniously falling off.

Concern raised Todd's thick brows. Even his dimples failed him, like they knew what kind of bad news was coming just from the tone in Buzz's voice.

"You had a…uh, a visitor," the barkeep stated, that hesitancy growing.

"Buzz, in the all the months I've known you I've never seen you hold your tongue. Out with it—I had a visitor, you say. Not that I'm expecting one, but you might as well spring it on me. It's already a surprise, how much worse of one could it be?"

"Okay. Now, before I say what she said, let me describe her."

Lana perked up now. "Her?"

Todd downplayed her sudden curiosity. Still, despite the air-conditioning being on full blast, he began to feel beads of sweat form on his forehead. "Buzz?"

"One of the most gorgeous creatures I've ever set these tired eyes on, truly. Creamy skin, and with hair the color of fire, eyes as emerald as the motherland…sorry, I dabbled in poetry as a youth and when I saw her, well, let's just say she would have inspired a number of poems, and quite possibly suicides. No man could ever possess a thing of such exquisite beauty." And then came the dramatic pause. "Except perhaps the luckiest man on earth."

"Buzz?" Todd repeated. "What did this apparent Helen of Hamilton have to say?"

"She was looking for one Todd Gleason."

"Who was she?" Lana interjected.

Buzz gave Lana a look before he answered Todd.

"I only know by what she said."

"Buzz? You're killing me here."

"She said she was your wife."

The next thing Todd remembered was the stinging slap against his face. The upside was, despite the hot, lingering sting, he was cooled off immediately. Because right after feeling the sharpness of Lana's open palm against his cheek, she had thrown her drink in his face, ice and all. Not the glass, though. And then she'd promptly left the bar. The door was on a hinge, but somehow Lana managed to slam it shut. With no goodbye to "Toddly."

The bar quieted down, all eyes on Todd.

Buzz, handing Todd a fresh drink and a napkin, said, "The, uh, wife…she said to give you this envelope. So, I'm guessing you know the woman I'm talking about."

Taking the envelope, he settled his wobbly legs back down on the bar stool. That's when Todd breathed one simple, debilitating name.

"Cindy."

And then thought: how the hell had she found me?

"**MY WIFE.** That's a good one."

"It got your attention."

"It got me here, that's all."

"That's a start."

"Should we start sparring now?"

"Oh, Todd, I know it's been a few years, but surely we can skip the *un*pleasantries."

"And what, go right toward the making up?"

For the first time in the five minutes they'd been back in each other's company, the flame-haired Cindy Scanlon allowed a frown to cross her otherwise flawless face. And of course, the preceding dialogue hadn't taken a full five minutes—rather, Todd had knocked and Cindy had answered and for a good long minute neither had said a word, they'd just stared at each other, the kind of stare that only came from years of history and lots of regret.

"Why don't we just start over," Cindy suggested, opening the door to her hotel room, encouraging Todd to step inside. With a hint of reluctance and an undeniable knowledge that he couldn't resist her pull, like he was caught in the Death Star's tractor beam, he followed her lead. Before long he was inside and the door was closed and Cindy was offering him a drink. Grand Moff Tarkin was never so hospitable.

"Scotch, if I remember."

He shook his head. "I think I'll keep my wits about me. But thanks…for the offer, and for…well, for remembering."

"I remember a lot, Todd." With her lips painted blood red, her nails scarlet-stained, and her still amazing body draped in a red sundress, she was a devil in drag, and Todd couldn't help but feel her fire. As though his fingers were singed, he let drop to the floor the letter she had left for him. The one that stated where she was staying and that she would be waiting for him. No phone number, no alternate plan, as though she'd known he'd come at a moment's notice. She'd been right.

"So, what's her name?" Cindy asked.

"I don't know what you mean?"

"Silly, Todd, assuming I don't know you. The mark of her hand is still imprinted on your cheek. Sorry, was it the wife remark?"

Todd opted to say nothing and instead stepped away from her like a boxer sizing up his opponent. Wondering why said opponent was still so gorgeous, and swimming in a perfume that threatened to drown him. But he had to focus, keep up his guard. That much he remembered, too. So, digging deep into his masculine reserves, he fought to resist her devastating allure. "Actually, I'd like to ask you a few questions and I expect some honest answers."

"Todd, I've only ever been honest with you."

"Yes. Brutally honest—the wife part notwithstanding. Though I have to say, even for you that inside joke was inspired. I'm sure you had little doubt I'd know only one woman who would make such a claim. So, how is the woman who chose to marry my best friend rather than me doing?"

"Big picture, I'm fine. Little picture, I need your help."

"I didn't think it was a social call. What's Patrick done this time?"

"What makes you think he's…done something?"

"Already established—we both have memories like an elephant, Cin," he said, suddenly questioning the spelling of her truncated name. "Look, we all go back a long ways. You, me, Patrick. College chums we all were—well, chums most of the time. And even though we should have been concentrating on our studies, there was always some scheme that drew our attention away from our classes and homework and other…

activities. And Patrick was the worst. He was always trying to execute some money-making plan and more times than not they landed flatter than a body off the Empire State Building. Selling essays, seducing professors, setting up a lottery for school grants? Total busts. And I was always brought in to scrape up the mess, keep him from getting expelled. Am I to assume that's the case this time?"

"Todd, why don't I fix you that drink?"

"How about you tell me if I'm right, and then I may reconsider your offer."

She didn't like being told what to do, she never had. Todd felt a bit in the driver's seat, a rare advantage over her. So, after a slight pause, she said, "Okay, yes, Patrick needs your help. He's in over his head. But, Todd, this isn't some dumb case of expulsion, it's real grown-up stuff, you know, like life and death—maybe his death. Look, I know we have our past to deal with, and that involves Patrick and what he might think if he knew the truth about us. For now he needs your help. I need your help."

Todd could rarely, if ever, resist the requests of one Cindy Scanlon. Tonight was proving to be no exception. "Fine, you've got it. My best friend, his wife, and too much history between us all? Choice is not exactly an option. So tell me. What's Patrick caught up in now?"

"I don't know all the particulars."

"Gee, that's real helpful, Cin. And by the way, why isn't he here in person asking for my help?"

"Because he can't."

"He can't. This just gets better. Wanna explain that one?"

"It's simple," she said without looking away. "Patrick has disappeared."

Todd waited a beat before saying, "I'll take that drink now."

"Good choice. Why not wait for me on the terrace and we'll get down to business."

Todd tossed Cindy a withering look, but then did as instructed. As he opened the glass door and stepped out onto the sixth-story terrace of the Southampton Princess Hotel, he gazed out at the moonlight shimmering down on the rippling waters of the bay. He could hear voices coming from the pool—laughter and the genial sounds of soused vacationers. He thought of Lana and what she must be doing. Was she among those randy revelers? Or was she drowning her sorrows with her two friends? Maybe packing for her morning flight? Getting back at him by hooking up with some other guy? The last image faded from his mind as the world suddenly grew blurry before him, and he realized the reason for it was the glass now dangling before his eyes. He took the drink and knocked back half in one gulp.

"Sorry if I spoiled things with your latest conquest."

"It's okay," he said, his tone indicating otherwise. "She's leaving tomorrow. All we missed out on was our last night together."

"Todd, only you can take a fling and make it complicated. You never did know when they should be flung."

Todd swallowed that comment along with the rest of the burning scotch. "So, speaking of complications..."

"Right. Where should I begin?"

"The beginning," Todd cleverly suggested.

"Still the wise-ass."

"You came to me, Cindy. You know what to expect. And who."

She cast an arched eyebrow at him, as though to say "touché." Instead, she said, "Patrick owes someone half a million dollars."

Todd said nothing. His expression urged her to continue.

"Okay, gee, I thought that might get a reaction from you, but…fine, I'll keep going. I guess we'll begin with when I noticed the changes. A couple of years ago Patrick went to work for this company, Livingston Enterprises, they do something with…uh, computers, technology, IT stuff—or at least that's what he said they did. Only recently did I get the sense that the work they do is not always on the up and up. I mean, there had been clues early on, but I chose to ignore them. We were having too much fun. We were suddenly living in grand style—which in Los Angeles is no easy feat unless you're involved in either Hollywood's upper echelons, or its lower ones. Patrick had bought a fancy new car—a BMW convertible. It always has to be a convertible out there, work on your tan, talk on your cell, all while getting to your destination. Anyway, he had the car, he always seemed to have plenty of cash, and he started spoiling me with expensive purchases—jewelry, clothes, A-list restaurants, that kind of stuff. Not that I minded, you know how much I enjoy being…pampered. Patrick said it was high time he treated me like a queen. I suppose our new lifestyle also kept me from asking too many questions. So, things were great, no reason to complain. We'd even rekindled our sex life—which had started to wane after nearly seven years of marriage…sorry, you probably don't need to hear that part. Though it's hardly a surprise to you, considering…."

They had moved to the railing and both had barely looked at each other as the details of the Scanlon's glamorous new life unfolded, and now, as they reached a critical juncture of the story Todd found himself looking at the woman he always referred to as The One Who Got Away. The one who, at college, had toyed with him, teased him, and when push came to shove dumped him for the best friend who was always at their side. The reason, she claimed, was that, despite his faults, Patrick was more grounded in his ambitions, he knew what he wanted from life and could promise her more. "He has drive, Todd," Cindy had said all those years ago. "You never know what you're doing tomorrow, where your next paycheck is. Patrick at least has an idea of what he'd like tomorrow to be like. And I like the idea of his ideas."

"That's a lot of liking," Todd stated at the time.

Still, all that talk about ambition and drive and what did it get Patrick now? Some serious trouble from the sound of it, which of course left Cindy with only one place to turn. To ask for help from the one person whom she was probably most loathe to ask. For a passing second Todd felt sorry for her. Okay, second passed.

"This must have been difficult—coming to me, asking for my help."

"What's a desperate woman to do? Explore all other options or just realize the last resort is clearly the best resort?" she posed. "Todd, you're the only person who can help Patrick out of this predicament."

"Funny, after all these years I'm finally your first choice and my instincts are telling me to walk away," Todd said. And then quickly added, "But I won't. So, what do you want? Half a million of my hard-earned money, so you can pay off some goon and take the heat off Patrick?"

"Like you have that kind of cash."

Todd thought briefly of the wealthy windfall he'd scored from his London adventure, all of it nicely tucked away in an offshore account, ready for a rainy day. Last he looked, clear skies hung over the Bermudian night.

"As if," he followed up with. "So, you don't want cash. Spill it, Cindy. The real story."

"Okay. Look, last week, Patrick came home late from work—and he was not looking his best. He'd been beaten—a few bruises, a blackened eye, but thankfully no broken bones. He'd been warned, I suppose, a pretense of worse things to come. I nursed him, tried to get him to talk about what happened, but he just went to bed. When I woke up, Patrick was gone. So was one of our suitcases and a bunch of his clothes. He'd left a short note. 'Gone for help. You know who, and you know where.' Cryptic, but enough for me to know he'd gone to see you."

"Except I haven't seen him."

"Thank you, yes, I realize that, Todd," Cindy said, sarcasm dripping from her blood-stained lips. "Patrick no doubt hopped a flight to New York and went to your apartment. He had no idea you'd fled the city and were hiding out in Bermuda."

Todd excused her choice of words; fled, hide. Made him sound like such a...crook. Confidence man, sure, that had a dashing, rogue-ish quality to it. But crook? He shunned such a one-dimensional label. "So, Cindy, let me ask a couple preliminary questions before I ask—from my point of view—the all important one." She blinked her eyes and waited. "You said paying off the guy who's after Patrick wasn't enough. What is?"

"I don't really know too much of what's required. All I know is that three days ago there was a knock at my door. Some beast of a guy walks in—tall, thick, intimidating, straight out of central-casting. Asks for Patrick and I tell him he's gone, I don't know where he is. He owes something, that's what this beast tells me. 'Yeah, money, right?' I ask. 'That, sure, and something else.' Then the beast says, 'He calls, you tell him to get in touch—that is, if he values his life.' And then he was gone, faster than he'd arrived."

"Any idea what that something else is?"

Cindy stared right into his eyes when she said, "Not a clue."

"What do you want me to do, Cindy?"

"Easy. Find Patrick."

"In New York? A city of eight million people. Should I just stand in Times Square and call out his name?"

"Todd, how you disappoint me," Cindy said, suddenly moving her body in closer, the sheer material of her dress dancing close, nearly touching him. Her slender finger brushed against his lip, caressed it. Scratched at his stubbled chin. "You're a very clever and resourceful man, Todd Gleason. You always were. I'm sure your mind is already reeling with ideas."

Leaning in close enough to smell the scotch on her breath, Todd felt temptation washing over him. He reached out and pushed a stray lock of hair away from her perfect face. It was like she hadn't aged a day, that ten years hadn't somehow slipped by and they were still those raucous juniors in college, ready to take on the world, ready to one-up each other. Todd remembered Cindy as the kind of girl who didn't take no for an answer, despite the fact she was an expert at speaking the word herself. Suddenly, though, the past was tucked back where it belonged and Todd returned to this terrace and this situation… and this woman. He decided in that instant to accept her task, not for her but for his wayward friend Patrick. Because he'd rather leave the island to get him out of trouble than to attend his funeral. But he also made another decision, and that one definitely involved Cindy. Because he knew her, because he assumed she was leaving out certain details, he simply decided to not entirely trust her.

"One question," he said. "What's in it for me?"

"Todd, ever the mercenary...."

"That's not an answer."

Cindy paused, as if finally deciding what to reveal. "Let's put it this way: if you find Patrick there's a good chance that will lead to a big payoff. And yes, since I know it's you I'm dealing with, by payoff I mean 'financially.' Cash, hard and cold, and untraceable."

Now she really had Todd's attention.

"Fine," he said. "I'm in."

Cindy smiled. "I knew you would be."

Probably the first truth she'd spoken all night.

CHAPTER 2

THE DAY had started promisingly. It's ending? Not so.

As the midnight hour approached, Todd found himself suddenly alone, no Cindy and certainly no Lana. Not that he didn't welcome a moment to collect his thoughts. Life, in less time than it took for the sun to break and for night to fall, had become overly complicated. On his own since the end of his very profitable London adventure, enjoying this lush island paradise, Todd had for months called all the shots. Now, the real world was pulling him back, like some time machine had sucked him in and returned him to a place where someone named Cindy Scanlon could have encouraged him to leap off a bridge.

Hamilton was quiet at this late hour. The cruise ships were alive with action, but their gangplanks had been pulled up and only their own passengers were awake to partake of midnight buffets, late-night intoxications and all that came with such indulgences. Todd walked along Front Street, his feet scuffling against the sidewalk, clearly not pleased with the turn of events. Tomorrow he would leave, Cindy at his side. For now, he needed some down time.

That's when he saw the Buzz Factory beaming at him, a beacon beckoning him to its bar. That's just what he needed, to think and to drink in friendly surroundings. A beer to knock back, an ear to listen to his woes, Buzz was always good with both. Todd was about a block away from his oasis when, unannounced, that beacon became black. The outside light, so welcoming in this lonely stretch of night, had just been doused.

"Shit," Todd said to the quiet street.

It didn't answer, a breeze just took hold of his profanity and washed it out to sea.

Undeterred, Todd approached the Factory. Buzz had no business closing up early—but then, Buzz only did that when he had no business. Todd leaned up against the door, his eyes peering through the small pane of glass. He noticed Buzz behind the bar, furiously washing glasses and determinedly avoiding any activity at his front door.

Todd knocked.

Buzz looked up.

Todd pleaded.

Buzz relented.

Such was the friendship that had been forged between them, the symbiotic rapport of one man in sudden need and the other possessing a certain cure all. A father figure helping out his troubled son. Unlocking the deadbolt, Buzz could only sympathize with his nocturnal imbiber.

"At least the slap mark on your cheek is gone."

"My new wounds are hidden."

"Come in, my boy," the grizzled barkeep said. "You need a libation."

"What I need is to erase the day. Or, at the very least the second half of it."

Buzz slid a chilled bottle of Newcastle Brown Ale his patron's way, and Todd caught it just as he settled onto his barstool, a slim Norm Peterson with dimples. Todd took a quick pull, knocking back a good third of the bitter in one eager gulp.

"Two gorgeous women fighting over you, I can see why you'd need to pound down a few beers in an effort to forget," Buzz said, his sarcasm dripping like summer humidity. "Wanna talk about it?"

"In a sec—let me sip at my beer, visit with my old friend."

"You do that, I'm gonna get the lights in the back."

Now, most bartenders would assume "old friend" meant indulging a private moment with the drink before him, but not so with one Todd Gleason. Sure, he liked his beer. He liked his true companion, his pet, even more. Moving behind the bar, Todd approached the ten-gallon fish tank that was positioned on a ready-made shelf above an ancient cash register. With each sale, the arm of the cash register shook the tank and gave the water a little ripple, enlivening its only tenant. That tenant was, obviously, of amphibious nature. A frog. In this case, an aquatic one, who went by the handy name of Toad. For five months, ever since Todd and Buzz had formed their somewhat paternal relationship, Toad had called the Buzz Factory his home. Toad was a social frog, he liked the activity that came with bar-life. It he could talk, he'd say the Factory was much better than hanging out at Todd's cottage, where the only action he saw was the action Todd saw.

Todd rapped his knuckles against the side of the glass. His pet, seemingly down for the night, reacted to his owner's presence. Big eyes blinked back at Todd.

"Looks like I'm going to have to go away for a little while. Again."

Toad blinked.

"Yeah, I know. I left you for a bit last winter. But we've had a great time since then, living the good life in Bermuda. And you have to admit it, you've got it so much better here than in my tiny apartment in New York. Look at all the friends you've made at Buzz's. So, take care, Toad, and remember," Todd said with a wink, "My secrets are your secrets. Keep 'em that way. And don't forget, I'll be back. You know that, I always come back."

Toad blinked again. Then he just swam away, because that's what frogs do.

"You're so right. Thanks, Toad."

"Ya done talking to that there damn frog?" Buzz had come up behind them, tossing his barkeep's apron under the bar. His ever-changing accent had taken on a noticeably East End tone. "I swear boy, I just don't get what it is with you and that frog of yours. He's a good conversation piece on a slow night, sure, but you seem to think he really listens to you. So, what gives?"

"He's my good luck charm."

"Didn't seem to be working tonight."

"*Au contraire*, Buzz. Toad had some good advice for me."

"Yeah, what's that?"

"A frog always trusts its instincts, comes second nature to them. We fallible humans could learn a thing or two from our amphibious friends. So often our emotions get the better of us. So, I just need to heed his advice, follow the twists life hands me but always act on my instincts and stay aware."

"Looked to me more like he was turning his back on you," Buzz said.

"Gee, thanks."

"This got something to do with your, uh, wife?"

"She's not my wife, Buzz. But I think you knew that."

"Yeah, but whoever she is, she sure has got you jumping through hoops. Let me guess: you went over there and asked how many," he said. "Cause that woman had the look of someone who needed a favor. And by that I mean a big favor—considering she flew all the way here to track you down. A woman like that, she knows how to use her feminine wiles." Buzz paused. "I'm getting the sense you're about to ask me for a favor all your own."

Todd stole one last look at Toad. Rapped on the glass like it was code. "A simple one. I want you to take care of the frog for a couple of weeks. Looks like my island escape has come to an end—for now. Time has come for me to start figuring out where I go from here. But before I do, a friend needs my help and..."

"Whoa, hold on there, my boy. I got no problem dropping some pellets into the water and feeding your little froggie, but truth be known that's all I need to know about what's going on. The island tends to attract people who don't want to know from the real world, that's what's made living here these five-some years so ideal for me—and I can guess these past months have had a similar effect for you. I don't ask questions, Todd—not about money, not about motives, and not about any mischief someone might be up to. Keeps me just serving drinks and playing out life as I see fit."

"Sounds nice."

"Give it thirty years, play your cards right and you'll get there. For now, I think it's probably a good idea you venture off our fair island, a boy with your obvious talents, he can get soft here, complacent—and that's never a good thing. Do what you gotta do and don't worry nothing about your frog." Buzz poured himself a shot of whiskey, served up Todd a second Newcastle. "But seeing as though I'm older and therefore far wiser, time for you to do some good and listening. Let me just caution you some. About women."

With the lights on dim and the alcohol beginning to swim in Todd's bloodstream, he felt the world darkening, like the distance was fading from his view and all he could concentrate on was the here and the now—and the warning. Maybe it was that word—*women*—that brought on that effect, because he sure as hell fell victim to their charms easily. Too easily. "Yeah, I know, avoid 'em."

"Oh, no, my boy. You keep having that fun. Just don't let them in here," he said, poking at Todd's chest. "Not till you meet the right one, and are sure of it. Until then, stay wary and trust 'em as far as you can throw them. Take that Lana—sure, she was pretty and innocent, on the surface. But no woman who slaps like that is all pure sugar cane sweetness. And I only had to take one gander at that so-called wife of yours to know she was trouble with a capital you-know-what. So, whatever it is she's asking of you, know that she hasn't told you everything."

Todd nodded, letting the old man's hard-earned wisdom sink in before considering his next question. "Hey, Buzz?"

"Yeah, what's that?"

"Was there ever a Mrs. Buzz?"

Buzz sidled right over to Todd and placed a meaty hand on

Todd's cheeks, making sure the boy was "good and listening." Todd took one look at the mangled digit where his middle finger should have been. When he'd first noticed it, it had kind of creeped him out. Now he was accustomed to it, just part of the mystery that enveloped Buzz. "You see that sign above the outdoors, saying 'Established 2004?' That goes not just for the Buzz Factory, if you catch my drift. Before that time, this old bar belonged to someone else and it held someone else's memories. You want to know something else, it had a different name. Get it?"

"Got it," Todd said.

"Good," Buzz said. "Now go on and git. The mainland awaits you."

Todd was sorry to be leaving Buzz. He'd never really known his own father, not since that proverbial cigarette run back when Todd was five, and certainly he had never bonded with any elder statesman who could impart such genuine, world-weary wisdom. Advice like that could save your ass, especially when you had the taste for the con and you lived your life somewhere between honest citizen and sneaky opportunist.

Todd realized that description didn't only apply to himself.

As he sucked down the remains of his beer, one question ran though his mind: Patrick Scanlon, what have you gotten me into?

FIRST THING he noticed, his hair looked damned good—dark, thick, slightly tousled. He didn't feel good about himself until he was satisfied that his hair was just so. He was convinced it was the source of his luck. Second thing he noticed were the worry lines beginning to crease his forehead. He stole a look back into the mirror opposite him, looked north of those worry lines and attempted a smile again. The heck with the lines, the follicle gods sure had been good to him. Third thing he noticed: he was far from Los Angeles and still nowhere near to finding a solution to his problem.

Fall in New York City, where all the leaves were brown—not to mention yellow, orange, and a certain trashy grime color. Night was falling, giving the sky a gray pallor. The workday was done, regular folks with regular jobs were returning home to fix dinner and watch the latest reality craze dance across their television screen, go to sleep and then wake up and do it all over again. Traditional, unassuming, unexciting, even in the city that never sleeps there existed people who lived for their pillows.

Patrick Scanlon missed such a predictable life. But home and his former life were far from his mind, leaving him concerned only with the here and now. Wondering where his notoriously self-sufficient, go-with-the-flow, hard-to-track-down friend had gone off to. Todd Gleason's darkened apartment windows had stared back at him when he'd gone looking for him, and now, three nights later nothing had changed. Todd never did like adhering to anyone's schedule but his own, which meant Patrick had little choice but to wait for Todd's eventual return. He was camping out on the Upper East Side and he was beyond frustrated with his no-show of a friend. Didn't he know he needed his help? Sense it? Or better yet, couldn't he at least check his phone messages? Really, something had to give.

"More coffee, sir?"

"Oh, yeah, sure. I guess."

A dejected Patrick was sitting in a booth inside a diner on the corner of 89th Street and Second Avenue in Manhattan. Considering that the last two nights he had ended up staying beyond twelve a.m., he was thankful for the diner's all-too-convenient name. Midnight Express. The owner had come up with a handy slogan: The Neighborhoods 24-Hour Place. On the second night lazing about the diner, Patrick had wanted to grab a pen and stencil in the needed apostrophe.

The waitress refilled his coffee cup before removing the remnants of his late-hour dinner of Souvlaki. What was in it was all Greek to him, but it sure tasted fine. Healthy, stick-to-your-ribs fare, the kind of food he wouldn't be caught dead eating in L.A. where, ribs were something you had removed during surgery. The drawback was the heavy food made him sleepy, and the caffeinated coffee just wasn't packing as much punch as he would have liked. This numbing waiting around was draining, attacking his already fraying nerves. His eyes might want to shut tight for the night, but his fingers were doing a little tap-dance on the Formica table, the constant beat doing its best to keep his mind alert.

Being alert. That was a good thing. Especially now, watching the entrance to the diner. The door had just opened and in walked two of the most imposing figures Patrick had seen this side of *Easy Rider*. The first of them was large, probably six four and thickly-built, dressed all in black, tattoos on his bare arms and a dome so gleamingly bald you'd think he was Mr. Clean out for a night at the leather bars. The second guy was probably a foot shorter, but his body was just as thick and his face, with its bushy mustache and bristly cheeks, appeared to have scared off a razor a couple of weeks ago. Separately they were intimidating, together they were downright scary, and what made their presence at the Midnight Express diner all the worse was the fact that their beady, suspicious eyes had zeroed in on some guy sitting alone in a booth. Patrick realized he was that guy sitting alone in a corner booth.

His heart skipping a beat, he decided the better part of valor was to stop drawing attention to himself by staring at them. He looked away. As for the two burly men, they walked right past Patrick and sat down at a booth on the other side of the diner. He heard them order power shakes with a side of bacon.

Patrick drank his coffee. The infusion of fresh caffeine into his bloodstream did nothing to calm his racing heart, and his nerves tossed his dinner around in his churning stomach. That's when he felt a bead of sweat attach itself to his upper lip. Maybe it wasn't the caffeine making him sweat, maybe it wasn't the Souvlaki making him green, but the stolen looks he was getting from Hulk and Mini-Hulk. Questions peppered his mind: Friends? Foes? Were they following him? Wanting to hurt him? Who sent them? Who knew he was here? None of the questions good, all of the answers decidedly unfavorable.

Oh, and one more question: what to do about them?

The answer? Beats the crap out of Patrick.

That, of course, was what Patrick was ultimately afraid of. He'd already suffered one beating last week, and he wasn't all that keen on the experience. Here he came to New York to find Todd and lose himself in the anonymity of the city, and instead he had come up empty with his friend and somehow had been discovered by rejects from the WWF. What luck.

From his booth, Patrick let out an unavoidable laugh.

Luck.

Now if that wasn't a four-letter word, he didn't know what was. Nothing seemed to be going his way lately, and this impulsive decision to fly to New York City seemed right in line with the events of the past week, going from bad to worse to… what was worse than worse? Fucked, he thought.

Now, though, he had to make a decision and he needed to stand firm. And that decision was to slip into the night and try to elude these two thick-necked thugs. Unless of course his mind was just working overtime from being over-tired, maybe these guys just really needed that power shake to make it through an all-nighter. He stole a look at them, and the large one stared back at Patrick, folding his arms while doing so, flexing a set of incredibly impressive biceps. Perhaps this Popeye enjoyed Souvlaki too.

Just then Mini-Hunk scrambled out of the booth and made his way to the bathroom. In the silence of the late-night diner, Patrick could hear the click of the lock. This was his moment, time to make his move. Rising from the comfort and safety of his booth, he made his way toward the back of the restaurant, seemingly making as though he too needed the restroom. Hulk watched as Patrick stationed himself right near the men's room door. The big guy looked away, perhaps figuring Patrick couldn't go anywhere too far, not with the little guy so close by. And that's when Patrick pulled a fast one.

You see, Patrick, having already spent two nights inside the diner, had had time on his hands and given his propensity for tricky spots, he'd scouted out an emergency exit. So that's what he did, pushed open the door near the rear exit. The wash of cool night air rushed in, blowing napkins off the empty tables and eliciting a "hey" from not only the management but from

Hulk. Just then the door to the bathroom opened and the little guy joined the big guy and together they went running out the emergency exit.

As for Patrick, he watched the two bumbling beasts leave while he himself stood behind another door, this one the swinging set that led to the kitchen. Two waiters and a man in the big white chef hat behind a grill stared at him, all of them waiting for him to explain his presence in their sacred territory.

"Just wanted to say how much I enjoyed the Souvlaki, really, my hat's off to the chef."

The chef kept his hat on.

Then Patrick bolted from the kitchen, making his way out that same emergency exit he'd faked exiting before. By now he hoped those goons had realized he'd given them the slip and were probably regrouping at the front entrance. That's just what Patrick saw before he went tearing up 89th Street in an effort to lose himself on the streets of Manhattan.

His mind was racing. Okay, he'd proved one thing, that indeed someone was looking for him and that someone had sent the muscle-duo to find him. How they'd known to find him at the diner had him worried, because that meant whoever wanted him knew more than he expected them to know. They knew about Todd, where he lived, and they knew Patrick was waiting for him.

Patrick patted the inside of his jacket pocket, making sure the envelope he'd secured was in fact, well, still secure. It was. Good. If he was caught with it, that wouldn't be ideal, this was his ticket out of his current predicament—but he needed reinforcements, and that's what he'd come for in the person of Todd Gleason. Patrick realized there was no time to think of the consequences of his actions. He just needed to separate himself from the envelope's contents.

Doubling back along 91st Street and down a couple blocks, Patrick eventually made his way to Todd's apartment building, hiding in the shadows and keeping his eyes wide and alert. So far he saw no sign of his new workout buddies, but that didn't mean they weren't lurking around the near corner. Just then he saw a person approaching Todd's building; a man with a knapsack and a brown leather bomber jacket. Under the streetlights Patrick saw a balding head; couldn't be Todd. A neighbor? Maybe that would work.

As the man approached the building and withdrew a set of keys, Patrick boldly walked up behind him. Now, Manhattanites are suspicious folks by nature, and so it came as no surprise that Baldy turned around to see just who was creeping up on him.

"Oh, hey, I'm looking for Todd Gleason, he lives up on five," Patrick said. Might as well start with honesty and see where that got him.

"Haven't seen him around in awhile," the man said with a surprising jovial tone.

"Look, I just got into town and…"

"I'm not letting you in the building." Jovial only goes so far.

"No, no, I wouldn't ask such a thing…look, I owe him some money and I promised I'd drop it off in person, but he doesn't seem to be around. Could I leave something for him with you?" Patrick asked, withdrawing a letter-sized envelope from his pocket. "Just slide it under his door? Could you do that for me?"

The man looked at the innocent-looking envelope. There was no writing on it. He looked back at Patrick. His face didn't seem to say anything either.

"Yeah, okay, why not," the man said, all neighborly again. "We folks who live in doormen-free buildings have to look out for each other. I hate when I come home and find one of those UPS labels saying sorry we missed you."

"Thanks, I appreciate it."

With that, the envelope exchange was made, the neighbor went his merry way into his home, and Patrick breathed a huge sigh of relief. One that was, admittedly, short-lived. Because Patrick noticed newfound company striding down the dimly-lit street. Two huge shapes, their shadows seemingly possessing their own shadows. He could allow himself to get caught now, seeing as though he no longer possessed the envelope, right? But then again, they could always beat the truth out of him.

And that's when Patrick made a run for it.

And that's when the two men set chase after him.

Now, the thing about fine Manhattan folk is, sometimes people just like to mind their own business and even when they see a fellow neighbor in trouble they seldom do something about it. Which is why the sight of one man being chased down a darkened street by two thugly men gave no one pause. No cell phone calls were interrupted, and the bum digging through trash didn't even look up. A cab honked at Patrick as he crossed against the light, but that was the only involvement from anyone.

As he made his way to First Avenue, barely escaping the grill of another cab, Patrick chanced a look back. The two thugs had started to make their way across the broad avenue, but were stopped by the passing of the accordion-like M15 bus blocking the view. So, Patrick slipped down 87th Street, where he stumbled upon, of all things, a church. Sanctuary, he thought.

And so he raced up the stairs and went into the church, which thankfully was open. In the glow of candlelight, he made his way to one of the confessionals and slipped in, literally praying not to be discovered.

Wiping sweat from his brow, trying to silence his heaving chest, he had to hope that his pursuers had not seen the exchange between him and Todd's neighbor. Please let the excitement of the night be over. He allowed a few minutes to pass, in which time his breathing returned to a regular pattern, enabling him to keep a listen to the sounds inside the church. All was quiet; even the silence echoed, instilling within him a sense of calm.

The creak of the entrance door jerked his head up. He gave a listen as heavy boots hit the tile floor. One step, then another. Then another. Was that one person, or two? Was it a priest come for a midnight ablution, or someone else about to commit a mortal sin? Patrick burrowed further down into the confessional, kneeling on the cushion, his face against the mesh that separated sinner from forgiver. He looked down, and that's when he noticed his foot sticking out from the maroon curtain.

"Shit," he said aloud, and then quietly apologized for his language.

Still, that didn't keep God from handing out His penance.

The curtain was drawn back and Patrick looked up from his kneeling position. The big Hulk loomed even larger, more imposing. Lou Ferrigno on steroids.

"Patrick Scanlon?" the man asked.

Patrick could only nod.

Just then the little guy came up behind his partner. "Good job, Barney," he praised.

"Thanks, Fred."

And then, shock of shocks, Barney leaned down and planted a nice wet, lingering kiss on Fred's lips.

Patrick's eyes blinked once, then twice. Had he just seen what he'd seen? Then, despite his circumstances and the risk of retribution, he couldn't resist himself. "Uh, guys, do you really think you should be doing that…you know, in a place like this?"

In the shadow of the crucifix, the Hulk now named Barney grabbed Patrick by the collar and lifted him out of the confessional.

Patrick felt his dinner rising in his throat.

Fear had a way of doing that.

A DATE with destiny and a morning departure with Cindy Scanlon came quickly for Todd Gleason. His sojourn in Bermuda had come to an abrupt end, and never in his wildest dreams had he imagined he'd be leaving this particular island with this particular woman at his side, not unless it was their honeymoon and Todd just happened to be dreaming.

They'd agreed to meet at the airport and when Cindy caught sight of Todd getting out of the taxi about ten minutes past the arranged time, she wagged one of those scarlet-drenched fingers at him. "You're late. Though truth be told, you're earlier than I expected. Part of me had you pegged as a no-show."

Todd, ever so confident about his lack of confidence with Cindy, said, "No, you didn't."

"Oh, Todd, leave it to you to put a negative spin on this situation," she replied, kissing his rarely but now clean-shaven cheek. "Come on, let's check in."

Bermuda International Airport was brightly colored, and the sun streamed though the sheer plate-glass windows with streaks of appealing rainbows, as though calling out to departing tourists to not leave behind the island's temptations just yet. Todd, pulling his packed suitcase behind him, gazed about the semi-empty terminal.

"Looking for someone?" Cindy asked.

"Just people watching," he said, a hint of wistfulness to his voice. "Let's just get this over with, okay, Cin?"

"Face it, Todd. She's gone, just take your torrid little thing for what it is. Or was. You and she will always have Bermuda. But you'll never meet again."

"Ever the romantic," he said dryly.

Cindy decided the conversation was over. Silently they made their way to the U.S. Airways counter and hopped on the short line. Five minutes ticked by and then finally they were called forward to the waiting ticket agent.

"Hi, folks, I hope you had a lovely time on our island," the woman said, a slight British lilt to her voice. "Where are we flying to?"

Simultaneously the women heard, "Los Angeles" and "New York."

For a moment she was confused, there's no such place as Los York.

Todd looked at Cindy and found Cindy staring right at him.

"You said you would book your flight," she said.

"I did, to New York."

"Todd, you're coming to Los Angeles—with me."

"You said Patrick was looking for me. Where else would he go but to where he thinks I live? And where I do live?"

"Yes, that all sounds very logical, but..."

The ticket agent interrupted the volley. "Excuse me, if the two of you want to settle this and I can help the next person in line?"

"No, no," Todd said, thrusting forward his passport with purpose. "I'm traveling to New York, booked on the nine-thirty five. Gleason is the last name." Cindy, standing behind him and obviously not pleased with this turn of events, was curtly instructed to step back in line. As they were not traveling together, she'd need to wait for the next agent.

She did as asked, the words "not happy" slipping out from between her ruby lips. Todd couldn't help but allow a slight smirk. He'd won a rare victory. Yet as he was being handed his boarding pass and the agent was smiling at him and wishing him a great flight, he couldn't help but feel a false sense of security. Cindy Scanlon was not one who allowed anyone the upper hand for long.

As he cleared the counter, Cindy was called next. The check-in process went smoothly, Cindy would fly to Washington and from there get her connection to L.A. Before long Cindy was back at Todd's side and they were heading toward security.

"Frankly, Cin, I thought you had booked a flight to New York, too, I thought you wanted to help me find Patrick. You know, you and me as a team, like old times?"

Cindy was about to respond when suddenly Todd was no longer interested in her answer. He had stopped dead in his tracks. Because about ten people in front of him, just about to pass through the security checkpoint, were the two blonde friends that Todd had seen Lana with that first night at the Buzz Factory. Immediately he began to search out the line for the lovely Lana, the results not in his favor. She was nowhere near her friends; perhaps she'd already slipped through security and he'd missed her by mere seconds? That sounded right, right? He started to get antsy, waiting in a line that moved in slow motion.

"We'll continue our discussion once we pass through those machines. For now, can you cool it, Mr. Itchy Pants?" Cindy asked. "I hate attracting attention at the security point."

This from a woman dressed for the Devil's Prom.

Her words, though, had the desired effect. Todd stopped looking, not only for Lana but for her blonde friends, both of whom had seemingly been sucked into the great timeless void that is an airport terminal, the gates a mere portal between the now and the then, the here and the destination. In other words, Blonde #1 and Blonde #2 were gone. And like that, seemingly so too was his opportunity to explain his situation to Lana. He hated how their fling had ended, he flotsam, she jetsam, the waves of life tossing them in opposite directions.

Todd and Cindy passed through the security checkpoint without incident, and so, with shoes back on their feet and radiation possibly coursing through their systems, they headed toward their respective gates, side by side by silent.

"Look, Todd, I'll allow this—for now."

"Allow what? My returning to New York? It's a little too late for that, sweetheart, I've already got my boarding pass. Besides, you're the one who flew all the way across the country to get me to come back into your lives, so you can hardly have a problem with…" That's when a sudden realization came over Todd and words became difficult to pronounce, difficult to find, really.

Cindy merely looked at him, waiting for his apparent stroke to pass.

"You did it again," he finally said.

"I don't know what you're talking about…"

"Save it, Cindy, innocence doesn't dress like you," he said. "Last night you might have caught me by surprise—perhaps my guard was down and I let you too easily pull my strings—but now it's time for a reality check. Time to fess up and tell me what's really going on. What do you really want from me?"

"It's simple, I told you. I want you to find Patrick."

"In L.A. But you say he's in New York. Funny how your two plus two equals three. Suppose I fail in my mission and Patrick remains AWOL. What's the back-up plan?"

Before she answered the boarding call for Todd's flight to New York came over the speaker. "Cin? I gotta go."

Petulance was written across her face. "So go, Todd, fly back to New York and pull your hero act again, find my wayward husband. But hear this: you have three days and, successful or not, you then have to join me in Los Angeles. I'll arrange for your flight out West, and you had better be on it."

"What happens in three days?"

"I need Patrick in Los Angeles. Or else."

"Or else what?"

"Or else I need you in Los Angeles. Impersonating Patrick."

There it was again, that mini-stroke that cost Todd the ability to speak. It wouldn't be the last time that morning, either. When Todd parted ways with Cindy, her intriguing words ringing inside his brain, he boarded the plane only to discover he was on the same flight as Blonde #1 and Blonde #2. There he learned a shocking series of truths: they were from Long Island, not the South, they'd come to Bermuda to deepen their tans and heighten their blondeness, and here was the big one: they had only just met Lana at the hotel.

"She paid for all our drinks," said Blonde #1.

"And all we had to do was pretend to be her friend," said Blonde #2.

Todd said nothing, which also happened to be the sound of dumbfounded.

He'd had his fill of what any and all women had to say lately; truth seemed a challenge too great to overcome. Right then and there he reminded himself to stay far away from blondes, brunettes, and thinking of Cindy, of Lana, definitely redheads. That left him with little choice; no choice, really. Gee, just like his current situation.

Just then Todd felt the rush of the plane taking off, shooting safely into the sky.

Too bad, he wouldn't have minded crashing to the ground right about now.

CHAPTER 3

PATRICK SCANLON'S disembodied voice filled Todd's apartment, almost as if he was actually there. Would have been nice to see his old friend in the flesh, that way Todd could ensure that only his voice was separated from his body and not other, more vital parts. He had an image of legs in limbo, the rest of Patrick unable to catch up to them.

"*Hey, Todd…where are you? It's Patrick and I…shit, where do I begin? Not on the machine, I don't. Call me.*" Then he left a number.

"*Hey, Todd, where the fuck are you? I've been in town for two days, still no word from you. Call me. Same number.*"

"*Hey, Todd…what's the deal, don't you have a cell phone, don't you check messages?*"

Truth of the matter was, yes, Todd did have a cell phone but he hardly used it and almost never gave the number out. He also didn't have that many friends, mostly by choice, and so when he disappeared for weeks or months at a time, checking his home machine wasn't high on his list of priorities. But explaining all that to Patrick would take time, and right now Todd had no clue where Patrick was.

He'd phoned the cell number Patrick had left. And it had gone straight to voicemail.

So Todd, back home in New York all of two hours and stewing in his apartment, had nothing to do but wait, filling his time by endlessly playing Patrick's several messages and hear the increasing panic in his voice. Credit Cindy with knowing her husband: yup, he was in trouble, and he was in New York, and he needed Todd's help.

He took his finger off the answering machine, plopped down on the sofa, and then he sighed.

"Now what?" he asked the room.

The room said nothing, and that felt weird. Not that he expected answers from inanimate objects, it's just Todd was accustomed to having his pet, Toad, keep him company, answering his questions with a blink of his big, amphibious eyes, a plink of water. Nope, this time out, Todd was truly alone.

Or maybe not.

A knock came at his door. He turned toward it with surprise.

"Who is it?" he called out from the sofa. His eyes darted about, as though looking for an escape route. Patrick's messages had imbued him with a sense of paranoia already.

"Oh, it's your neighbor, Bob…from 5D."

Todd relaxed. Just his overly friendly neighbor who lived in the apartment behind him. Their bathrooms backed up against each other (and sometimes literally backed up together).

Todd made his way over to the door and opened it, where he was greeted by the bald, bespeckled, beer-gutted bear of a man who'd been a boarder in this building for decades. They didn't exactly hang out, but they'd shared a few drinks over the years, the neighborly thing to do, right?

"Hey, welcome back," Bob said.

"Thanks."

"Look good, nice tan."

"My business trip had certain fringe benefits," Todd said evasively. "So, what can I do for you?"

"Oh, right. Yeah, heard you knocking about in your apartment, so figured should bring this over. Someone dropped this off—well, tried but you weren't home and so I offered to hold onto it until you got back. Though truth be known, I had no idea when you were returning, it's been awhile since I've seen you."

Todd tried to process everything his neighbor had just said. That was a lot of words and he wasn't sure if there was meaning in any of them. He'd figure that out later. For now he took the proffered offering. An envelope, no lettering on the front or, when he turned it over, on the back.

"What is it?"

"Envelope."

"Gee, you think? I mean, where did it come from? You say a friend of mine?"

"Yeah, came by a couple days ago, asked that I give it you."

Was it him, or did this guy speak with a lack of pronouns?

"A friend? Male, female?"

"Oh, yeah, male. About your height...dark hair, curlier than yours. Looked sort of like you, but had uh, I don't know, a worried look on his face."

Lack of pronouns aside, Todd knew the description well: Patrick Scanlon.

"Thanks, Bob, I appreciate it."

"No problem. Seemed really worried."

Who? Todd wanted to ask. He'd go on the assumption he meant Patrick. Still, were full sentences too much to expect?

"He's been waiting for me to return home, but I was delayed. Look, Bob, I appreciate your helping out my friend by holding onto this till I got back. I'll take it from here."

That last line was Todd-speak for dismissal, and Bob finally picked up on it. He said goodnight, welcome back, let's have a drink soon, etc, and Todd said sure, can't wait, my place next time, and then he watched as his neighbor walked down the hall and went back inside his apartment. He heard the lock turn behind him.

Which made Todd think about his own lock. Bending down, he examined both the bottom lock and the top, checking for signs of any forced entry and scratches, perhaps made by lockpicks. Maybe Patrick had tried to get in, or maybe someone looking for Patrick? What he came up with was this: nothing. Nary a scratch, nary a hint of invasion. But he knew his friend had come to the building, how else had he encountered neighborly Bob?

That reminded him of the envelope in his hand. "Interesting."

He ripped open the plain white envelope and found inside two sheets of paper. One of them was a schematic drawing with a series of lines on them and a big X. He dismissed that one in favor of the sheet that had actual words on it. It was a printout from the *Los Angeles Daily News*, with the headline, "Fast Cash—The Final Word?" Written by a staff columnist named Carl Beaufort. Todd quickly scanned the article, and then wondered aloud, "Who the hell is Fast Cash?"

And what does the story of a bank robber from seven years ago have to do with Patrick Scanlon and his apparent disappearance?

Todd took another look at that first piece of paper, the drawing. It looked like the floor plan for a house, with an emphasis on the lower level—the basement, where the big "X" marked the spot. He couldn't help but think this was a map of sort, leading him to what…a treasure? He thought of Cindy's words about a fortune waiting to be found and he had to think her comment and this map were more than coincidence.

For the first time in months, Todd saw dollar signs, and maybe just another generous and untraceable paycheck. He liked those, they kind of come tax-free. This case had suddenly piqued his interest; or is that self-interest?

He thought again: Somewhere out there existed three million dollars in unrecovered money. He had a few thoughts about that.

First thought: wow, three million dollars.

Second thought: finding it could be nothing but trouble, a financial Pandora's Box.

Third thought: yeah, but wasn't three million dollars worth the price of admission?

WHILE TODD decided what to do about Patrick, he knew the time had come to spring into action. He sat down at his desk, fired up the laptop, logged online, and through the simple beauty of a Google search he'd found more information than he needed regarding an L.A.-based bank robber of yesteryear who went by the less-than-witty name of Fast Cash. Correction, the nickname wasn't his doing but had first been coined by that reporter. The rest of the press had taken his lead, so to speak, and so after twenty-four robberies, Fast Cash's name had not only stuck, it had become legend. Todd was surprised to find that no one had done a television special on the case, like the E! Network's True Hollywood Story. The story was rife with all that made reality television so repugnantly fascinating—crime, pseudo-celebrity, scandal, mystery, and something Hollywood seemed especially adept at: a thoroughly unsatisfying payoff. Because the question begged: what really happened to Fast Cash?

Todd leaned back against the back of his chair, absorbing all he'd just read. Some articles were short, especially those about the early robberies; before the two-year epidemic had taken on such newsworthiness. Many of the accounts were dry and lacked any of the romance of the crimes, and Todd figured that ate at Fast Cash's craw. Where's the glory in an article that follows the rules of Who, What, When, Where, and Why? In fact, the most interesting feature Todd came across was also the most recent one, penned just six weeks ago, and it put a fresh take on a chapter in L.A. history that barely required a footnote, much less a retrospective. And it happened to be written by that same reporter who had come up with the nickname: Carl Beaufort, still of the same daily. Looked like Beaufort was now a regular columnist, free to write about what interested him, and after seven years Fast Cash seemed to still fill that bill.

CARL'S CORNER: "WHO'S TO BLAME??"
By Carl Beaufort, Daily News Columnist

Seven years ago, I lost some money—and so did you. As a loyal customer to California Fidelity, I'd had the same account longer than I'd been with some women. That's loyalty. So, why then didn't the bank return that sense of loyalty when it came to the matter of their Public Enemy #1: Jack "Fast Cash" Cashman?

Surely you remember Fast Cash. He's the guy who made off with nearly three million dollars and on his last mission was shot and killed—supposedly. As a journalist, I'm expected to be impartial and to deal only in the facts, and back when I had the crime beat I tried my best to stick to the facts as presented to me. The joy of being a columnist is, I get to write what I want and toss my opinion around like one of those talking heads on the cable news channels. So back to that "supposedly" comment of mine. Fast Cash was definitely shot that morning in early September, the blood on the ground matched his, and his picture was identified in security cameras and then verified by his wife, Lottie Cashman.

But since that fateful morning, Jack Cashman has disappeared. No body has turned up anywhere, and none of the money has either. Did Fast Cash pull another fast withdrawal—this one of his own doing? Or did he just deposit himself far, far away and live out his existence with the comfort of my (and your) money?

If the "widow" Cashman knows, she ain't saying. Except, maybe she is. A recent court filing has Lottie petitioning to have her husband declared legally dead, and if she gets her wish, well, won't that just be the final nail in the coffin of Fast Cash's life? He'll be dead, and you know, he'll still be rich. Now, if the court allows such a travesty of justice, we'll have no one to blame but California Fidelity.

Oh, you wondered when I would get back to them, didn't you? You see, my beef is not with Fast Cash or with *his wife or with his final robbery accomplice, Marty Beam. I'm also not mad at the cops, they've got lots of criminals to catch and if truth be known, Fast Cash never physically injured anyway, he just stole money, and like a greedy Robin Hood, he kept it for himself. Nope, I'm mad at the bank. For allowing Fast Cash to so blatantly get away with it and not care a whit.*

"Hey, we're insured," said one bank official. Like we need any more reasons in this day and age to dislike the banking industry. But there you have it folks, this is L.A. and as we all know by now, you can get away with anything here. Rest in Peace, Fast Cash. Oh, and spend well.

Todd had to admit, he liked this Beaufort guy's style. Leave it to a seasoned, jaded reporter to write an article about a criminal and have him look like the good guy. Todd thought perhaps he would enjoy the Los Angeles perspective more than he expected.

But back to the situation at hand: obviously Patrick himself was somehow interested in the story of Fast Cash, why else would he have stuck the article inside the envelope he'd sent to him? And what was with the map, what did it represent and just what was buried at the X? The obvious thought flashed in his mind again: the unrecovered three million dollars? Could it be possible? Did Patrick know the location of the house indicated on the map? How much did Cindy really know? Not enough, he assumed, otherwise why had she come seeking out his help?

Enough background, enough speculation. Get off the sofa and seek out your friend.

Night had fallen on Manhattan, and for Todd that was always his favorite time of day. Action was best served under a cloud of darkness, when you could skulk about without anyone really giving you a second thought, because they were busy doing the same. Problem was, Todd wasn't sure where to start, where to skulk in tracking down his wayward friend.

Todd thought about Patrick, about their past and about how they had played, scammed, and conned their way through college. And then they'd lost touch after the move to L.A. Patrick had always been the reckless one, and Todd supposed he felt a bit responsible. Maybe that's why he so easily gave in to Cindy's request, not out of some lost desire for her but as a way to make up for his past mistakes. Those thoughts, at least for now, he pushed aside. Oh, it had gotten complicated, and so quickly.

Dressed in dark clothes, Todd started out of the door when he realized he'd left his cell phone charging on the table in the corner. Going to retrieve it, he stopped in his tracks and once again surveyed his apartment. Had someone been here? Who, and why? An idea flashed into his mind. He picked up the receiver of his landline and for fun, maybe for luck, he pressed that old reliable "redial" button. Maybe someone had goofed, maybe an electronic clue had been left? A series of sounds and clicks echoed in his ear and finally the connection was made and an answering machine popped on.

"Hi, you've reached the Two Dicks Agency," said a deep, scary-sounding voice. "Leave a message, a phone number, and a short description of your problem and we'll get back to you." A second voice ended the message by saying, "Have a super day."

Todd set the phone back down without leaving a message.

He was too busy wondering who these guys were, and more importantly, why someone had used his phone to call them. The case was early still, but already the questions were starting to mount. Better that than the body count.

MEANWHILE, IN Los Angeles, the story of Fast Cash had reached an end game.

The morning smog had burned off, leaving powerful rays to beam down on this sun-kissed land. Every day in the City of Angels it seemed the sun shined brighter for one particular person, as though they had been singled out by the gods above. Today, after quite a considerable wait—years, really—it was the widow Cashman's turn in the spotlight. Thing of it was, the sun could be blinding, making you oblivious to hidden dangers.

At this very second, Lottie was shielded from those harmful rays and instead was busy fending off the intense, questioning glare of the judge. Sitting in the witness chair, she was busy giving testimony in Los Angeles Superior Court, Family Division. Judge Harry Butz presiding.

"Mrs. Cashman, would you please recount for the court one final time the events of the morning in question. The final morning shared between you and your husband?"

Fifty or sixty-something (she wouldn't say) Lottie Cashman took a breather to compose herself, to get her thoughts organized in her usually muddled mind. This was her moment—yes, in the sun—and she wanted to look her very best. For the court, sure, and inevitably, for the cameras. This was L.A., where cameras seemingly outnumbered people and where even a hint of scandal could land you on the news—or better, YouTube. She'd already encountered those slimy paparazzi on her way up the court's cement steps, making her feel like a heroine in one of those legal thrillers she liked to read. She imagined herself a Grisham title—"The Widow." With one camera practically in her face, she'd wiped away a tear for good measure, and good effect. The subsequent flash had nearly blinded her. But that was okay, she knew how important it was for the press to get "the before shot." That "after shot," though, is really what had consumed her thoughts since waking.

Thankfully, Lottie had slept well, her beauty sleep for once working in her favor. After years of heavy smoking, her complexion had gone sallow and her skin leathery, and the aforementioned sun had done its fair share of damage as well. Her blonde-to-graying hair was streaked with the yellow-stain of nicotine, and her teeth at least matched. Carrying about forty pounds more than her doctor advised, Lottie Cashman looked like a woman running out of time.

Yet think as you might, today's proceeding was no divorce of the L.A. kind. This was more mandated by that old chestnut "till death do us part." Trouble was, her husband wasn't officially dead. After more than seven years of silence, Lottie had followed her heart's fondest wish to find, finally, closure. That meant having one Jack Cashman declared legally dead.

"Mrs. Cashman, your story?" the judge prompted.

"Oh, yes, my apologies your honor," she said, wearing her best manners alongside her unfortunately colored canary yellow suit. "My tale."

And so it began, in a courtroom not exactly overflowing with interested parties. Sure, there were those curious folks who filled their days attending various trials and such, there were even a couple reporters jotting down notes for a story that had about three seconds of interest. Otherwise, Lottie's voice echoed in the otherwise spacious chamber.

"One thing you have to understand about the man I married, the man to whom I gave my heart to," began Lottie, "he was a secretive snake, and could seldom be trusted to tell the truth. Especially when it came to his business. The robberies, all those banks he hit, that was purely a business transaction to him, and as such, none of my business. I only knew after the fact, after that last caper when… (she paused, sniffled for effect) that trigger-happy guard shot my Jack and took him from me."

"Mrs. Cashman, we already have Mr. O'Brien's account of what happened that day he was working security detail at the bank. What we need, please, is your accounting of that final exchange between you and your husband. His mood, his frame of mind—that sort of thing. If you please…."

"Certainly, my apologies again. Being here…in court, answering to the law…it's new for me," Lottie said. "Jack woke that morning like any other morning, at six on the dot. The alarm went off, he switched it off, and then he was ready to begin his day. Jack was not the kind of man to ever hit the snooze button. He was a doer, and he saw every new day as a brand new opportunity to…do. So, really, that morning was no different from any other. I stayed in bed, under the comfort of our covers, while he got up, made coffee, went down to his first-floor office and clicked on the computer for the latest headlines. He was a big fan of the Internet, amazed always at the information you could find out there. Anyway, he returned to the bedroom with a cup of coffee for me—he made the best, it almost feels as though I haven't had a decent cup since he died, uh, left, uh…see, judge, I don't even know how to refer to my situation…."

"Yes, I can see it's all very troubling for you. After all this time, to still live with such uncertainty…"

"No, judge, I've long given in to certainty. My Jack, he's no longer…among us."

"If you'd continue…"

"Yes. So, he shared that last cup of coffee on the edge of the bed and I do recall him saying to me, "Lots—that was his nickname for me, as in Lots O'Woman. Weight has never been my friend—well, actually it's more like it's been my best friend, if you know what I mean." She laughed at that, and her nicotine-flecked laugh boomed throughout the courtroom. Lottie looked around at the newly startled folks in the room, and realized she was losing the interest of her audience.

She continued, no more interruptions, no commercials during this program.

"Next thing I know, Jack kissed me once and then announced he needed to get ready for a business appointment. I knew better than to ask, so I told him to have a nice day, dinner was at six, I was making lamb chops. And he turned to me, and gave me that loving look of his, and with the zeal that carried him throughout his life, Jack said to me, 'I love your chops, I wouldn't miss them for the world.' Still, judge, there was a tone to his voice, a wistfulness if you will. As though he knew something no one else did. Like he'd never get to enjoy my chops again."

There was a slight muffled sound of laughter in the courtroom. Lottie was oblivious to it.

"I wonder, your honor, if people have this sense of when they are about to die, do they know it somehow?" Lottie Cashman paused for dramatic effect and then said, "Anyway, I suppose those are questions we ourselves can only answer when our day of reckoning comes. But let me say this, judge, those lamb chops were not cheap, and it was such a waste to see them languishing first on the dinner plate, then later in the trashcan. But if that doesn't sum up that entire day, then I don't know what does—it began with promise and ended up just being tossed out with the rest of the fauna. Jack never returned to our lovely home and it wasn't until three days later that I found out what had happened."

"From?"

"Why the police, of course. Certainly I had filed a missing persons report after Jack went missing, but I had to wait until the requisite twenty-four hours had passed. Actually, it was two nights without him before I notified the police, because…well, I just couldn't imagine anything untoward happening to my Jack. I'd called his friends, my friends, anyone I could think of. No one had seen—or heard from—Jack. Then came that fateful knock on the door, and I thought that sympathetic desk officer I'd spoken to about Jack's disappearance had come with good news. But at the door was a different policeman—two of them, actually, and they were anything but understanding. They were LAPD detectives. And that's when my life unraveled."

Lottie looked up at the judge, then back at the courtroom. Everyone was hanging on her every word, the use of the word "unraveled" was good, dramatic without being melodramatic. Her lawyer just nodded once at her, as though to say, "Good job."

"Anyway, your honor, you know the rest, the whole world does. The testimony of the police about the alleged actions of my husband, claiming he was that notorious bank bandit known as 'Fast Cash,' the video from the bank, the forensics from that poor actress's Hollywood star, all splattered with my Jack's blood…"

"Yes, Mrs. Cashman, there's no need to rehash the previous two days of testimony," the judge said. "As important as those facts are, what helps me most in rendering a verdict in this difficult case is your accounting of Mr. Cashman's frame of mind. And to that point, I do have a question for you."

"Certainly, I'm happy to answer any you might have."

"Very good," Judge Butz said. "Now, Mrs. Cashman, since the morning of your husband's disappearance was anything different from your usual routine? I wonder, after seven-plus years, how is it you can recall the matter with such clarity, even to go so far as to say your husband may have suspected his oncoming death?"

"Oh, your honor, it wasn't the actions of that morning that made me remember them, it was the night before."

"And what happened then?"

Lottie Cashman squirmed in her seat, as though searching for the right sequence of words that would give the judge the answer he needed. Then she said, "Because the night before my Jack left me for good, he and I shared a most profound evening of love, one I will remember to my own dying day. He made love to me as though it was our last time, and I'll tell you judge, Jack Cashman was not the type of lover to savor the experience. Except on that night of nights…even in the darkness of our room, colors exploded in my mind. That's how I remember that final morning as Mrs. Jack Cashman. A satisfied one."

Just then a small sound was heard in the otherwise quiet courtroom. It was Lottie's lawyer, who had accidentally dropped his pen. Sure, it wasn't a pin dropping, but there was no mistaking it as the only sound to echo in the suddenly hushed hall of justice.

After a moment of studied silence, Lottie looked up at the judge, noticed he was still a bit red-faced from her revelation. "Will there be anything else?" she asked.

Judge Butz excused her, and then he excused himself, rendering court in recess for thirty minutes. It was an excruciating wait, but as her lawyer reminded her, "You've waited seven years for this, Lottie, surely another half-hour shouldn't matter. You were brilliant up there, I couldn't have scripted it…uh, said it better myself."

"And that pen hitting the floor, Dustin," she said, her hand reaching out to touch the sleeve of her lawyer's threadbare suit. "It was perfect, even better than when we rehearsed it."

Finally, Judge Harry Butz returned to his bench, dropping the gavel down with one eager motion. He had a full docket, and it was best to get this messy matter cleared up now.

"It is the judgment of this court that after careful consideration of the testimony heard before it, and of the learned opinion of said witnesses, that I declare Mr. Jack Cashman as death in abstenia—legally deceased—and that all his assets are hereby the property of his widow, one Lottie Cashman. This matter is closed, and this court is adjourned."

He banged his gavel again, and, quite like Jack Cashman did seven years ago, Judge Butz disappeared from Lottie Cashman's life.

As her lawyer hugged her, Lottie wiped away a tear, and this time the appearance of said tear caught even her by surprise. It was one thing to work the court to your advantage and play the role so many other actresses…uh, women had played in this town, but it was quite another to hear such a definitive note of finality.

Whisked away from the prying eyes of those assembled in court, Lottie knew she had one more gauntlet through which to pass, and it was this one she had practiced the most for. Because it was one thing to address the judge, it was quite another to star on the local news. With her lawyer by her side, Lottie emerged back in the L.A. sunshine, where she donned a pair of sunglasses. Nothing unusual about that, a private moment being exposed to the public, you needed a little protection, right? Especially from those flashing bulbs.

Several reporters shot questions at her, but she fended them all off, thinking it was best to retain an air of mystery about her feelings. Until one reporter, well, he just asked the most perfect question of all and called her by just the most perfect name. Lottie, suddenly conscious of her new-found celebrity, removed those sunglasses when she heard the following:

"Mrs. Fast Cash, Carl Beaufort here, L.A. Daily News—how does it feel, now that it's all over?"

"Over?" Lottie marveled, smiling as she said that one simple little word. The cameras all zoomed in for their close-up, and as though Mr. DeMille was yelling "action" in the background, Lottie Cashman put her best foot forward on those steps of the courthouse and said to the world, "Mr. Beaufort, you of all people should know nothing is every truly over. Why, my life is really only just beginning."

CHAPTER FOUR

TODD GLEASON liked when quick leads led to good progress. Before leaving his apartment, he had gone back online and found the website for "Two Dicks Agency," which on its home page revealed both a Manhattan street address and a photograph of the two, uh, detectives, a pair of scary-looking guys dressed all in black who more resembled bodyguards or thugs or mercenaries. One short and the other tall, but both had muscles upon muscles in common. Neither of them did Todd wish to encounter in a dark alley. Not for the first time did he wonder what they had to do with what was going on, and who might have called them from his apartment?

It felt weird being back in New York, riding the subway while staring into space and not caring about your fellow traveler. Bermuda had been so warm and welcoming, so down home—there was something to be said for being hospitable. He might never have met the lovely Lana if not for the simple island-greeting that Buzz had taught him: "Smile, be welcoming. Lose that inherent New York skepticism." It had worked, several times. But no more notably than with Lana. He thought about her. He wanted to talk. He'd like to explain himself to her. For now, he'd have to continue to miss her, especially now, since the train conductor had just garbled an announcement that they were approaching 18th Street. Todd's desired stop, finally, after two transfers. It was time to get to work.

He hopped off the #1 train at the back, perfectly positioned to leave via the 19th Street exit. Back topside on Seventh Avenue, Todd scoped out the neighborhood. Chelsea, it wasn't a place he hung out in normally, and on this balmy September Thursday the sidewalks were hopping. Men alone, women with friends, men holding hands with other men, muscle boys walking tiny dogs that yapped at Todd when he passed by, diners enjoying their meals outside. Just another night in Manhattan.

Todd slipped down 19th Street and quickly found the address he was looking for. An office building circa 1972, with white cement moldings and a rather boring edifice. There was no doorman on duty; instead there were buttons to press to allow entry into the building. At seven minutes past eleven in the evening, Todd had to wonder if anyone was inside still working. He checked the listing of companies, and there on the sixth floor was listed "T.D. Agency." Guess they didn't want to advertise too blatantly, with a name like Two Dicks you were asking to be fake-buzzed. Could be mistaken for another type of service. Still, detectives keep odd hours and there was every possibility one or both was inside, so he crossed to the south side of the street and gazed up at the sixth floor, looking for any sign of life, of light. A faint glow came from one of the windows, but otherwise he couldn't see anything. No figures, not even shadows.

He scanned the rest of the building, just in case his counting was off as to which floor was which. Hard to tell, what with the high-ceiled lobby. On the top floor, he saw a bright light bathing the night sky in its glow, only to be doused mere seconds later. Todd's mind raced. A late worker, shutting down for the night? On his way out? He thought quickly, his eyes darting left and right down the street. An idea came to him, but he had to act fast. Dashing down the street, he ran into the corner deli, where he asked for a pack of smokes.

"Which kind?" asked the guy behind the counter.

"I don't know…um…"

"You don't know what brand you smoke?"

I don't smoke, Todd thought, and then said, "Marlboro."

"Box, light, menthol?"

Christ. Box sounded sturdy. "Box, plus matches."

"Ten fifty."

God, cigarettes cost even more than an arm or a leg. More like a lung.

He got his smokes, unwrapped the cellophane and tossed it aside as he ran back down to the street. Catching his breath easily (good thing he didn't smoke, he would have lost valuable time), he lit up and tossed the match aside just as the front door to the building opened.

Todd, leaning against the façade, let out a puff of smoke.

"Hey, lucky you, done for the night?" Todd said, acting all casual-like.

"Yeah, finally," the guy said. Young, probably early twenties, just out of college, trying to prove to his boss he was dedicated, a real company man. Didn't matter, the system would eat him up eventually and he'd come to regret all those late hours.

Happened to everyone.

"Me, I gotta go back in, damn reports."

"Don't work too hard, man," the guy said, and then headed off down the street.

What the kid had failed to see during their exchange was Todd tossing the pack of cigarettes into the doorframe, stopping the door from closing all the way. With the kid now gone out of sight, Todd tossed the burning cigarette to the street and then easily slipped inside the building. He bypassed the elevator for the more surreptitious approach of the stairs. Six flights was nothing for a guy who lived on the fifth floor of a Manhattan walkup, though as he made his way up that final flight Todd had admit to feeling somewhat winded. Geez, he'd barely taken a puff.

Hiding in the stairwell, Todd considered his next move. He decided to wait it out and see if something happened that would decide his move for him. As luck would have it, ten minutes later the elevator "pinged" and out stepped the little guy—Todd recognized him from the picture on the website. Not the best thing for a private detective to do, advertise so publicly but hey, no website these days and you might as well just close up shop.

So, the little guy, he got off the elevator and took out keys and opened the door to the "T. D. Agency," as the black-stenciled lettering on the door stated. Then he closed it behind him with a turn of the lock. Okay, he's being cautious, that's a good quality in a detective. Not helpful to Todd, though. He'd have to take more of a chance if he were to learn anything about who these guys were.

He pressed his ear up against the door and tried to listen.

He heard the scrape of a chair and a voice; then he heard another voice, and even though it was muffled he was certain he'd discerned two distinct, separate voices. Okay, so there were two people inside, and they were having a conversation. But who was the second person? The Big One? Could it possibly be Patrick? Or that mysterious stranger who had used his phone? And what were they talking about? Todd considered just knocking on the door and asking what was going on—I mean, these guys were detectives, not criminals, so what was he so nervous about? Well, first of all, their look—they could probably bench press the Empire State Building. Second of all, you can't con a con, everyone had their own motives for doing what they did, and who knew what had motivated these two goons to become private detectives? Could be a front for something else, right?

One of the voices was getting louder and Todd realized someone was making for the exit. Scrambling back to the stairwell, he left about an inch of space so he could observe what transpired next. The agency's door opened and out stepped the other guy—the one we were now calling The Big One. Todd slowly closed the door a bit more, he'd hate to be discovered by that beast.

"Okay, Fred, I'll see you in about a half-hour at The Raven," he said, the voice deep and gravelly, the same one Todd had heard on their voicemail. "In the meantime, take care of our guest, make sure he doesn't go anywhere."

Laughter could be heard coming from inside the office.

So, they weren't alone. It was easy math here: a phone call to the Two Dicks Agency made from his apartment and a missing Patrick Scanlon, he'd say two plus two just equaled four. Before he could process what to do with this new information, Todd heard the Big Guy say something else and he had to rewind his own mind before he conceded that's exactly what the man had said.

"Love ya, babe."

CINDY SCANLON'S connecting flight was delayed, but at last she made it back to Los Angeles. She bypassed baggage claim and went directly to Patrick's beloved BMW, parked in the long-term parking lot. She'd only been gone three days total, but the trip could have lasted much longer, especially had she gone to New York with Todd.

But that wasn't possible. She needed for him to find Patrick, and in the meantime, she had her own things to get ready for.

From LAX, she joined the familiar start-and-stop of traffic on the 405, heading south to the home she and Patrick shared in the small ocean-fronted village of Manhattan Beach. She'd liked its name, giving her one piece of her previous life in New York to hang onto, that's what she'd said to Patrick when they were searching for the perfect place to relocate. "We may be in L.A. babe, but living here we can be reminded to never lose our New York attitude."

"Like that would be possible," had been Patrick's reply.

That had been almost five years ago, Cindy reflected, as she drove down the freeway. Their lives had changed so much since making the decision to go west. It had been after her mother's funeral when Cindy felt a sea change, and so she told Patrick they needed new scenery, and with the small inheritance from her mother's estate Cindy and Patrick Scanlon packed up their stuff and made the cross-country trek in search of a new beginning.

As she headed for the freeway exit ramp, her cell phone rang. She grabbed at it, checking the caller ID. Not Patrick, and not Todd. The number was a 323 exchange; local. She swallowed once, considered letting it go to voicemail. Instead, she picked up, she had to.

"Hello," she said, her voice like stone.

"Welcome home," a man's voice said.

"How do you know I'm back?"

"Cindy, you disappoint me. You don't think I know all your movements?"

"Look, I'm tired, I feel like I've been on planes for the last three days and I need to take a shower, pour myself a glass of wine, and take in the sunset."

"Sounds nice, care for some company?"

"Do I have a choice?"

"We all have choices, my dear. But alas, I have business to attend to tonight."

"So then what was the point of this call?"

"I think you know," he said, and then said nothing else.

The connection broken, Cindy threw the phone down on the passenger seat and narrowly escaped banging into the car in front of her. She cursed, and not because of the near crash. Finally, the light changed, and she and her near miss went their separate ways. Paranoia crept into her mind as she stole a look back at the limo that she had nearly rear-ended. Had he been that close? Limos were as prevalent in L.A. as palm trees, so who was to say her "friend" was in that one?

Because it's just what he would do.

At last, Cindy pulled into her driveway and killed the engine. She made her way into her house, dropping her carry-on and phone at the entrance, and then she removed her shoes. Padding barefoot into the kitchen, she went straight for the refrigerator and did as she'd said she would, she poured herself a glass of wine. A Chardonnay from the Central Coast, and the first sip helped soothe her nerves, the second sip doing an even better job. Knowing she needed a moment to collect herself, she slid open the glass doors that led to their backyard.

The time was seven forty-five in the evening, the sun was starting to dip beneath the horizon and cast rippling shadows on the water's surface. As much as she loved New York, there was nothing like the crashing sounds of the Pacific so nearby. Still, that didn't stop her and Patrick from buying a house with a pool; come on, this was still L.A. and privacy was as necessary in this town as publicity.

She made her way to the pool, where she sat down in the chaise lounge, enabling her to stretch her long, supple legs. Her eyes closed, she took another sip at her wine and allowed the warmth of the alcohol to spread throughout her body. The temperature outside was warm, also, and she considered going for a relaxing swim. Not having the energy to change into her suit, Cindy considered a skinny dip.

Her plans for an evening's swim, though, were about to be interrupted.

Because when she stood up, she looked at the calm waters of the pool and realized there was already someone in there. He wasn't swimming, nor had he been for some time, considering there wasn't a ripple coming from the undisturbed water. Nope, he was just floating there, face down.

Now Cindy, she'd always prided herself on her calm nature. So she didn't scream at the sight of the dead man, she just allowed a sense of shock to overcome her. The glass of wine slipped from her hand and went shattering onto the ground. She didn't notice the cut on her foot, or the blood that seeped from her fresh wound. Nope, Cindy was concentrating on the pool. And not just on the dead body.

She was curious, ridiculously so, on not who he was or why he was in her pool or how he might have ended up there, but why, surrounding him, like green leaves blown from the trees, were dozens of bills in all denominations, twenties and fifties and hundreds.

TODD WASN'T naïve, he'd never lived his life under a rock. He'd had his share of adventures, of pulling scams and working the innocently rich to his own financial gain and reward. That was his only offense, really, and it's not like he drove anyone to bankruptcy or any kind of monetary ruin. The people he stole from, they were richer in experience having been bilked—they would keep better control of their cash, and not fall victim to perhaps some worse predator than himself. After all, he'd taken the money with no more threat than his crooked, dimpled smile offered, a promise of some quick investment payoff. And then he'd run. Ponzi he wasn't. He'd pulled his schemes by acting under the guise of one Richard Booker.

A man and a name and an identity he had thought were behind him.

Except Todd's current situation demanded that he slip into another role, assume a new identity, one that would gain him entrance into a world that was far removed from naïveté, from innocence. Here's the deal:

The Raven Club was a bar that catered to Manhattan's vibrant gay community and the more you were into leather, whips, chains, and other such fetishes, the more you fit in. Todd was, at the moment, standing across the street from the 12th Avenue bar, watching as an assortment of characters made their way toward the entrance. Time was midnight, and it appeared the party was only just getting started. All the men were dressed similarly, in leather pants and tops, some with just vests open to their gym-toned bodies; almost like a costume party that celebrated that motorcycle guy from the Village People. Todd took one look at his own style of dress—black jeans, black T-shirt, denim jacket, he thought maybe he could sing the construction worker's vocal track. Then he thought: am I really contemplating going inside?

Yes. See, in the half hour he'd been scoping out the neighborhood and weighing the odds of whether to go inside or not, the Little Guy, aka Fred, had showed up and after giving the bouncer a kiss quickly went through the door. Not his first time here, Todd deduced. He'd seen the same thing happen with the Big Guy.

Todd, after seeing said Big Guy leave the office, had retreated back down the stairs and simply followed him to his night's destination. He supposed he could have found the bar all on his own, but just in case it was one of those "secret" locations that only the night owls knew, he thought it best to trail him. That's how Todd had come to be on the western-most avenue of Manhattan, in the Meatpacking district, ready to join the throng of people eager for a night that the bar's outside banner called "Bear With Me" night. From what Todd could see, this happened every Thursday night.

Could he really have been in the magical world of Bermuda just this morning? Awakening in his cottage to the calling sounds of the ocean, to the birds' cawing love song, to the sweet memory of his and Lana's last beach excursion. And now he was getting ready to enter a big-gay-daddy-leather-bar-type-place. Talk about life changing on a dime. He considered his options and realized that if he didn't go forward with this plan and find out if these guys were his link to Patrick, he might have to go someplace far worse and far more west than 12th Avenue and 16th Street.

He might have to go to Los Angeles.

"Okay, to the Raven I go," he said aloud, and then, as he crossed the street, silently said to himself that after tonight, "nevermore."

Todd was twenty feet from the entrance when he heard someone with a high-pitched voice say, "You'll never get in dressed like that."

He continued on, assuming whoever had spoken those words was addressing a person other than himself. Until he heard this:

"Seriously, dude, it's not cowboy night."

Todd stopped on the corner and turned to see who was talking. He saw a kid, probably on the wrong side of the age requirement to get inside, his feathery blonde hair and smooth cheeks proving a fake I.D. isn't all you need. Puberty might work, too. Still, Todd thought, the kid at least was dressed in the proper attire for a night of whips and chains. Though his leather pants did carry some fringe on the side (talk about cowboy night!), and a black T-shirt and vest, metal chains linking the spots where his nipples jutted. He also wore six earrings (in each ear!). Todd would hate to get caught behind this kid at airport security.

"Thanks for the advice, but my friends are already inside."

"Sure they are. They've got strict rules, you'll see."

Ignoring the kid, Todd continued toward the entrance to the club, where he joined a line of leather-clad men and their leather-clad dates, he standing out like a sore thumb on a leather glove. The bouncer took one look at him and just shook his head.

"But my friends, they're inside."

"Not happening man, leather night. Gotta be dressed in leather."

Todd considered his options. It was important to get inside, to see what Fred and the Big Guy were up to, perhaps even get close enough to overhear something. Or maybe get his hands on a set of office keys, see who else might be inside their agency. Had to be Patrick, there had to be a connection.

As he stepped away from the club's darkly-lit entrance, he emerged under the glow of the spotlight, and as though a light bulb had gone off over his head, he called out to the kid with the earrings.

"Hey, kid."

"Hey yourself—don't call me a kid."

"Fine. What's your name?"

"Scooter."

"Sco…" Todd stopped himself. Come on, wasn't Kid an improvement over that?

"How much for your vest?"

"One hundred."

"One hundred dollars? Christ…"

"How about twenty…and you get me inside."

"Deal."

And so an exchange was made for their shared, mutual benefit. Scooter kept his fringe-laden leather pants and t-shirt, Todd divested himself of his jean jacket and donned the kid's leather vest over his t-shirt and together they looked like a cowboy had met a leather boy and they had fallen in love and realized they were the same size and could double their wardrobe. Mix and match, and ready to go.

"Wait, you don't look right yet," the kid said. "The T-shirt, it's gotta go."

"Excuse me?"

"Trust me, it'll do the trick, I can tell."

So there, as the clock struck twelve thirty in the morning and the nocturnal activity was just heating up, Todd was shucking his T-shirt off in the middle of the street, whistles and catcalls filling the night air. Tucking the shirt into his back pocket and letting it dangle, he then threw the vest back over his exposed chest. He felt cold all of a sudden, the light wind making his nipples perk up. Truthfully, he felt ridiculous. He supposed that was the point.

"Perfect," the kid said, ruffling the hair across Todd's strong chest.

"Uh, I thought you guys liked 'em smooth."

The kid laughed. "Man, you don't know anything, do you? Not this crowd, no waxing here, they like it rough…you catch my drift."

"If I have to."

"Relax man, you're gonna stick out—and not in a good way. Wait, one more step…"

Scooter removed his nipple clips and instead fastened them to Todd.

"Now you're perfect."

This kid… Scooter, turned out he knew how to work this crowd, or at least the bouncer. Because acting in tandem, when it came their turn to be accepted or rejected, the bouncer grinned once and then opened the velvet rope for them. A new world awaited him.

You know, this kind of education, you just can't get in books.

CHAPTER FIVE

OBSERVATIONS: THE lights were low, giving the club a dungeon-like feel; the music pounded against the walls, surprising Todd that he hadn't been able to hear it out on the street. Place must be soundproofed to within an inch of its life. The other thing he noticed was that the main room, where he saw two bars and a dance floor, was over-crowded with men, lots and lots of men. Not that he expected to find many women, he was just taken aback by the sheer number of people who were here. And it was only a Thursday night. Todd wasn't a prude by any stretch of the imagination, but even he had to admit this party-till-dawn lifestyle would drain him.

Frankly, he liked to keep his wits about him.

Which is why he said no to a drink when Scooter asked him.

"Dude, you're gonna stick out again. Everyone's drinking."

"Okay, a beer, any kind. And that dude stuff, it's gotta go."

"You want me to try for honey, sweetie, looover?"

"Dude, just get me a beer."

So while young Scooter went for their drinks, Todd surveyed the room, locking eyes with numerous guys as he did so.

Whether he knew it or not, he was cruising and he was getting some eager return glances. On the dance floor, he watched as two men climbed atop a small stage and together began to bump and grind to the music, which sounded distinctly like electro-pop Pet Shop Boys. Todd remembered listening to them in college; did people still listen to them? If nothing else this night was entertaining and it brought a smile to his lips. Said smile attracted all sorts of new attention.

"I could do shots from those dimples," Todd heard.

"Excuse me?" he asked, suddenly aware he wasn't alone.

Standing before him was a large, hulking man, fifty-something, about six seven, goateed, with a chest so massive and so furred, Todd wasn't sure if this guy was human or animal. He wasn't sure he wanted to ask. So he pretended not to have heard.

"Hey, I was talking to you," human or animal said.

"Oh, hey, the music…it's so loud."

"I like your dimples, man. You want to get naked?"

"Uh, not right now. Just got here, not ready to leave."

"Who said anything about leaving? What are you, some kind of…"

"Oh, hi, sorry I was late, babe," said Scooter, ready with a rescue by planting a kiss on Todd's cheek.

Todd looked at the big guy and then back at Scooter. "Sorry, like 'em young."

"Damn twink," human or animal replied, disgust in his voice. Then he took off.

"Thanks," Todd said.

"Anytime," Scooter said, and then smiled.

"Look, Scooter, I'm here on business. So, don't get any wild ideas.…"

"Oh, honey, you're as straight and narrow as the Upper East Side. I knew you didn't fit in here the moment I saw you, but you sure made me curious. What's going on? Are we tracking a criminal? Ooh, are you an undercover cop?"

"Sshh, no. But do you want to get us…me, killed?"

"Sorry, mum's the word."

"Look, let me just wander. You go and have fun—I got you in, surely you had something else in mind than hanging around with…someone so straight and narrow."

"Sweetie, you're just my type," Scooter said.

"Except for one thing."

Scooter smiled. "Oh, a few beers would take care of that. It always does."

Todd reminded himself to limit himself to the beer in his hand.

With a wave and a smile, Scooter flitted off to make some new friends, leaving Todd to himself and a host of leather daddies with eyes for something a bit fresher. He opted to move on through the crowd, figuring an object in motion was harder to catch. Besides, he had people to scope out.

The music changed, this time to something Todd didn't recognize. Some kind of combination of dance/disco/hip-hop/house that just sort of tunelessly but relentlessly blended into the background. Not that the crowd wasn't happy, a whole new contingent of dancers went flocking to the dance floor, nearly catching Todd in its crush. The chain link he wore nearly got stuck on someone else, and he felt a sharp tug at his nipple. That was enough, he took off the nipple chain and tossed it to the floor.

"Dangerous in here, isn't it?"

Todd had slipped away from the crowd and was standing between a large speaker and a line for the bathroom. A guy on the line was talking to him. Todd looked up, and lo and behold, there was the Big Guy. Bingo.

"Sure is," Todd said, his voice taking on a Southern accent. Where had that come from?

"Name's Barney," Big Guy said, extending a massive hand.

"Uh, Richard."

"Where you from, Uh Richard?"

"Virginia. Just visiting for a long weekend."

"You up for some fun this weekend?"

"Maybe, Barney, maybe I am." Todd smiled, got one in return.

That's when Barney stepped off the bathroom line and moved in tight against Todd, practically pressing his large body against him. "You're very hot, Richard. What are you into?"

"Uh, at the moment, just chilling. You know, just got here, wanna check out the scene. Don't have stuff like this where I'm from, you know?"

"I could show you around. They have a nice downstairs, uh, lounge. My partner is there right now."

"Oh, you have a partner?"

"Yeah, but that doesn't matter. He'll like you, too."

Todd had a mental image suddenly of Barney the Big Guy and Fred the Little Guy doing all sorts of things together, and now Barney wanted to get Todd in the middle of things—literally. A little bam bam. And that's when the ridiculousness of the situation hit him. A pair of gay private detectives named Fred and Barney and together they ran an agency called Two Dicks, and now they were out at a leather club and attempting to pick up the guy who was trailing them. You know, you just can't write this stuff.

Invitation extended, though, Todd knew he had to react quickly. He'd been hoping to find his prey first and plan his attack, and now the tables were turned, the hunter had become the hunted. Well, in for a dime, in for dollar. Had enough clichés? Okay, let's move on.

"So, Barney, what do you have in mind?"

"Follow me."

Todd did as instructed, watching as Barney expertly moved through the thick crowd of bodies, emerging from the dance area to a spiral staircase. Barney started down them, and Todd, well, he hesitated just a moment.

"What's wrong?"

"Nothing," he said, and attempted a smile. With the aid of the dim light coming from the staircase, Todd could finally take in Barney up close and in person. Not that he was checking him out, he was scoping out his skintight leather outfit, noticing he seemed to have a thing for thick metal chains. Where did you put normal stuff, like a wallet, or…keys. And then he saw them, dangling from a chain on the side of his pants. Well, you weren't going to lose them that way, secured like that. Just how far was he going to have to go in his search for Patrick?

"You coming?"

"Yeah."

The downstairs was more dimly lit, or he supposed, less brightly lit. But when you're already dealing with an upstairs that barely allows you to see a foot in front of you, this basement was downright suffering from a power outage. Still, Todd could make out several couples (or several groups), all of whom were blatantly making out. Hands were everywhere, lips moved in hungry, drunken motions, and as far as he could tell no one seemed to be with any one particular person. Todd realized he was staring, blinked once, then moved away from the throng of horny guys and followed just the one big horny guy. Down the hallway they went until they at last came to a door. Barney took hold of his keys and unlocked the door.

"We're regulars, we get special treatment," he said. "Which means, so do you."

Todd was escorted inside a small room, aglow with red light. There were a series of hooks on one wall, and against the other wall, a small cot. He turned to find Barney coming at him. The large man pushed Todd against the wall, staring into his eyes as he did so. With his hand he brushed at Todd's chest, following the dark trail down his belly and eventually, the guy's hand found something to cup. Except what he found was nothing much happening down there. That just spurred Barney on, and he pressed his body so tight against Todd, his breath heated his neck.

Todd had to act fast.

"Owww."

Barney suddenly pulled away. "What's the matter?"

"All those chains, that big bunch of keys, they were digging into my skin."

Barney grinned. "Easily, uh, erectified."

Yeah, funny pun, Barn, Todd thought.

Still, it seemed to have worked, as Barney busied himself with removing his pants. He tossed them onto a hook, where Todd watched as the keys dangled in mid-air. Now, talk about something tempting.

Barney, standing there in leather shorts (wow, he really carried the theme all the way), his legs thick and hairy, told Todd he might be more comfortable if he took off those jeans. Not happening, Todd, thought, and then thought about how best to get Barney temporarily out of the room.

"Hey, thought you said your partner would like me, too?"

"Oh, is that what it's going to take to get you...going."

"Well, I didn't come to a place like this to meet just one guy."

"You know, I'm liking you more and more, Uh Richard," he said. "Don't go anywhere, Fred is just outside in the big orgy we passed."

Barney opened the door and exited, and just as he did Todd went for the man's keys. He fumbled with the chain, trying to disconnect it from the pants. He realized they were part of a complex series of bolts and that the only way he was going to leave with the keys was to leave with the pants. Quickly, he put Barney's pants on over his jeans; they were massively baggy on Todd. So much for skintight.

He opened the door, looked down the hallway. Saw Barney and then saw Fred, the two of them talking ear to ear. Todd stole a glance the other way and saw nothing but blank wall. Well, wasn't that great, he was trapped. And he didn't have long before company would be arriving back, and this time with reinforcements. Todd was rightly assuming that Fred the Little Guy was the brains of the outfit.

Just then the door opposite him opened and out stepped that human or animal from earlier, the one who had wanted to do shots from Todd's dimples. He paid Todd no mind this time, apparently we was already satisfied and was ready to go back upstairs. Good thing, because his size blocked the rest of the hallway, keeping Todd, for now, still hidden. That's when he heard, "Dude, that you?"

He looked at the room from where human or animal had come from. And there was Scooter, half dressed and with a big smile on his face.

Todd had no choice, he dashed across to the room and closed the door.

"Dude...those pants..."

"Ssshhh."

There was a commotion happening in the other room. Todd couldn't hear everything, but he did catch the word "Fuck" a few times. Then he heard the slam of the door, and the sound of retreating footsteps.

"You want to tell me what's going on?" Scooter asked.

"I'm trying to save someone's life," Todd said.

"Yeah, from the looks of it, your own."

MONEY COULD buy many things. But sometimes, cold hard cash just wasn't enough to get you out of a sticky situation. Sometimes you needed a little help from your friends, and barring them, your enemies could sometimes be counted on in a pinch. Cindy Scanlon knew one thing: somebody, anybody, had to come and deal with the floater.

Cindy Scanlon had, since the discovery of the body in the pool, patched up the wound on her foot, thinking her injury a bit more serious than the dead man's, considering, well... she was alive. With a band-aid over the cut and a fresh glass of wine at her side she could finally contemplate the situation at hand and figure out just what to do about it. The obvious choice would be to call 911 and have the police deal with it. The second choice was to do the first, but first clean the pool of all those appealing bills. Her third choice was to call Todd and inform him of this latest development, which might encourage him to hop on the next flight and come to her aid. Because someone was sending the Scanlons a message, and it was clearly not a good one. They—whoever they were—had killed the messenger, and hey, aren't you not supposed to do that?

A gentle knocking came from her front door. She jumped a bit out of her skin and off the sofa and realized the wine had still not done an effective job of calming her frazzled nerves. Pausing in the living room, she waited for the knocking sound again; perhaps she had imagined it, perhaps the wind had…

Knock, knock.

Okay, the wind rarely announced itself, it just sort of swept through unannounced.

Cindy approached the front door, not before checking her appearance in the mirror. Her face was a bit flush, highlighting the already red locks that framed it. Dressed casually in sweats, she wasn't exactly up for company. A feeling inside her said the visitor wouldn't go away until she'd answered, and perhaps not even then.

"Who is it?"

"Oh, I think you know."

Yes, she did. She knew that voice. Turning the lock, Cindy opened the door wide and let in her sizable guest. For such a corpulent figure he breezed in quickly, moving past Cindy and into the living room before she'd even had a chance to close the door. Stealing a glance outside, she saw the limo pull away, the driver knowing not to hang around the neighborhood. This wasn't exactly typical limo territory, so no sense sticking out and alerting the neighbors.

Cindy then joined her guest, who had taken a seat on the black leather sofa, a smile perfectly pasted on his pudgy face. He was dressed sharply in a fancy business suit, probably some Prada label or something, extra big. Nails perfectly manicured, his thick steel-colored hair coiffed, his tan healthy, he was very much the image of the successful businessman. Except for that weight problem, which made him look jowly.

"No sign of Patrick yet?" the man asked.

"No, Langston."

"Pity," he said, patting the available seat next to him.

"Is it?"

Cindy had no choice, she sat next to him, allowing him to run his meaty fingers across her face. "Even when you've displeased me, you're still quite beautiful. But you know that."

"Yes, I do. Vanity was always one of my strong suits."

"So is lying."

"Langston, let's not go there. Okay, not now, not after…"

"Not after what? Is it Patrick, are you feeling a tinge of guilt? Or is it this guy you went to see, the one you said could fix all your problems?" He grinned, his perfectly white teeth practically glowing. "Yes, Cynthia, I know all of your moves. New York, Bermuda, you've been a busy lady these last few days. But I do see that you are alone here—which makes me believe you have not found your wayward husband—or found rescue from your mysterious friend. Regardless, my dear, what I'm most curious to know is this: where is my money?"

"I don't have it yet."

"I figured as much," the man named Langston said. "That does not make me happy. As a result, it won't make you happy either."

Langston placed a meaty hand inside his suit jacket, fumbled in the pocket. Cindy, by instinct, moved back. Was he going to threaten her with a gun, or worse…use it? What he withdrew was gun metal in color but a weapon it wasn't. He took hold of Cindy's hand, kissed it once, admired the perfectly manicured nails. "You have lovely hands and fingers, my dear," he said," and that's when he displayed the item in his hand. A nutcracker. With gentle motions, Langston placed one of Cindy's delicate fingers between the metal teeth of the device. Her eyes opened in fear and his eyes widened with pleasure and suddenly he began to squeeze…

Snip.

No, it wasn't her finger that fell to the floor but rather the long sharp nail at its edge.

"Let that be a lesson to you," he said. "Fail me again, and the pain will be far worse."

He squeezed again, lightly, against the finger.

Cindy had to think, she had to act fast.

"Langston…please. There's…" And then inspiration hit. An easy distraction. "…some money, I've got some of it. It's out by the pool." She laughed a bit, amazed at the words about to spill from her mouth. "Actually, there's money in the pool. Along with something else."

"Beautiful, and now intriguing. It will be a dark day when our business is concluded," he said, rising with a huff from the sofa. "Show me the money."

Langston followed her out to the patio. The moonlight was bright tonight and it shimmered down on the pool, which made it quite easy to show her guest her other guest.

"Well, well, what do we have here? Isn't this the shocker of the night," Langston said. "No wonder you hit the wine. Any idea who the poor schmuck is?"

Cindy tossed him a look that could only be read as "Duh."

"He's not exactly showing his best side," she commented.

"A fine point. And something we can figure out later. For now, I suppose you want me to get rid of this little problem for you?"

"Well, if I was going to call the police, don't you think I would have already?"

Without a moment's hesitation, Langston pulled out his cell phone and spoke a sharp order. "Garth, Mr. Livingston here. Bring the limo, and a blanket. Oh, and douse the headlights when you pull up to the bungalow."

"Thank you, Langston," Cindy said.

"Don't thank me yet, dear," he said. "We'll just add this little favor to your account. In the meantime, why don't you fish all those delectable bills out of the water. Consider them a down payment on the interest this task is going to cost you."

As she fished the bills out of the pool and did her best to avoid looking at the floating dead body, Cindy Scanlon realized sometimes in life you had to make adjustments. She was the kind of person usually comfortable in her own skin; she wouldn't ever think she'd be happy to be anyone other than herself. Except maybe now. New York sounded good, far from L.A. and floaters and thugs with strange torture devices, she'd rather be at Todd's side. How bad could it be for him right now?

LEAVING THE Raven turned out to be easier than expected. All Todd had to do was wait twenty minutes in that downstairs room with Scooter, who thankfully had been satiated by the big thug and had dropped any hint of attraction toward Todd. Deciding to take a chance, Todd, with Scooter at his side, made for the stairs and then once back on the main level went for the exit. No one was paying him any mind. There seemed to be some sort of fashion show happening on the stage, with the leather men modeling the latest in whips and chains. The crowd went wild, and Todd slipped out into the night.

Scooter, Todd noticed, remained inside for the festivities.

That was fine, sidekicks weren't his speed.

The question was, where were Fred and Barney? Had they taken the hit on the pants and stayed inside the bar, or had they gone back to the office? Did they suspect anything of Todd other than being a chicken-shit and a thief? He couldn't think of the consequences, all he knew was that he had possession of Barney's keys and that meant he had access to their office, where he could check in on their "guest."

Todd removed the leather pants; they were hindering his walk. Comfortably back in his jeans, he grabbed his t-shirt from his back pocket and slipped it back on. He tossed the vest in the garbage, apologizing to Scooter as he did so. Now, feeling like his old self again, all he needed now was a shower. Or three. That would have to wait.

He was going back to the offices of the Two Dicks Detective Agency.

Fifteen minutes later he was back at 7th Avenue and 19th

Street. It took several minutes before he found the correct key for the building's front door, and then a few minutes more as he took the stairs back up to the sixth floor. He emerged from the stairwell to find everything dark—the vestibule between the elevator and the office, even the office itself, which earlier had emitted a slight glow.

In the dark, Todd again fumbled with keys, but finally he found the right one. He turned the lock, easing himself inside the office, pausing briefly to see if any kind of alarm might sound. Why should one, he'd used a key, he hadn't broken in. Still, there could be a silent alarm that might have been triggered. He had to assume yes on that one.

Okay, then, work fast.

He did so. He checked the main office, which was little more than a desk and computer, pretty untidy. There were also file cabinets, and assorted other office furniture. Really, nothing very distinct, and nothing very modern either. Todd had to imagine it was tough work keeping up with the bills; how much work was out there for these two, uh, dicks?

Todd made his way to the back, where he found two more offices, both of them with window views of 19th Street. In the first one, marked "Barney Stone," it was business as usual. In the second one, marked "Fred Halpern," it wasn't business as usual. Because stretched out on a green-colored couch was a person, sleeping soundly. Todd noticed the handcuffs on the man's wrist, the other handcuff connected to a metal handle on the wall. Someone didn't want their guest going anywhere.

Todd leaned over to the desk, turned on the small lamp. A soft light gave the room a warm glow. It also stirred the person from his gentle rest, who rose from his sleep and quickly smoothed down any stray hair that might have been sticking up. Always had to look his best.

"Hello, Patrick," Todd said.

"Oh, thank God, Todd, you wouldn't believe what I've been through."

"Yeah," Todd said, a sour look on his face. "Back at ya, dude."

CHAPTER SIX

CLOSURE SURE had a funny way of opening up the world.

Take Lottie Cashman. She awoke on this fresh new morning feeling more alive than she'd felt in, oh, at least seven years. As she slept, the dawn crept up on her, and when it sliced through her eyes she eagerly embraced it, beginning the first day of her brand new life with a vigor and enthusiasm she thought had left her long ago. Out of bed, into the shower, where the hot water prickled away her tired skin, leaving it reddened and revived. A quick layer of moisturizer, a dab of makeup to her cheeks, she dressed in a smart eggplant-colored suit, and then carried herself with studied composure down the stairs, as though the cameras were still focused right on her.

She headed for the kitchen and turned on the small TV set. She distinctly heard the name "Fast Cash" broadcast over the airwaves, and quickly she grabbed the remote to turn up the volume. "That and more, when we come back."

"That? What about that?" Lottie screamed at the television. G-D commercials, she hated the way those perky news folk teased the news rather than read it, and then broke for an ad while they freshened up their hair and make-up. Did it really need so much fixing? That woman with the blonde hair, a strong wind couldn't move that helmet. Those were Lottie's musings while she waited out an ad for Metamucil. G-D, who was watching TV at this hour, only those with digestive problems?

"Good morning again, I'm Logan Morgan and you're watching KABC-TV."

"And I'm Mark Logan," mouthed her preserved counterpart. They smiled at each with gleaming white teeth, joking like they did every day about their Logan link. It had grown stale over the six months since the station had put these two together. Then male Logan continued. "The body of noted L.A. Daily News columnist Carl Beaufort was found early this morning alongside an exit ramp off the 101. Police have no leads or suspects at this time, and are calling it a crime against the good name of professional journalism as well as a crime against humanity. Carl Beaufort was a twenty-two year veteran of news, first in his native New Orleans before making his home—and name—in Los Angeles. He was best known for his regular and wildly popular column, 'Carl's Corner,' for which he won three local Pulitzers. Here he is in his final interview, captured just yesterday morning on the steps of the L.A. Country Courthouse, where he was working the notorious Fast Cash case."

"Notorious?" Lottie questioned to no one but the breakfast crumbs. To her Logan's comment sounded inflammatory, as though stoking the flames of speculation would start a ratings bonfire. Ratings made reputations, perhaps more so than criminal behavior.

The screen then went to the videotape, which showed

none other than Lottie Cashman descending the steps of the courthouse, her yellow suit making her looked like a fattened banana. Luckily, she didn't slip on herself, and instead looked confident as questions were hurtled at her. Then came the image of Carl Beaufort, slightly overweight, slightly balding, slightly ordinary looking, his sound-bite question about the affair of Fast Cash being over. She listened to her quote, just as she had on last night's news, but this time it was tinged with a bit of sorrow, since here she was proclaiming her life about to begin, and poor Carl Beaufort was just hours from meeting his maker.

"Serves you right, nosy bastard," Lottie said to the frozen image of the doomed reporter.

"Carl Beaufort, dead of a single bullet wound to the back of the head. He was 57," said Mark Logan. "Logan, what else is going on today?"

"Oh, big doings with Britney and Paris..."

Lottie flicked off the television and calmly finished her breakfast, careful to wipe away all the crumbs of her low-fat bagel. She liked to tidy things up, especially before starting something new. In her mind, it's always better to be done with one project before embarking on another. Otherwise you're just left with lots of unfinished business.

Speaking of business, she had some to attend to. With the traffic on the freeways always so bad, Lottie figured she should get going, she did not want to be late for this very important date. So, she grabbed her purse and her keys, double-checked her appearance in the mirror—G.D. she didn't want to show up with lipstick on her teeth, now did she? All systems go, she left her home and got behind the wheel of her ancient Porsche.

Jack's old Porsche. You just had to indulge when in L.A., that's what Jack always said. For a moment, she thought of her beloved Jack and how much he'd loved this car.

She left her modest estate in Palos Verdes, and made her way through bumper-to-bumper traffic, stopping practically at every light until she at last came to the 405. She headed north, unable to use the commuter lane, since the only passenger she had at her side was impatience, and if that qualified than everyone would be in the fast lane. So, she listened to music, not caring today to listen to those talking heads talk their heads off. At last she exited at Santa Monica Boulevard and went east, driving past such places as the Los Angeles Country Club and the Beverly Hilton, then onward to Rodeo Drive, where she managed to find a parking spot just in front of the Porsche dealer. Well, perhaps that was karma working for her.

But an upgrade in car wasn't her intent today. Nope, today was about real estate, and in her eggplant suit and feeling every much like she belonged on this very exclusive street, Lottie jostled her way past curious glances and to the address she'd been given over the phone. The building was actually just a block off Rodeo, on Wilshire, but she had a feeling when the owner spoke of her address, she was careful to include Rodeo in every mention. It was a small, pale yellow structure, beautifully kept green grounds, which positively gleamed in the L.A. sunshine. Then, again what didn't gleam under such glorious conditions?

The touch that Lottie truly appreciated was the lack of vulgar signage. Rather than a huge billboard announcing the business, a simple, elegant gold-crusted plaque, letters written in script, was embedded in the wall just to the right of the entrance.

Beverly Mills of Beverly Hills. Realtor.

Simple, elegant. No doubt just like the lady herself.

Lottie Cashman depressed the buzzer once, and then calmly awaited a reply. Just then a voice crackled. "Yes, may we help you?"

"Lottie Cashman, I have a ten o'clock appointment with Ms. Mills."

There was silence on the other end, as though the voice was confirming the appointment. Guess she was given the okay, since the lock was disengaged and Lottie was allowed entry in the hallowed halls of one of Beverly Hills' newest and reportedly exclusive offices. Really, Lottie was beginning to think she'd arrived.

Just then an attractive women in a perfectly tailored dark suit emerged from the back, extending her hand as he did so. "Mrs. Cashman, pleasure to see you again."

"Well, hello….Ms. Davies, is it?"

"Wonderful of you to remember," said the beautiful young woman who admitted her. "Won't you come this way?"

They made their way back to a smartly appointed room, more sitting room than office, with lush floral prints on the sofas and chairs, and antique, cherry wood desks. The computers were equally sleek, dark, flat screen, with nary a wire in sight. Simplicity and elegance, this was clearly a message that Beverly Mills wished to enjoin to her staff and her guests. Guests, Lottie thought, so much classier than customers.

"Ms. Mills will be right with you, may I get you a cappuccino or espresso, green tea—or perhaps a simple cup of coffee?"

"Oh, my, well…"

Before Lottie had a chance to answer, a booming voice

echoed down the stairs, followed by a body that perfectly matched said voice, which by that is meant: large. Think Ethel Merman gone to seed, but with gads of new money. And what she had to say, well, it could have knocked Lottie over with a feather.

"Hells bells, they'll be no coffee right now. We've got a real-life celebrity in our midst, and for that we'll have us some champers. Whaddaya say, Lots?"

"Oh, uh, sure, that sounds, uh, lovely," Lottie said, trying to retain the composure she'd gathered within herself when she'd crossed the border into Beverly Hills. A town with such a reputation, well, you just wanted to fit in, right? And she was, wasn't she? After all, she was Lottie Cashman, a bonafide celebrity.

She couldn't say the same for the big, booming, brassy Beverly Mills. Lottie took in the unexpected sight before her.

Beverly Mills. She was easily late fifties, five eleven, and her frame was more linebacker than runway model, and she wore her dyed-black hair in a thick helmet. What Lottie couldn't help but notice was the size of Beverly's uh, bosom. They came at you like twin cannons, and they bounced as though they had no support. Either that or Playtex just didn't make 'em in that size. Add to this image her bravado and well, Beverly Mills was a character straight out of…no, not central casting. Someone created her, mold broken after birth.

"Lottie Cashman," Beverly stated with a thrust hand, "what an absolute, utter thrill to meet you. Just yesterday we were all watching the news and I said to my girls, 'girls, we're having us a celebrity in the office tomorrow.' Isn't that right, Ms. Davies?"

"Yes, Ms. Mills, quoted exactly."

"Ha ha, of course. Steel trap, right up here," Beverly said, trying to put a finger through her shellacked hair. "Okay, Lots, what do you say, let's find our way to my office, grab us that champers and have us some profitable business talk. I've got a good feeling about this, you and I and that house of yours, it's gonna go like that." She snapped her fingers. "And make us both a tidy little sum."

Tidy, that was the first thing Beverly had said that Lottie found herself relating to.

"Okay, Ms. Davies will be right up with our beverage, and then she'll join us. After all, it's her ingenuity and aggressiveness that have brought you to Beverly Mills of Beverly Hills. With us, you get the best service in the world. Ha ha."

Lottie followed that voice, that presence, up the stairs, where she was brought into an office quite unlike the rest of the place. The room reeked of cigarette smoke, despite that fact that the windows were open and a cool, steady breeze was blowing in. Like smoke lived here, had insinuated itself into the rug, the furnishings. Speaking of, her furnishings were more down to earth than the rest of the office, and Lottie supposed few got to see the inner sanctum very often. Really, this woman was the last thing she expected to have achieved such success in Beverly Hills.

Just then Ms. Davies appeared, and set down the chilled bottle of Dom Perignon and two glasses. She poured, and Lottie watched as a trace amount of liquid gold bubbled over the side of the crystal.

At last, they were settled in their seats, with Ms. Davis sitting to their side with a notepad and no champagne. Someone was keeping her wits about her. Ms. Davies seemed no more than a glorified secretary, but obviously was eager to make her mark on the realty world, how else could she put up with the daily contradiction that was her boss.

"So, let's cut to the chase, Lottie—can I call you Lottie?"

"Oh, yes, certainly."

"Good, I like using first names, Lots. Makes for a more convivial relationship," Beverly said. "Okay, here's the scoop. Ms. Davies has already done all the preliminary work—you know, getting the estimates, checking out the market in your neck of the woods. Your initial meeting six weeks ago laid the groundwork, and now that you've been granted legal possession of the estate we can move as quickly as you like. You're ready to move on and the house just holds too many memories of your late husband? That's it in a nutshell, Lots, right?"

"Yes…" Lottie said hesitantly.

"So, I was tossing around ideas on how best to go about selling your house. You realize there will be curious folks, celebrity stalkers, and people who just want to see the house where the infamous Fast Cash lived. Right, you do get that, this town—well, Goddamn, this town just makes me howl. It's predictable, but it's lovable. With me so far?"

"I'm listening," Lottie said.

"Anyway, we were tossing around a buncha ideas yesterday once word came down about the Fast Cash judgment, and I'll give credit where credit is due, Ms. Davies here came up with the winning idea. What do you say, Lots, if we just hold an open house for all interested parties, and then we take it from there to deal with any serious bidders. It will cut down on the amount of showing we do, plus it enables us to get the word out quickly. We want to capitalize on your current celebrity, a week from now—heck, a day from now—you could be as old as my ex-husband. Ha ha ha."

Lottie wasn't sure why that was funny.

Ms. Davies leaned in and said, "Mr. Mills has been dead for nine years."

Beverly Mills drowned her glass of champagne and then said, "So, what'll it be, Lots. Sound like a plan?"

"Why, yes…I suppose…you're the experts…"

"Great, we'll get back to you with all the necessary details, including the date. But keep in mind, we're moving fast so I want you to be ready to sell, sell, sell. Really, great to meet you, Lottie, I'm looking real forward to selling your house."

Lottie assumed she'd been dismissed, and so she followed Ms. Davies' lead and headed back down carpeted stairs. She was a bit woozy from champagne on a near-empty stomach, not to mention the whirlwind that was Beverly Mills.

As she was making her way out the door, Lottie turned back to the lovely creature named Ms. Davies. "I suppose you too can call me Lottie, also, since we're going to be working together. But, please, not Lots. That was my Jack's pet name for me."

"Yes, I understand," Ms. Davies said with a perfectly lovely smile, one that highlighted her auburn-colored hair. "And please, you can call me Lana."

"**SO, YOU** wanna tell me what the hell is going on?"

"How much do you know?"

"Try nothing," Todd said.

"Wow, that's a lot not to know."

Todd wasn't amused by Patrick's obsequiousness.

Still, it was good to see his old friend. Todd realized he had missed his partner in petty crime. Six months in Bermuda, complacency had set it. Now the hunger was back.

Seated across the street at a true dive named Rudy's, a bottle of Irish whiskey between them despite the morning hour, time had no meaning as Patrick regaled Todd with a sordid tale of ambition, greed, intrigue, and oh, the discovery of a certain map.

"Two years ago I began a new job at this company named Livingston Enterprises. A cushy one that paid extremely well and had all sorts of fringe benefits—like a car and driver, cash. Oodles of cash. I came and went as I pleased, and my boss, Langston Livingston, practically treated me like a son. But really, this Langston guy? Get on his bad side and even the original Godfather would find him scary."

That statement was dramatic enough to warrant a break in the story, allowing Patrick a sip of his whiskey.

Then he said, "What, no reaction so far?"

"Consider me your therapist."

"Right, okay, you're the listener. And I guess that means I'm paying the bill. Anyway, Livingston Enterprises is, well…let's call them diversified."

"Diversified?"

"You're talking, not listening."

"Patrick…"

"Okay, I know it sounds bad when I say 'diversified,' but I truly thought everything was on the up and up."

"In Los Angeles?"

"Hey, you've never been there. There's legitimate work out there."

"Not that you found it."

"Christ, you can't resist twisting the knife, can you?"

"Just remember, Patrick, I'm not the one who put it there," Todd remarked. "Now, the story."

"Okay, so, Livingston Enterprises. We're importers of wine, fabrics, spices, food, other stuff."

"Just importers? Not exporting?" Todd asked.

"Uh, yeah, of course we also do some exporting of wine, food…uh, and other, you know, stuff."

"Stuff. Real specific, Patrick. Sounds remarkably reputable."

"We also deal in electronics, real estate, the movie studios, assorted other lucrative companies who are always in need of a quick infusion of cash."

Todd nodded, not happily. "In other words, you went to work for a professional money launderer. A loan shark."

"Don't judge…well, don't judge me. I didn't know. All I knew was I met this man at some party and he says, 'I could use a resourceful kid like you, why not come by and talk to me.' What was I going to say, no? Cindy and I had been in California for a couple of years and neither of us was having much success. Just dumb office jobs, temp gigs and such, we hadn't really settled on what we wanted to do out there. So, here comes this opportunity of a lifetime and I talked about it with Cindy and she urged me to call Langston the next day. Langston, that's what he insisted I call him. You know, getting chummy. It was far easier to call him Mr. Livingston."

"So I presume," Todd quipped.

"Funny as always."

Todd poured them each another shot, and before the story continued they saluted and downed the amber liquid in one pleasing, throat-burning moment. They smacked their shot glasses back down on the rotted wood table in satisfaction. It had to be five o'clock somewhere.

"So, you went to work for this Livingston fellow. How long until you suspected things weren't as legit as you'd been led to believe?"

"At work there was no indication of any trouble. I made deliveries—well, my driver did, but I was always in the back seat, usually on the phone with Mr. Livingston, making a list of the warehouses I needed to check on, the employees I needed to talk with. A few of our clients had accounts past due, and I was there to hand them a bill. You know, a reminder."

"You were the heavy?"

"Not that I ever suspected. Anyway, I think Mr. Livingston was very careful about the assignments he gave me, especially in the beginning. I guess he wanted to ensure that I didn't know too much about his business."

"When did you learn that your boss was a crook?"

"After a couple months I started to get an idea. But by then, you of all people know, you get used to a certain lifestyle…"

"Yes, Cindy mentioned the nice cars and expensive jewelry. Which I bet Mr. Livingston had no problem handing over to you. Extended credit, good terms for good employees, that kind of thing?"

"Sort of."

"You got over-extended?"

"I thought you didn't know anything?"

"Patrick, I can see this coming a mile away. Hollywood has made this story a gazillion times. Local good guy gets caught up in a web of intrigue, gets seduced by the glamorous life, takes out a loan to clear his debts, only the person he gets the cash from turns out to be far worse than a bank. A bank would only take your house; said 'person' will take your life. Of course, in the movies, the local good guy ends up turning states evidence and flees the country. Didn't you ever see *The Firm*? From what I've gleaned, you haven't exactly informed the police about your involvement with this Livingston character?"

"That would be a 'no.'"

"And yet you fled anyway—to New York, to find me. To what end? To clear your name? To pay your debt? Or worse, have me pay it?"

"Now you're being sarcastic," Patrick said, reaching again for the bottle.

"I'm being the realist. Don't you think it's time you played that role, too?"

Patrick was silent, out of words. And out of options.

"Let me ask you this—how much are you in for?"

"Don't ask me that."

"Patrick? That does not sound reassuring. Cindy mentioned half a million, but I have a sinking feeling it's more than that."

"Truthfully, I don't know the total. But I'd place it somewhere around three quarters of a mil. Interest, which happens to grow exponentially when you've skipped out on a payment. It's not exactly a fixed rate, Langston could charge me whatever he wants."

That bit of news required another shot. Todd, on little sleep and no breakfast, was getting a little woozy. Better to finish this conversation before either of them couldn't remember it.

"Tell me one last thing, and then we can figure out our next move."

"Shoot."

"Poor choice of words."

"Yeah, okay."

"The map you left for me," Todd said. "What the hell does this Fast Cash guy and his unrecovered fortune have to do with your money situation?"

"See, that's just it. That's the easy way out of this whole thing. Simply, we find the stolen money and I can pay back Livingston."

"Simply. I like that. Do you even know where the money is?"

"Yup."

Okay, that perked up Todd's drooping eyes. "Where?"

"The map is of Fast Cash's house in an L.A. suburb. Called Palos Verdes Estates. The X references the basement—that's where the money is buried. See, we just need to gain entrance to the house and bingo, the money is ours and my problem goes away. See, easy."

"So why didn't you just break into the house and steal the money?"

"I was going to, but that's when Garth came and beat the crap out of me."

"Garth?"

"Livingston's goon."

"Guess everyone's got to have a goon," Todd said. "Still, that doesn't explain why you need me."

"Look, Langston is watching my every move, he finds out I'm on the trail of Fast Cash's money, he'll take it all. Come on, Todd, put yourself in my shoes. Let's say you owe some guy a cool mil, you gonna pass up an opportunity to score triple that? The deal is this: you come back to L.A. with me, break into the Cashman house and find the money. I pay Langston the money I owe, and you and I split what's left."

Todd hated to admit it. Patrick was talking in a language he could understand.

Still, he was skeptical.

"Sounds too easy."

IT WAS close to eleven in the morning when Patrick and Todd finished the bottle and stumbled out into the September sunshine of a warm New York day. Hailing a cab, they sat back and waited out the fifteen-minute ride up to Todd's apartment in the East 80s. To say they were a little drunk was to say Patrick was in debt for two dollars.

But truthfully, they'd both had a good time getting reacquainted and plotting the details of this new scam. Old friends with many years between them, they realized there was a trust factor here and Patrick thanked his friend (over and over again, forgetting in the boozy haze that he'd already done so) for being there for him.

"See, I knew exactly where to turn. And so did Cindy," Patrick said. "You and she, you always had a special bond, don't think I don't know it, Todd. She loves you in her own way, it's just…I don't know, she picked me. You know?"

"Drop it," Todd said.

Fortunately, that conversation was put to a stop as the cab

pulled before Todd's building. He paid the twelve-dollar fare, tossed in a generous tip, and then helped Patrick out of the cab and into the vestibule of his building.

"You need an elevator."

"Too bad."

Somehow they made it up the five flights of stairs, and then Todd dug out his keys and inserted them in to their respective locks. Then he opened the door and let himself and Patrick inside the quiet apartment. Patrick went right for the sofa, where he dropped like a stone. He was asleep faster than you can…

Todd didn't have a chance to come up with a metaphor. He ended up on the floor, but of course it wasn't the booze that caused his sudden encounter with slumber. Nope, it was thanks to a certain intruder who hit him over the head with a kibosh. Todd never felt a thing, he wasn't even sure he heard what his attacker said to him as he fell:

"Steal my leather pants, that'll teach you."

Okay, he heard that. But nothing else, not for awhile.

CHAPTER SEVEN

THINGS WERE getting interesting, weren't they?

And they were about to get even more so, as seemingly disparate people came together with a seemingly common bond. Certain motives were coming to light and no one would rest until they could say "Mission Accomplished." With most of the players in place for this unfolding scheme, the ante had just been upped. But let's see what's about to transpire, and also see who else might find this puzzling case of interest.

The promise of riches, after all, tends to attract all types.

CINDY SCANLON paced. She could barely conceal her annoyance, her…impatience. She'd called Todd on his cell phone, asking for the simplest of things: an update. Granted she didn't have a great track record when it came to asking simple things of Todd, but still, couldn't he at least have had the courtesy to call her back? She hated voice mail, it put the control in the pocket of the receiver, not the dialer. Now she either had to keep calling back and making her look desperate (wasn't she?), or wait it out until the ingrate decided to phone her back.

She hadn't heard from him since they'd parted ways at the Bermuda airport. And while she certainly had had her own distractions to deal with since returning to L.A., she wished he would just pick up the phone and call her.

About to wear out the carpet and about to give in to an inner urge to light up a cigarette, Cindy's patience reached the boiling point.

"Call me, damn it," she screamed to the walls.

Apparently the Verizon Gods were listening because just a second later her cell phone did ring, deafeningly loud in the echoing silence of the room. It didn't take her long to answer, the phone was practically burning a hole through her palm. The called I.D. said "Private Number."

"Shit," she said, pressed the green button, then said, "Hello."

"Five minutes. Outside."

The call was disconnected.

Like she had a choice. Cindy quickly gathered herself together. She wore simple blue jeans and a navy blue blouse, and that morning she had put her hair up in a tight bun. Now, as she saw the sleek limo approaching, she removed the pin and let her radiant red locks flow naturally against her shoulders. Might as well look her best, perhaps by giving her hair a quick fluff she might distract him from the worry lines creeping around her eyes. Then for good measure she undid the third button of her blouse. Tired of playing wallflower, tired of control being something held by others, Cindy needed to channel her inner vixen.

She grabbed her keys, her purse, and oh yes, her phone, and then emerged into a Friday morning that was wholly uncharacteristic of Los Angeles. That meant it was raining.

Garth, all six ten of him, dressed in a black driver's suit, stood with the rear door open. Cindy dodged the raindrops and quickly climbed into the back seat, where Langston Livingston sat in relaxed comfort while talking on the phone. He held up his stubby finger, indicating Cindy should be quiet. Garth closed the door, got behind the wheel, and the limo took off.

"Very good, very good. Sounds like a perfect plan," Langston was saying into the phone. "Fine, I'll see you in thirty minutes."

He put the phone down and said to Cindy, "I have a favor to ask of you."

"I figured."

"You're not exactly in a position to pull the attitude card, little lady. Considering the ginormous favor I did you."

Between this car and his driver and his own body, Langston was one to speak of things ginormous. Asking him to get rid of that body from her pool, she'd thought of little else over the last day and a half. Why hadn't she just phoned the police? It's not like she'd murdered the guy, someone had just dumped the body there....for some reason. She had to wonder though, just how much was that favor going to cost her? From the smirk on Langston's puffy face, plenty.

"By the way, I take it you heard about that body being found alongside the freeway?"

"Yes, some newspaper reporter."

"Indeed. Now, Cynthia, why do you suppose someone would want to kill Mr. Beaufort?"

"Reporters are nosy by nature, perhaps he angered the wrong person."

"Apparently. Shot in the back of the head. They call that execution style."

"I wouldn't know."

"Indeed," he said again. "Still, I find it curious that Mr. Beaufort's final act on this planet was to go for a swim in some backyard pool in Manhattan Beach. First of all—there's the ocean, not fifty feet away. And, he wasn't exactly dressed for a swim now, was he?"

"Langston, I have no idea what you're talking about. Mr.... Beauman, is it?"

"Beaufort."

"Right. He was found by the side of the road. That's what the police said, I heard it yesterday morning on that annoying morning show, *Logan & Logan*."

Langston snorted, his version of being semi-amused. "Indeed. A true tragedy, wouldn't you say? Human beings, they are so callous, and careless. To take such a life and toss it by the side of the road like trash from a fast food meal. Anyway, I did not summon you to discuss Mr. Beaufort. Rather, I've been given advance information about a small function happening this Sunday afternoon, and I would like for you to attend on my behalf." He took out a piece of paper from his suit jacket pocket, handed it to Cindy.

She looked at the address. "An open house?"

"Yes. For a property which may be of interest to me. Of you too, I would assume. Your own motives, though, are neither here nor there. All I'm concerned with is not driving the price up unnecessarily. I would hate to tip off the real estate agency as to my interest. Normally this is something I would have an employee of Patrick's stature handle. But seeing as though he's proven himself to be unreliable of late, I thought you would be the perfect person to enlist."

Cindy Scanlon did her best to hide her expression from Langston Livingston, indulging an inner poker face she'd perfected years ago. Simply, she didn't want him to know how she truly felt. Because if you want to know the truth—well, some of it—Cindy had already seen the small ad in the classifieds this morning and had marked the date on her calendar.

She wouldn't miss the open house at Fast Cash's place for all the wine in Napa.

And Langston was right, she did have her own motive for wanting to be there.

"OH, THAT would be lovely, I'll have a bottle of wine chilled…oh, or perhaps a pot of tea would be more appropriate."

Lottie Cashman could barely contain her excitement over how quickly things were happening. A phone call yesterday afternoon from that sweet young thing at Beverly Mills of Beverly Hills had confirmed that the Open House was scheduled for this coming Sunday, from noon to five, and that both she and Beverly would be there to help her play host to the festivities. She had said there were a few matters to attend to, and could she drop by in the morning.

Now morning had arrived, and despite the foul weather sweeping across the area, Lottie's mood was as bright as sunshine. The teakettle began to whistle just as a smart-looking

Jaguar pulled into her driveway, parking behind Lottie's aging Porsche. G-D, people sure had a lot of money in this town, she thought. Then she turned off the kettle, bustled her way to the front door and let in that sweet Ms. Davies before she got too wet.

"Oh, nasty day. So unlike Los Angeles."

"The weatherman said the Santa Ana's were going to pick up," Lottie said. "Rain and wind, a day to stay inside."

Lottie escorted her guest into her kitchen, poured tea for them both.

"I'm sorry, I should have a pound cake, also. I'm a bit distracted lately."

"That's perfectly understandable, Mrs. Cashman."

"Oh, please, you must call me Lottie. I feel such a connection with you, young lady. It's like you've known all along what I've needed, and you've responded with such kindness."

"What a nice thing to say. And remember, first name basis goes both ways."

"Yes, Lana."

Lottie sipped at her tea and then said, "I really must remark on how professional you've been—and how much of a go-getter you are. Ms. Mills must be quite pleased with how you go about your job. How you ever knew to contact me, I'll just never know."

"If you're going to work in real estate, you have to act fast, especially if you're going to succeed at such a prestigious agency as Beverly Mills of Beverly Hills. When I saw the news article about your upcoming court case, I wondered if there might be some way we could work together. You had a house to sell, I sell houses. And with Ms. Mills' blessing, I contacted you. It's really very simple, and very much by-the-book."

"You're quite a sweet thing," Lottie said. "Men must be banging down your door."

A sour expression crossed Lana's face, and she quickly redirected the conversation.

Ten minutes of amiable chatter ensued, and when they had equally exhausted pleasantries and tea, Lana suggested they get on with the business at hand. Gathering an umbrella, the two ladies ventured outdoors into the rainy mess. While Lana went to her car's trunk, Lottie looked back at the house she and Jack had shared, a spacious, faux Beaux-Arts style mansion, with incredible views of the ocean. Yet something about it looked so forlorn against the day's gray landscape, and Lottie actually shed a tear as she realized that part of her life was truly over. The house was as empty as her life. She would be moving on.

"Let's get this done with quickly, so we don't get too wet."

Lottie agreed. With the umbrella shielding her from the blowing wind and cascading rain, she watched as Lana Davies went to her trunk and pulled out a "For Sale" sign. A diagonal strip had been placed over the sign, announcing the Open House.

With the aid of a hammer, Lana placed the sign into the ground.

As for Lottie, she looked first at the house and then at the sign. Finally, in a wistful, quiet voice, she said, "My Jack, he really is dead, isn't he?"

Lana found herself just staring at the grieving widow.

ANOTHER PARADISE, an ocean away.

Patrick Scanlon hadn't exactly packed for island living, but dressed in jeans and a T-shirt, we supposed he was comfy enough. He had little choice, not as though he booked the flight himself. The temperature was only in the low seventies that day on Bermuda, and the forecast held for cooler temperatures. That was a good thing he was told, this was Hurricane season in the mid-Atlantic region, and so it was lucky to avoid the hot, steamy, muggy conditions that made such violent storms possible. Even so, the cooler air and fresh floral scents of the island were doing wonders for Patrick's hangover.

As he stood on the beach, allowing the water to chill his toes, Patrick contemplated the situation as he knew it. The last thing Patrick remembered, he and Todd were climbing the stairs to his apartment in New York and then he was crashing on the sofa…and next thing he knew, he was waking on an altogether different, yet familiar sofa. He realized he'd been brought back to where he had been before, handcuffed to that smelly sofa in the offices of the two thugs. He had to wonder then: had he dreamed the entire rescue by Todd, the bar, the…no, that was too real. So, what the hell had happened?

"All answers will come to you soon," had said the little guy called Fred. There'd been no sign of Barney.

Trouble was, if Patrick wanted answers of any kind, he had to do as instructed, and that included hopping in a cab, going to LaGuardia and boarding a flight to Bermuda. He didn't put up much fight, given that he knew the island paradise had been where Todd had been the past six months; perhaps this was part of Todd's plan? No, even in his hung-over haze, to Patrick that reasoning made no reasonable sense. During the two-hour flight, he had his thoughts to occupy him.

The morning arrived and Fred emerged from the cottage by the beach and said, "Come on, Mr. Beachcomber, we're going into town."

"What for?"

"You wanted answers?"

So Patrick gave in, as he so often did, wishing he hadn't gotten so used to playing the role of the Defeated Man lately. A cab came and claimed them, and after cutting around cautious curves, they arrived in the harbor town of Hamilton. Patrick had never been to Bermuda before, and he thought the city looked like a mix of Colonial, British, and some tiny little Western town from yesteryear. The huge cruise ships docked to his left let him know he was in the present day, and in the midst of tourist central.

Except where they went, few tourists would dare to venture. It was a rickety old dive bar, and once Patrick walked in from the bright light of outdoors, he needed a good minute before his eyes adjusted to its dark interior. He followed Fred to the long wood bar, where they both took up seats.

"What'll it be boys?"

"Beer. Whatever's on tap," Fred said. "Two of them."

Still feeling the effects of yesterday's whisky, Patrick wasn't sure alcohol should be on tap for him. Still, when the cold lager was placed before him, he happily took a sip. It felt good going down and for a second he imagined everything would be fine.

"Just arrive, boys?" asked the barkeep.

"How can you tell?" Patrick said.

"In the darkness of the bar, your pale skin kind of glows."

"Thanks."

"Name's Buzz," said the barkeep. "Welcome to the Factory. You going to be staying awhile?"

"Depends," Fred said.

"That right, depends on what?" Buzz asked.

"Yeah, I'd kind of like to know the answer to that, too."

Just then Buzz held up his hands. "You know, boys, I think I'd prefer not to know anything. Just enjoy your beers, let me know if you need another." With that, the crusty old barkeep backed away, back to his bar and the polishing of glasses. Patrick watched the guy for a second, noticed behind him the big antique cash register, the fish tank above it. Something was swimming inside the latter, but from here Patrick couldn't make it out. Not a fish, something else.

Patrick gazed back at Fred. "You want to tell me what the hell is going on? Why are we here?"

"All in good time, all in good time," said Fred, who, despite his tiny size, still maintained a threatening air to him. Must be those muscles. "We may as well enjoy ourselves while we wait out whatever's happening on the mainland. Shall we have a toast?"

"What are we toasting?" Patrick asked.

"A man named Fast Cash," Fred said.

And then he waited for Patrick to clink glasses. It took a second.

"What do you know about Fast Cash?"

Fred pulled out from his pocket a photocopy of the map and article about the legendary bank robber.

"Lot of money seems to be floating out there, ready for the taking by the first one who finds it."

Fred smiled. Patrick didn't.

Both men clinked their glassed with a hint of reluctance, and then looked over at Buzz for a refill.

But Buzz was busy, dropping a small pellet of food into the tank.

"What the heck is he feeding?" Patrick asked.

"Looks like a frog."

Toad! Patrick thought. And that's when he realized he was now where Todd had been just days ago.

But why?

BEVERLY MILLS had her feet up on her desk, and she was chugging away at a cigarette, more eating it than smoking it. Damn she loved these things. So what if they would one day put her in her grave, damn well she was going to enjoy herself as long as she thrived on this planet. She always did.

Her phone buzzed. "Yes, Veronica."

"No, I'm Vera."

"Oh, right, whatever."

"You have a guest. He said he was expected, but he won't give a name."

Oh right, Vera was new, she'd replaced Veronica, who had replaced Lana, and maybe that's where the confusion set in? Ever since Lana had done so well bringing in the Cashman account to get promoted, Beverly had been through scores of assistants and none of them lasted long enough to remember who to let in and who not to, and frankly, Beverly was tired of trying to keep all these newbies straight in her own mind.

"Just send him up."

Heavy footsteps pounded on her stairs and she winced at the scuffling. She needed to have the carpet cleaned, such a brute he was. She opened a drawer to her desk, double-checked the device was there. Staring at it, she spoke aloud, "Langston, is that you?" and watched the spirals begin to spin.

"Beverly Mills of Beverly Hills, who the hell else would it be?"

"What can I do for you?"

"I think you know."

"You're so boring, Langston."

"I like to play it safe. Now, shall we get down to business?"

She knew the drill. First the payment. Second the interest due.

Atop her desk was a plain white envelope, not the fancy kind used by her agency. Why waste taste on a vulgar man like him? She tossed it Langston's way and he just scooped it up and placed it within his suit jacket pocket.

"You're not going to count it?"

"You haven't disappointed me yet, why should I start to distrust you now?" he said. "And now that you've covered the base payment, let me enjoy the interest."

She just closed her eyes and allowed it to happen. Langston Livingston buried himself in the mounds of her stupendous breasts, gobbling every last inch as he lifted her dress. With his clothes still glued to his skin, he unzipped and hoisted himself out, then slid in easily and quickly, and thrust and thrust and then, well, he was done. Quickly, thankfully.

The man grinned at her as he rose from his position.

"One of these days you'll realize that you can't live without me," he said, and then with a more pointed tone, finished by saying, "Esther."

"Yes, I'm perfectly aware that my life—and livelihood—is in your hands," spoke the woman who insisted she be called Beverly Mills.

God, she hated that all of that had been recorded.

AND WHAT of Todd, what's become of him?

Well, right this very moment he was at JFK International Airport, boarding a non-stop American Airlines flight to Los Angeles, and he was not a happy camper…er, flyer.

He had to wonder: they say you shouldn't fly when you have a cold; did that same rule apply to headaches? His hangover might be long gone, but damn if that bump on his noggin still ached. Regardless of his injuries, Todd Gleason had no choice but to board, this was the last flight out tonight and he had promised Cindy he would not let her down, Patrick or no Patrick. When he'd woken from his thug-induced slumber to find the apartment empty, he'd quickly gathered his wits about him and started planning for the next stage of their scheme. What he knew was this: Patrick was gone, the map to Fast Cash's house was too, and Todd had run out of time.

He'd had no choice, he returned Cindy's five phone calls.

"It's about time you called back."

"Look, it's complicated."

"Did you find Patrick?'

"Yes…and no."

"You want to explain that one?"

"I will, later. Pick me up at LAX at nine forty-five tonight."

"Todd, what's going on?"

"I'll see you soon. I've got a flight to catch."

And now, here he was, in seat 16F, staring out the window at the tarmac, waiting for them to close the door and begin the arduous taxi to the runway. He was looking forward to six hours where all he had to do was sleep and think. That was the nice thing about flying. You were trapped not in your current world or your next one, you were suspended in time and not in control. Might as well enjoy it. Especially since no one was sitting beside him.

Whoops, thought too soon.

"Is this seat taken?" said the man who hovered above.

Todd wasn't even going to look up, but there was something familiar about those pants.

"Oh, Christ."

"Hello, Todd. Or is it Richard? This flight is going to Los Angeles, not Virginia."

"I think you know I was lying."

"How about that, the first honest thing you've said to me." The Big Guy sat down beside him in the middle seat, crowding him. Those thick muscles, they needed room to expand. "And by the way, my name really is Barney."

"I know," he said. "Something tells me this is not a coincidence."

"Nope," Barney said, and from his tight leather pants pocket he withdrew a single sheet of paper. It was, of course, the map. "You and me, we've got some business to attend to in the City of Angels. I hear it's a place where you can make your fortune."

"One question—where's Patrick?"

"I don't know who you're talking about."

"Fine. Play it that way," Todd said. "Another question."

"You got too many questions."

"Yeah. Then try answering one of them. Where's your little partner, Fred? I doubt he's playing house with Betty."

"Funny. And Fred's none of your concern."

Todd did the math. Barney at his side. Patrick missing, Fred missing.

"Just tell me one thing. Patrick, he's not hurt, is he?"

"Are you?" Barney asked, his eyes baring down on Todd with a hint of menace.

"Not currently."

"Shut up, it stays that way. For you both."

Todd's intended reply was interrupted by an announcement from the flight deck. "Ladies and gentleman, a reminder to please keep your seatbelts fastened at all times. As we get closer to Los Angeles, a storm is brewing with possible strong winds. We could be in for a bumpy flight, folks."

No kidding, Todd thought.

Just then the plane went hurtling down the runway and shot its way into the night sky. Next stop: Los Angeles. Or Bust.

BAD ENOUGH Carl Beaufort would be buried with a gaping wound in the back of his head, but did they have to slice and dice him, too? Murder victim translates to autopsy, no matter how obvious the cause of death is. Those cops, they like to dot their t's and cross their eyes.

For Los Angeles Detective Earnest Dalrymple, autopsies always made him queasy, and this one had been scheduled for just after his designated dinnertime. That beef burrito with extra rice and beans just wasn't going to last that long in his system.

Dalrymple entered the County Morgue building, made his way down the corridor and eventually found himself standing outside Examination Room #4. Gazing in, from the looks of it the coroner was finished with her primary exam, but hadn't yet…closed the guy up. No wonder Carl Beaufort had been such a damn fine reporter, Dalrymple, thought, what with guts like that.

Just then the door opened and Dr. Emily Marcus stepped out. She was a real looker, the detective had always thought so, and found it curious that a woman with such beauty would choose a profession that was so ugly.

"Perfect timing, Ernie," Dr. Marcus said. "I just filed the report. Just as you and Benes suspected—definitely it was the gunshot. The guy was alive before then, no question."

"And the wet clothes?"

"Oh yeah, he was definitely killed somewhere else, then dropped alongside the 101."

"Ocean?"

"Nope, chlorine in his lungs. Guy went swimming in someone's pool."

"Anything else?"

"Oh yeah, you may want to have a look at this. We found it stuffed down his throat."

Protected in an evidence bag was a tiny slip of paper.

"Well, I think we've got our first lead," Dalrymple said, reading the name written on the mysterious piece of paper. "Just who are you Patrick Scanlon, and are you my killer?"

PART TWO

CITY OF ANGLES

CHAPTER EIGHT

IN A world renowned for its laid-back approach to life, its grand lifestyles and Olympic-size swimming pools, its luxury cars and ready-to-glow tans, how appropriate was it that Angelinos referred to their main airport as LAX. As if upon on second landing it was called RELAX. Such was Todd Gleason's appraisal as they began their initial descent into the greater Los Angeles area. From his window seat he watched as the voluminous streaks of illumination on the ground grew ever closer, as the wings worked overtime to lower the plane to the runway.

That earlier storm had blown through quickly and so, by the time they had flown all the way across the country, the sky had settled and the air was calm and they near-glided their way to a smooth landing. The jet touched down, the pilot applied the brakes, and gradually they were reduced to a more manageable speed. In other words, they were on the ground safely and without incident. Except for the fact that Todd's companion hadn't bailed on him mid-flight, as he'd hoped.

Todd turned toward his unwanted seatmate and said, "Well, we're here. What next?"

"You tell me. Like I said during the flight, I'm being paid to act as your bodyguard."

Great, in L.A. not even a minute and already this guy was taking acting lessons.

"I don't need a bodyguard."

"Consider it a gift."

"Can I return you for store credit?"

Barney smirked. "You're lucky I'm harmless."

"Good thing to have in a bodyguard," he said. "Though my head stills begs to differ. Just who are you protecting me from—yourself? You still haven't told me who hired you."

"Who said anyone did? What kind of detective would I be to reveal client secrets?"

"See, you're contradicting yourself—pick one, private eye or bodyguard?"

That was enough conversation for now, frankly more than they'd shared the entire trip. Todd had slept, Barney had watched a movie, Todd watched a movie, Barney slept, Todd tried to move to another seat, Barney had awakened and stopped him. A volley at 37,000 feet, to be continued at sea level.

They slowly shuffled their way off the plane, followed their fellow passengers toward the baggage claim and the exit. On Todd's shoulder was a weekend bag, not unlike the one Barney carried on his own massive shoulder. But Todd claimed he had a larger suitcase to pick up at baggage.

"You're kidding. Who checks bag?"

"I do. I hate lugging those damn things through the airport when my gate is usually six miles away from the security point."

This was utter bullshit. Of course Todd did not have a bag to collect. Of course he was lying. Of course it was step one in ditching his cross-country shadow. Next thing to figure out was how to work this sudden ruse to his advantage.

Todd said, "Why don't you wait at the carousel while I use the bathroom?"

"Nice try."

"What, I can't go anywhere without my luggage, and I can't leave without peeing."

"Why didn't you pee on the plane?"

"I hate those tight quarters. Big Guy, you should relate."

"We're like an old married couple, the way we bicker."

"I won't tell Fred if you don't."

He rolled his eyes. "As if. Fine, go pee. But I'm waiting right by the door, you're not going anywhere. So don't try something stupid like standing on the toilet so I can't see your legs and think you're somewhere other than the john."

Todd put his hand on the thug's shoulder. "You're just too smart for me."

Todd started toward the men's room when Barney said, "Oh, and leave your bag with me. Who knows what tricks you got up some shirt sleeve."

Doing as requested without complaint, Todd then made his way into the men's room. He went right for the last stall, closed the door. From there he withdrew his cell phone from his pocket; dumb Barney. Immediately, Todd set his thumbs to work on the keypad, sending a text message to Cindy. What he wrote was simple enough: *Come to Exit. Pull Long Lost Friend. Like College. T.* Then he peed and flushed the toilet for good measure, just in case some cop or U.S. Senator was nearby. By then, Cindy had replied. *K.*

The whole thing had only taken three minutes and Barney

was waiting outside the men's room just as promised. He said the bags should be unloaded by now, let's go get your suitcase. That's when Todd confessed it had been part of a trick he was trying to pull.

"You saw right through that. Guess you're right, there's no getting rid of you."

"The sooner you realize it, Todd, the better we're going to get along."

The two unlikely travelers then headed toward the terminal exit, Todd searching for signs of Cindy. There she was, just beyond the ropes. With that flowing red hair and gorgeous body, she was unmistakable, even in a city where beauty was so common the ugly people tended to stand out.

As Todd and Barney joined the waiting throngs of people who anticipated the arrival of their friend, family, lover, mistress, agent, a sudden commotion caught the attention of many of the onlookers.

"Leopold! My Leo, oh my goodness, my love…my…huge, hulking love!"

That declaration of love was coming from the mouth of Cindy Scanlon and she wasted no time in running into the surprised arms of one Barney Stone. Cindy peppered his scruffy face with kisses and he had no choice but to run with the moment, and besides, even considering his bulk, the forward motion of her body worked in tandem with his natural resistance and it in turn created a near-aerial swirl, almost a dance. The crowd erupted into applause so loud that Todd couldn't even hear Barney's protests. Well, mostly he couldn't hear them because he'd slipped away from the shameless display, making his way into the dark night of Los Angeles.

Barney gone. Now he needed to reconnect with Cindy. And hand her an Oscar.

Really, that was some introduction to life in Hollywood.

"LEOPOLD?"

"It was either that or Loeb, and Leopold just had the right number of syllables."

"You're awful."

"I thought a crook like you would appreciate it."

"Hey, I'm nowhere near in their league, thank you very much. Besides, you know I don't like that label. I'm more like Robin Hood."

"Robin Hood shared with the less fortunate."

"So we don't have everything in common."

With the aid of further texting, Cindy and Todd had surreptitiously met up at the United terminal, and now they were driving—well, Cindy was driving, Todd was just chatting—south on the 405 and destined for the Scanlon bungalow in Manhattan Beach. They'd discussed whether it was safe to go there, and Cindy wondered did the Lug in Leather know who Todd was meeting and where they were going? Not to my knowledge, was Todd's hopeful reply. For now, they'd take a chance. Barney had already proved not to be terribly smart; twice now in fact.

"He'll turn up at some point, he's like a bad penny."

"This is L.A," Cindy said with a throaty laugh. "We don't do pennies."

Todd stole a look at his friend—a real look, not at the teasing temptress he'd seen in Bermuda, but the real woman, in her element, hurtling down the freeway and reveling in the night breeze as it brazenly whipped through her hair. For a second he was reminded of the sprightly young co-ed who had pierced his heart upon first sight, and only the memory of her pulling a figurative knife out a couple years later reminded him to watch his step. Hollywood might enjoy making romances, but they also did thrillers, and Cindy could no doubt play either the love interest or the femme fatale.

"Patrick," Cindy finally said after a few minutes of silent driving. "You saw him?"

"Sure did."

"Where is he now?"

Todd told her. The rescue, the retaliation. "So Barney's on my trail, and Fred has Patrick, I guess like an insurance policy. Hopefully our ditching Barney won't have any harmful repercussions."

"No matter, we're on a mission, and the sooner we bring it to a close the better."

Cindy then dropped the subject altogether.

A short while later they pulled into the narrow driveway of a cute little bungalow.

"But at least it's a house, tiny as it is. And it has a pool. Patrick and I just didn't want to live in one of those fabricated apartment complexes filled with wannabe actors and washed-up, uh, actors. We didn't come here to seek fame—fortune, yes. And as you can see from the modest little bungalow we call home, fortune has yet to return the favor. Despite the promises of Livingston Enterprises. The house was one thing I wouldn't upgrade, not right away."

"It's cute."

"So are puppies."

"And they're just as small."

"This from a guy who calls a closet home."

"At least my studio is paid for."

For that, Cindy punched Todd in the arm. He didn't mind, the more time they spent together the more natural their friendship felt, their connection. Because once upon a time their friendship had come with lots of fringe benefits, and they rarely missed an opportunity to take advantage of them. Nights, mornings, lunch breaks, in between classes, there were days you had to peel them off each other. She had wiles, this one did, and now she was older, wiser…and what else? Todd would have to watch his step, danger and temptation lurked on every block.

"Are you tired, do you want to just crash?" Cindy asked.

"At this point, I'm running on pure adrenaline. Now that I'm here, might as well keep going. Besides, we have a lot to talk about and I think the cover of night might serve us better. There's something about moonlight that's good about getting to the heart's soul."

"Todd Gleason, when did you become such a poet?"

"Maybe you bring it out in me."

Okay, wrong thing to say, wrong part of the "heart's soul" to reveal. "So, how about that pool, we can catch a swim and then talk?"

"No!" Cindy said, more sharply than she intended. Todd picked up on her slight loss of cool, this noticeable deviation in character.

"Uh, Cin? What's wrong with the pool? You were just bragging about it…"

"It needs to be cleaned, Patrick usually takes care of that and well, he's nowhere to be found is he? Or, in your case, re-found. Look, how about we go down to the beach, it's not far, we can take a stroll along the cool sand. If your Frigidaire-sized bodyguard decides to make an appearance, at least we won't be home."

Todd found himself agreeing, though mention of the beach reminded him of Bermuda and of Lana and of…oh, never mind such wistful thoughts. Focus on the here and now.

So Cindy changed into jeans and sandals, and Todd refreshed himself by leaving on the same jeans he'd worn on the flight, but changed to a looser, blue chambray button down, which he left untucked. Casual and beachy, perfect for a moonlight stroll along the beach with… Really, he had to stop thinking that way. In the bathroom, he splashed water on his face and said to the mirrored-image of himself, "Cindy is the past. Even the recent past, it's still the past." Like Lana…

Enough.

Okay.

There, that was settled, wasn't that easy?

A doubtful expression faded from the mirror as Todd made his exit.

Cindy was waiting on the porch, and together the two of them wound their way down a worn, darkened path, the crashing waves of the ocean growing louder with each forward step. As though calling out to them, leading them toward its undercurrent of temptations. At last they emerged from a copse of thick green brush and their feet hit the soft, surprisingly warm sand; a breeze was blowing off the ocean and Todd immediately felt a chill. Would L.A. make up its mind what weather pattern it wanted?

Still, he had to admit, the view was incredible, with intermittent clouds hanging over the horizon, and the near-full moon bathing the water with shimmering ripples.

"So, where do we begin?" Todd suddenly said.

"Cut right to the chase, huh, Todd?"

"I think our small talk wouldn't fit in Whoville," he said. "Look, Patrick filled me in on a few things before I…lost him. But I get the sense that there's a whole lot more going on than just Patrick trying to clear his debts to a boss who doesn't exactly look after his employees best interests. The map, Cin? Patrick seems to believe a fortune in stolen money is waiting to be found in the old Cashman estate. Patrick says we find it, we split it."

Cindy said nothing. Todd had no choice but to continue.

"Silent treatment, huh? Okay, so the map, this whole Fast Cash business, I'm guessing it's actually got nothing to do with Livingston Enterprises but yet has everything to do with what the two of you are mixed up in. Which tells me you two are mixed up in two things, and I think you're trying to play one against the other and see which of them gives you some kind of upper hand."

"Wow, that's a lot of deduction."

"It was a long flight."

"Well, you're right about one thing," Cindy said. "We are going to find that missing money, that's why I needed you in Los Angeles."

"But what's it all about? Really."

"Todd, do you remember when we met in college, what bonded us?"

"Sure. You were beautiful and I wanted to sleep with you."

"After that, Todd. More than the physical. What was our emotional bond?"

Todd swallowed, a sudden heavy lump appearing in his throat. He knew the answer, of course he knew, but that didn't mean he liked to talk about it, even now, even after so much time had elapsed and the wound should have long-healed. But it hadn't.

"Fathers," he finally said.

"No Alzheimer's here, good," she said, linking her arm in his as they walked. "I remember that one night our sophomore year, lying in bed and realizing how quickly I was falling in love with you and then suddenly asking you if you ever saw yourself getting married, having kids. You know, the whole white picket fence thing. I thought you were going to freak, thinking I was looking to get hitched right then and there. Do you remember what you said?"

"Yeah. I said, 'I don't want to be a father.'"

"You hadn't spoken much about your family; you didn't see eye to eye and you seldom, if ever, went home. But at least you mentioned a mother, three sisters—I do remember all that, Todd. I remember all of our conversations. I listened to the pain behind the words. Including the fact that the one subject you wouldn't discuss was your father."

"Sure I did. I said he left to get cigarettes when I was five years old, but those cancer sticks must have gotten to him before he'd even reached the store."

"A flippant remark that hid deeper emotions."

"So, my father left us poor and starving. Whatever, happens all the time."

"And what did I tell you about my father?"

"That he got your mother pregnant, married her, then three months after you were born he said he couldn't do this and he left. See, I too remember our talks, Cindy. In fact, I fancy a conversation we had during our senior year, just after you'd broken up with me. You said that you wanted to have the stable family life that you'd never had growing up, and that you'd found a man who could give you everything you wanted and who wanted everything that you wanted. Trouble was that someone happened to be my best friend."

They'd been walking aimlessly down the lonely stretch of beach, and at the moment had stopped before a wall of crumbling stone and rock. Without saying so, they both climbed atop the stone wall, dangling their legs over the side. They sat side by side, each of them lost to their stories of yesterday.

Cindy turned to Todd, placed her hand on his scruffy cheek. Even in the darkness the red of her nails looked like fresh blood. As though a fresh wound had been opened, or maybe just an old one. Except one of them was chipped.

Todd took hold of her hand, felt the electric tingle between them.

"What happened here? You're usually so well put together."

"Slight mishap, haven't had a chance to have my nails done again."

"Well, chip or not, you still have lovely hands, I remember their touch…"

She pulled away. "And you're still as irresistibly charming as ever, Todd Gleason," Cindy said. "I can't take back anything that happened between us…in college, and certainly not after. Right now, in this perfect moment where neither of us has to think of anything but the person before us, it would be the easiest thing in the world to give in to an attraction that obviously still exists. But I can't do that to Patrick, not now, I can't allow vulnerability to feed desire. There's too much at stake, and my emotions are too raw."

"Why?" Todd said, his voice a whisper, his mouth so close to hers.

"Our bond, remember, that's where we started this conversation. And as much as you say you never want to know what happened to your father, I do. That's what this is about: my dad. Todd, everything my mother told me about him was a lie."

"How can you be sure?"

"Because she told me so herself."

"Cindy, your mother died four years ago, right before you moved to…"

"Los Angeles."

"Is that what prompted the move? That night, after your mother's funeral, you were a bit of a mess and…"

"Todd, please. Don't go there. Not now."

She'd always been such a strong woman, rarely was there a tone to her voice that brought to mind a frightened little girl. But it was there tonight. Cynthia O'Neil Scanlon did not scare easily, and picking up on her vulnerabilities Todd swallowed the past, forgot it. But then again, he always did what Cindy asked. Love me, break up with me…other stuff. Find Patrick.

"Okay, some things are starting to make a little more sense. You and Patrick pulled up stakes just weeks after your mom died and you moved to Los Angeles. I never knew why and neither of you gave me a satisfactory answer. Felt a change, that's what you said, had some money from her estate. Now you're telling me the reason was to get reacquainted with the father you never knew. Why? He didn't want you then, why would you think he'd want you now?"

"Todd, don't transfer how you feel to me," she said. "The fact of the matter is my father never knew I even existed. Yes, he got my mother pregnant, but she never told him about the pregnancy, not then. They never got married, he never left me. By the time he did learn about me, so many years had passed and he'd found himself a new life. A life he'd found in California, a long way away from the Long Island of his teen years."

"Why did your mother contact him—I mean, years had passed. What did she expect him to do about it? About you?"

"Typical Mother O'Neil," Cindy said. "She found him because she wanted some financial help. She tracked him down, told him about me, insisted he pay for my college education. Which apparently he did, even though he didn't really have the money. That was just the start of what would become a history of financial troubles for him, something he never recovered from. Something that led him to do something that was strictly out of character for him—or so Mother claimed."

"Look, this is a lot to take in. Can we just cut to the chase? What does your father's past have to do with what's going on now? With Patrick?"

"I made us move to L.A., because I wanted to find out who my father was."

"Was? That sounds definitively past tense."

"Not necessarily," Cindy said. "See, according to my mother—and remember, this was on her deathbed four years ago, so what reason would she have to continue to lie?—she said my father had simply disappeared one day, about three or so years prior."

"So that would make it about seven, eight years ago?"

Just then a light bulb went off over Todd's head, brightening the sky better than any old glow of starlight could ever wish upon. After all, he'd just done all this reading and research on the man Cindy was talking about. Yes, lots of pieces were now starting to fall into place. "My God, Cindy, your father is Jack Cashman—that crook known as Fast Cash."

Cindy simply nodded. "How about that, Todd, I'm the child of a criminal. No wonder I found you so appealing, huh?"

"Gee, funny," he said dryly. "Want to tell what your plan is?

"Easy. Find my father's fortune and use it to get Patrick out of trouble. And maybe, just maybe, once I have his money I can finally learn the truth about what happened to him. I mean, no word for seven years? Not even a body turning up? He's got to be somewhere. And I think someone knows exactly where."

"**MOTHER, I'M** home. Are you awake? Mother?"

Announcing her arrival back to the small apartment they shared in the enclave known as Glendale wasn't rude, if Mother was sleeping she wanted to be awakened. Her daughter's safe return from the evil that insidiously dwelled in Los Angeles was worth being roused from even the deepest slumber. Not that Mother could fully rest that of the weary until her only child had returned home, and in one piece.

"Mother?"

"What is in the den?" came a voice from another room, ostensibly, from the den.

"Someone's watching *Jeopardy*."

"And someone else is late."

Lana Davies walked into the over-crowded den, removing her indulgent Prada high heels as she did so. Back to her comfortable five-foot-five, she bent over and kissed her pale-skinned mother on the forehead, brushing back the wispy gray hair, and said, "I called from the office over two hours ago, said I was working on a potential big sale and then had to drop something off. Said I'd be home before *Law & Order*."

"You didn't specify which one," Mother asked. "I don't like these new responsibilities of yours, they have you working many more hours than necessary. And those shoes, have I seen them before? They look expensive."

"Mother. It's worth it, both the job and looking the part. You need to trust me."

"Like I did when you insisted I trust you about that little trip out of town. Darling, you came home so…I would call it dispirited."

"Mother, everything is fine. I'm fine."

"I've missed you, dear. Come and sit by my side, at least watch until the double jeopardy round is over. I used the DVR to record it, so I could watch all the news shows live. I'll pause it while you get your dinner, which is still heating in the oven."

Dinner was the last thing on Lana's mind. She assured her mother she'd already eaten and said, "Let's just watch the show." Actually, the concept of "double jeopardy" caught her off guard, and she sat there and contemplated its meaning: not being able to be tried a second time for the same crime. The law always seemed to side with the criminal, as though Section IV, Article 2 of the Criminal Code said, "Oh, yeah, well prove it!" Before she knew it the program had ended, she missed out on not only

Double Jeopardy but Final Jeopardy, and golly if that concept didn't appeal to her. She'd also missed what followed, which was a question by her mother.

"What? Oh, I'm sorry. I drifted."

"Lana Davies, where is your mind tonight? Or for that matter, lately."

If only she knew. Life was just not something that seemed to be going her way lately, not since before her trip to Bermuda and not since. But she was working on it, determined to get them out of his dingy cheap-but-not-really apartment. It was Lana and Mother against the world, and now that young Lana had grown into a magnificent beauty of such radiance, why, nothing was going to stop her. Like when she decided the real money in L.A. was not in movie making but in land dealing, and she'd strived every day since moving into this imaginary palace to make it in the exclusive, backstabbing world that was California real estate. Five years of grunt work, low pay, and lower expectations, she'd finally gotten her big break—working the receptionist's desk at the newly formed Beverly Mills of Beverly Hills. After lasting longer in her position than her previous eleven predecessors, the big-as-life Ms. Mills had taken the wet-behind-the-ears Ms. Davies under her sizable wings (read: bosoms) and began to shape her in her own image. Okay, not an exact physical match, but all the same she instilled within her a drive that Lana always knew breathed beneath her constricted lungs.

Cut to a year and a half later, and at last her moment was here. Her big "get."

"Lana, darling, what's troubling you? You look like a deer who has just learned hunting season begins tomorrow."

"Well, I do have to talk to you—and by that I mean I talk and you listen. You do have a tendency, Mother, to shoot your mouth off before you hear the whole story," Lana stated, uncharacteristically outspoken. Maybe she was changing, maybe thanks to Ms. Mills she was learning to stand on her own two feet.

Sitting down beside Mother, she took hold of the woman's craggy hands and said, "Mama (not the formal Mother she usually used, she needed her to hear these words from her heart, not her mind), I've got a lead—on Daddy...."

"Lana, darling, what have you been up to?"

"Just wait…listen. I told you, it's about Daddy."

"Your father is dead, darling. If I've been able to move on, they why can't you?"

Lana swung her arms wide, nearly knocking over the cheap lamp on the end table. "You call living in this place moving on? It's like hanging out in purgatory, Mother, like an airplane that hasn't been cleared for landing, just flying in circles waiting for someone else to tell us its okay to land. And it's been like that since…well, since you know when. I think it's time we landed. And don't tell me you're satisfied…"

"Lana, I'm fifty-nine, I've long given up on being satisfied. Content is a more suitable word. To me, I exist until I don't, and what life hands me, that's what I take."

"Sometimes, Mother, you have to give back to life the shit it's trying to shove down your throat."

"Lana!"

"Oh, Mother, don't get me wrong. I appreciate and love you for all that you've done for me. But I'm twenty-six now, and I need to get my sea legs, so to speak. I need to not only ride those waves that are breaking out there, I need to conquer them and prove that I matter. That I can win."

"Such colorful language, Lana. Full of metaphors tonight."

"Yeah, well, someone taught me that life is what you make it, and he…"

"He?"

"Forget about any 'he,' it's just someone I met who got me thinking," Lana said. "Look, here's what I wanted to tell you before we got sidetracked. Mother, work requires my time—only for a few hours—over the weekend, and yes, I know we usually spend all day Sunday together, but this is so vitally important to my career—and beyond—that I'm hoping you don't fight me on it. I'd rather go with your blessing than go with you disappointed in me."

"Lana, I could never be disappointed in you. But let me ask you this—this work on Sunday? Is it really for your career? Or does it have to do with this lingering mess about your father?"

"Actually, Mother, the two are kind of related."

"Meaning what, exactly?"

"Meaning I think I know where Daddy is," she said. "I'm just waiting for confirmation. By the way, any mail for me today, or any calls from a lab?"

"Lana Davies, honestly, some days I hardly recognize you anymore. Labs!" she said. "You sound like you've got something cooking, and by that I don't mean dinner. Which by the way you should eat because I know you and you didn't get food earlier." Then she paused, and Lana saw the sad look cross her Mother's face. "Lana, please, be careful of your dreams, you didn't exactly inherit good genes when it comes to success."

Lana looked again at their Spartan apartment, wondered if Mother meant herself, or Daddy. Then her stomach grumbled in protest. In *Jeopardy* speak: What is Mother knows best?

CHAPTER NINE

"ANY CHANCE of you waking today?"

The voice was vaguely familiar, and when he managed to open still-tired eyes, the vision brought certain recollections to light. The walls, the bed, the general surroundings, they were all a bit fuzzy to his eyes. Then the fog lifted and he remembered it all: the long flight, the arrival in Los Angeles, the walk along the beach, Cindy's revelations about the search for her presumed dead father. Todd was conscious, suddenly aware that beneath the blankets he was quite entirely naked. He looked at himself, and then he looked at her.

"Don't worry, champ, nothing happened."

Todd gazed up from the comfort of his downy pillow. Cindy wore different jeans and a fresh blouse, but otherwise she was the same temptingly infuriating woman who had in recent days managed to scam both a private detective and a con man. Damn, she was good.

"Wanna tell me what did happen last night?"

"I told you—nothing."

"Then why am I not wearing any clothes?"

Cindy placed her hands on her hips, gave off a hint of a smile. "It's not as though you packed your wooly pajamas and I'm not inclined to have you sleep in your clothes and then have to do your laundry. Check the chair, your clothes are all neatly laid out."

"Yeah, but who put them there?"

"Todd, you were so exhausted when we returned from the beach, you passed out like a drunk on a bender. So I removed your clothes and tucked you in nice and tight. No harm done."

"You had to remove, uh, everything?"

Cindy, laughing, dropped to his bedside. She ruffled his bed-head. "Oh, Todd you don't wear modesty very well, do you? Besides, it's not anything I haven't seen before. You keep in very nice shape. Nice all-over tan, too."

He pulled the cover up to his neck.

"Get up, shy boy. Clock's gone past noon. You want to succeed in this town, you get up with the sun."

She left the room and then Todd did as instructed and in less than twenty minutes he'd showered and dressed and when he appeared in the kitchen for a cup of Cindy's coffee, she remarked on his appearance.

"Don't you ever shave?"

He rubbed a three-day growth of dark scruff. "What, are we going to visit the Queen?"

"Come on, lazy boy."

Shy? Lazy? She was positively oozing charm today. Made Todd want to spend lots of time with her. All sarcasm aside, that actually was the case. More to learn, more to uncover. He felt closer to Fast Cash's money already.

She claimed they had a series of errands to run, and for the next couple of hours the two of them did lots of running around, spending more time getting to places than spending time in them. Life in L.A. Finally, Todd and Cindy had all the provisions she stated they needed. Shovel? Check. Pick? Check. High-beam flashlights? Check. Bottled Water? Double-check. It was good to stay hydrated when doing physical labor, especially when you weren't sure how long said labor was going to take. Oh, and the last item, heavyweight trash bags, "you know, for the take," Cindy had said.

"Aren't you the optimistic one."

"Todd, you said it yourself: three million dollars in unrecovered cash. Even if it's all big bills you can't just stuff them in your wallet."

"Well, you can, you just won't sit very comfortably."

"Ever the wise-ass."

They sped easily along the freeway, allowed to bypass much of the traffic since they could use the HOV lane; two or more in the car bought you such favors in Los Angeles. Before long, though, Cindy had to make the difficult change of lanes—make that four lanes—to get all the way over for their upcoming exit ramp. It wasn't easy, and Todd just shook his head at the insanity that was California driving.

"Give me the subway any day," he said.

"Said the man who's been riding motor scooters for the past six months."

Okay, so every place had its mix of danger and practicality.

As they hit the exit ramp for Palos Verdes, Todd watched Cindy's studied expression. He admired how determined she was to find out the truth about her missing father, a man she had never known but somehow felt responsible for. He couldn't imagine such a circumstance where he would help the man who had done little more than provide a shot of sperm one night to help create him. Their situations were so different. Jack Cashman hadn't known of his daughter's existence until it was too late; as for Todd's father, he'd gotten to know his kids and decided he wanted nothing more to do with them. Nice.

"You've gone quiet, Todd."

"Just wondering."

"About?"

"Actually, several things that still don't add up."

"Like what?"

"Okay, retrieving the money—just how is that going to help you find out what happened to Jack? And what about this accomplice I read about, this Marty Beam character."

"I don't care about Marty Beam, he's probably responsible for whatever truly happened. Slimy snake, he was. The money is to get Patrick out of trouble."

"And the way to do that is to track down three million dollars that was stolen from a bunch of banks seven years ago? And the reason the fortune is still supposed to exist is because the bank robber was shot during his last attempt and has never been seen or heard from since? And has just been declared legally dead? So, if Fast Cash isn't alive to spend it, the money must be somewhere, right?"

"Stands to reason."

"What if this Marty Beam took the money?"

"Excuse me?"

"You say you don't care about him, but you should. Look, you read Carl Beaufort's column that imagines the morning when Fast Cash and Marty Beam went to the Fidelity Trust branch on Hollywood and Vine. There was a lot of confusion, shots rang out, blood was found on one of those Walk of Fame stars, even the cops admitted that they couldn't exactly be sure what might have happened after the getaway car drove off. The security video was just a bundle of images, none of them gave a clear picture of the sequence of events. And afterwards, no phone calls to either of their wives, and more importantly, no bodies have ever been found. It's one thing for one man to disappear, but both of them?"

"You think they both might have run off with the money?"

"Not a chance."

"Why?"

"Crooks don't think that way," Todd said. "Every report prior to the final incident has Fast Cash working independently; even Beaufort wondered about the sudden change in M.O. For some reason, Fast Cash deviated from his prior modus operandi and invited his friend Marty to accompany him on that jaunt. The question begs: why involve someone new in his scheme, especially if he'd planned all along that this would be his final take? Why would he reveal himself as the notorious Fast Cash after so many successful, anonymous strikes? Unless…"

"Unless what?"

"Good ol' Fast Cash was being the farthest thing from a friend. He was using his pal Marty—and what happened on the morning in question was exactly as it was supposed to have happened, scripted. As difficult as it may be to consider, you've already established that your father wasn't the most upright of citizens."

"No, no, I've long given up idealizing the man my father became."

"Smart decision," Todd said, a distant look to his eyes.

"So what are you saying—that someone else was in on Fast Cash's scheme? Someone else helped orchestrate the entire scenario? A second accomplice is something nobody, not even Carl Beaufort, considered. Who?"

Todd considered his answer before replying. "Either someone very powerful or someone very skilled at intimidation. Or maybe it's just the opposite: someone who plays the role of the innocent extremely well. Know anyone who fits any of those descriptions?"

"Todd, what are you getting at?"

"I'm just talking it out, trying to see where all these questions and coincidences collide. If you've been looking into this for some time, maybe you stumbled across some knowledge—or a person with knowledge—but you just didn't know how to interpret it."

"Every angle I've tried comes up a dead end."

Speaking of dead ends, they had arrived at the Cashman estate. The house looked empty against the cloudy backdrop of sky, like a black-and-white photograph in a colorized world. It was real, though, right down to the "For Sale" sign bending in the slight wind that blew off the cliffs. Cindy pulled up to the curb, let the engine idle as she put the gear in park.

"What now?" Todd asked. "We can't exactly bring all our spoils right up the front door, knock and ask to go excavating in her basement. The widow Cashman still lives here, right?"

"Yes. Just stay here, I'll be right back."

"Cindy…"

She wasn't listening to him. Okay, not totally true. She'd heard him, she just decided to ignore his protests about her calling attention to herself. Closing the driver's door behind her, Cindy waltzed right up the pathway toward the front door. She peered through the window situated on either side of the door, cupping her hand to see inside better.

Todd didn't like this, this blatant middle-of-the-day scope out.

He wasn't going to like what happened next, either.

In the rearview mirror he saw a car pull up behind theirs, and Todd had enough experience living life on the edge of the law to know an unmarked police car when one drove up behind you. Especially considering two middle-aged men where inside it; neither looked like a vacuum salesman coming for a house call.

Todd watched as the action unfolded. The two men (cops, Todd thought, cops…) got out of their vehicle and traced the same steps Cindy had made. By now, Cindy had noticed them and she turned to them with a wide smile and that alluring look she was so very good at. There were benefits to being a beautiful woman, and one of them was swaying cops into buying your side of the story.

Todd listened.

"Miss, you do realize this is private property?"

"Of course, I wouldn't just walk up to someone's house and…are you part of the security detail for the neighborhood watch? That's a good first sign to find such dedication to one's job—you know, in case my husband and I decide to move here, it's nice to know someone is looking after us."

"Miss, you do realize the Open House is tomorrow," said the first man (cop).

"Of course. Sorry, I just wanted a little sneak peek, you know how it is?"

"Is that your husband over there?"

They'd pointed to her car; they'd pointed to Todd. He looked over at them, waved.

"Yes, yes of course."

Okay, Todd didn't like that answer, nor the way both men scrunched their faces at him. Cindy didn't realize it, but she was being interrogated. What Todd wanted to know was: over what? Did they have any particular interest in Cindy Scanlon herself, or was their arrival just happenstance? Todd believed more in coincidence, and this had coincidence written all over it. In his mind, Todd kept saying, "Shut up, shut up, shut up."

"Well, gentleman, I suppose if you're working security than I'll see you tomorrow for the Open House. It's rare that such a beauty like this house comes on the market, and with an Open House—well, I'm sure there will be lots of interested parties."

"Why is that, Miss?" asked the second man (cop).

Okay, just call them cops, no more of this first man, second man stuff.

"Isn't this the house where that criminal Fast Cash lived?"

Oh, no, she did not just tip her hand.

"And what's your interest in this Fast Cash person?"

"Oh, curiosity factor, I suppose. Like being part of a Hollywood True Story."

"Yes, of course. But now is not the time. If you'd kindly move on."

"Of course, gentleman. My apologies if I seemed—well, eager to see the house. Getting a jump on all the other interested parties, I suppose some might consider it cheating a bit. But certainly I've done nothing wrong. And I doubt seriously I'm the first person to do a drive by."

"Just don't do any shooting," said the first cop.

Cindy excused herself and retreated to the car, and when she sat down she did not like the expression on Todd's face.

"What?" she asked.

"Just drive."

Finally, for once, she listened to him. When they had cleared the hill's incline and the Cashman house and those cops were gone from the rearview mirror, Todd said, "You do realize those guys were not security. They were cops."

"Cops?"

"Yeah, like plain clothes detectives. LAPD."

"So," Cindy said, hesitancy creeping into her voice. "It's not like I did anything wrong."

"Which you carefully pointed out to them. Cindy, why would the cops be pulling a stakeout on the Cashman house—it's a seven-year-old case and besides, Fast Cash was just this week declared legally dead. The trail should be colder than…well, I'm not sure what's so cold anymore, all this global warming shit they try and scare us with. Look, the point is none of this stuff about Fast Cash should matter to the cops. Yet it clearly does. So, something else must be going on."

"Well, it doesn't involve me, certainly."

Todd thought the lady doth protest too much. "I hope you're right. Because you want to know what those guys are doing right this moment?"

"What?"

"Running your plates."

Impulse took control, and Cindy's foot jammed on the brakes. The seatbelts kept them from flying through the windshield and thankfully no one was behind to crash into them. Still, sitting in the middle of the road wasn't the safest thing for them to be doing. Todd told her to pull over, and the forceful tone in his voice made her do as he asked. He thought about those cops and whether they might be following them. A double-check of the rearview mirror allowed him to breathe a bit easier. Nothing.

He turned to his old college lover, the woman who had chosen his best friend over him with the simple phrase of, "Todd, we need to talk." Now was the time for that kind of discussion again. It was time to reveal another truth.

"We need to talk," he said.

"I gathered."

"It's just like when you dumped me for Patrick, you're holding out on me, and this time I've got my wits about me. You're not going to blind-side me. Fess up, Cin. What aren't you telling me? What about the cops got you suddenly spooked?"

She looked away, checking the side view mirror. Without looking at Todd, she said, near silently, "It's serious."

He nodded. "I gathered."

"It's about a murder."

That, Todd hadn't gathered. And what he had to say about that was simple enough.

"Shit."

"COME ON, Buzz. Surely you've got a story."

"You ain't telling your tale, I don't got one to tell either."

Patrick had been held captive in far worse places than a tavern, which really doesn't say much about the way you're living your life if you can compare hostage situations. Still, this beat that crappy Chelsea office of the Two Dicks and certainly beat that time a couple weeks ago on his boss's yacht. That time, that's when he'd known he was in deep water, and only help from someone like Todd would allow him to at least tread water. A yacht sounds nice and all, but not when it's called *The Nutcracker* and not when you're getting the shit beat out of you and you're tasting your own blood and then the motion of the water is threatening to upchuck said blood, you can see why that not-so-pleasure cruise didn't make his Top Ten list. Patrick wasn't good with boats. But Bermuda and this dank place called the Buzz Factory, with its Mai Tais and Rum Swizzles and an assortment of imported draft beers, why it was easy enough to drown your sorrows and forget your troubles.

"Give me something to cling to," Patrick said. "Why does a guy go about opening a bar in an island paradise? I mean, how resourceful must he have been in his former life to end up with a retirement plan like this? Okay, you don't have to tell me your financial secrets, fine. But give me something…oh, tell me how you lost the tip of your middle finger. That's got to be a good story."

Buzz was behind the bar and he was washing a glass and his finger lay dead against the glass while the rest of his hand busily attacked it. "No story, dumb accident."

"You're a bartender, Buzz, aren't you supposed to tell stories?"

"No, that's a cabbie you're thinking of. Bartenders, we just listen and dispense advice. Me though, I like to skip all the stories and all the advice and just stick to what works: serving up drinks till you leave, pass out, run out of money, or the dawn comes. Whichever comes first. So, refill?"

"Sure."

Buzz pulled the tap on the Newcastle Brown Ale that Patrick was drinking. Yesterday it had been Fuller's Pride. Tomorrow's brew of choice, well, he didn't have to decide that right now, did he? Though the Boddington's was tempting…or the Smithwicks. Might as well save some of the fun for then, since it didn't look like he was getting out of this situation any time soon. Before long, Patrick had taken a sip of his beer—his third that day and it was only three in the afternoon—and considered what next to do. He turned toward the front door to the tavern, where Fred the Little One was standing guard. Patrick waved at him, and he received back nothing in return. The guy's job was to keep tabs on Patrick, not be his friend.

"Hey, Pat, I gotta head to the head, keep an eye on the bar, would you? If you're going be an all-day loafer, might as well help a guy out. But no helping yourself to the taps—only the boss man gets to do those honors."

"That's fine, Buzz, I wouldn't want to upset the boss, not with my track record. Though I can't imagine you'd be as bad as that bastard Langston Livingston."

"That's quite a mouthful. Who might that be?" Buzz asked.

Patrick swallowed down a bit of beer. "When you get back, I'll tell you my story. Might as well pass the time some way."

"I think I'd like to hear about this Livingston character," Buzz said. "Now take the bar, why not drop some pellets into

Toad's tank. He's good at making new friends. We could all learn a bit from our amphibious friends."

DETECTIVE EARNEST Dalrymple was eating a cheeseburger at his desk and waiting for a phone call. His partner, Detective Sandy Benes, was stealing his French fries and also waiting for that phone call. That's what it meant to be partners.

"Can't you get your own meal? I'm not your wife, I don't provide your dinner."

"I spend more time with you than my wife."

"Please don't ever say that again, Sandy."

At the new Police Administration Building on West 1st Street, both detectives had worked out of homicide for the past five years, having transferred from the decrepit Parker Center, and they'd reached the point where not only could they finish each other's sentences (and French Fries), they could tell what the other was thinking (extra ketchup). This made them very effective detectives, with a high percentage of solveds. But their co-workers were always commenting on what a bickering old couple they were.

"Should have got onion rings instead."

"I don't like onion rings."

"But I do."

The ringing of the phone spared them any further conversation about meal choices. "Dalrymple, whaddaya got for me? Un-huh, uh-huh," he said repeatedly, jotting down notes on a pad stained with coleslaw. "Right, thanks." He hung up and looked up at his partner.

"Am I gonna like this?"

"Depends."

"Out with it."

"The car we checked out? It's registered to a Cynthia Scanlon, of Manhattan Beach."

"Scanlon, huh?"

"Husband's name is Patrick."

"So, he was right there under our noses."

"In the passenger seat."

"You got more for me?"

"Yup. Guess who our Mr. Patrick Scanlon works for?"

"Oh, don't leave me in suspense."

"Livingston Enterprises."

"Our old friend, Langston. Oh, this is getting very interesting."

"And now we find out the Scanlons are interested in the Fast Cash case," Dalrymple said.

"So, what's our next step?" Benes asked.

"Tomorrow, I think we should make an appearance at…" Dalrymple began.

"…an Open House?" Benes finished.

See, these two knew how to work together, the good guys always do.

CHAPTER TEN

A BIG day had arrived in the saga of Jack "Fast Cash" Cashman, perhaps the biggest and most eventful since that fateful morning when Jack and Marty went cruising down Sunset Boulevard en route to not only a daring daylight robbery, but also to their own destinies. Time had passed, people had moved on, and unless you were directly affected by the circumstances that had taken place, the legend of Fast Cash was relegated to nothing more than another story of another brazen criminal who tried to make Los Angeles his kind of town. Filler for the six o'clock news.

Today could be considered Lottie's coming out day, and she wanted to look perfect for it. Her yellow suit having already seen the light of day this week and that luscious eggplant having been used for her meeting with Beverly Mills, Lottie surveyed her closet and debated between Easter-egg blue or slimming, sultry black. She chose the blue, it's not like she was headed to a funeral and besides, who was she looking sexy for? Lottie hadn't attracted the attention of a man for years.

Her outfit justifiably chosen, her make-up applied, Lottie

realized that no matter how confident she appeared, on the inside she was nervous and found herself pacing all around the furnished apartment she'd rented the other day. The Open House might not begin until noon, but surely she should be there beforehand. So, with that resolve instilled within her, she put herself behind the old Porsche and made the short journey from Torrance to Palos Verdes Estates. The car easily made the cresting hill, and at last she emerged before the house she and Jack had shared, once their prized possession. It already looked unfamiliar. Another car was already in the circular drive, parked under the portico.

"Could there already be someone so eager to buy our home, Jack?" she asked to the air.

As Lottie pulled in behind the car, she suddenly remembered whose car that was.

"Lord, where is my mind," she said, again to the air.

That's when the front door opened and out stepped Lana Davies, looking every much the successful businesswoman, her lithe body tucked into a smartly-tailored black (black, the young ones like those dark colors, see, good thing she wore the blue suit...) suit. Her rich, auburn hair was piled up nicely, as though she'd gone this morning to her salon, telling them she needed to look her most professional, her most grown up.

"Well, Ms. Davies, am I to assume you got the worm?"

She laughed politely. "Oh no, I didn't arrive that early; but I also didn't want to chance unexpected traffic, coming all the way from Glendale."

"Oh, Glendale, is that nice? You have a roommate, boyfriend?"

"No, I live with my mother. I've been looking after her for

many years. I was just getting a few matters settled inside. Shall we go in?"

"Admirable of you, looking after your mother. But yes, by all means let's go in. This is a big day for me, Ms. Davies."

"It is for all of us, Mrs. Cashman."

Neither of them remarked that they'd regressed to a more formal way of addressing each other. As though after working together just this short amount of time, they each recognized that there was no love lost between them, and had just now established themselves in their respective corners. Let the first round begin.

Ding.

HAVING BEEN presented with so many scenarios of what was going on and how many secrets Cindy was keeping, Todd had decided not to get angry. Not about her keeping quiet regarding the body she'd discovered in her pool, or about the fact that Langston Livingston had done her a "favor" by removing it from her residence. Instead, he would concentrate on the matter of the un-recovered bank money and paying off Patrick's debts. At least be cleared of one problem. Then they could go about solving the rest of the Scanlon's problems.

"You've really managed to make quite a mess of things here in L.A., Cin," Todd had said before heading to bed last night.

"Tomorrow. The clean-up begins tomorrow."

Tomorrow proved not to be a day away, because the cloud-shrouded moon had gone to sleep and the sun had made a welcome, brilliant return to the sky, cutting through Todd's eyes to the point where he could ignore it no more. He'd risen from his bed in the guest room—in a pair of shorts, yes he'd undressed himself last night, thank you very much—and padded down to the bathroom. The door was closed.

"Sorry, busy, but just you wait…it will be well worth it."

It took thirty more minutes for that statement to be given a test ride, and guess what? Todd was buying.

Cynthia O'Neil Scanlon, nearly once Cynthia O'Neil Gleason, came down the stairs—no, make that…arrived down the stairs like a visionary vixen who could vex any unsuspecting victim. She loved the color red—and how it loved her back. Her tailored suit highlighted her slim waist, her long legs, her bosom, her flame-enriched hair, her…okay, you get the point. She looked amazing, drop dead gorgeous, so alive the color looked painted on.

"You approve?" Cindy asked, stopping at the foot of the staircase for effect.

"Uh, yeah. You always knew how to make an entrance."

"Good, that's the point," she said. "As for yourself, you'll certainly stick out, too. For the wrong reason."

Todd was wearing his jeans and a simple white button shirt. His beard was looking a bit too scruffy. "What, I thought L.A. was casual."

"Los Angeles is glamour, my dear. Haven't you ever watched the Oscars?"

"That's Hollywood. This is the real L.A. Crooks, bank robbers, murderers."

"Here a couple of days and already you've got this town figured out?"

"Yup. Use it how you see fit."

"Could you at least put on a suit jacket?"

He pointed to a blue blazer draped against the back of a chair. "Give me a little credit. I raided Patrick's closet."

It was already noon by the time they left. As they pulled out of the driveway, Todd stole another look at his fabulously dressed companion. Dressed to kill, he supposed was the phrase that worked here. Except for the slight pout on her face.

"What?" she asked when he pointed out her imperfection.

"You didn't really expect me to wear…you know, a business suit, did you?"

"It would have been nice. Patrick has some very nice ones that would have fit you."

"Patrick has a few things that would have fit me well over the years."

Cindy opted to ignore that one, changed the subject. "So, any new thoughts how we're going to get the shovel and other supplies into a house teeming with people? I mean, the very definition of an Open House is to be nosy. Everyone will be looking everywhere."

"Actually, I haven't come up with a solution yet."

"What kind of crook are you?"

"Would you please stop calling me that? As far as I know, I'm not the one who has broken the law. Well, this time."

Cindy opted to ignore that one, too, and this time she just shut up and drove.

When they arrived at the Open House thirty minutes later, the joint was jumping. Cars were parked along both sides of the street and they could see dozens of people milling about the lawn, checking the outer structure of the house, the well-kept grounds, poking and prodding at anything that struck their curiosity. Oddly, many of them were carrying newspapers. Oh, and those papers weren't the only media presence. Two news vans were parked nearby, Fox and the local ABC affiliate. Since when was an Open House fodder for the evening broadcasts? Todd told Cindy to keep driving since it was better to park away from the action. Enable them to take in this unusual sight from a safe distance.

"Did you expect it to be this busy?" Todd asked.

"No, I wonder has something happened. I mean, FOX I can understand, the Fast Cash story has always been tailor made for the tabloids…but ABC, too? I wonder if *Logan & Logan* will be here?"

"Who?"

"Never mind. Must be a slow news day."

"More like a busy one—right here at the Cashman house," Todd said. "I think we should find out what's really going on before we venture inside."

"I think I agree with you."

And with that Cindy started to pull away from their hard-earned parking spot. She swung back around the neighborhood, slowing down when she drove by the Cashman estate. There it was again, that nagging feeling that something unexpected was going on. Several people were pointing first at the newspaper, then at the house. A reporter with a microphone was talking to a camera, indicating the house behind him.

"You don't think someone beat us to it—you know, the money?" Todd asked.

"Who? We have the map—or, we did have it."

Todd had told Cindy about good 'ol Barney having a copy of the map Patrick had left for him. But he didn't know the location of the house. So the money, they had to assume, was safe.

All speculation would have to wait. Cindy wasn't completely familiar with the neighborhood of Palos Verdes, but she had to assume there was a store somewhere. This may be L.A., but still, people had to eat, right? She found a grocery store, pulled up right in front of the entrance, and, leaving the car idling, told Todd to wait. Todd hated this kind of waiting, it was like saving seats in a movie theatre, you always had to explain yourself to people who arrived behind you.

Fifteen minutes later Cindy emerged, the Los Angeles Daily News in her grasp.

"What took so long to buy a newspaper?"

"Even the express checkout line was long—but at least I got to read the paper while I waited and I gotta say, Todd, I'm glad we followed our instincts. Check out the headline."

DID FAST CASH KILL COLUMNIST?

"CAN'T WE close the front door?"

Beverly Mills of Beverly Hills, currently of Palos Verdes Estates, tossed a noticeably disheveled Lottie Cashman a look of utter horror. "Hardly! That sort of defeats the purpose of an *Open* House, dear."

"But all these people, all those reporters…oh, how could such a thing have occurred?"

Lottie had been so preoccupied with getting ready this morning that she'd failed to notice the headline in the Daily News, nor the subsequent speculation that was suddenly all over the morning newscasts. Beverly, for her part, was extremely pleased, and as she watched Lottie go bustling away from the crowd, she moved through the open door and from the porch listened to one of the reporters she had tipped off.

"It's a case that had grown colder than winter in Alaska, the notorious Fast Cash crime wave of seven years ago. But events in the past week or so have given renewed interest in this puzzling case. Just last week, the widow Cashman had the courts declare her husband legally dead, and then the next morning one of our colleagues in the press, noted columnist and Fast Cash enthusiast Carl Beaufort was found shot to death, his body left discarded along the freeway. The final story filed by Mr. Beaufort was all about the Fast Cash case, and it was filled again with speculation as to what truly happened. Now, days later Mrs. Cashman is holding an Open House hosted by Beverly Mills of Beverly Hills in an attempt to sell her late husband's estate. Judging by the huge turnout today, offers are sure to pour in. Either that or it's morbid curiosity, which wouldn't exactly be a first in this town. Speculation has a way of taking to these Santa Ana winds like fire, and the police are once again wondering if Fast Cash—aka Jack Cashman—is not only alive and well, but perhaps has gone from bank robber—to murderer."

Cut and print. Beverly grinned. She couldn't have scripted it better. Especially the nice plug for her agency. So, with the publicity machine well oiled, Beverly began to take in all that she had masterminded.

Masterminded, indeed. You don't succeed in a town such as Los Angeles—much less an enclave as exclusive as Beverly Hills—without knowing how to spread the word—and feed a crowd. So the assorted hangers-on and curious alike mingled with the serious real estate buyer, all of them contentedly chatting about the day's news and the actuality of owning a place once the domicile of someone so infamous. The crowd could even enjoy little hand-held quiches to nip their appetites and cold "champers" to help wash it down while satisfying their curiosities. Caterers and waiters circulated the rooms of the main level with tray after tray and no one went untended.

Of course, Beverly had a nose for a sale, can smell the buyer from the time-waster. Someone could say, "Wow, look at the inlay on that ceiling" and Beverly would continue walking. Designers! Someone else could say, "After three years, the value on this property can exponentially increase at a rate which would further speed up our retirement." House flippers! Someone else could say, "How much do you think a place like this goes for?" Poor people!

The foyer had grown crowded, and Beverly was just about to retreat to the kitchen for a breather when she noticed an intriguing couple walking up the pathway. He was typical male slacker, thinking jeans and a white shirt could be dressed up by adding a blazer as a finishing touch; still, she had to admit with his shades and his nine o'clock shadow, he had a certain devil-may-care Hollywood appeal. The woman beside him, though, now that's who got Beverly to sit up and truly take notice. Granted, ol' Bev had already been standing, but with such a vision coming toward her she stood that much more at attention. She knew new money was headed her way, and didn't new money like to spend like they had old money, buying their way into a world which otherwise was closed off to them? That was a theory Beverly Mills of Beverly Hills could relate to.

Beverly remained at the front entrance and decided to personally greet the fashionably late, fashionably hot couple—Red and Whiskers, those were the cute monikers she assigned them. They stepped over the threshold and that's when Beverly Mills put on her best Beverly Hills charm. She knew when to be her brassy self; she also knew when to be the picture of elegance.

"How do you do?"

"Oh, hello. What a wonderful event."

"Kind of you to say. Allow me to introduce myself, I am Beverly Mills of..."

"...of Beverly Hills. Yes, your reputation precedes you. It's one of the reasons I insisted we come by just as soon as we could. I am Cynthia Cash-Scanlon."

"Cashscanlon, what an interesting name."

"No, it's two names—you can't hear the hyphen. 'Cash-Scanlon.'"

"Cash, you say? An interesting maiden name, considering the circumstances that bring us all together today. Well, this is one modern woman you've married, Mr. Scanlon," she said to Whiskers.

"What's that...oh, no, I'm not..."

"What my husband is trying to say," Cindy quickly interjected, "is that, his appearance notwithstanding, he left his caveman instincts way back in the last century. He quite respects a woman who needs to hold on to a part of her true self. You don't lose your individuality just because you say 'I do.' Patrick is a darling."

"And he's a very handsome darling, if you don't mind my saying so," Beverly said, baring her baleful smile at Whiskers. The smile, though, was just for effect, because inside Beverly felt a sudden chill. The name had nagged at her initially, but the "Cash" part had thrown her off. Oh, this could be intriguing, Beverly thought. "You know, the two of you would make this lovely home that much more beautiful. People Magazine meets Architectural Digest. I assume it is the house that interests you and not…the current spectacle."

"The house," Cindy said confidently. "Definitely the house."

Beverly smiled, eager to keep them in her good graces—and in her company. "Such a pleasure to hear that. May I get you some champer…er, a glass of champagne and then perhaps I can personally escort you around?"

"That would be lovely. Patrick, isn't that very hospitable of Ms. Mills?"

"Remarkably hospitable."

Beverly's smile faltered just a bit. She knew they were a couple on the make and that they had come to the Open House with an agenda. Then again, all of L.A. comes with an agenda, and it didn't hurt that these two were remarkably beautiful to boot, giving them higher chances for success in this town. To which Beverly reminded herself: don't trust them a whit.

"Shall we?"

Champagne was served, glasses clinked in the glare of mid-afternoon sunlight that streamed through the windows, and a small toast was raised.

"To Fast Cash, for bringing us all together," Beverly spoke.

"To Jack Cashman," Cindy said.

Todd said nothing, too busy was he choking on his champers.

And with that, the grand tour began.

STUDIO-DWELLING TODD could never live in such a palace, his feet hurt after their twenty-minute tour of the place. He couldn't possibly imagine getting up from watching the game on the sofa in the den (not living room or sitting room, you don't put electronics in such a room…) to grab a beer from the kitchen fridge. It was like…miles.

So, as they wound back down the front hall staircase, Todd watched as Beverly shooshed away a few curious onlookers and then closed off the velvet rope. He wondered what had made them so special that they'd been singled out for such high-class treatment. Still, despite having seen all the bedrooms, all the baths, all the places to eat, drink, have sex, Todd couldn't help but feel a portion of the house had been left out. Come on, you can't exactly call it a grand tour if you don't get to see every inch, every…level.

"So, what about the basement?" Todd suddenly asked. His answer came in the form of an elbow to the gut, courtesy of Cindy. He tossed her a look that said, "What did I say?"

"Really, Beverly (they'd moved onto first names when they hit the master bedroom), I don't know what my impulsive husband is thinking. The basement, of all things. I'm sure it's just dank and dark and…"

"And off limits," said a new voice to the conversation that until now had been a volley between Todd, Cindy, and Beverly. Now the sides were even, double match. "Hello, I'm Lottie Cashman and this is my home."

Cindy stepped forward with an eager hand. Todd watched her carefully, wondering how she would feel finally shaking hands with the woman who technically was her stepmother. But Cindy was gracious and revealed nothing except her lovely smile. "And it's a pleasure to be here, Mrs. Cashman. I'm sure it must tear at your heart to part with such a beautiful home."

Okay, Cindy's sucking up to the real estate agent was one thing, her tone now bordered on the sickening. Or maybe it was those spinach quiches…

"Thank you…Mrs…"

"Cynthia Cash-Scanlon," Cindy said in that fake upper-crusty don't-take-a-breath way of talking.

"Cashscanlon," Mrs. Cashman said. "What an interesting name…"

Again…

"It's Scanlon," Todd interceded. "Patrick Scanlon, how do you do."

"Scanlon you say?"

Okay, now that was another voice altogether. Seems their party was growing larger by the minute. This time it was a gentleman in a floppy brown suit with equally floppy brown hair and at his side was a blue-suited man, also lacking refinement. Todd of course recognized them from yesterday, when he'd glimpsed them in the rearview mirror of Cindy's car.

Cindy noticed them, too. From the look she gave Todd, she remembered them, too.

Cops.

At this point, Beverly stepped in to control the group. "Gentleman, if you don't mind, I can be right with you if you just allow us to finish with the Scanlons, we were just nearly done with our tour. Now, Cynthia, let me get you that paperwork I was telling you about upstairs…"

"Actually, ma'am, we do mind." That's when Floppy reached into his jacket pocket and withdrew a shiny shield, gleaming even without the benefit of the L.A. sun. "Detective Earnest Dalrymple, this is my partner, Detective Sandy Benes. LAPD. Homicide."

They sure liked to toss around those labels, as though Beverly would introduce herself as Real Estate Agent Beverly Mills or Todd would introduce himself as Confidence Man Todd Gleason…you see, sometimes labels were just wholly unnecessary. Especially on these guys, they just screamed career law enforcement.

"Police? At an Open House? Oh, Beverly…I just knew something like this would ruin my day," Lottie began. "Officers, if it's about all those newspaper articles and reporters…"

"Actually, it is, and we'll take it from here," said Dalrymple. "Mr. Patrick Scanlon, may we ask you a few questions?"

Now, Todd didn't normally like the police, and he didn't like them knowing he was Todd Gleason. But at the moment being Todd Gleason was far better than being Patrick Scanlon considering the story Cindy had told him of finding a body in their pool. Suppose these cops were working the Beaufort murder case and they'd found out that Cindy had arranged for the body to be moved, and who better to do so than her big, strong husband. So, what was a man to do at this point? Tell the truth.

"Actually, detective, I'm not Patrick Scanlon, I'm just a friend of the family…"

"Mr. Scanlon, what are you saying?" Beverly interjected.

Cindy said, "Oh, crap."

"You were just identified as being Patrick Scanlon and we have some questions for you. And if you're not him, then we have even more questions for you. Either way, I think it would be good for you—and your wife or not-wife—to accompany us downtown."

"Really, officers, couldn't this wait?" Lottie asked. "Everyone is staring at us and my Open House is in tatters; I'll never sell this house now!"

"Ma'am, please, we'll be out of your hair in a moment. Mr. Scanlon…or whoever you are, if you'll come with us."

Sometimes life just doesn't work in your favor and the cops come and lead you away and expose your lie and probe everything about you and you end up in jail for the rest of your natural-born existence. And sometimes that scenario is just a case of being overly melodramatic, because sometimes opportunity arrives and allows you the chance to get yourself out of trouble. Opportunity here arrived in the form of one more person to their assemblage, and it was what she said that put everyone into pause mode—except for the man she was talking to.

"Toddly?!"

With both a new voice and a new name added to the mix, everyone spun in different directions to see who was speaking and to whom she was referring. Todd took this moment to do what came natural: he slipped away. Losing himself in the crowd, he distanced himself from not only Cindy and Beverly, Lottie and the Cops, but from the other woman. The woman who knew his name.

He thought to himself: what the hell was Lana doing here?

TODD GLEASON was literally in the dark. Clever boy that he is, he did the one thing those wily detectives hadn't expected him to do: he never left the Cashman house. Consider it killing two birds with one stone, as he was able to outwit and outmaneuver the cops, plus do as he had been planning on all along, which was to stay behind long after the last morbid onlooker had left the premises. Where had he hidden? A closet in the servant's quarters, just beyond the kitchen. It was neither roomy nor well lit, and now that evening had fallen and the lights had been doused and he was alone except for the creaking winds off the bluff, Todd was…well, in the dark.

He'd had a lot of free time and little else to do but think.

The first thing he did was shut off his cell phone. He didn't need any calls, text messages, expected or unexpected. Even putting a phone on vibrate made some noise. So, not only was he immersed in the dark, he was also incommunicado. Hence, all of this time to think.

First he'd thought about Lana, his mind trying to play tricks on him and getting him to believe it hadn't been her but merely a pale (okay, tan) reflection of her. He'd only caught a momentary glimpse of her, her auburn hair and her sweet smile that was slightly crooked and overly sexy, but since he'd had to skedaddle faster than an Olympic sprinter on steroids maybe he'd just been imagining her. He'd gone back and forth and then gone around for another round and in the end he decided he was crazy. It were merely his own proximity to Cindy these past few days which had fueled desires that lay dormant and now he was trying to transition them from a real-life Cindy to an imaginary Lana.

Still, there had been that voice, the way she'd said his

name...Toddly. Only Lana called him that.

Then his thoughts moved onto the more pressing and intimidating matter of the police. Never a good sign of a scheme going well when you had the police enter the picture, it meant loose ends weren't as tied up as you'd thought, and other people were working their own angles. What surprised Todd was their interest in not Cindy but Patrick. Hadn't it been Cindy who discovered Beaufort's body? Hadn't it been Cindy's brilliant idea to ask the unforgiving Langston Livingston to get rid of it for her? So if Cindy was guilty of tampering with the scene of a crime, why did they want Todd...er, Patrick, to "come downtown." Just like in all those Hollywood scripts, there were no new phrases under the bright lights of the soundstage.

All of those questions would have to wait, because now that night had fallen it was time for all nefarious activities to begin. Problem was—why must there always be a problem?—his tools to aid him in the planned nocturnal dig were still stuck in Cindy's trunk, and he had to assume Cindy wasn't anywhere near the Cashman house, not with the police sniffing around her and on the lookout for her (not) husband. Too risky. Todd, his eyes long ago adjusted to the darkness of the closet, looked down at his hands. Could they dig into the hard ground and find Fast Cash's lost treasure?

Maybe there was a spoon in a kitchen drawer.

Anyway, at least he'd have a chance to scope out the basement. With the house now silent as a church mouse, Todd eased himself from his hiding spot. Again, he listened for the sound of someone else lurking inside the house. Why would there be? Who remained behind after an Open House became a Closed House? Making his way through the kitchen and into the hallway that led to the foyer, Todd continued to keep both eyes open and his wits about him. He stole a look outside at the circular driveway, saw nothing—no cars, no lights, no sign of any activity beneath the streetlamps.

Retracing his steps back to the kitchen, he then moved beyond to where the schematic map he'd seen back in New York had indicated the entrance to the basement. As he stepped forward, a sudden creak caught his attention. Did the sound come from stepping on loose wood flanks? Or did he have company? He listened again, and this time he heard it again. And again. He looked upwards, and realized the sound was coming from directly above him. He wasn't alone in the house, of that much he was convinced.

Now there were more creaks, the sound of feet on the staircase.

With all these creaks in the woodwork, Todd felt the house's resale value depreciating.

He made to retreat to his servant's hiding place, but realized he might not make it across the kitchen in time. Turning his head to and fro, he looked for any hiding place and found to his left the pantry, complete with a swinging door; he hoped the hinges were oiled. Acting quickly, he tossed himself inside, where once again he was bathed in darkness. His pupils dimmed then widened and at last he had his night vision back.

He listened again. Footsteps, gentle against the floor but definitely noticeable, came closer. He heard the door to the kitchen open and knew that whoever else was in the house, well, that person was getting hotter. Todd considered his options: surprise his guest, grab his guest, knock out his guest? Or just hold steady and hope that they moved on.

Todd looked around at the bare pantry, wondering if in this hiding place was some better place to hide. There was a large box marked "supplies" but he supposed opening it up and removing probable kitchen appliances might make a lot of noise. Then he noticed a blanket and then he noticed…a shovel?

Had Cindy somehow managed to get their stuff inside?

Actually, she hadn't, those belongings belonged to someone else entirely, and it was at that precise moment the unknown person came to retrieve them. Todd was stuck, and worse, Todd had just been discovered.

"You're not going to go running off on me again, are you?"

"That depends, are you going to slap me like you did the last time I saw you?"

Lana Davies said, "Todd, what the hell are you doing here?"

"Thought you might need a hand with the digging," Todd said, and then with a dimpled smile directed at his Bermudian paramour, he lifted the shovel.

"**WHERE DO** we start?"

"How about where we were supposed to leave off."

"I'm being serious."

"You think I'm not?" said Todd, tossing a smile Lana's way that even in the darkness of the closet she couldn't help but notice. He used a good whitening toothpaste. Reaching out to feel her silky hair, its touch brought him hurtling back in time to those sultry nights in Bermuda, at the Buzz Factory and at his cottage and lost together behind a rocky wall, their shared times were as vivid now as they were then. They were good images, even that nasty slap of hers—because it just meant she had cared. But then she had disappeared before he could explain.

He supposed he was being given a second chance. She hadn't exactly backed away from his caress, her eyes still gazing longingly into his. He could feel a palpable zing bounce between them, ricocheting off the walls of the pantry. He knew just how to make the moment perfect, to make now then. His lips bent down and actually, they very nearly made contact with hers.

"Wait," Lana said, her voice filled with a sudden trembling.

"What is it, tell me what you're feeling, Lana," he whispered, and not just because he was feeling the tender exchange but because it was still wise to keep their location hidden. If he had the idea to hide out in the Cashman house and Lana did too, the possibility, however remote, existed that together they weren't alone either. Still, he wasn't going to screw up this moment. "Please, Lana…"

"Answer me…who is it that wants to kiss me?"

"Me. Do you see anything else hiding in this closet?"

"Yes, I know it's you. But who are you? Are you Todd, or are you Patrick? And that woman from before, can I assume that's the wife who came calling for you? She's lovely."

"I never lied to you, Lana. My name is Todd Gleason, and I am definitely not married. I am free and clear of any and all complications." He stopped, looked around at their ridiculous situation. "Wait, change that. Free of any romantic complications. Besides, speaking of lying, who was it who claimed to be on vacation with her two college friends? I ran into them on my flight back to New York—a couple of legal aids from Long Island who you paid to pretend to be your friends."

"Oh, right, that."

"So if anyone here was pulling a scam, Lana, it was you," Todd said. "Which I've got to tell you I find incredibly sexy."

"Oh, Todd…"

"Oh, Lana."

Or words to that effect that didn't quite sound like soap opera. They stopped listening and talking and trying to outsmart the other and instead threw themselves at each other. The fact that they were hiding out in a pantry in the soon-to-be-sold estate of a known criminal, surrounded by tools designed for digging into the hardened dirt of the earth, Todd and Lana, like when they first met, realized the moment was bigger than life.

His kiss was strong and urgent, and she replied in kind, pressing her slinky body against him, grinding her hips with a need that seemed to have been on hold since they had parted ways, now unleashed and unstoppable. His mouth found her neck, and she groaned with pleasure as his cheeks scraped against her skin. Nails dug into the back of his shirt, while his hands reached under her shirt. His tongue tasted skin gone hot.

"Oh, Todd, my God, we can't…we shouldn't."

"Two negatives, I think they equal a positive," he urged, his subsequent kisses mirroring his words. Lana's protests grew weaker as her arms encircled him, gently squeezing him to an excited state—not that he needed help in that department. Suddenly her hands were fumbling with the buttons of his shirt, unwrapping him like a dirty-minded Christmas present.

"Yes, Todd, Todd, yes, take me…"

"Oh, God, Lana, I want you so badly…"

Okay, enter a slight change of plans. Enter the following

rude interruption into evidence: "Look out honey, he may only be after your keys."

Todd suddenly, amazingly, stopped. "Huh?"

Lana, too, whimpering, stopped. "What?"

They both looked up in confusion and complete dissatisfaction, where they noticed that the door to the pantry had been opened, but yet seemed blocked all the same. A huge, bald hulking man in leather pants stood in the door frame, making any kind of escape impossible. Not that they were properly dressed to be making any fast exits.

"Who the hell are you?" Lana demanded to know.

The huge hulk didn't answer. Todd, instead, took care of the introductions.

"Lana. Barney. Barney, Lana."

CHAPTER ELEVEN

THE OFFICES of Livingston Enterprises were nearly darkened on this Sunday late night, as most businesses were apt to be on the weekend. Perhaps just the cleaning crew bustled about, readying the office for the start of the new work week. That couldn't be further from the truth, because the light was emanating from Langston Livingston's very own inner sanctum for one reason and one reason alone: Langston was there, and though he was alone right now, that didn't mean he would be for long.

Just an hour ago he had dispatched chauffeur slash goon Garth to play a game of "fetch," and Langston was looking forward to seeing the person his right-hand man was chasing down. But even a patient gentleman such as Langston Livingston had his own levels of tolerance, and the creases in his brow indicated he was reaching it. Garth had phoned ten minutes ago, saying he had their guest secure in the backseat of the limo but that for some reason the traffic was a bitch.

"I think it's the Emmys," Garth had said.

"I don't want an Emmy. I'd like a different woman, and I want her here now."

"Doing my best, sir."

This was his best, stuck in an awards-show induced traffic jam? Christ, why didn't he just move his operation to Vegas or something, sometimes he thought it was time to get out of this town. That was just reactionary talk, Langston Livingston had been part of the Southern California culture since he was an eighteen-year-old-thug-on-the-run, a poor kid with a major attitude and a desire to grab some of the money which seemed to flow through these people's systems like urine. He was fifty-eight now, a good forty years had passed and he had his fortune, he had his power, and at the moment, he had nothing else.

Langston decided to pour himself a rare drink; usually he kept it for guests, it was good to get them loosened up, get their tongues wagging. A couple Scotches could sometimes be more effective than other forms of getting the answers he wanted. Tonight, though, the Scotch called out to him and so he poured two fingers worth of Johnny Blue into his Waterford tumbler, then carried it to his window, where he could gaze out over his own criminal empire.

Los Angeles. Living here was not an easy prospect, what with all the accoutrements required to even attempt to make it. A car, that's your first priority, more so than a house or an apartment or a cardboard box; the car you could always sleep in and the next day, no one was any the wiser as you tooled down the freeway, just another wannabe being a doobee. Some cash, that was important, too. You didn't get anywhere in this town without being able to grease the right palms, get your way, hook that desired table at that hot restaurant, and those earnings from In and Out Burger won't cut it. Thing is, not everybody who comes to LaLa Land has the natural talent to make their mark, so they need a little help: acting classes, headshots, surgery, each of them were expensive propositions and sure, the payoff could be great, life-changing, even life setting. It's that time in between arriving and Arriving when Langston stepped in to offer his brand of help. Most folks were good about paying him back, they were smart. Every once in awhile though, some sharp-talking kid from the hicks comes along and thinks he can one-up Langston Livingston.

He had a way of dealing with them. You see, for a man like Langston Livingston, being owed money was really just a means to a profitable end. Sure, you could collect on that debt, settle your account, and then be on your way. Those people served their purpose, they kept his cash flow, uh, flowing, but from a business perspective they flat-out bored Langston. It was the kid who got in over his head, the smart-mouth who spent first, rationed later, those were the clients who made Langston grin like an alligator waiting to move in for the kill. He didn't just hold their marker in his jaws, he held their very souls, their very lives in a death roll.

From the reception area he heard the ping of the elevator. Langston returned his portly self behind his desk, set his fingers into a church steeple. Hey, even he was not without his Hollywood influences. He waited for the door to his office to open, and it did so less than a minute after he settled into the comfortable leather-backed chair.

"Your guest, Mr. Livingston."

"Thank you, Garth. You'll wait in the lobby for my call?"

"Of course, sir."

Garth closed the door behind him, leaving Langston with his evening's guest.

"Hello, Cynthia."

He noticed she didn't return his greeting, merely took a seat opposite him, letting out a heavy sigh as she did so.

"Please, have a seat," he said, deadpan.

"Langston, not tonight. It's been a hell of a day."

"Yes, so I gather. But aside from your personal troubles, today was a day in which I had handed you an assignment—in lieu of your husband being available, that is. Now, since you don't normally work for me I'll forgive this little transgression. Next time, I expect a phone call from you, reporting back on what transpired."

"Nothing happened. The day kind of got…aborted."

"That does not please me."

"Langston, can we cut the crap? You know as well as I do that I spent half the day speaking with the police—downtown. And by downtown I mean the PAB. The big joint. It was an experience I did not enjoy."

"I'm sure not."

"Langston—you were supposed to do me a favor by getting rid of that body in the pool. A body that turned out to belong to a nosy reporter who was far too interested in the Fast Cash case. A body that was supposed to have no connection to me or to Patrick. But somehow the police linked him and Patrick. Care to explain that one?"

"Nothing ferrets out a missing person like the formal interest of the police."

Cindy sat there, fuming. "You know, just when I was beginning to think you couldn't be more cruel—you go and do this, and for what? Your amusement? It's not enough that Patrick owes you money, now he's wanted for murder. A murder which both you and I know he could not have committed."

"So we are led to believe," Langston said. "However, don't you find it curious the body of Carl Beaufort ended up in your pool? His killer must have chosen that location for a reason, and I for one am darn curious. So I tipped off the police, I'm nothing if not a good citizen."

"You're not a good anything," Cindy quickly said, her temper flaring.

"How droll. Oh, Cynthia, your attitude is showing, and for the first time since meeting you I don't like what's on display," he said. "Forget about dead bodies and the police and where Patrick might be, I think we need to re-establish the dynamic of our relationship. Let me ask you this—how long have we known each other?"

Cindy said nothing. She just sat there, refusing to answer.

"Cynthia, the sooner you talk, the sooner you get to leave. Simple, really."

"Fine. We've known each other about two years."

"About right, yes. Do you recall the situation which brought us together?"

"Yes. I rear-ended your limo."

"Indeed."

"And you let me off the hook—no police report, no reimbursing you for the damage to your taillight. At least, you didn't ask for any financial payback then. You just let me go on my merry way that day, all you said was 'a beautiful lady like you should be more careful who she drives into.' That was it, until two months later, when out of the blue…"

"Yes, I called you."

"And we met right here."

"Because I had done a background check on you."

"Langston, do we really need to rehash the past?"

"It would seem that way, yes. Because from all that's been happening the last couple of weeks, it seems the past keeps creeping into our present-day lives—and mucking them up, you might say. So, let's continue, I'm enjoying our little stroll down memory lane."

"You learned who I was, and you called me in for a meeting."

"Who are you, Cynthia Scanlon?"

"I'm the daughter of Shannon O'Neil and Jack Cashman."

"Yes, the elusive Fast Cash. You never knew him."

Cindy flinched, a sore subject had been broached, that much Langston knew. She asked, "Is there a point to all of this?"

"Well, you may never have met Jack Cashman, but I certainly did. You know for a fact that he worked for me and for a while he was quite a capable...collector. I liked his spirit. He and I shared a similar appreciation for the finer things in life. You think he came by that nice estate in Palos Verdes easily?"

"You shared a love for money."

"Such a dismissive tone, Cynthia. You yourself have been as guilty as your father, you didn't exactly say no when Patrick started raking in the big bucks. But yes, Jack and I each had an affinity for cold hard cash," Langston said. "But like most people who get too close to the sun, their wings melt and they fall back down to earth. Not everyone is as lucky as Icarus, he had the sea to break his fall. Jack, his crash was a bit harder, the cement paving of a Los Angeles sidewalk is not as forgiving. I'm afraid the apple doesn't fall too far from the tree."

"Are your numerous metaphors supposed to mean something? I mean, something new? None of this would interest a beat reporter, much less a columnist like Carl Beaufort."

"Ah, yes, the news folk. We'll get to that," he said. "But just to return ever-so-briefly to our past history, I confronted you with the idea that you had deliberately crashed your car into my limo. Gave poor Garth a bit of whiplash that lasted for a couple months, I don't think I ever told you that. Don't worry, I covered the medical bills. Anyway, as I understood it, you were trying to find out what happened to your father and you thought maybe a businessman such as myself might have had something to do with it. And what did I tell you?"

"You told me my father ran out on his debts."

"Indeed. Even after he'd begun his little bank robbery operation, he had the money to pay me back but obviously he had other plans for that money. Guts, he certainly had those, a fearless quality that made him so good at his job. You're a bit like him, Cynthia, you have moxie, which I admire. Even if you do sometimes take certain liberties with my patience. So I arranged for you and your husband to attend a party, and I pretended to like your Patrick enough to grant him an interview. Of course I had every intention of hiring him; wasn't that just perfect, the son-in-law of Jack Cashman filling a position within my company was karma's way to settle lost debts."

"This is water under the bridge, Langston. You gave Patrick a job and made it easy for him to have access to all those finer things in life. Your way of ensuring his loyalty—and mine. Am I to assume that's why I've ultimately been dragged here tonight?"

"Such a clever girl," he said. Langston leaned forward and

depressed the buzzer, where a waiting Garth picked up on the other end. "You may join us now, Garth."

Only a moment passed before the gargantuan Garth returned to his boss's office, closing—and locking—the door behind him.

"Now, Cynthia, we're going to play a game. Twenty questions; I assume you're familiar with it?"

Cindy replied with studied silence.

"I'll take that as a yes," he said. "Now, when I ask a question, you'll answer truthfully and honestly."

Garth moved forward and sidled right up beside Cindy. From Langston's desk he took hold of a simple, effective nutcracker that was lying atop a bowl of shelled walnuts, pecans, almonds. Garth took Cindy's hand into his, more specifically her middle finger. Which he then proceeded to place between the hungry, powerful jaws of the nutcracker.

"Remember, Cynthia, answer my questions truthfully and honestly and no harm will come to you. And no nails tonight, we're going for honest to goodness tender flesh. We'll cover several topics you'll no doubt be familiar with, including your wayward husband, your still-missing father, and the unrecovered fortune he supposedly left behind. But first, I want to discuss that curious fellow you are currently keeping company with. Seems quite the…rogue, I believe is the correct term."

"He's an old friend," was Cindy's less-than-helpful answer.

Langston nodded.

Garth squeezed, ever-so-slightly.

"That's Mr. Todd Gleason, is it not? The man you went to find in New York?"

"Langston, if you already know the answers to your

questions, why bother with me?"

Langston nodded, Garth squeezed some more.

"Did it ever occur to you I'm testing your honesty? If your answers match up with mine, perhaps you'll walk away with all ten fingers intact. The choice, my dear, is yours. Think carefully before you answer. Where is Todd now?"

Her silence was not to his liking. Another nod, another squeeze. They could be in for a long night. He knew pouring that glass of Scotch had been a good idea, the heat of the alcohol would help dilute the screams of his victim.

"Let's try this again, shall we? Where is Todd Gleason?"

"**WHO GOES** first?"

"Who goes second?"

"Who goes third?"

Three people, all willingly locked inside a deserted house, all of them with stories of their own, secrets and motives that none of the others were familiar with. Todd supposed, looking at Lana who was looking at Barney who was looking back at Todd, that all their explanations might take away valuable time from what they had all seemingly come for: Fast Cash's hidden treasure. So he suggested a season of détente, where they all worked in tandem on their common mission and after the cash was found, they could get the hell out of here and sort out this complicated mess.

"Sound like a plan?" he asked.

"Deal," Lana said, extending her arm.

Barney did the same. "Deal."

Todd, the organizer of said deal, said, "Deal."

And like the motliest crew this side of the Three Musketeers, the three of them shook and raised their arms like sportsmen rallying to defeat their opponent. Then they went to work.

Lana grabbed the blanket and began to lug it down the basement stairs, wiping away at cobwebs as she did so. Todd followed with the shovel and a pick-axe, and Barney grabbed the two high-beam flashlights. Seemed Lana and Cindy had more in common than just a history with Todd and that red-hair which made them both so devastatingly alluring. They both shopped at Home Depot. Todd felt a stirring in his loins, silently cursed Barney for his bad timing. He supposed one would call it poetic justice, Barney being the one to catch him on the verge of having sex in a private chamber.

Before long, the thick beams of the flashlights were in place, and the dank basement was alive, at least, with illumination.

"I doubt even the rats have been for a visit lately," Todd said when he looked at the caked dirt floor, at the occasional rock which protruded from the ground, at the crumbling effects of the cement foundation. "You sure this place is secure?"

"Yes, we had it thoroughly appraised once Mrs. Cashman and I came to contract."

"I'm curious to know how that came about, and why."

"Our stories, I thought we were saving them for later."

"Can't I get a sneak preview?"

"Short story? I'm the real estate agent on this property, and I was co-hosting the Open House with Beverly Mills. It's where I work, Beverly Mills of Beverly Hills."

"Catchy name," Todd said, nodding. "So that explains why you were able to smuggle all these digging goodies into the house without anyone watching. Why now, though? Why wait until after the Open House to go on an archeological dig?"

"I didn't want to take a chance that anyone discovered something before we had all those people traipsing in and out of the house. Who knew if someone was going to insist on seeing the basement, I couldn't exactly have an excavation site exposed."

"The basement was off-limits, that's what Beverly told me during our tour. I asked."

"Hey, you two…" Barney interjected. "Do you even know each other? Or was that little display in the upstairs pantry for my benefit? God, you breeders. You have some weird mating rituals."

This statement from a leather-clad, goateed muscle man who had once tried to do Todd in an underground cave inside a 12th Avenue bar. But Todd let the picturesque image go, no time for judgments now. "Barney's right, we're deviating from our agreement, let's get back to the task at hand." With that, he picked up a shovel and said, "Where do we start…oh wait, Barney, since you're here, I don't suppose you brought the map you took from me."

It was Lana who spoke up and said, "The map? I have the map."

Barney reached into his rear pocket and withdrew the familiar piece of paper. He unfolded it, and in the shadowy light Todd compared it to the one Lana had. Could only surmise one thing:

"Same map."

"Where did you get yours?" was asked simultaneously.

Barney answered first: "From him."

"And you, Lana?"

"I…it's a secret…"

Todd moved beside this double bill of mystery and desire, his hand touching her cheek, feeling the heat beneath her skin. He said, "Lana, I think you need to spill some beans. Who gave you the map, and what's your interest in all of this anyway?"

"The map arrived in the mail one day, about six, seven weeks ago. Days after Lottie Cashman had petitioned the court to have Fast Cash declared legally dead. There was no return address, only thing I know was that the postmark was Los Angeles. But I knew what it was, I recognized the schematic because it's similar to the one our consultants were using when doing their estimate on this house."

"And so you decided to buy a shovel and see if X really did mark the spot?"

"Todd, can we dig now, ask questions later?"

"She's got a point, *Toddly*. We're wasting valuable time."

Todd turned to him. "You got a hot date, Barn?"

"I'm just saying, given the interest the police seem to have in this whole matter and how you had to run from them earlier this afternoon, it's possible they may do a drive-by tonight and it's also possible they may see the light coming out from the basement's little windows."

"You were here, at the Open House?"

"Even a guy who looks like me can blend in quite well when the crowd is thick enough."

Lana stepped in and said, "I'm sorry, I know we need to get to work, but I need to know…who are you, and what exactly do you have to do with any of this?"

"Barney Stone. Licensed private dick from New York. I

was hired to look after Todd, even though he doesn't appear to want my protection. He ditched me at LAX the other night, and I've spent the last couple days waiting for him to make his next move. See, I'm not a bad detective after all—found you, Todd, and right where I needed to find you. Now, can we cut the chatter, let's just dig."

Under the glow of the flashlight, they pointed directions out, north, west, east, south, trying to gauge their positioning and where best to start digging. Without proper calculations or actual numerals marked on the map, they did their best to estimate the distance between the stairwell and the far wall, as the X had been placed somewhere between the two. Unfortunately for them, there'd been no actual X marked on the floor.

Todd took the shovel and Barney took the pickaxe and Lana grabbed one of the lights and for the first time they were truly working as a team. They picked their spot in the floor. And the digging began. The ground was hard, but not impossible to cut through. With huffs and puffs, Todd dug his foot into the shovel's head and watched as the blade sliced through the caked floor, turning it into chunks and crumbles of dirt. He cleared the loose dirt away from the hole he'd begun to create, repeated the entire process a second, a third, a dozen more times. He was starting to make some progress, and as he dug more and he dug even more the ground opened up to him like a pliant mistress, ready and willing to be plundered. Sweat began to drip from his face and down his back, his shirt becoming stained with the fruit of his labor.

As for Barney, those leather pants weren't exactly ideal material for strong physical activity, so he'd done his best to keep himself cool by removing his own shirt and vest, exposing a powerful torso of both graying fur and corded muscle, from his chest to his back and shoulders. Like an angry tennis player, he grunted with each heave of his pickaxe. Though he was making good progress himself, without benefit of a shovel he was having trouble keeping the hole clear of the ground's remnants. A second shovel would have been good, he commented.

Todd agreed, and thought of the two shovels in the back of Cindy's trunk. Oh well, this was better than having to use his hands, as he'd earlier imagined. He wondered briefly about Cindy, what she was up to, what kind of trouble he'd left her with.

About a half hour had elapsed since they'd begun their dig in earnest, and each had created a hole of about three feet deep and though they had their sweat and exhaustion to point to as evidence of their hard work, they had little else to be pleased about. In other words: it was nothing but dirt and rocks and the occasional slimy little bug that scurried away after having its home disturbed. No cash.

"So," Todd began, taking a break, wiping his brow with the tail of his untucked shirt. "Any chance someone was playing a trick on us, sending us on a wild goose chase? That perhaps Fast Cash's fortune being buried here was about as real as the rest of this town?"

"Why would someone go to such trouble?" Lana asked. "The mystery of Fast Cash remained dormant for so long, and only in the wake of his being declared legally dead has anyone found his story remotely interesting. I mean, that's where this whole thing started, when Lottie Cashman petitioned the court to put her husband at last to rest."

"And why do you think she suddenly decided on this tactic?"

"Because it had been seven years and there'd been no word from Fast Cash, so I guess she felt she finally had a legal leg to stand on. Look, Todd, that money exists somewhere, even if it's not buried here. Fast Cash is long dead, has been since that morning he took a bullet while trying to escape from the robbery."

"How can you be so sure?"

"I...I just know."

"And what about his accomplice?" Todd said.

"What about him?" Lana suddenly said, anger reflected in her tone, barely a space between each word.

"Well, there were two of them that morning—Fast Cash, and some guy named Marty Beam. He's missing, too, don't you think maybe he could have double-crossed his partner and made off with the money? All this speculation by the news media about Fast Cash still being alive, I think it's all a lot of bullshit. The guy's worm food, and has been for years. I think it's time people started focusing a bit more on this Beam character. Maybe he killed Fast Cash and..."

Todd didn't have a chance to finish his sentence. Because Lana had unleashed the anger that had been building up inside her and she lashed out, and this time she didn't slap him across the face as she had done in Bermuda. Nope, Lana curled her fist together and with the force of her convictions she pummeled Todd with a major blow to the solar plexus.

Todd went reeling backwards, he tripped on the shovel, and as his body twisted in mid-air in an attempt to break his fall, he saw in that slow-motion kind of way that it wasn't the dirt floor he was headed for. His body was going to hit the cement wall, and that…that was going to hurt a lot more.

Except it didn't.

Todd went right through the wall. As it turned out, the cement wasn't so thick where he landed. Pieces of cement crumbled around him like rotted plasterboard, and that's when Todd realized he wasn't alone in the crevice his body had created.

Another body fell right on top of him, bones crashing over him and onto the dirt floor, where they came to, ironically, a peaceful rest.

Three things happened next.

Barney said: "I'll be a son-of-a-bitch."

Lana, staring at the mix of Todd's body and the skeletal bones, well, she just let out one mother of a scream.

And Todd, he had his own reaction. He simply said, "So, Fast Cash, you've been home all along."

"**SO, YOU** want to explain yourself, punching me like that?"

Lana, seated in the rear passenger seat of her own car, held her arms tight around her body, still trying to shake off the chill of what she'd just seen, what she'd just witnessed. Even if she felt like responding to Todd's question, she wasn't sure she could.

Todd was behind the wheel of the car, still looking every bit the dusty, filthy mess he'd been in the basement of the Cashman house. Sitting beside Lana, all dirty and also silent, was Barney, who looked a little green around the gills. Guess this private detective hadn't seen many bodies, especially bodies that no longer had any flesh to cover their bare necessities.

They had all agreed to make a fast exit from the house, though that was easier said than done. Into the trunk had gone the shovel and the pickaxe, the two lights, the blanket, and absolutely none of Fast Cash's long-rumored money. With their own shirts, they wiped down any surfaces they may have touched, and even some they knew they hadn't, just to play it safe. Who wasn't in the trunk, or even riding shotgun, was the person whose skeletal remains they'd unexpectedly uncovered. Until they knew what to do, the bones of Fast Cash could remain just where they were.

Keeping an eye out on the road ahead of him and in the rearview mirror, Todd didn't get a sense that they were being followed. He also wasn't sure they were necessarily headed in the right direction; L.A. driving was not exactly his specialty. But pulling up a mental image of the drive from this morning—which truthfully felt like weeks ago—he did the reverse of what he imagined, hit the freeway, and before long he began to see signs for Manhattan Beach. With little choice of where else to go to, he'd decided to head back to the Scanlon house.

He realized there'd been no communication from Cindy; not a phone call, no voicemail, not a text message. He'd checked. Better to drive there, check in on her, let her know what had happened. And get cleaned up a bit, maybe get Lana a cup of tea or a shot of brandy. He looked over at her, and still she was quiet, distant.

When they pulled into the driveway of the intimate bungalow shared by Cindy and Patrick Scanlon, Todd breathed a heavy sigh of relief. Cindy's car was parked before theirs, a light shone from the living room. Todd checked his watch: nearly midnight.

With Barney's help, they escorted Lana out of the car and up the porch, where they were greeted at an open door by a sallow-eyed Cindy Scanlon.

"I heard the car doors," she said as she welcomed everyone into her home. "Wanna tell me who everyone is, and why you all look…oh my God, Todd, did you find the money? Please, tell me you found the money…"

"Hardly," said Barney.

"Oh, Leopold," Cindy said, "nice to see you."

"You're greeting now doesn't rival the one at the airport."

"Yes, well, the circumstances are a bit different," Cindy said, followed by, "And who may I ask, is this?"

This…meaning her. Meaning Lana.

Cindy wasn't looking her best, and Lana certainly didn't quality for Miss America at the moment, but yet both women's hackles were raised, cats circling each other, trying to figure out the other's agenda. Lana was agenda-ed out at the moment.

Todd interceded. "This is Lana. From Bermuda…."

"Bermuda?"

"She of the slapped face. Lana, this is Cindy—she of the wife comment. Look, it's a long story and even I don't have everything straight—wait, check that, anything. Can you, for now, help Lana? Get her cleaned up, maybe into some fresh clothes or something, you both look to be about the same size."

Cindy took control of Lana, leading her forward. That's when Todd noticed thick white gauze wrapped around Cindy's middle finger. "You okay?"

"I'm fine. For another time, trust me, I'll fill you in," Cindy said. "I think we've all been through enough tonight, let's get all of you cleaned up and rested."

"Good idea. Barney here, I think he could benefit from a shower, too. Please."

"And what about you, Todd?"

"I'll be okay, they can shower first. I've got a few things to sort out in my mind. But I'll tell you, I'll be glad to get out of these filthy clothes…"

That wasn't to be the case, though, not now anyway. The doorbell rang, and Todd told everyone to clear out of the living room, he would deal with whoever was at the door at this ridiculously late hour. Really, who did a drop by at midnight, and on a Sunday night to boot? Well, who it was, they rarely needed to phone ahead, Emily Post's manners weren't exactly part of the criminal code.

Todd opened the door and found himself face to face with his new old friends, Detectives Dalrymple and Benes. As the senior member, Dalrymple got to do the honors.

"We meet again," Dalrymple said. "Mr. Patrick Scanlon, you're under arrest for the murder of Carl Beaufort…."

While Todd listened as the rest of his rights were read, Benes slipped a pair of handcuffs on him. Now where were those when he and Lana had been alone in the pantry?

CHAPTER TWELVE

THE WIND swirled in the early morning sky, blowing strong off the ocean, causing the fronds of the palm tress to twist sideways and on occasion claim a weaker frond and toss it aside lazily. To think that was a metaphor for the role of Patrick Scanlon in this entire unfolding drama was to think accurately. Patrick had always had these grand ideas, such great plans, first for him and then after Cindy entered his life for them both. Dreams of avarice, though, had led to nightmares of glutinous proportions, and the real problem was, there was nothing Patrick could do to rectify the situation now; he may as well have been a sloth.

Sloth or palm frond, whichever applied, we find Patrick sitting on the beach watching the sunrise on a Monday morning in mid-September. The forecasters were not exactly predicting a hurricane, but the threat of gale force winds had sent a wave of panic around the small island, and the night before residents and tourists alike had started to batten down the hatches. Neither Patrick nor his little bodyguard Fred knew what to do about Todd's tiny rented cottage, or who to call about it.

Lost in thought on the beach, Patrick suddenly heard sounds behind him. He turned and of course, there was little muscle-bound Fred in his little muscle-T, encroaching on Patrick's peaceful and private piece of the world. His ruminations were taken with the wind, and instead new questions formed when Fred merely said, "Let's go."

"Uh, where?"

Fred hadn't proved to be the most amiable or chatty bodyguard (what the police would call kidnapper), and had mostly kept his conversation to one-word utterances. Like now.

"Now."

See?

Patrick knew he had little choice but to acquiesce. This little guy Fred, he might be short in stature but he was all meat and no gristle, and though Patrick was loathe to admit it he knew that the L.A. lifestyle of driving everywhere—even to the gym—had made him soft. Any resistance, Fred would rake him good over the dunes. So he followed after his captor, saw that a taxi was waiting just past the cottage. He saved himself some words by not asking where they were going. He had a sense, and a short while later that sense proved to be accurate. The taxi dropped them off in front of the Buzz Factory and this time Patrick did turn to Fred and said, "Isn't it a little early to be imbibing?"

"We're not here to drink."

Sure, Patrick asks a rhetorical question and finally this guy speaks a full sentence.

Fred knocked once, apparently a prearranged signal, because Buzz appeared right away and opened the door for them. Patrick stepped in, Fred behind him. Buzz turned the lock and

Fred took up his usual stance by the door. Thick, corded arms crossed.

"Come on, kid, let me get you a coffee," Buzz said.

Patrick sidled up to the bar, put his butt on a stool. Outside he heard the wind picking up, rattling the rafters of the rickety old saloon. The water in Toad's tank stirred, and the frog happily rode the fresh wave. Buzz ignored the building storm and simply poured the coffee, one for Patrick and one for himself and a third for Fred, who actually left his post to retrieve it, but quickly returned when the front door rattled. Patrick stole a look back; was that the wind, or was that company?

Buzz leaned against the bar. "Oh, don't worry your head about a little wind. 'Tis the stormy season down here. It's just wind, I've slept through worse and that's without the need of my sleeping pills. Yup, I've been through a few fits of Mother Nature's fury, the Factory always remains fit as a fiddle."

"Consider me reassured," Patrick said, grateful for the steaming hot coffee but kind of looking at the bottle of Jameson on the top shelf. An Irish coffee might be nice. "So, do you know what's going on, Buzz? Why I keep getting brought back to this place?"

"Me? What do I know about anything? I'm just a tavern owner, I serve drinks."

Patrick gave the man a smirk. "I don't think you've ever been just anything, Buzz. But fine, we'll play it your way and I'll continue to remain in the dark. Though between you, me and Toad, I think I'm here for a reason."

Buzz shrugged, kept washing glasses.

Fred had come up behind him, tapping him on the shoulder.

Patrick turned, looked down at the bulky little guy.

"Join me," Fred said.

Patrick's eyes widened. "Oh, now you decide to have a chat?"

"Complaining?"

So, Patrick joined Fred at one of the back tables, settled across from his mysterious friend (what the police would call his captor). He stared right at him and said, "So, are you going to finally explain why am I here, of all places?"

"You don't like Bermuda? Could be worse places."

"Like that grimy sofa in your office? Still itching from it," he said. "So, spill. What do you and your partner have to do with me? Are you here to hurt me?"

"What makes you think this isn't just some ordinary business arrangement?"

Patrick rolled his eyes; he couldn't help it. "Let's see—for starters, I'm being held against my will by…well, you, and in association with your partner, Barney. At first I thought you two might be working for my boss, but then when I was kept in New York and not returned to Los Angeles to face his music, well, there went that theory. So, I get rescued by my friend, at the request of my wife. Somehow she was able to find Todd, even when I couldn't. Turns out, he was in Bermuda and that's where I am now, and in the hands of some guy who could probably bench press a Volvo. What's the matter, you feel slighted as a kid, only way to overcome was to overdevelop?"

"Picking on a man's foibles, not very nice, Mr. Scanlon," said Fred, his thick muscled arms twitching. "Just consider yourself lucky to be away from California. From what I've been able to learn, this entire scheme has gotten rather complicated."

Patrick drank from his coffee, realized it was nearly empty. Just then Buzz came over with fresh refills, the aroma of the coffee bean filling his nostrils. Fred took a sip from his.

"Can you tell me this: what's the point of keeping me captive?"

Fred set down his coffee cup. "Maybe someone wants you out of the way—at least, temporarily."

"By someone, I assume you mean the person who's paying you," Patrick said.

Fred shook his head, obviously tired of hearing the same questions and not wanting—or being able—to answer them. "Whoever is paying us is of no concern to you."

"So, is there a point to why I'm being held in this particular place? In Bermuda, staying at Todd's cottage, hanging out in the bar where Todd has left his pet frog?"

Patrick didn't get his answer. Because just then Fred let out a sudden yawn, and then his head drooped to his chest. He'd gone all quiet. Patrick looked around, found Buzz watching the unfolding action.

"Uh, hey Buzz, what's going on?"

Buzz innocently stood behind the bar, polishing a glass. "You know, sometimes it's not what's in coffee naturally but what you add to it."

"I don't get the sense you're talking about milk and sugar."

"Shame really."

"Buzz?" Patrick asked. "Why? I thought you preferred to stay uninvolved."

"Consider it a favor. Don't worry about him, you just busy yourself by getting the hell off this island before the wind cancels any flights and you find yourself back where this day started," he said. "And son, just between you and me, sometimes I do get involved—you know, when there's something in it for me.

"Fred could be dangerous, Buzz."

That's when Buzz pulled out from under the counter a shiny, well-oiled pistol. Ready for action.

"I'll be just fine. Now go."

Patrick wasted not a second longer.

During the long flight he could think about what the hell was going on.

"COME ON, hop to it."

Back to Los Angeles, back to Todd, who after eight hours and lots of questions, was unfortunately still in the hands of the local gendarmes and at the moment, back in the holding cell they had put him in around three that morning. They had come for him at five, asked him some more questions and then instructed the kind uniformed officer whose care he was under to escort him back to his cell. In all his years of pulling small time cons (and even fewer larger ones) he'd never before been in police custody and it figures doesn't it, that he'd lose his virgin status in a big way. Suspected of murder, but also, suspected of being someone he knew he was not.

Those detectives, Dalrymple and Benes, they weren't convinced of Todd's claim that he was, in fact, Todd Gleason and not Patrick Scanlon. His track record with them wasn't so good: first, being at the Cashman house in Cindy's car the day before the Open House; at Cindy's side and playing the dutiful husband during the Open House—not to mention running from the cops when they asked to question him; and lastly, answering the door at the Scanlon house at midnight on a Sunday. Add up all those instances, and it was easy to side with the cops.

"But we'll look into that identity," Benes had said, none-too-convincingly after the first round of interrogations.

Fortunately, the severity of the crime he'd been accused of had landed him single occupancy status; he had his cell to himself, and even if he'd been forced to share with drug dealers, pimps and other assorted colorful California characters, Todd was certain they would have kept their distance. Dressed still in his jeans and white shirt, still caked with dirt, his hair a disheveled mess and his face now officially sporting a start-up beard, he suspected he didn't smell all that great. Nor did he imagine his mug shot was anything to post on Facebook.

The clang of bars broke Todd of his reverie, and he watched as Benes approached his cell. He nodded once at an officer, and the cop, who looked not even thirty with a pale, pasty complexion (in L.A.?), unlocked the gate and pulled it wide open. Todd waited for Benes to say he could step forward.

"You didn't say Simon Says," Todd said.

"You're a funny guy, Gleason," Benes said.

"Thanks, I try…wait, what did you call me?"

"You checked out. But, we're not done with you just yet. A few more questions, if you don't mind."

"It will be my citizenry pleasure," Todd said.

Back upstairs he was escorted to where Interrogation Room #3 waited for him. As did Detective Earnest Dalrymple, a cup of coffee and a doughnut on the tabletop. The cop stood when Todd was brought in.

"Wow, now I'm getting some respect."

"Doughnut, Mr. Gleason? Coffee?"

"Sure, don't mind if I do," Todd said. He hadn't eaten since yesterday's breakfast and he was admittedly a bit woozy from lack of nourishment. He sat down without having to ask, such was the power of being wrongly accused of a capital crime.

"Is there anything else we can get you, sir?" Benes said, closing the door behind him.

Todd stole a look from one cop to the other, and realized they were playing that old police chestnut, good cop-good cop. "Look, detectives, you can relax for now. I don't have any intention of suing the Los Angeles Police Department for false arrest. Like I said—for now. Can we just talk honestly, now that you know who I really am?"

"We'd appreciate any help you can offer the department on this puzzling murder."

Okay, so they were going to continue to speak in that smarmy official suck-up language, it was something like Article 42, Section 4: Be Nice to Those You Falsely Arrested. Todd took a bite of Dalrymple's doughnut, savored the gooey sweetness.

"A couple of questions, Mr. Gleason?"

"Certainly."

"What's brought you to Los Angeles. We see that you are a resident of New York City."

"The Scanlons are old friends from college. I'm helping them out with some personal business."

"And that involves the Fast Cash case?"

"Not really. Patrick and Cindy are interested in the house, Patrick is out of town and so I accompanied Mrs. Scanlon. It was through an innocent, but still mistaken, assumption that people thought I was her husband."

"I see. And you have no other business here in Los Angeles?"

"None."

"Your clothing. You never did provide a satisfactory answer when we questioned you about how you got so filthy."

"What, everyone has to be a neat freak?"

"Mr. Gleason, you can do better, I'm sure."

"Look, you guys were trying to pin a murder on me, and you didn't even give me a chance to say my constitutional right to 'no comment.' So I ran. And after running from you guys—after you'd scared me into thinking I was going to be hauled off to jail—I ran into the backyard of the Cashman house and ended up tumbling down the cliff, dirtying myself in the process. I got quite banged up, actually, I hope I haven't suffered any broken bones." Todd smiled. "I assume this conversation is being recorded?"

"Sandy, you got any more questions for this joker?"

"Nah, let's just cut him loose."

"Fine," said Dalrymple. "But Mr. Gleason, I would appreciate that if you leave town you'll first check with us, leave a forwarding address—of course, we do know how to reach you in New York if anything of importance were to come up about this case. However, before you go, let me just say this."

"I'm listening."

"You're good, Mr. Gleason. A spotless record, not even a speeding ticket…"

"I live in New York, I ride the subway…"

"…and that just plain puts my panties in a bunch, if you know what I mean."

"You could try briefs, they'll keep everything secure…"

"What I'm trying to say is: we'll be watching you. Because twenty years as a detective tells me you're anything but just a caring friend helping out with some, as you say, 'personal' business. Just keep your nose clean, and everyone, especially the LAPD, will be happy."

"I would love to keep my nose clean, as well as the rest of me. I really do need a shower."

"Sandy, get him out of here."

And like that, Todd found himself released from police custody. He was all alone, no one to greet him in the wee hours of the morning. Not Lana, not Cindy, heck, not even Barney. Tossed into the Monday sunshine of the actual downtown Los Angeles, this was essentially a lost world to himself and a host of others who called SoCal home. He wondered, was it as easy to hail a cab in here as it was in New York?

Luck found him instead, so he wouldn't have to find out.

"You look like you could use a shower," was what Todd heard from the car that pulled up beside him. It wasn't the car that was speaking (no *Knight Rider* here), but rather the lovely driver situated behind its wheel.

When he saw who had come to rescue him, he smiled, his dimples catching the gleam of the sun, as though it had been scripted that way.

"Only if you join me," was what he said before getting into Lana's car.

NOW CARL Beaufort, what about his murder? Frankly, that's what Beverly Mills wanted to know, not only who did it but why. Why. That's the eternal question, isn't it? How far did one person have to go to push another person to actually pull the trigger of a gun and end a life? It was a brutal scenario, awash with desperation and blood. It was also a chancy question, because pursuing the truth about such a terrible crime, there was every possibility you could anger the killer so much they might come…uh, gunning for you. Beverly Mills, though, if she had learned one thing about life in LaLa Land, watching your back was that thing.

Hence the voice-activated tape recorder she kept hidden in her desk drawer.

Call it a bit of an insurance policy against unseemly types, and none came more unseemly-er than the malicious money marauder Langston Livingston. What he held over her was far more than the deed for her real estate office and a couple hundred thousand in cash debt. Those were mere possessions. Beverly Mills valued her lifestyle, the sun-drenched California sky and everything this gilded city had to offer for a wily operator. She hadn't changed everything about her just to have it blow up in her face.

Monday morning at Beverly Mills of Beverly Hills had Beverly placing a number of calls, follow-ups to the Open House. Poor Lana was tuckered out from the unexpected drama of the day, she'd been given the day off. But Vera was here, or was it Veronica…no matter, she was buzzing Beverly's phone with news that she had visitors.

"Plural?"

"And they say it can't wait."

"Why is that, dear?"

"Because they say they are from the police."

Beverly swallowed hard at that bit of news. "Oh, well, send them up."

It didn't take long; Vera or Veronica escorted the two men inside and not to Beverly's surprise did she know they were the same two who had pulled a surprise visit at the Open House. Formal introductions were made. Dalrymple, Benes. She nodded politely, extended her big hand and hoped it didn't have too much sweat on it. Beverly was a cool character normally, except when in the face of authority. Langston had that effect; and now the police.

"We hope not to take up too much of your time, Ms. Mills. Just a couple of questions."

"Certainly, gentleman...officers..."

"Lieutenant, actually," the rumpled one offered. He was Dalrymple.

"Forgive me. I suppose this is about the Open House, the man you were looking for."

"Actually, it's not. We're here about Carl Beaufort," said Benes, shifting on his feet, gazing about the nicely appointed office. "Guy was a gritty reporter, he liked to tackle subjects some other journalists might have been afraid to cover. And he had free reign, what with his column. Gave him the chance to speculate, that's what made his pieces about Fast Cash so intriguing, the way he imagined how that all went down."

"Yes, yes, I read them. He was a talented writer."

"We've been going through his stuff, Ms. Mills. And what do you think we found among his notes?"

"I would have no idea?" she said.

That's when Dalrymple pulled from his coat pocket a microcassette, just like the kind Beverly used for her tape recorder. "There were a few of these tapes in Beaufort's possession, locked in a safe deposit box, but we found them and gave them a good listen. Quite interesting. Seems when he was done with his Fast Cash obsession, Carl was going to be moving onto a new subject. Guy by the name of Langston Livingston, according to his notes. And these tapes…well, they just happen to have Livingston's voice on them. His, and from what I can gather, yours."

"Ms. Mills, are you in some kind of trouble?" Benes asked.

"Why ever would you think that?"

"Sounds like you owe him money. That he stops by regularly for payment. Makes threats from the sounds of it," Dalrymple said. "So, you wanna tell us what you're up to? Seems you're already on Livingston's bad side, he finds out about these tapes you've made, the fact that you've handed them over to a reporter…I'd say you're playing a very dangerous game."

"Perhaps a game that's already gotten one man killed."

"Poor Carl," Beverly said. "So you think Langston…that he killed Carl?"

Both men shook their heads. "We know a lot about Livingston and his high-end loan sharking and money laundering…just don't have a lot of evidence to arrest him. Still, what we can surmise about this guy is, he prefers his victim to stay alive. He likes to collect, he likes to threaten, but he's never smelled of murder before. His fingernails may be dirty, but his nose is clean, if you catch my drift."

"My, such colorful language," Beverly said, reminding herself to play up the damsel in distress role. Who knows where this might lead.

"Ms. Mills, forgive me," Dalrymple said, "but at yesterday's Open House, we saw a completely different woman in action than the one we're seeing right now. Seems you adapt your personality to the situation, whether it's the overbearing real estate agent or now, the quivering wall flower. Makes me curious, a chameleon such as yourself, what might she be hiding."

"Gentleman…detectives, let me assure you. Beverly Mills of Beverly Hills is a lot of things, career-minded, perhaps a bit too driven…but I certainly have nothing to hide. Truth of the matter is this: Langston Livingston holds quite a few things over me, it all kind of snuck up on me and now…well, I'm caught, as they say, between a rock and a hard place."

Dalrymple gave Benes a look. Benes gave Dalrymple one in return.

Beverly watched the exchange with curiosity. Shit, she thought, they know.

"Ms. Mills, before we meet with people of interest—which you currently are—we like to do our homework. One of those assignments was to run the prints on this particular cassette. And do you know what we found?"

Beverly nodded. "Yes, you found out that my name is not Beverly Mills." She paused. "And that I'm not from Beverly Hills."

Again, those detectives exchanged looks. Then they settled down in the chairs that faced Beverly's desk, like they were going to be here for a while. She, too, finally sat down. With the window open and a breeze blowing, she picked up her cigarettes and lit one. The smoke felt great, the nicotine raced through her system. Okay, she felt more like herself now.

And that's when she said, "Okay, guys, what do you need from good ol' Esther."

"We'd like your help in nailing Langston Livingston," Dalrymple said.

"Yeah, I figured. What do I get out of it?"

Benes had that one. "Immunity."

CHAPTER THIRTEEN

EVEN THOUGH she didn't know it, Lottie Cashman's days were numbered, certainly when it came to her old life. She started her morning with a low-carb bagel with low-fat cream cheese. You had to be careful what you put into your system these days, the experts would have you convinced just thinking about certain foods will kill you. So she was being extra careful.

Otherwise, the day had begun fairly routinely. She enjoyed the yucks offered up by the staged bickering of Logan and Logan, and today in particular she enjoyed them because during their news segments there had been no mention of her beloved Jack; the story of Fast Cash had had its renaissance, and was now, again, relegated to the proverbial back page. The Open House failed to get a mention, too, which pleased Lottie to no end. Reruns might get you residuals, but first run got you ratings, and in this town that was the difference between has-been and tabloid fodder.

After her recent experience with the press, she'd happily accept has-been status.

The hosts said "Have a great day," with L.A. smiles plastered (botoxed?) to their faces, the credits rolled, with promotional consideration given by Princess Cruises, and that advertisement got Lottie moving at last. She had things to do, and most importantly a plane to catch. Putting away the dishes, wiping away the last of the crumbs from her bagel, Lottie turned off the kitchen light and headed upstairs to her room.

For the next hour she readied herself—shower, dress, make-up, and then she gave herself a long stare in the floor-length mirror. She was dressed in strawberry red, and it looked as though if squeezed ripe, red juice would seep out of her plumpy sides. To add the final touch (and to complete that berry image) she topped her head off with a jaunty green beret, just enough panache to give her step added bounce. There, she thought, eminently pleased with her colorful palate, ready for anything. Life had been building to this point since the court case began—for the anticipated and long-awaited reunion.

Lottie Cashman checked her watch. Closing in on noon. Her flight was not until eleven that night, a red-eye to the East Coast, where after arriving in DC in the early morning she would wait out a short holdover until her connection. So yes, she was slightly ahead of schedule, but she also had a few errands to run and didn't relish the idea of driving all the way back home. One thing she wouldn't miss about L.A. was the freeway traffic.

With that in mind, she grabbed hold of her bright yellow suitcase—Lottie was definitely a primary colors kind of gal—she wheeled it out of her bedroom, only to stop at the top of the stairs.

"Oh dear, I didn't plan very well, did I?"

Not that she was tiny or weak, but what she had packed

would last her weeks and as a result the bag was ridiculously heavy. She could imagine the woman at the airline counter smacking the bag with one of those "heavy" tags, and then charging Lottie for the extra weight. Just then she laughed; now there was a diet plan, you get charged for weighing too much. People didn't like to pay fines, they put more energy into fighting them than facing up to what they've done. She laughed again.

"Okay, Lots, you're just putting off the inevitable."

Indeed she was. And so by summoning an inner strength called determination, she grabbed hold of the handle and lifted the bag from the landing's top step. She stared down the remaining steps and told herself to have patience, *you have all the time in the world*. Which is exactly what James Bond said to his wife in *On Her Majesty's Secret Service*, only to have their marriage last only longer than George Lazenby's 007-minutes of fame. Okay, stop with the distractions, concentrate. Another step, *that's it ol' girl, here comes another*.

"You're doing great, Lots."

She was, and then all of a sudden she wasn't. Lottie Cashman was between steps when the doorbell rang out. Ding-dong. Ding-dong.

"Who could that be?" she asked, causing a shift in her focus.

Two-thirds down the staircase, Lottie found herself losing her grip on the suitcase, her hands slippery from the exertion. The bag separated from her hand and went noisily tumbling down the stairs. Lottie let out a short scream as the doorbell started up again. Ding-dong. Ding-dong. Well, that's when Lottie's flailing arms missed the railing, and she too went the way of the suitcase. Her screams mixed with the sound of her body hitting the wooden stairs, until at last they subsided when she hit the base of the staircase with a noticeable thud.

"Ugh," was the sound that came out of her mouth shortly before her eyes closed.

But not permanently.

Not yet.

Lottie Cashman's eyes flickered open, and disoriented as she was she found the energy to focus on her surroundings. She was neither at the base of the stairs nor still lying atop her luggage. She was lying on the sofa in her rented apartment. What she didn't realize was just who had moved her there, and whether or not said person was still there. She recalled the doorbell, and wondered if her savior and the ringer were one in the same.

"Mrs. Cashman, can you hear me?"

"What...yes. Who are you? Wait, are there two of you, or am I seeing double?"

"No, no, you're correct. Two of us. I'm Detective Dalrymple, and this is my partner, Detective Benes."

"Ma'am," said Benes with a nod of his head.

"I'm guessing our arrival surprised you. How fortunate you are that the suitcase broke your fall. You could have broken your neck or worse. As it is, how do you feel?"

"Surprisingly...I feel just fine. Foolish, perhaps. And I suppose tomorrow the pain will hit my big backside." Lottie paused then, as though tomorrow's oncoming pain was nothing compared to her current situation. "Wait a minute, did you say detectives?"

"Yes, ma'am," Dalrymple said. "We're the lead detectives on the Carl Beaufort murder. We have some questions for you. Do you feel up to answering a few of them?"

"I can't possibly imagine what I would know about… something so sordid as murder."

"We understand Mr. Beaufort had a well, how shall we say, an unhealthy interest in your late husband's case."

"Unhealthy to the point it got him killed," Benes added.

With that, Lottie perked up. "What makes you think his incessant stories about Jack got him killed? As far as I understand it, Mr. Beaufort was an investigative journalist and no doubt he had many such stories he was working on. Perhaps it was someone who didn't like being investigated that caused his unfortunate end."

"Like your husband?"

Lottie didn't like the way Benes said that. Not a question, not completely a statement either—and he'd left off the "late" that Dalrymple had respectfully added. Lottie's mind was beginning to clear, and what she saw was trouble ahead.

"Detectives, I'm really not comfortable discussing this, and besides, I really have nothing to add."

"Mrs. Cashman, do you have any reason to believe your husband may be involved somehow with Carl Beaufort?"

"Detective, I resent that implication. My husband is dead."

Benes again. "Legally."

"Exactly, so he can have absolutely nothing to do with this matter."

"I understand you're selling your husband's home."

"It's mine now, as anyone familiar with the recent court case knows," she said. "Wait a minute, you're the two from the Open House…you almost ruined a perfectly good potential sale, that Scanlon woman…"

"I'm sure there will be plenty of offers, such a desirable location and all…"

"Not to mention the notoriety," Benes said. "Mrs. Cashman, I'm guessing from the suitcase that broke your fall that you're planning a trip?"

"Yes. My late husband's case has taken its toll on me, too many memories have recently been unearthed, and I need time to think about my future."

"May we remind you that you're a person of interest in an active murder investigation?"

"Actually, I am not."

"Excuse me?"

"Detective, are you about to tell me that I cannot leave town?"

"It would be in your best interest to stick around, yes."

"But you honestly cannot stop me from leaving. Can you?"

"Not unless we charge you with a crime."

"And are you?"

A definite lull had hit this fast-moving conversation, as both detectives exchanged looks. Blank looks, from where Lottie sat.

"Well, detectives?"

"No, we're not charging you with anything at this time, Mrs. Cashman. However, given the circumstances here—your husband recently declared legally dead, the reporter's murder, your decision to sell the house, not to mention the hefty suitcase in the hall—a combined thirty-two years of police work make us think there are too many coincidences."

"Coincidences, detectives," Lottie said, "will get one acquitted."

There was really nothing further to say. Lottie knew she had won this round, and if she had her way it would be a knockout punch, a kibosh on this case that would render any future contests unnecessary. Lottie, with their help, got up from the sofa and escorted the detectives out of the living room, and ultimately out of her house.

"You may want to see a doctor, Mrs. Cashman. You know, that fall?"

"I appreciate your concern. Good day, detectives."

Lottie closed the door on them, watched as they retreated to their unmarked vehicle parked at the curb. They remained for no longer than two minutes before driving off. As for Lottie, she started to shake. She didn't like close calls, not with the police and certainly not with her life. Screw that low-carb crap. Time had come for Lottie Cashman to start living. And, with a smile toward the future, thought: not alone.

"**DON'T SAY** a word."

"Your command. My wish."

"Toddly, you're quite silly." A pause. "I miss that."

"I miss hearing that—Toddly. What else do you miss?"

"Such a sweet talker," Lana said. "Just you wait until I show you."

Whether that last bit of banter was truth or the heat of the moment, it seemed to carry them forward on a cascading wave of desire. Lana had parked her car in her allotted space in her complex's underground garage, and with her hand locked in Todd's she led him out of the maze and back into the bright sunshine of the waning morning. At last they reached the front door of the apartment, and that's when and where she issued her cautionary statement of staying quiet. As for Todd, he didn't question why the monk treatment, he just hoped the vow of silence was the only one he was required to take.

Turned out, someone else should have listened to Lana as well. As they opened the door, they were met by a blast of noise and for a second Todd thought he heard applause. Wait, change that, more than a second and more than applause, he heard screams, too, and he imagined they had walked onto a Hollywood sound stage and the studio audience had erupted with sudden excitement over their arrival. Until he realized both sounds were kind of tinny, definitely not live.

"What the hell is that?" he whispered. Why he whispered, he didn't know.

"Sshh, it's the television," Lana whispered back.

"Are you kidding with all this whispering? The dead can't sleep with that racket."

"If we—meaning you—get discovered you may get to test out that theory."

More threats. This one intriguing. "Wanna elaborate?"

Lana closed the door on them. "Let's just say my mother would not take kindly to my inviting a boy home."

"Ooh, that sounds risky. Almost like sex on a public beach."

"Todd?"

"Yeah?"

"Don't say a word."

Okay, this time he really listened. He even fake-zippered his mouth, and mixing his silent metaphors he tossed away an imaginary key. Lana rolled her eyes while stifling a laugh.

For now, though, they tip-toed through the entranceway of Lana's home, sneaking into what Todd presumed was Lana's bedroom. They had skirted a small den, home to the television, home to that blaring sound, home to, apparently, Lana's overprotective mother. As Lana closed the door to her room, Todd had an image of the actress from *Throw Momma from the Train*. A woman who would toss Todd from a train without a shadow of a doubt.

So, behind closed doors without a hitch, safe for the moment, Lana slid right up the still-dirt clad Todd, placing her hands upon his chest.

"Where were we?" she asked.

"I seem to recall a filthy basement, some shovels, oh…and a dead body falling out of a wall you pushed me into. And a night in the slammer—one with no shower."

"I was thinking of a different time, a different place. Say… Bermuda?"

"Ah, well, if you want to go back that far in time, your hand was challenging my cheek to a duel. Your hand won."

"Todd?"

"Yes, Lana," he said, a smirk crossing his face, his dimples cracking the caked dirt on his cheeks.

"Do you always have to remember the bad times?"

"Well," he started to say, only to be stopped by Lana's lovely fingers outlining his lips.

"Sshh, we only have a half hour before *The Price is Right* ends. The noon news, it's just not as…raucous."

"Oh," Todd cleverly retorted.

"Oh, indeed," Lana answered, the only further word she was able to get out before their lips met.

As they kissed, the confined space that was Lana's childhood bedroom gave way, returning them to a place in their hearts and their minds, to a secluded beach where nothing and no one existed but them. Todd even thought he could smell the ocean air, but perhaps that was the power of memory forcing its way to the forefront of his mind. But like the waves that crashed to shore, so too were the motions of Todd and Lana, themselves crashing to the sand-like softness of her bed, comforter and pillows breaking their fall. And even though they were indoors, locked (right, she did lock that door?) behind closed doors, there was a sense of *From Here to Eternity* to this situation, imaginary water crashing over their bodies, their embraces taking on greater urgency as each piece of clothing was shed.

"Todd, I sorry I slapped you."

"Lana, I'm sorry you slapped me, too."

Smart ass. Lana let out a throaty laugh, then caught herself as the sound bounced off the walls. That was Todd, though, and that's what Lana responded to, a bad boy who was really a good guy, and it was both of them that she gave herself to right then and there, on a Monday morning in Los Angeles, while a decomposed body lay newly discovered but still unrecovered, where a woman lost herself to the showcase shenanigans of *The Price is Right*, where a case filled with discrepancies and disappearances threatened to overwhelm them. Todd Gleason and Lana Davies took this lost moment in time to rekindle a romance which had ended as quickly as it had started, and truth be told, the conflict that had caused their rift came with newfound benefits, because Todd and Lana, well, what happened between them now was bigger and better than anything they'd experienced in a place called Paradise.

"Wow," Lana said, her skin sweaty, her breath gradually coming back to her.

"I second that motion," Todd said, smiling down at Lana, her hands brushing the sweaty hair away from her face.

Lana laughed again, her fingernails lightly scraping against his back. She leaned up, kissed him again. Neither of them said anything, not even to remark how restrained they had been, their motions saying what they were thinking, what they wished to give voice to. With her mother in the other room, they had played it safe and silent, but no less passionately. Todd had the gentle bite mark on his shoulder to prove that point.

"So, it's three minutes to noon," Todd finally said, breaking the silence. "What next? You sneak me out the window?"

"Nothing so high school…"

"You know, I think I would have liked you a lot back then—"

"Why do I suspect you've had lots of practice making such escapes?"

"Just means you're getting to know me."

Playfully, she pushed Todd off of her, and then Lana got up from the bed, giving a listen at her door. Turning the lock, she cracked the door ajar, giving life to the blare of the television once again. He watched as Lana locked them inside and returned her beautiful naked self to the bed. She slid under the covers and slid right next to Todd. She kissed his rough chin, his softer lips, his tender tongue. Her fingers found their way to his chest; she gently stroked the hair. Todd felt himself getting excited again, especially when she pressed herself hard against his body. He wanted her again, there was no question about that, but yet his mind was suddenly filled with question upon question, and if he was to give himself fully to Lana this time he wanted to know answer upon answer. Like what was really going on, and where did they go from here.

"What's wrong?" Lana said, suddenly breaking free of the embrace.

"Sorry, it's just…"

"Is it Momma?"

Well, yes. But no, he thought.

"Well, yes. But no," he said.

"Then what?"

"It's you. Me. Us. This situation. What's our next step?"

"Oh, Todd," Lana said, "can't we just enjoy this moment? Life is going to intrude upon us real soon, and I for one am not relishing having to deal with it. I know what we have to do, and I suppose I just wanted a little escape." She kissed him again, her tongue slipping between his lips. He responded in kind, he responded with recharged enthusiasm.

Except he had to stop a moment later.

A knock came at the door.

"Oh shit," Lana suddenly said, shoving him beneath the covers.

"Lana, is that you? What are you doing?"

"Hang on, Mother," Lana said, and then, peering beneath the blanket, said to Todd: "I'll be right back."

Lana quickly wrapped a bathrobe around her, rearranged the pillows on the bed to cover Todd, and made her way out of the bedroom. Todd heard the door close and then he poked up from the covers. This was ridiculous; Lana was a grown woman and shouldn't she have every right to have a man in her bed if she so desired. Through the door he could hear voices but failed to pick up any words. He didn't like the tone, though.

Taking a chance, he got out of bed and threw his clothes on as quickly and quietly as possible. Then he eased himself over to the window, looked out. Luckily they were only one flight above the ground and a big green bush fortunately grew right beneath the window. Gave him something to break his fall. He opened the window, slipped out, dropped. The thick bush caught him, but not without the prickly branches sticking him in painful spots.

"Ouch," he said, allowing his body to slide off the bush and onto the ground.

He lay there, thinking, panting, breathing…

"Hey….you! You keep well away from my daughter…."

He looked up at the sound of voice, saw a woman with long silvery hair peering down at him. He didn't wait for introductions, he scrambled up and away, not even sure where he was going. Not even sure if he should be waiting for Lana or if once again their romantic moment had been interrupted from an unwelcome woman. That's when Todd saw Lana emerge from the front door, running quickly away from the house. Todd followed her, caught up to her back in the parking lot.

"So, Mother Davies wasn't so keen to find a boy in your room after all."

Lana looked frazzled, like she'd just taken the brunt of an argument with her mother. "No, definitely not. She's rather over-protective, ever since my father…look, Todd, about all that. You see…oh crap, I might as well just blurt it out."

Todd looked more than ready for some explanations. "Blurt away."

"Beam," she said suddenly, "It's not Momma Davies. It's

Momma Beam."

Todd's expression faltered. "Beam? Why is that name so familiar…oh no…"

Lana nodded. "As in Marty Beam."

"You're his daughter," Todd said, feeling a bit of déjà vu.

"Look, I can explain…"

"This ought to be good," Todd said.

OKAY, HERE'S a question: What rational person willingly walked into a hungry lion's cage?

Of course, such words were sheer metaphor, right? The man behind this sudden act of bravado considered the reputation of the man he was going against, one Langston Livingston, and that's where he came up with the lion analogy. He supposed the ferocious businessman would be angry, hungry even—for blood and for money, certainly and quite possibly for revenge. Langston was an unforgiving sort, and so this step of his was what some would call brave. Or plain suicidal.

Good thing he had an ace up his sleeve.

The time was just after six on this busy Monday evening, and most of Los Angeles were stuck in their cars on crowded freeways as they made their escape from downtown and back home to the various suburbs, whether beach or valley or canyon. Which meant a villainous sort like Langston Livingston was just getting started with his day's work. Not the day and not the night, a guy like him tended to favor when dusk's shadows came out, they were sometimes easier to hide, better to fool the unsuspecting.

Patrick Scanlon knew the building, obviously, it was his place of employ. Just off Sunset at La Cienega, he knew which floor was his ultimate destination. He counted up five, found the large corner on the southeast side, where you could easily waste the day away by watching the steady influx of planes touching down at LAX. He'd been there just recently. Light filtered out into the encroaching night from the office window. Langston was there; target found.

The front entrance was patrolled by security, so he quickly dismissed such an approach. How many times had he entered through the front, confident about his job, filled with optimism that all his problems would work themselves out. But as the job—and Langston—had revealed its true colors, the rear entrance took on brand new importance, a level of needed privacy, and so it was there he directed his feet. Through the parking lot he went, to the literal back door, withdrew his access card and for a split second wondered if his membership had been canceled. The quick release of the lock answered that question. He pushed open the door, and a second later had gained entry. The plan was working perfectly so far.

From here he had two options. There was a creaky old service elevator that would announce his arrival with more fanfare than a horn section, or a back staircase that was as quiet as a fresh corpse. Easy choice, though why he'd gone with that particular metaphor he couldn't say. Not a nice image. Ensuring his silence he slid off his shoes and carefully trod his way up the five flights. Ha, the stealth bomber had nothing on him.

Easing open the door, he peeked one way and was greeted by an empty hall. Then he peeked the other way—and that's when a he felt a big, thick hand grab his shoulder and pull him from the stairwell and out into the open space. Without a word, he was dragged much like an disobedient child into the foyer of a tastefully appointed waiting area. He was tossed into a chair, the impact causing him to drop his shoes.

"Wait until summoned."

Though left alone, he knew that wasn't truly the case. Cameras everywhere, damn them. He sensed eyes on him, several pair, watching his every move. In the corner of the room, a small red light caught his attention. Yup, there it was, a surveillance camera mounted upon on the wall.

"Oh, crap."

Did he really expect otherwise? That's what you get for working for a paranoid criminal, his characteristic suspicious nature making for one cruel, awful individual. For an amateur con man, he realized he'd been beat before stepping into the building. So he resigned himself to whatever his fate held.

Just then the door to the inner sanctum opened, seemingly automatically. Like a magic trick, complete with the reappearance of that callous, calloused-handed thug.

"Join us," was all he heard.

Rising from the chair, he felt ridiculous that he hadn't thought to put his shoes back on. There was no time now, so he padded through the doorway in his socks. Not exactly dressing for success, was he? And if this were an interview, from all appearances he didn't have a chance in hell of getting the job, not if you could read body language. Langston Livingston remained seated behind his huge desk, his hands clasped in their best Brando. People in LA, their frame of reference seemed limited by those who appeared in frames.

"Well, well, the Prodigal Thief returns."

"Evening, Mr. Livingston."

"So formal, Patrick? I think we are well beyond that."

"I guess so."

"Garth, frisk him, would you?"

So, was it any surprise that Patrick Scanlon's return to his place of employment was not exactly met with any level of trust? Garth, trusty handyman, bodyguard, driver, all around thug, with less-than-delicate hands roughed him up a bit while patting him down. Patrick detected an extra effort at his balls, a slight squeeze that made him wince from the pressure. Finally, though, Garth was done feeling him down, and up.

"He's clean."

Patrick scoffed. "Langston, you insult me. I had hoped we could be civilized."

"Is that why you opted to sneak in the back way?"

Patrick decided he had no response to that.

"Though, Patrick, I do appreciate your level of discretion. If no one knows you're inside the building, they'll never know if you left it or not." Langston smiled, albeit briefly. "So, I suppose there is a reason for your return to the city of angels? Sudden as it is."

"I thought we could talk."

"I hate 'talking.'"

"Okay, perhaps we could…compromise."

"Compromise does not rank above talking."

Patrick stole a look back at the behemoth that was Langston's bodyguard. "Look, I'm a bit nervous with him…uh, hovering. Do you think you could call off Garth Vader?"

Langston actually laughed at that, dismissing his trusted employee as his laughter faded.

"You have my money?"

"See, that's what I came about…"

"Patrick. Answer the question. Do you have the money you owe?"

"Not yet."

Langston let out an audible sigh, his discontent obvious. "All this time you've been away and you still come back empty-handed? How you disappoint me. Though I'm hardly surprised. You never really lived up to the potential I saw in you. You wife has more gumption and guts in her pinky than you have all together."

"I'm here now, aren't I?"

"Foolishly, yes, you are. So, you want to talk…talk."

"Look, Langston…Mr. Livingston, I'm onto something—a big hit—and when it comes in I'll be able to pay you back every cent plus interest. I just need more time, and I need to do it without having to look over my shoulder every second, if you know what I mean. Just give me a chance."

"Patrick, I always know what you mean."

"Are we just going to trade insults all night, or are we going to conduct business?"

"I respond well to business talk. Fine. Speak."

"It's this Fast Cash business…"

"Ah, Patrick, I was afraid that's where you were going with this. Look, that crook is long gone, and may I emphasize, so is his fortune. Anything else you hear about him is pure myth."

"Maybe not."

"Maybe? If you're not fully convinced, why should I be?"

"Okay, definitely not."

"Aha. So, you have proof that Fast Cash's stash—rumored

to be nearly three million dollars—really is hidden somewhere, and it's just waiting for some clever upstart fellow such as yourself to figure out where it's been stashed?"

"Well, no. And no. But I do have a hunch."

"Patrick, hunches are for men without instincts."

Patrick looked visibly insulted. "Look, I know I don't bring a high level of trust at the moment, but you're going to have to trust me nonetheless. Something very odd is going on here. There's this map—which some think is of the old Cashman house, but I think is a fake out. I've had time to do some thinking and see, here's the thing. There's a clue in the map, for sure, and that will ultimately lead to the true location of the unrecovered money. It has to exist—look at all that's happened since the *widow* Cashman sought to have Fast Cash declared legally dead."

"There has been an unusual amount of activity surrounding this case—especially for a guy everyone thinks is dead."

Patrick smiled, sensing that Langston was coming around to his side and was just waiting to hear more. He decided not to say anything further, not yet. Let the boss initiate the next step. He crossed his arms, body language taking over. Waiting, waiting, still the boss remained silent and seated. Patrick realized sweat had begun to form on his brow. He felt his nerves tense up, his advantage begin to slip away....

"What do you have in mind?" Langston finally said.

"I have a plan."

"I assumed so."

"We get all the players in one place. Somewhere they can't escape from."

"You suggest a kidnapping?"

"In a manner of speaking," Patrick said, his voice taking on new urgency, as though he truly felt in charge. The fool. "You entice them, Langston, individually. But ultimately they all find themselves gathered in the same place. You're still in possession of that yacht you had to take as a down payment from that studio exec who got fired? *The Nutcracker*?"

Langston Livingston blinked. Then he smiled. "Interesting. Very interesting," he said. "Sit down, Patrick, take a load off. Let's hear what you've got to say. Oh, but could you put your shoes on? I don't want you feeling too comfortable. That's hardly my style."

CHAPTER FOURTEEN

THEY'D MADE their escape from Mother Beam, her feathery silvery hair just a distant memory. Her voice though, lingered, nagged at Todd like a schoolmarm who disapproved of the truant actions of an irrepressible schoolboy. Finally, Todd had Lana truly to himself, but what was on his mind was something other than things of a carnal nature. Time had come for some answers.

"Promise you'll tell me everything? About this crook Fast Cash and your involvement in selling the Cashman house, how you came to be working with Lottie and Beverly Mills, and why your mother's last name is Beam and your last name is Davies."

"Wow, that's a lot to reveal."

'Oh, and what exactly you were doing in Bermuda."

"Right. That one might be a bit more complicated to explain."

"Doesn't matter where we begin, just so long as we cover every topic."

Ah, L.A. at night, a time for secrets to slither out from the shadows. Tonight was one lit by blinking gold and red intermingling with streaks of blue and green, a sleek rainbow set amidst an otherwise black canvas. The towers of downtown rose high above the backdrop of mist-covered mountains, a juxtaposition of cosmopolitan city and land ruled by coyotes and other creatures. Todd had to admit, even when the film industry wasn't even trying to set the scene it still magically appeared.

Gazing out the windows of the car, watching the city grow more distant as they climbed higher into the hills, Todd said, "We're away from your home. Everything else, too, it seems. So, your story, I'm eager to hear it."

Lana, all curves herself, clutched the steering wheel and negotiated the winding curves of Mulholland Drive as though she raced with NASCAR and this was a course she was all too familiar with. As she took the next bend she didn't even look, her eyes fixated on Todd. "Let me guess, patience was never one of your strong points."

"Patience is overrated. There's something to be said for knowing what you need to know when you want to know it."

"Or wanting to know when you need it," she replied with more than a hint of a smile.

Todd tossed her a withering look. Smart-ass comments were his playground, and he didn't like when others jumped the fence. "I think I've been plenty patient, seeing as you've kept me waiting ever since you picked me up outside the PAB."

"You didn't want to hear it earlier. You were distracted."

"You're good at distracting me."

"See, we all have something we're good at," she replied.

"Okay, so far we've mastered the art of bantering, but substantive conversation I have to say is severely lacking."

"Todd?"

"Yeah?"

"Can't you just be quiet and enjoy the view?"

"Sure, if you tell me where we are, and where we're going."

Lana had told Todd she would reveal all, but she wanted to do so at a special place. That's all she said at the time as the reunited lovers hopped into her car and sped off into a moonlit, Hollywood-scripted night. Now, they were rounding the endless bends of Mulholland, putting more and more distance between themselves and the reality that lived down in the valley. Up here in the hills, fantasies rented space, behind iron gates and brick walls, in the shimmering waters of a blue-lit pool, on the flickering images shown inside home screening rooms. In a place like this, where the city fell at their feet, you could almost imagine that the story of Fast Cash and the search for his fortune and the body in the basement existed only as a reel inside some director's mind. That all you needed was a movie theatre and a spare two hours and soon the last frame would flicker and all secrets would be revealed.

Real life, however, seldom resembled reel life.

And in this forced silence, Todd figured they were in danger of losing their "talkie" status.

"So, did I tell you I like your tan lines?"

"It's dark outside, you can't see my tan lines."

"I have a flawless memory."

"Todd?"

"Yeah?"

"I don't remember you being such a talker."

"Fine. I'll be quiet. Especially when we get to where we're going. Because you'll be doing all the talking."

"That was a pretty wordy way of shutting up."

"Nice," he said.

"Better."

This time he closed his mouth.

"Ever better," she said, and ended her victory with her lovely, enticing laugh.

For two people who really knew very little about each other—when you removed that biblical element to their relationship—Lana Davies and Todd Gleason had a good read on each other's personalities, their temperaments, which boded well for them working together as a team.

For now they managed to co-exist with the silence between them until they made their way to their (Lana's) desired destination. Todd needed a bit more help, the signs were darkened in the parking area and only a strong glow from higher up gave him any sense of being near civilization. Griffiths Park, Lana explained, and then pointed upwards.

"It's the Hollywood sign," Lana explained.

Now, you can't get too close to the sign anymore, since the Chamber of Commerce had it all fenced off, fending off graffiti artists and suicide attempts with one fell swoop. But you could ride up the mountainside and park in the shadow of the sign, sit in the glow of the lights and stare down at the neon streaks of the city, watch as planes landed on a continual basis at LAX. And that's where Lana took Todd, settled on the grassy edge of the hill.

"I love coming up here, it's the perfect place to think."

"Uh, Lana?"

"Yes, Todd?"

"I thought we were here to talk. Thinking is kinda too quiet for me."

"You're incorrigible, you know that?"

He grinned, and it was like his dimples caught the light of the sign. As if Hollywood was saying we like your smile, come, stay, audition. Lana wasn't to be swayed by his charm at the moment and he noticed a sad expression take up residence on her face. He leaned in, brushed a hand against her cheek. Not a romantic move, but rather one of comfort. Letting her know it was okay to talk. To confess.

And so began Lana's tale.

"Life can get complicated and well…everyone needs that one spot on this planet which is yours and truly yours. This is mine. Like your beach in Bermuda, your so-called 'corner of the world.' When you brought me there, all I could think about was this place, high in the Hollywood hills. It's brought me such comfort, especially when I needed it most. It's amazing to think that in a city of six million people, I could find a private spot to call my own. And I'm in real estate, so that's saying something."

Todd smiled at her attempt at levity. "Want to tell me what were you running from?"

"A bad marriage."

Todd didn't react. He opted for his poker face. "You're married?"

"Was—hence the Davies last name. It lasted two years, less in the honeymoon sense if you can crack that code. He was older, I was really young, and even though I was stupid to get involved with him…well, he was even more stupid. Getting caught up with the wrong crowd, promising me the world. In the end, we just went our separate ways, no hard feelings. I haven't seen him in three years. Still, even after the divorce I never considered going back to my maiden name, I couldn't, knowing people remembered the Beam name." She paused, then gave him a curious look. "What about you, Todd?"

"I kept my maiden name."

"Why do I bother?" she asked the sky. The stars twinkled at her. Turning back to him, she said, "Seriously, were you ever married?"

"Nope."

"Ever want to be?"

Todd said nothing. He too looked to the sky, as if for answers. His mind flashed back to those days of college and to Cindy, to the once upon a fairy tale dream he'd had of the two of them running off, eloping into a sunset that still held a bit of burn to it. Danger of the unknown, comforted by the fact they were in on it together. Then he blinked and the image was gone. "I think marriage and me are a bit like oil and water."

"Kids?"

"I use protection."

Okay, for that one she hit him. "Are you ever serious?"

"Not if I can help it," he said. "Can we get back to your life story? Tell me about Marty Beam. He was your father."

"You say that like it couldn't be possible."

Todd thought of Cindy and the story she told him on the moonlit beach just the other night. About the father she'd never known, a guy by the name of Jack Cashman. And here he was days later, in a spot just as romantic and with an equally beautiful woman, and she was telling him about her father, a guy who went by the name of Marty Beam. Disney claimed it was a small world, but if what Cindy believed and what Lana stated were both true, than the world could fit on the head of a pin. Two fathers, partners in crime until they turned on each other, and now years after they had disappeared both of their daughters were looking for them. And here was Todd, smack dab in the middle.

"Did you ever know him?" Todd found himself asking.

"Of course I did. He was my father. All through my childhood, my teen years, he was always there for me. A doting father, they call them. Until one day when…"

"He disappeared."

"Todd, why do I get the sense you know more about this story than I do?"

"My tale soon. Continue yours."

"Look, I'll keep this really simple. On the last day my father was seen, he walked into a bank with his supposed friend Jack Cashman and robbed a bank. During the escape, one of them got shot and the other drove off alone. After that, they both disappeared. I want to know what happened that day, and where my father is today."

"Why now? Why seven years after the fact?"

"Because of Lottie Cashman and her ridiculous petition to have Jack declared legally dead," Lana said. "I'd put it all behind me, or so I thought. I'd married Chuck, who my mother always hated and thought was a poor substitute for a father figure—which, after hours of contemplation up here in the hills—I supposed there was some validation to that. But then one day in the news is this report—in 'Carl's Corner' in the *Daily News*—about Lottie Cashman's appointment with the courts. Suddenly my father's unresolved legacy came screaming back. I did everything I could to shield my mother from what was happening, but she's such a crazy news junkie, sits in front of the television all day, the task was near impossible. So I decided

I needed to do something about it. I wasn't sure what my angle was going to be with Lottie. I thought about confronting her; I mean, our families never really knew each other, Jack and Marty were more bar buddies than barbeque ones. So that's when I began to get the idea—Lottie wouldn't remember me, she'd probably only met me once or twice."

"So that's when you decided to pursue the real estate angle?"

"Almost. I had thought about testifying against her, since it had never been satisfactorily explained what happened to her husband—or my father. I thought I could produce enough doubt in the judge's mind to render a verdict against Lottie. But in the end, that's not how it was destined to play out."

"What happened?"

"The map arrived."

Okay, poker face gone, Todd was showing his hand. He thought about the map that Patrick and Cindy had, and he thought about how it was considered so valuable that some other people were after it. All of them believing that Fast Cash's fortune remained to be found.

"And that's when the real estate scam happened."

"I was already working for Beverly Mills. After my divorce, I got my license, applied and got hired—as her assistant. Beverly had been through so many, I think I was the only young woman left in the L.A. area who hadn't been fired by her. But I was strong-willed, put in my time, and when the time came I took some initiative and set up a meeting with Lottie."

"Okay," Todd said. "So I've got your motives, your means, and your opportunity. You faked Lottie out so you could gain access to the house, follow the directions on the map, and what? Dig up the fortune?"

"I never believed there was money down in that basement."

"What then?"

"Exactly what we found," she said. "Given the court case, I had to figure someone was pulling Lottie's strings, finally trying to bring the whole story to a close. Trouble is, we've got another mystery on our hands. We're not sure who wanted closure, because we're not sure whose bones those belong to."

"You don't think he's Fast Cash?"

"He could be. Or he could be my father," she said, dramatic silence giving pause to the scene. "In any case, someone put the body there, which is fishy unto itself. And you know what else it means? That person in the basement of the Cashman house was probably murdered, and the killer was hiding the body from discovery for a reason."

"And that reason would be?"

"To keep the trail alive. To keep the questions alive."

"So, you're saying that either Marty Beam killed Fast Cash, or the other way around, and that whichever one is the killer is still out there?"

"Bingo," Lana said. "Living off three million dollars."

"Any idea where he might be?"

Lana looked away, not ready to reveal her final secret.

But Todd, his mind worked in mischievous ways naturally, and his thoughts took him in only one direction, as though on a non-stop flight. From the slickness of the Los Angeles lifestyle to the simple existence of an island retreat, Todd's thoughts flew faster than the Concorde.

"Lana?"

"Yes, Todd?"

"Wanna tell me just what you were really doing in Bermuda?"

She shook her head. "I don't know anything yet, can't we leave that for another time? As it is I've said too much. It's your turn."

Todd decided to give the questions a rest, Lana obviously had said all she was going to say for the moment. "Fine, my story. I was already in Bermuda. Innocently vacationing."

"Todd?"

"Yeah?"

"Give me a little credit. I'm not sure anything you do can be qualified as 'innocent.' And besides, I wasn't talking about why you were in Bermuda. I meant Los Angeles. Just what are you doing wrapped up in the case of Fast Cash? What do you know? And more importantly, who do you know? Does it have anything to do with that woman, the one who claimed to be your wife? Who is she, really?"

Your rival, he thought.

"TODD, DID you even hear me?"

The answer was: apparently not. Because the moment that Lana inquired as to who had involved Todd on this crazy adventure, a picture had begun forming in his mind. Actually, the image was blurry, as though he'd been hit over the head and was seeing double. Double as in both Cindy Scanlon and Lana Davies. Perhaps it was his mind working overtime, but darn if they didn't look alike. Not exactly sisters; a few years separated them. The daughters of Marty Beam and Jack Cashman, unaware of each other, working separate angles but looking to achieve the same goal. What he thought, ultimately, was this: huh.

"Hello, Earth to Todd. Did you hear me?"

The thing of it was, it took a second time for Lana saying this that finally brought Todd out of his reverie. His last conscious thought before focusing back on Lana was the fact that without even knowing it he'd been working both sides of the same case. Todd focused back on the here and now because Lana hit him upside his head.

"Ow."

"Serves you right."

"What did I do?"

"I pour my heart out—take you to my special place. And what do you do? Ignore me."

"Lana, please, you gotta stop hitting me."

"Oh right, I forgot. I kind of slapped you in Bermuda," she said. "Did it hurt?"

"Let's just say the pain of that memory just came screaming back."

"Next time, answer my question."

Todd wasn't ready to answer her question, and he supposed ultimately that's why he'd zoned out. The timing was off, he couldn't yet reveal the truth to Lana about Cindy, and vice versa. In fact, loaded with the information Lana had just revealed Todd had more than a few things to figure out. How had this day gotten away from him? From being released by the police, to the gymnastic routines he and Lana had indulged in back at her place, to his near miss with Mother Beam, one big piece of the puzzle still glared like the L.A. haze.

What to do about the body in the basement.

As far as Todd knew, only three people knew about the body: himself, Lana, and a private eye slash bodyguard named Barney.

Neither he nor Lana were apt to say anything, not purposely and not yet, and he figured Barney was safe from telling all to the police. What did a private dick from New York want with a seven-year-old case of murder in Los Angeles? Todd still didn't know how Barney and Fred fit into the equation, only that they had an unhealthy attachment to Patrick and a dislike of Todd. Two plus two had to, in this case, equal five. Someone was missing.

Which made a light bulb go off over his head.

Cindy.

"Todd?"

He got up off the ground and started back toward her car.

"Todd, where are you going? Come on, we're not done yet. What aren't you telling me...Todd?"

He heard her footsteps behind him, making him pick up his pace. His mind was working just as fast, and suddenly none if was making sense. Lana and Cindy and Marty Beam, Lottie Cashman and the now-legally dead Jack Cashman, Patrick and his boss, Langston Livingston. There was Beverly Mills of Beverly Hills, and then there were Barney and Fred. And lest he forget, there were the two murder victims—one from seven years ago, identity unknown, buried behind a basement wall, the other a pesky reporter by the name of Carl Beaufort with a penchant for exposing big-time crooks. Somehow all of these people were connected, and what seemed to be the common denominator was a stash of money that so far showed no evidence of actually existing.

Lana caught up to him, tugging at his arm. "What is it? Was it something I said, or did you figure something out?"

"Lots of pieces, Lana, but none of them fit."

"Maybe you're looking to solve the wrong puzzle," she said.

That statement got Todd's reeling mind to suddenly stop reeling. It actually got him to focus.

"Cindy, you're brilliant."

"Excuse me?"

"Wait, what...Lana, I'm so sorry."

Todd had shared so much with Lana, made memories both in Bermuda and now in Los Angeles. Could make a person believe in destiny, those two finding each other again. The memories they had shared...including a painful one Todd would sooner forget. No chance of that happening, not now. Lana, for her part, made sure to remind Todd.

"Owww," he said.

Yup, she had slapped him again.

And this time she didn't just run out of the Buzz Factory, she ran out on him. She got in the car, locked the doors, gunned the engine, and sped off.

Todd just stood there, watching as the taillights disappeared from view.

"Sorry I had to do that, Lana."

But it was the only way he could think to get rid of her. Not that his heart wanted to, but he'd been brought to Los Angeles to help his friend and so far he didn't feel as though his mind had been completely focused on his assignment. Certainly not since Lana had re-entered the picture, distracting him from the mission at hand. She would forgive him. He knew she would. So long as he got her the answers she herself was seeking: the truth about her father.

Todd had plenty of time to figure out his next move. After all, he'd been left to his own devices in the Hollywood Hills, and there were no cabs to be hailed, no rides being offered. Just one foot in front of the other, and soon he'd be walking into town. Fortunately, he had an idea of where he was going.

Sunset Boulevard.

Because he had something important figured out and that something was the common link between past mystery and current predicament: Marty Beam and Patrick Scanlon. And that link had his offices on Sunset, in a small office tower. Todd thought it was about time for him to meet the wily Langston Livingston.

"Okay, this one's for you, Patrick," Todd said to the wind. "Wherever you are."

THE POOL held her captive. Like the black waters held certain secrets and she only had to overcome her fears and reach down and grab hold of them. In her mind, though, she saw Carl Beaufort floating to the top. Yet he remained face down until she went over and tried to assist him. Of course it was Patrick's face that revealed itself when she flipped it over.

That's why she was self-medicating with a bottle of Russian River Valley Chardonnay at her side, her glass half-empty and the bottle even emptier. Metaphor for her life? She could laugh if she wasn't so worried. But somewhere she had to find the strength to continue, to push until she had learned the truth. These setbacks were a challenge to her inner self and her belief in all she could achieve. Tomorrow, she thought to herself, tomorrow she regains control.

Patrick getting into this mess to begin with? Not the way

she would have handled it.

And Carl Beaufort taking a final swim in her pool? Again, someone else pulling the strings.

She had to hope that Patrick, impulsive fool that he was, didn't meet a similar fate as the reporter.

For that matter, Todd, too.

She hadn't heard from him all day, but had to assume he was better off than Patrick. One of them was self-sufficient, the other self-destructive, and if you had to ask which was which you just haven't been paying attention.

Cindy drained her glass, reached for the bottle, slippery from the condensation of the warm night. She poured the last remains of the wine into her glass, took a sip. Glancing at her watch, she saw that it was ten twenty-one...two. She was staring, she was lost, for the first time since Patrick had disappeared she failed to realize her next move.

That's when the phone rang, the ringing of the cell jolting Cindy from her thoughts. Without thinking, without even looking at the caller I.D., she said, with perhaps more anxiety than she intended, "Todd?"

There was silenced breathing on the other end, and then a voice said, "No, this is your husband."

"Patrick?"

"You remember my name, I see."

"Your name is Mud, capital M, if you ask me."

"Still, it's not Todd."

She ignored that one. "Patrick, where the hell are you?"

"Where do you think?"

"Don't play games with me...crap, wherever you are, at least you're safe...let me rephrase. At least you're alive."

"So glad you care."

"Of course I care, Patrick. All of this has been for you... everything I've done."

"Now that's the first thing you've said that I don't believe a word of. But we'll forget it for now, we'll talk later. Why don't you pour me a glass of that wine, because I sure could use a drink."

Cindy dropped the phone, stood from her chair, and turned around, all in a split second. What she saw, when she allowed her eyes and brain to fully process the image before her was her wayward husband, standing at the edge of the patio, his arms outstretched.

"What the hell are you doing here?" she asked.

Okay, not exactly the generous greeting one might expect but that didn't stop Patrick from embracing his wife, from kissing her neck and holding her body tight against his. She squirmed at first, and then she allowed herself to relax. Her eyes, though, were wide open and aware, searching out the space behind them.

"I'll explain everything, later," he said. "Right now, I was serious. I need some of that wine, and I need too the loving arms of my beautiful, hot, sexy wife."

"I like the sound of that—of all of that."

That's all it took for Cynthia Scanlon to realize the full power of herself once again, that control. For now, she knew it was them against everyone else, and they would prevail so long as Patrick listened to her. They would somehow pay back Langston Livingston and rid him from their lives, and she would at last put to bed the mystery of Jack Cashman.

Confidence, though, has a way of waning, far faster than it

takes a bullet to down an innocent man. As Cindy and Patrick were headed to the bedroom, fresh bottle of wine in hand, the doorbell rang. Fear found its way to Cindy's face, and she hated herself for revealing herself so…fully. Patrick, though, showed no hesitation as he simply opened the door, held out his hand, said thank you before closing the door. He returned with a small white envelope in his hand. Cindy looked down and found their names written in a beautiful script.

"What's this?"

"An invitation," Patrick said.

"You make it sound like you were expecting it."

"Oh, I was," he said, a bit too proudly. "Go ahead, open it, I think you'll like what you see. And then we need to get some sleep. Reporting time is 8:30."

Cindy read the carefully worded invitation, then looked at up her stupid, foolish, naïve lug of a husband. She knew one thing, and that was the fact that he should have stayed where he was, far away from Los Angeles. Such a stupid plan! "Pier 44 in Marina del Rey? Oh, Patrick, you can't be serious. Why not just crush all of our fingers at one time?"

Not to mention our dreams.

CHAPTER FIFTEEN

TO SAY nothing had gone as planned could easily be considered an understatement. For all concerned with the Strange Case of Jack "Fast Cash" Cashman, it was amazing to consider the man's impact on so many people, especially since there had been no word from the man for over seven years. No phone calls, no emails, no text messages, no tweets, no telegrams, postcards, or skywriting. If it was possible for a man to still be alive on this planet and to have kept such a low profile, then Fast Cash should be writing the definitive text on how to disappear. Though his promotional tour might be a bust.

As for the others—his wife, Lottie, who declared him legally dead; the reporter Carl Beaufort who had been intrigued enough by the case to lose his life; the daughter of his accomplice who was still seeking answers as to what really happened; and a host of others who thrilled at the idea of finding his lost fortune—too many questions prevailed and not enough answers surrounded them. Too many people had become caught up in a case that seemed to have been inspired by Shakespeare, and indeed, there was much ado about nothing here on this late summer's night.

Much had happened on this Monday, the day after much had happened on Sunday. Lovers and spouses were reunited, new alliances had been formed, the shadows had revealed themselves in the day's blazing sun, old crimes and fresh motives had risen to the surface. But that was nothing compared to the surprises yet to come as the sun closed up shop for the day and the moonlight illuminated the next turn of events.

"MS. MILLS, if it's okay with you, I'm going to head out for the day."

The time was ten-thirty at night, and Beverly Mills was still behind her desk, hard at work on a couple of mansions along Sunset that she hoped would soon come available. A couple of power couples were seemingly having an outage in the love department (at least with each other), and the settlement might make them both give up their dream home.

"Yes, Lana, that's fine."

"I'm not Lana—she wasn't in today, remember? I'm Vera."

Beverly looked up from her desk, pushing her glasses down to the bridge of her nose. She smiled. "Oh, yes, of course. You're the new girl. Have a lovely evening darling, see you here at nine sharp."

Beverly was a stickler for regular working hours.

In any case, Beverly decided to settle in for a late night of work. She hated going home at such an early hour; she wasn't much of a sleeper, and to spend so many hours in her spacious home all by herself just didn't hold much appeal. So, with the office to herself—so much more intimate, so comforting—she got up from her chair and made her way to her mini-bar, where she withdrew a cold bottle of a New Zealand Sauvignon Blanc. She poured herself a healthy-sized glass, then retreated back to her desk.

The chirping of her cell phone broke Beverly's concentration. The number on the caller I.D. did not look familiar, but she took it anyway. Being in real estate, you did not ignore certain things and those included late night phone calls that held the possibility of a rich-bitch having passed and a house in sudden need of a new owner.

"Hello, this is Beverly Mills of Beverly Hills."

"Ma'am, it's Vera."

"Who?"

"Your assistant."

"Oh, hello dear. Didn't you just close up shop?"

"Yes, ma'am. But as I was leaving, a limousine pulled up next to the building and a rather large gentleman handed me a most lovely looking invitation. It has your name written upon it. Shall I bring it up to you?"

"No, dear. Just read it to me."

As she listened to what Vera had to say, Beverly found herself leaning forward. Her heart was racing, as though someone had dealt her a really good hand—and the house dealer was suddenly revealing all he had. She was expected on board tomorrow morning.

"A yacht named *The Nutcracker*, how cruelly appropriate," Beverly said. "And what a fascinating invitation. I've changed my mind, please bring the envelope up to my office at once. Especially considering I need to be there at nine in the morning. Thank you, Lana."

"It's Vera," the woman on the other end said.

"Since when," Beverly Mills said to an empty line.

WHY HAD she slapped him? Why had she left him alone in the Hollywood hills, left to his own devices in a strange land? Why had she gotten so mad at him?

Easy. A woman did not like to be called by some other woman's name.

On the drive back to Glendale, Lana Davies had turned over the idea of returning for Todd dozens of times, to the point where the very notion became as twisted as the return trip along Mulholland. But she wasn't even sure where he was at this point, and the last thing she felt like doing was driving around for hours and hours looking for him. If she knew anything about Todd Gleason, he was a resourceful guy and would find his way back.

Probably find his way to that woman—Cindy. The supposed wife who wasn't his wife but still held some kind of power over him. Made him do and say things that he normally wouldn't do or say. A woman like that, even in theory, was tough to compete with. And Lana, having seen her yesterday at the Open House and briefly at her bungalow, theory had given way to reality and she liked the result even less. Even Lana could tell that Cindy Scanlon was nothing short of luscious. How to compete with that?

A half hour later, home was where she found herself, and after parking her car in her allotted slot, she started up the walkway to the apartment complex. A series of headlights caught her eyes, and she had to blink them away. She was left with spots before her eyes, making her stops in her tracks. Like the driver had done that deliberately, as though trying to get her attention.

"Ms. Lana Davies?" said a voice through an opened window.

"Yes?"

"For you."

Lana's eyes were starting to lose the blinking dots and her pupils were refocusing, and that's when she noticed the car that had blinded her was a big ol' sleek limousine, and that the driver was dressed in central-casting wardrobe.

"What is this?' she asked, taking hold of the envelope. She noticed her name had been written upon the front in beautiful, scripted lettering.

"Inside the envelope, it explains all. Have a pleasant evening, Ms. Davies."

As the limo sped off into the L.A. night, Lana found herself tearing apart the invitation. She read it once, and then she read it a second and third time. She was scheduled to report at 9:15, leaving her less than twelve hours to gather her wits and figure out just what was going on, because she didn't feel like walking into the lion's den without at least some training.

She unlocked her door, where she was immediately met by the blaring sound of the television. Applause again greeted her, and for a second she grew morose over thinking about Todd, about the morning they'd spent together that her mother had so predictably ruined. Then she heard the TV host announcing that the next celebrity couple would be dancing the tango.

"Too much reality," she said, and decided to bypass the living room. "Mother, I'm home but I'm going right to sleep.

Long day today, longer day tomorrow."

A message light on her answering machine caught her attention, and so she depressed the button and listened. What she heard would keep her from falling asleep for quite awhile. She kept hearing the words of the man on the other end.

"Your lab results are in, Ms. Davies."

A voice "hurrmumphed" behind her. Lana turned, and there was Mother Beam.

"Lana, dear, I think we need to talk."

"Mother, I'm too tired."

"Too bad. This nonsense about your father…I heard that message on the machine. Lab results? Just what have you been up to? And what does that man I caught leaping from your bedroom window have to do with all of this?"

"Tomorrow, Mother. I'll explain everything tomorrow. For now, I have to get some rest. It's a big day tomorrow."

"Hmmph," Mother Beam said. "Guess I'll go see which stars can't dance."

And with that, Lana closed her door and Mother Beam retreated back to the den.

A SCENE was unfolding at the Burbank airport at the JetBlue baggage claim, a reunion was taking place much to the shock and surprise of those assembled waiting for their loved ones. Among them was Barney, who quite frankly was getting tired of all this sunshine and all the evasive maneuvering that went along with the L.A. lifestyle. Give him the face-to-face insincerity of New York; that he could deal with. Actually, he could put up with either as long as he had his partner to share it with.

God he missed Fred.

So that's why, when it was announced the flight from JFK had landed, Barney—big hulk that he is—jumped up and down like a schoolchild, clapping his hands with glee. A woman to his left moved just a bit more to his left, and if there was a political statement in such a move Barney was too revved up to get offended. Fred's call from the plane before it had taken off had included the important info that he was "toward the front of the plane, so I should be one of the first off."

"You'd better be," Barney had said.

He'd been at Bob Hope Airport in Burbank for hours, he was that impatient to see Fred. Say what you will about their lifestyle, they were every much the couple that anyone else was, and when circumstance broke them apart, well, that was the only thing that would.

"Barney!" came a deep voice from the middle of a pack of people.

Barney knew he was there, somewhere, the way he said his name…but he couldn't see him. Fred was noticeably (or perhaps not so) short, and Barney had to search below and beneath the crowd of other folks who were filing out of the exit area to the outside baggage carousel. At last, though, there he was, and Barney went running up to his compact muscle boy and lifted him high above even himself. They embraced, they kissed, all to the astonishment of nearly everyone else.

"Really," one woman remarked, "it's not like this is LAX."

So, what's one bad apple in a crowd of fruits. That's what Barney thought as he escorted his life and business partner from the baggage area. Above them a plane took off, the sound deafening. Neither of them had said much, just hi and so glad to see you and I missed you and other sweet nothings, they were just happy to hold hands en route to the taxi stand.

They wouldn't get that far.

A limo pulled up beside them, and a darkened window whirred down to where a lone face peered back at them.

"Ride, gentlemen?"

Barney looked at Fred who looked back at Barney. Seemed too convenient, but then again everything and nothing about this case that had taken them to LaLa Land had been easy. Why should this situation be any less confounding.

"Do you know where we're going?"

"Tonight, you tell me. I'm already here, might as well give you a lift downtown since I've got to head that way anyway. Tomorrow—here, this will explain it."

And from the front passenger side of the limousine came an outstretched hand, and attached to it was an ivory-colored envelope.

FRED and BARNEY was written across the front in Cyrillic script.

"Uh, do we even know you?"

"You don't need to. Consider me the messenger. And the driver. Now get in."

Barney and Fred needed no other urging. Into the back of the limo they climbed, and as the car took off into the dark night, they settled back to see just what surprise awaited them. Ripping open the envelope, Barney extracted the parchment inside and read.

"What is it?"

"We've been invited to a party," Barney said.

"But we don't know anyone out here."

"Oh, we know more than we think we do," Barney remarked. "We know our client. So buckle your seats belts, it's going to a bumpy ride."

"Oh, Barn—I love when you quote Bette Davis," Fred said, leaning in to kiss his big lug of a boyfriend.

The partition dividing passengers and driver slid upwards. There was much catching up to do before their report time of 9:30 in the a.m.

LANGSTON LIVINGSTON had remained inside his office until past the midnight hour, waiting for the report on the developments of this latest scheme. This one he particularly liked, not only how it had been presented to him from that scoundrel Patrick Scanlon, but what possibilities it held when played out. A yacht full of unusual suspects, all of them with different knowledge about the same case, and perhaps when all their motives were revealed—at force, if necessary—a brighter picture of just what was going on would present itself to him.

But with such an early morning planned, he realized it might be wise to go home for a few hours of rest. So he called to Garth, who stated he was just two blocks from the office.

Langston took his private elevator down to the main lobby, and after bypassing the night security guard, he stepped out into a warm breezy Los Angeles night. He could almost smell the desires percolating around the city, could almost feel the pull of money and all it meant in this town. Speaking of which, Langston's limo appeared as if out of nowhere, pulling up curbside. The large chauffeur unfolded himself from the driver's seat, and then opened the passenger door for his employer.

"Garth, I assume all the invitations have been handed out?"

The behemoth nodded. "Invitations have been delivered in hand to the following: both of the Scanlons, those two curiously dressed and rather conspicuous private detectives, Ms. Mills of Beverly Hills, and to the beautiful Lana Davies as well. Two invitations remain in my possession and, as of yet, have gone undelivered."

"Mrs. Cashman?"

"Nowhere to be found," he said, nodding. "I tried both the Cashman estate, as well as the new apartment she recently moved to. Both of them—darkened."

"And the other?"

"As expected, the Gleason fellow, as you call him. He's not staying with the Scanlons and I don't have any other idea of where he might be."

Langston nodded. "Without the widow Cashman, the entire plan may just be a bust."

"I'll do my best, sir."

"Lottie Cashman is the key to everything. Do better than your best, and if you need to grease some palms to find out info, do so," Langston said. And with that, Langston Livingston withdrew a packet of cash from his pocket and tossed it to his hired hand. Garth quickly deposited the money into his pocket.

"Now drop me at the pier, I'll stay overnight on *The Nutcracker*, enabling you to continue to search for Lottie," Langston said. "Oh, keep up your search for that Gleason fellow, all night if you have to. He's the wild card in this whole caper, he's unpredictable. We must keep our wits about us, Garth."

"Indeed, sir. Next stop, Pier 44."

THERE WAS an art to running a successful con. Have a plan, stick to it, execute. It was really that simple, if you thought about it. One of the ways to achieve success was to always stay one step ahead of your competition, your enemy, your opponent. The problem with this California scheme was that it hadn't been Todd's from the start, so he had hardly felt in control at any time. Patrick had devised the plan, Cindy had altered it, and neither had executed it well at all. If this was death row, the execution would have been called "botched." So, that's why, starting this very moment, Todd Gleason, sneaky opportunist, was taking control.

From the corner of Sunset and La Cienga, the limo carrying Langston Livingston pulled away, leaving behind a mostly empty street. Todd's feet hurt from the too long walk from Griffith Park, and he was also hungry after waiting outside the building for so long.

But all had been worth it.

Pier 44, tomorrow morning. *The Nutcracker*. Something was going down.

Todd would be there, too.

"Even if I haven't formally received my invitation," he said to the waning night.

Morning was coming, and the game was afoot. The con was on, and the con was all his.

Yet, little did he know, one more piece of business was still to happen on this busy night, one that been set in motion for quite awhile, and it was a very nasty bit of business that nobody saw coming. There was nothing Todd Gleason could do to stop it.

There was nothing anyone could do.

Sometimes destiny wears a face of evil.

THE CASHMAN Estate was black against a black canvas, nearly lost in the night. Faint moonlight kept it from being completely swallowed into anonymity, as though it didn't really exist to begin with, only in the minds of those who sought out its secrets and those who visited its hidden rooms. A car sat parked halfway down the street, adjacent to the bluff that led directly down to the pounding Pacific surf. On this quiet street, and on this quiet night, about the only audible sound came from the waves crashing against the shore.

She made her way into the house through the back door, dropping the key back into her coat pocket. Gloves covered her hands; she would hate to leave fingerprints behind.

The basement door was to her left, just past the kitchen. Easing it open, it squeaked just once from years of neglect, not unlike those old bones of hers. She made her way down the open, wooden steps, carefully holding onto the rickety handrail nailed precariously to the wall. At last she was free of those stairs, and her feet touched down upon a dirt floor. By now her eyes had adjusted to the darkness, and it was as though she were a cat able to see in the blackness before her. Trouble was, she wasn't a cat and she didn't have nine lives.

"Hello, dear," a voice said, cutting its way through the dark.

"Who is that?"

"It's Jack."

"Jack…why don't be ridiculous…" she said. She took a step forward to get a better look at who had decided to join her in the basement of the old house. Really, this wasn't in their script, this was pure improv with a noticeably dangerous edge. Talk about walking on a high wire. "Who are you? Let me see you," the woman said.

Just then a flashlight was switched on, but its powerful beam failed to illuminate her path. Rather it fell on a crumbled wall and on a particular sight that lay just before the collection of dust, rock, and cement, revealing a collection of bones that when put together equaled that of a man, one long deceased. And that's just when her eyes went wide.

"Aaaaaaaah," she screamed.

It was the last sound she would make.

The gunshot blast was deafening in such a confined space, and it shook the walls of the basement. Combined, scream and shot were almost loud enough to wake the dead.

PART THREE
MAMAS AND PAPAS

CHAPTER SIXTEEN

DETECTIVE EARNEST Dalrymple hated early morning calls even more than he hated an unsolved murder or a partner who stole his French fries, and oftentimes the three went hand in hand in, er…hand. Take for example Tuesday morning, not even twenty-four hours had passed since he and his partner Sandy Benes had come to the unlikely aid of the stair-challenged Lottie Cashman and then afterwards satiated their hunger for burgers and fries. Enjoy the greasy goods, because guess when your number is up fate finds a way to clog your arteries some other way. Whether through accidentally falling down the stairs or, as was the current case, by gunshot.

"Oh, shit, really? Are we certain?"

Dalrymple listened to what the caller on the other end had to say.

"Oh shit," he said again.

The dispatcher informed him of the details of the anonymous tip which had come to them at just after three in the morning. Nope, didn't leave a name, couldn't even tell if it was male or female, the person had disguised their voice. Person, meaning the killer.

"Yeah, that was my thought, who else would know but the killer," said the dispatcher.

"You got a trace going out on the call?"

"Of course. Trouble is…"

"Yeah, I know. Wasn't on the line long enough. Shit."

Dalrymple then called Benes and together they made their way through the light traffic of an unsung morning in Los Angeles, en route to a murder scene that was unfortunately not their first of this case but hopefully their last. Still, this one hit hard. This one felt almost…

"Personal?" Benes asked while they drove toward Palos Verdes on a freeway devoid of Angelinos. As though the folks of Los Angeles knew that only bad things happened in the wee hours of the day and they were smart enough to stay secured in their home and leave the deadly roads to the police. Sure, when the body was already cold, that's when traffic was nil.

"We talked to her just yesterday. And now we're en route to deal with her body."

Benes checked his watch. "Mere hours that separate life from death."

Dalrymple acknowledged the profundity of such a statement with studied silence. In his mind, he hoped that the scene they came upon was something less than the carnival atmosphere that pervaded Sunday's Open House. Trying to keep an early morning murder quiet was like asking a Hollywood Madam to keep her clients secret—the truth would win out sooner rather than later.

Thankfully, Dalrymple noted, time was still on the side of the law.

All was quiet outside the Cashman house in Palos Verdes Estates, and even more so at the neighboring homes, where it appeared the neighbors were not yet wise to the violent event which had transpired inside the empty house. A lone police cruiser waited in the Cashman driveway, and its presence could be interpreted as cautionary at best, the officer leaning against the trunk with his arms crossed, waiting for someone else to take charge

"Morning, detectives," the officer said as both Dalrymple and Benes approached.

"Officer Meehan, you discovered the body?"

"Me and my partner—Vazquez. He's in the front seat, still a bit green."

Dalrymple nodded. He needed no more info.

"Rookie, eh?" Benes said, a slight grin elevating his cheeks.

"Sandy—we were all rookies once."

"Right, Ernie, sorry," Benes said, his comment directed more at Meehan than at his partner. Part of living by the code was having respect for all—rookies, veterans, the retired ones who had taken studio security jobs. They all earned the shield the same way, and if they were lucky they went out with dignity, their pension, and their lives.

"Take us inside," Dalrymple said, "and fill us in as you do so. Start before the beginning. The coffee was hot..."

"And the doughnuts were fresh. Yeah, typical morning, cruising the burbs. Pretty quiet, but then again it's early in the week. Weekends, Vazquez and I would have busted any number of DUIs by now and been consumed with some case or another, domestic disturbance, burglary. Just luck of the draw we caught this one; dispatch called and said for us to check out a possible 10-80 over in the Estates. Way we heard it, an anonymous tip came in—probably the killer toying with us, not wanting too much time to pass before his trophy was found. Even so, voice was disguised, used a pay phone. You believe that—people still use pay phones? Me, can never find one that works. Killers though, guess they're kind of determined, perhaps they MapQuest them before they do the deed. Anyway, dispatch asks us if we need back-up, we say not yet, let's get the lay of the land. And we did."

"Scene like this?"

"Quieter still, darker. No sun breaking over the horizon yet, not like now. Death just moved in, you know, while a bunch of people nearby slept through the night. Neighborhood like this one, nice and all, you kind of hope the whole thing's a hoax. Whole lot easier grabbing a prankster than a murderer."

Dalrymple liked this guy. He was good with the details and colorful with the commentary; showed he still had a case of optimism in a job known for stealing it quicker than the academy passed you.

"How long you on the job?"

"Six years," Meehan said.

Dalrymple nodded his approval.

All the while they talked, Meehan was leading the two detectives inside the home and back through to the kitchen. They stopped at the basement door, where Dalrymple instructed the officer to remain upstairs.

"From here I like to take a fresh approach, let my eyes see

what they want to see." He paused. "CSU been called yet? Medical Examiner?"

"No, sir. Waiting on your lead. Dispatch, when they were told of the identity of the vic, they ran a cursory check of the system and said it might be related to an active case you've been working. So I did as told, kept the scene fresh until you arrived."

"Good job. You ask me, all those tech folks are just plain pains in the ass. Too much science, not enough…you know."

Dalrymple tapped his temple

"Thinking," Benes added.

Meehan and Dalrymple just gave him a look.

With that, Dalrymple started down the stairs, Benes close behind. Weapons were drawn, just in case. It wasn't death they feared, but the living. It was always the living one who seemed to have no respect for the living, the dead knew the meaning of quiet. They also kept off the lights, opting instead for the beams of their flashlights. That is until they could survey the immediate situation before them. There was something about coming upon a body that required the stealth approach afforded by the dark.

"Wish you were somewhere else?" Benes suddenly asked.

"Sandy, when it comes to murder, there are always better places to be. Especially for the vic."

Enough chatter, a crime scene awaited them. With their high beams guiding them, they stepped off the stairs, including a creaky one about a third of the way down, and onto the hardened dirt floor. They followed the glow as it scoped out the enclosed space. There was something decidedly unfinished about this place. The hairs on the back on his neck stuck up as though struck by electricity—or by something more powerful.

Inherent, pervasive fear. To think, just the other day this house was over-crowded with potential buyers and media whores, and now what locked up the lease was death. It would soon become part of Hollywood lore; a lurid place for the curious.

At last the flashlight beam found its intended mark, and when Dalrymple saw what he saw he froze in his spot. Benes did the same, light finding the exact same thing.

"Hey, boss, that ain't the widow Cashman."

"You got that right, Sandy. Because that's a skeleton, and it's been dead for way longer than a few hours. You wanna go upstairs and flick on the lights, and also ask Meehan what the hell he was thinking? How did he think this could possibly be Lottie Cashman…unless, oh crap."

"Yeah, crap kind of applies. Guess you're thinking the same thing I am."

"Meehan didn't exactly scope out the entire area, did he?"

"I think he found what he found, and we found what we found."

"Right. Lights on, so we can all see everything—and everyone—there is to see."

Benes did as instructed, dashing back up the stairs, where he found the light switch. In seconds the entire basement was flooded with flickering florescent lighting, and though it wasn't the best in terms of revealing deep truths, it was good enough to reveal what lay on the surface of their discovery.

New light had been shed upon the ever-confounding case of Fast Cash. A gruesome scene greeted them, one that not even Freddy would imagine in his worst nightmare no matter how many sequels hit Elm Street. The woman's body lay face up, her face frozen with surprise, all the while a bullet wound to the chest held that expression for all eternity. Blood stained her canary yellow outfit. Her left arm was outstretched, and when you followed its snaking loop you saw that it connected with the fingertips of another body. No easy I.D. with that one. Not with no clothes, no flesh even, just dusty old bones. The scenario appeared almost staged, with the woman reaching out to the skeletal fingertips, which seemed equally eager to take hold of her cold hand. And, oddly, surrounding both bodies were dozens of bills, cold hard cash. Twenties, fifties, hundreds.

Benes bent down, examined the spot where finger met finger. On close inspection, he discovered an interesting development. He'd been pre-med one day and so knew a thing or two about anatomy and from what he could see, this skeleton was missing a bone on his middle finger.

"Almost like it had been cut off," he said.

"Is that supposed to mean something?" Dalrymple asked.

"Just something I remember from the old case files. Fast Cash's accomplice, that guy Beam, he was missing the tip of his middle finger. Jeez, Ernie, you think the Fast Cash case is moving from cold to hot?"

"It's certainly getting warmer. Good job, Sandy. Good memory. We have what the press might call a lead."

"Imagine losing a fingertip? Jesus," Benes said.

"Or your life."

"Still, had to have hurt."

Dalrymple reminded himself to teach his partner the meaning of "rhetorical." For now, though, he wiped a brow that had suddenly become drenched from sweat. "You want to know something, Benes?"

"What's that?"

"This case grew cold over seven years ago, but you're right, someone's turned up the heat and its threatening to boil over. A small-time thief hits a slew of banks, makes off with a pretty decent fortune. And all during his reign not one person was hurt, not wounded or shot or killed or nothing—well, not until that final robbery. Now years later the courts have determined this so-called Fast Cash is dead, at least from a legal standpoint. And what starts to happen almost immediately? The bodies start piling up. First Beaufort. Now her. Not to mention this bony fellow, buried behind a wall for who knows how long. This case, I don't like it one bit."

Benes stared down at the bodies. "So what next?"

Dalrymple frowned, obvious frustration on his face. "What comes next is we smoke out a killer." Then he looked around the basement and said, "Hate to be the person moving into this house, wasn't exactly a lucky place for the Cashmans."

As he said that last statement, he stared down at both bodies.

CONSIDERING THIS wasn't a true social occasion and none of these folks would normally be caught dead together at a dinner party, cocktail gathering, or funeral, their common enemy sure knew how to put out a nice spread. Imported cheeses, exotic and tropical fruits, croissants, scones, and other pastries, bloody Mary's and Mimosas, coffee and tea, all of it was beautifully assembled on tables inside the boat's main cabin, ready for the picking.

Of course, nerves taking the place of appetites, no one had dared touch the buffet yet.

Scene: *The Nutcracker* yacht, owned by Livingston Enterprises, captained by none other than the entrepreneurial Langston Livingston himself. Oh, that didn't mean he did the driving, that was still left in Garth's capably large mitts. He would steer them from the dock and out into the bay for a cruise that hopefully held better promise than the one Gilligan and the Skipper chartered. From Pier 44 in Marina del Rey, the boat would make it's way toward Catalina Island, but as their able host had announced to them as they had shoved off, "We won't be stopping at any ports of call. This is strictly an on board experience." Then he grinned. "We wouldn't want anyone getting left behind would we?"

None of the guests responded.

"You all act like this morning cruise was forced upon you, like you had no choice."

Langston Livingston found himself staring at the motley crew...crue. Patrick and Cindy Scanlon, looking surprisingly cozy together; he surmised neither knew the truth about the other's involvement in this case. Then there was Beverly Mills of Beverly Hills, who only had such a lofty address thanks to yours truly. A woman with such ambitions and appetites was so easily controlled and manipulated, especially when they were as hungry for acceptance as the formerly named Esther Grajkowski. Then there was this rather charming newcomer, Lana Davies, who he wished to get to know much, much more. Of course this troupe wasn't complete without the misfit couple of private detectives from New York, Fred and Barney, whose last names escaped him at the moment. They looked completely baffled as to what was going on.

"This silence, surely it cannot persist for the duration of the trip. We have way too much to accomplish, to discuss. So, let's say we just get the party started. Beverly, I know you'll join me in a glass of champers, you've never resisted my requests before, have you?"

"Fine, I'll have an L.A. Mimosa."

"What's that?" asked Barney.

"No O.J."

Langston laughed, his big belly roiling with amusement. "That's the spirit. Let's go everyone, let's get ourselves a juicy cocktail before we get down to business. If you can't enjoy the company, at least enjoy the spread and the weather and the gentle breeze that comes off the ocean. We couldn't have asked for a more pleasing day or backdrop to complete our mission."

With little choice but to partake, the assembled guests started to get up from their seats, but held their place when Langston stated he had one more announcement.

"Oh, a reminder: if any of you are thinking about pulling some funny stuff and think I'm not being guarded, you have another thing coming," he said.

"Think," Cindy said.

"Excuse me?"

"It's think. You have another think coming."

Langston's florid face scrunched up with confusion. But when he thought about it, he supposed she had a point; funny, did everyone misuse that common phrase? Anyway…

Resigned to their fate, the corks popped, the fizzy sounds of bubbly being poured started to fill the room, and it was almost as though with the release of pressure from the bottle the entire group suddenly relaxed and became quickly animated.

Beverly greeted Cindy. "Nice to see you again, dear. The house, I assume you have interest in it other than moving in?"

"Time will tell, " Cindy said.

Fred reconnected with his old friend Patrick. "That sedative that wily bartender gave me left me with a nasty headache."

"I have a backache from your lousy office sofa."

Langston greeted Lana. "I don't believe we've had the pleasure."

"If pleasure is the right word."

Small talk dispensed with, the small crowd resumed their seats on the various cushions and chairs, and waited for Act II.

"LET'S TALK about something called motive," Langston began.

Patrick looked first at his host, then at his wife. Had her gaze come from the sun, he'd have a considerable burn going at the moment. With his own eyes, he urged her to give this scheme he'd masterminded a chance, as though his brown eyes were promising that he had everything under control. As he'd explained the night before, this entire cruise had been his idea, a way to get everyone involved in one place. Of course the one person he needed the most was nowhere to be seen. Damn that Todd. Where are you?

"It's a selfish emotion, this thing we call motive. Derived from the word motivation, if I'm not mistaken. Meaning: the reason we do something. Motivation, though, has a positive spin to it, it's what gives us all the drive to accomplish something. Like my motivation for this little meeting—too many people have been running around trying to control the show and no one seems fully to have a grasp on the action. So I decided we needed to all sit down and talk—that's my motivation."

Langston paused to ensure his guests were with him.

Six pairs of eyes stared back at him waiting for more.

"Ah, but motive, that's a different situation altogether. There's a negative connotation to the word, isn't there? Police use it all the time when trying to prove why a certain person performed a criminal act. The courts love when they have motive, brings them that much closer to a conviction when they know the reason behind the crime. And that's what we're here to talk about today—crimes, motives, opportunity, culpability. You see, there's a murderer amongst us, and as much as many of you would like it to be me, the big, mean, greedy businessman, I hate to burst your bubble. I am no more a killer than I am thin."

With that, Langston Livingston took a deep breath, filling his considerable lungs with a refresher course of oxygen. He was usually not a man of so many words, preferring one-word responses better. Like yes, and no. Actually, just no. It was so much more effective, and offered up little chance of a comeback. In his world, no meant shut up and just do what I said.

"Exactly what crime are you referring to, Langston? Embezzling money, loan sharking, money laundering?" Cindy said, the juice-free mimosa fueling her tongue.

"How crude, Cynthia, to point fingers like that," he said. "And no, as charming as you attempt to be, I believe I mentioned murder."

"Carl Beaufort," said Beverly.

"We know who killed him," Lana suddenly said.

"Oh, and who might his killer be?"

Lana looked at the guests, then pointed. "The police are looking for a man named Patrick Scanlon."

"Excuse me? Why would they think it's me?" Patrick said, standing up to defend himself to Lana, to Langston, to Cindy and to everyone else who looked at him. This was ridiculous, he plans this party and he's the one who gets slapped with an accusation of murder? "I was out of town when it happened, and I can prove it. Besides, where would you get a stupid idea like that? Who are you, anyway?"

It was Beverly's turn to add to the story. "Seems when Carl's body was found alongside the freeway, the medical examiner found a piece of paper stuffed down his throat. That's what I read. The name Patrick Scanlon was written upon it. So, naturally, the police want to talk to this guy—and they thought they had him. Except he slipped through their fingers."

"I've never spoken to the police, not about Carl Beaufort or anyone else, and I've certainly never tried to evade them," Patrick said, confusion written across his face. He looked down at Cindy, looking for any kind of support—or explanation. "Wanna back me up on this one, sweetie?"

Cindy fessed up a bit. "That was Todd who gave them the slip. But they came back for him again, found him at our bungalow Sunday night. They had the mistaken impression he was you. And though I know he's been released from their custody, Todd hasn't been seen or heard from since."

"Actually, that's not true," Lana interjected.

"Oh?" was the reply from at least three people.

"I picked him up at the PAB Monday morning."

"And just how is it you know Todd? Who are you again?" Cindy asked. Patrick detected a slight sneer at the woman who was obviously giving his wife a run for the money in the looks department today. True, their hair color was similar, and there was a slight similarity in their high cheekbones, but Lana's glow was more innocent than that of his wife's.

"I met Todd recently," she said. "Let's just leave it at that."

"Wait a minute," Cindy said. "You're *that* Lana? The woman from Bermuda."

"Yes. Which would make you the wife."

Patrick's eyes opened wide on that one. "Uh, wife? My wife, not Todd's."

"Settle down, Patrick, it was a necessary ruse," she said, tapping her true husband's hand in support. "At least I didn't slap Todd upside the head. And I find it doubly curious that you failed to mention any of this when we crossed paths Sunday night."

"Ladies, ladies, can we get back to the matter at hand? I believe we've gotten off topic with this discussion about the elusive Mr. Gleason," Langston said. "I believe Ms. Davies had the floor, and was accusing Patrick of the reporter's murder."

"Which I've denied, and which I can prove. Besides, as Langston himself has said, it's all about motive and I couldn't possibly have one. I didn't know the columnist, and I certainly didn't have any problems with anything he ever wrote."

Beverly said, "Then why was his body found floating in your pool the other night?"

"Excuse me? You said he was found by the side of the road…" Patrick stated, his voice falling off.

Cindy grabbed at Patrick's arm, urging him to sit down. He wiggled away from her grasp and stepped away. "Is there something else you've forgotten to tell me?"

Langston stepped forward. "In the interest of time, let's move forward. Carl Beaufort, intrepid columnist for the Los

Angeles Daily News, was found shot to death and floating face down in the Scanlon's pool, that much is unfortunately true. Cynthia here didn't know what to do, and so rather than do something sensible like phone 911 she instead called me because Langston Livingston knows how to clean up messes. Anyway, Garth removed the body from the pool, seemingly taking away any responsibility from the Scanlons. But yet I didn't think that was entirely fair, since the Scanlons had already proved to be less than reliable when it came to returning my favors. Her husband skipped out on a major debt, and Cynthia, well, she just never seemed grateful for the favors I afforded her. So I made up an insurance policy."

"You slipped the piece of paper down Carl's throat?" Cindy asked.

"Desperate situations call for desperate measures. So yes, I instructed Garth to write Patrick's name on a slip of paper and to place it in the victim's throat. I was simply trying to cause some trouble, to force a situation. Perhaps smoke out Mr. Scanlon."

"So all this proves is that I'm not a killer," Patrick said.

"Neither am I, I found the body," said Cindy.

"Which begs the question," Langston said. "Who did know the reporter? Ms. Davies? Ms. Mills? The two of you work together, perhaps you had uncovered some real estate scheme which required the services of an investigative journalist?"

Beverly stared at Langston when she stated, "I'd nothing to with the man."

That's when Lana spoke up, and darn if she didn't just tip her hat a bit. "I objected to his obsession with the Fast Cash case—why he couldn't leave it alone I'll never know."

All heads, eyes, ears, whatever, were focused directly on her.

"Well, ladies and gentleman," Langston said, "I believe the first motive has revealed itself to us."

"No, no, that's not what I meant, it's hardly cause for... murder," Lana said, "I didn't know him, I didn't care. It's just... he upset so many people by constantly wondering about what happened to Fast Cash. I'm no killer..."

Patrick watched as Langston surveyed his room of suspects. He was trying to figure out the next step, what could possibly happen next. This was his show, his orchestra, wasn't he the conductor? Why did Langston seem to possess the baton?

"Wait a minute, wait a minute," Patrick said. "We've heard from everyone is this room except for these two goons who kidnapped me and held me against my will. Fred, Barney, you want to chime in here? Just what are you two doing here? What's your involvement in all this?"

Fred stood up, though that didn't make much of a difference to this height-challenged detective. "We're just hired guns, private detectives. We solve crimes, we don't perform them. When necessary, yes, we do bodyguard work, too."

"And we certainly don't go around murdering people," Barney added. "Before this week, we'd never before been to LA—unless you count a quick weekend during Gay Pride. Man, the parades, the costumes, gave New York pride a real run for its money."

"Charming," Langston said, bringing a close to the subject.

Patrick, though, wasn't done. "Hired guns. So, just who hired you?"

"We don't divulge our clients' names," they stated together, simultaneously.

A silence hung over the room, because until now each time a question had come up an answer had been forthcoming, no matter how much the person didn't like fessing up, no matter how much their disclosure cost them. This time, though, this particular question of who had hired these two men just seemed to hang in the air.

"Anyone?" Patrick asked.

Just then a suddenly timid voice spoke up, one lacking any strength. As though with such a revelation, she had lost any of her hard-won confidence, the bravado with which she carried herself. "I'm sorry, Patrick," said his wife. "I paid Fred and Barney to well…to kidnap you—but not to harm you. Just to keep you out of the picture until I could find us a way out of this mess. You see, that's why I hired an agency with two detectives. Their ad even said it, 'Two Dicks.' It was perfect, one could keep an eye on you while the other tracked down…"

Patrick, disgusted, cut her off. "Todd."

No one said a word. No one wanted to intervene during this moment of marital betrayal, one that on the surface seemed far worse than cheating, than lying. This was an unmistakable case of a lack of faith. Of trust.

"I'm sorry," Cindy said. "I thought it was for our own good."

Patrick said nothing, he just stormed toward the exit door, only to be stopped in his tracks by Garth, who suddenly appeared inside the stateroom. Langston's hired goon just shook his head, as though saying, "Don't even try it." As Patrick resumed his place, the remaining guests gazed at each other, all of them with the same blank expression on their faces. What next, they all seemed to be asking.

Langston urged Patrick back to his seat. He was once again

taking command of the situation. "Now, this is the part that intrigues me the most. This character I keep hearing about, this Todd Gleason. I've yet to meet him, and I seem to be at a loss as to why everyone thinks he can act as their savior. So, I suggest we just ask him ourselves." And then, dramatic pause in place, camera zeroed directly on Langston's puffy, florid face, he said with absolute glee, "Garth, would you do the honors?"

Garth stepped forward, made his way to a closet at the edge of the stateroom. He opened the door with a flourish, and there, behind door number one stood none other than Todd Gleason. His clothes hadn't completely dried from his earlier swim.

"I just love surveillance video," Langston said. "Now, Mr. Todd Gleason, join us. I trust you're up to speed, it's not like those closets are sound proofed."

CHAPTER SEVENTEEN

HE WASN'T Hercule Poirot and he certainly looked nothing like Jessica Fletcher and it's not like he had any pronouncements to make, but still, as Todd Gleason stepped out from his discovered hiding spot he gazed out at the entire crowd of suspects and said, "And the killer is…"

No one laughed.

Okay, Patrick smirked, but otherwise the gang was back to playing the silent game.

Langston, able host that he was, extended a pudgy hand and said, "Mr. Gleason, I trust. I've heard so much about you but was beginning to think you were pure fabrication, a myth. But yet, here you are in the living—and wet—flesh. We've never had the pleasure to be officially introduced. Langston Livingston."

Todd took the proffered hand and they shook. "So I presumed."

Langston frowned. "Why people think that's funny is beyond me. The explorer's name was Livingstone," he said. "Anyway, let's move on. There really was no need for you to board *The Nutcracker* under such surreptitious circumstances, swimming out to meet us as you did. We had an invitation all prepared for you. Just couldn't find you to give it to you. No matter, you found out about our little cruise somehow—quite resourceful of you, I might add. I trust you know everyone here?"

Not sure whether he'd been tossed a rhetorical question or not, Todd took a moment to survey the crowd and decided to answer regardless. "Well, let's see, Barney and Fred are old friends from New York, I'd recognize them anywhere—who else wears black leather in the L.A. sunshine; and certainly Patrick and Cindy, we go back even further. Beverly Mills of Beverly Hills, who I'm afraid mistook me for Patrick at one point—ma'am, my apologies for the duplicity; not exactly my choice."

"So Cindy has explained."

"As for this lovely creature, I'm not sure about…there's something familiar about her," Todd said, of course staring directly at Lana.

"Do I know you?" Lana asked, sarcasm laced with bitterness.

"I'm Luke Skywalker, I've come to rescue you," Todd said.

Langston emitted a short laugh. "Oh my boy, I do admire your fortitude—and your knowledge of film, you'd do well in this town. You've got what some might call balls. Certainly you're foolish, too, in case you were thinking of something heroic. No, not today, I'm afraid. No one is going anywhere until we figure out who our killer is, and when I'm going to get all the money due me."

"With all due respect, Mr. Livingston—our killer is obviously not here among us. Remember, I heard nearly every word inside your little closet. So why don't you just send your boat back to the dock and let us all off and we'll go about our business and you can go about yours. Seems fair, right?" Todd paused. "As for your money, your little boat may have many amenities but an ATM doesn't seem to be among them."

"Has anyone informed you that you are not funny?"

Luckily that question went unanswered.

A sharp, insistent ringing interrupted the growing standoff. Langston, keeping a watchful eye on Todd, went to the side panel and picked up the wall phone on the third ring. "My office, excuse me…Yes? I see, that's an interesting—and unfortunate development."

Todd watched the corpulent crook's face as hung up the receiver, and he didn't like what he saw. Confidence had given way to concern, worry gone to dread. Something had happened, and that something was very bad. News about someone who was supposed to be here but wasn't, and there was probably a life and death reason why they couldn't be here. More death than life.

"Well, it looks as though we may all be innocent after all," Langston said, once again addressing the entire group.

"You want to explain that one?" Cindy stated.

"I'd prefer to let the television do the talking," he said, and then he grabbed hold of a remote control within easy grasp, which both opened a black wood cabinet and turned on the large flat screen television revealed behind it. He opted for KABC, where Logan and Logan were at it again, their plastic faces gazing out at their camera and into living rooms all across L.A.

"When we come back, an update on our top story," Logan said.

The other Logan remarked, "It's a shame, really."

And then the show broke for commercial.

"Not like what happens when people on a television show turn on the TV and they just happen to hear the exact event they tuned in to hear," Beverly said. "Real life, you can't avoid the commercials."

Two minutes later, Metamucil was sold, hair color and deodorant shilled, and *Logan & Logan* returned to the airwaves with the "a breaking, developing story." Which was it? Their hair looked as perfect as ever, as though it had been freshly coiffed only seconds ago, and the hair and make-up people had just managed to escape the camera's stare.

"It was a gruesome scene inside the old Cashman estate in Palos Verdes Estates. Just one day after Lottie Cashman hosted an open house in hopes of selling the place and building a new life for herself, her body has been found in the basement. Shot to death."

"And that's not all, Logan," said her counterpart. "According to LAPD spokespeople, Mrs. Cashman's was not the only body discovered on the scene. A long forgotten body, now reduced to just bones, was found lying beside Mrs. Cashman's body, and police suspect it has been hidden away in the basement all these years. It's alleged that the skeleton may be that of her husband, Jack Cashman, who everyone knows was the notorious bank robber Fast Cash, who disappeared seven years ago, and just last week was declared legally dead by the courts."

Other Logan said, "A strange case, ladies and gentlemen, and a tragic one. We will keep you posted on further developments as they happen. Now, it's time for our first guest of the day, from the show *Campfire Meals*, celebrity chef and hunting enthusiast...."

Langston turned off the television, and then he stared back at the rest of the group.

"I'll leave you all for a moment to digest this latest piece of news," Langston said. "Garth, please keep an eye on them, though they are of course free to roam around the boat. It's not like they can go anywhere but overboard. And in these choppy waters that's not something I would recommend. Oh, but Mr. Gleason, I would suggest you accompany me."

Todd's eyebrows shot up. "And why is that?"

"Simple really. As much as people consider me a ruthless businessman—and don't get them wrong, I am, quite—what I don't condone is the selfish act of murder. What good is intimidation when someone isn't around to be afraid of it? These bodies turning up willy-nilly, I think it's time for all of this inhuman nature to stop."

"Murder, Mr. Livingston, is very much human nature."

"A shame, really," he said, and with not even a trace of irony said to his hostages, "Can't we all just manage to get along?"

"**YOU'RE A** curious fellow, Mr. Gleason."

"Is that supposed to be a compliment?"

"Merely an observation."

"Now I feel insulted."

"Come now, Mr. Gleason, you don't strike me as someone who takes offense easily," he said. "From what I've been able to surmise, you're far too clever for that."

Todd wasn't having any of this soft sell. "So, exactly what is you want from me?"

"So, that's the way it's going to be, all business?"

Gazing up at the sun, Todd felt the day getting away from them. "Time's a wasting."

"Indeed, you are correct, Mr. Gleason."

"Please, you can at least call me Todd."

"Yes, you youthful folk and your casualness. I suppose your smart-ass remark would be akin to saying 'Mr. Gleason is my father.'"

Todd's voice deepened as he said, "Hardly."

"My apologies if I touched a chord."

"I believe we had settled on you calling me Todd. Shall we just move on?"

"Indeed. Look at that, we're making progress already. Perhaps a friendship is not out of the realm of possibility."

What they were also making was waves. From their position up on the main deck, Todd could see vast stretches of ocean, the safety and security of land far, far away. He was vulnerable here to the whims of the sea, of nature, and Todd supposed to the whims of a businessman who liked to threaten, intimidate, and on occasion snip off the tips of his victim's fingers. Todd wondered which tactic was being used on him, and for the moment decided to keep his hands in his pockets.

"As I said, you're a very interesting fellow in that you go back a long way with Patrick and Cindy—all the way to college if I'm not mistaken. Me, I never went to college, never was afforded the possibility. I had to earn my keep on the streets and make my fortune with my wits and my smarts. And I've succeeded even beyond my wildest imaginations."

"The criminal life will sometimes do that for one."

"Oh, Todd, it's never good to minimize someone's accomplishments. You, for example, you should be quite proud."

"Of what?"

"Keeping your nose clean," Langston said. "You see, once I learned that Cynthia went to you for help I had no choice but to research your background. I like to size up those I might be pitted against, and I was correct in looking into your past. Because you want to know what I discovered? Not much. A clean record, for one."

"That's funny, the police said the same thing."

"I find that suspicious, not even a speeding ticket."

"Do you know Detective Dalrymple, you and he go to the same interrogation class?"

"Fine, Todd. We'll skip the niceties. Let's just say that I know you're not the innocent bystander your non-record claims you to be. Cynthia came to you for a reason. You're an operator, a crook."

"I really hate that word."

"Fine. Con man, you like that?"

"Sounds better, doesn't it? Your friendly neighborhood con man."

"Semantics. But if you insist, confidence man it is. The point is this: someone who is able to live the life you do with so little money in the bank—and yes, I have the capability to uncover such information—must have an ace or two up his sleeve. He's got to be clever, resourceful, and able to improvise when the moment requires."

"Am I to assume said moment has arrived?"

Just then Langston covered his eyes, the sun's glare having

shifted with the passage of time. He invited Todd to join him, and together the two men wound their way around the deck and found themselves settling inside a private stateroom, one that was not unlike Langston's own office on Sunset. Complete with desk, lamp, Scotch, and a bowl of nuts. Oh, and a nutcracker with which to open them. He offered his guest a seat and told him to relax.

"Let's cut to the heart of the matter. Patrick Scanlon owes me a fair amount of money, totaling nearly one million dollars given my current interest rates and mood. Oh, and the fact that he skipped out on me does not instill within me any confidence that I'll be seeing my money anytime soon. So that's where you come in."

"I don't have a million dollars," Todd said.

Langston waved off such a foolish notion. "I hardly expected you to pull out your checkbook, boy. No, it's really very simple. Bring me Fast Cash's missing millions and I'll consider Patrick's debts fully cleared—he and I will part ways, never to be heard from again. A fair bargain, I say."

"You sound like the Wizard asking me to bring back the witch's broom," Todd said. "And your request has perhaps as much fantasy to it. Because the fact of the matter is, even if Fast Cash's money still exists, that gives you a bonus double the amount of the original debt."

"What did you think, I would allow you to keep the other two million?"

"Finders fee?'

Langston grinned, and not in a nice way. "I don't think so," Langston said. "I'm out of pocket a fair amount of cash, and not just from Patrick. Other debts still need to be cleared off the books. That is, if I kept any."

Todd considered his options. Find the money, hand it over, end this saga. Or, find the money, keep the money, figure out how to sick detectives Dalrymple and Benes on the portly Langston. Another unfavorable scenario had him looking for the money, not finding the money, and being stuck with the status quo. Or, he surmised, the outcome could be a combination of all three. When had it gotten so complicated?

"I'll do this on one condition."

"You're not in any place for negotiation."

"From my point of view, I am. See, if I don't do as you say, you're no closer to getting any of your precious money back and you've already said Patrick can't pay you. That leaves us sitting here with a stalemate on our hands. Neither of us conceding, no new game to play."

"Not that I'm agreeing to anything, but let's hear what you have to say."

"Who else on board this less-than-pleasure cruise is in debt to you? Ms. Mills? Lana?"

"Would that the lovely Ms. Davies was indebted to me somehow, I see how taken with her you are. A further point of motivation on your part. You defended her honor moments ago with a considerable amount of chivalry. But alas, yes, it's Ms. Mills who remains heavily in my debt. Maintaining the Beverly Hills lifestyle—her agency, her couture, her expensive taste in 'champers,' if it weren't for me Beverly Mills of Beverly Hills would go back to being Esther Grajkowski of Peoria. But it's not Ms. Mills I necessarily have a problem with, she entertains me with that big…personality of hers. And she's regular with her payments, her benefits, so I have little to complain about."

"Except you still wield a certain power over her. A not so gentle form of intimidation?"

"We all have certain ways of conducting business."

"Yes, wishing to avoid mutilation can be quite motivating," Todd said, leaning forward, taking in his hands the nutcracker which sat atop the nut bowl. His fist played with the implement, considered the effect it could have on a shelled walnut…or worse, a fleshy finger and hard bone. He thought about Cindy's bandaged hand.

"Here's the deal, Mr. Livingston. I'll go find Fast Cash's lost fortune, and when I find it I will dispense with the money as I see fit. I will clear Patrick's debt and I will also clear Ms. Mills's. I will pay you—let's call it a kill fee—for your being inconvenienced these past weeks. And then I pocket the rest of it. Also, while I'm gone on my little treasure hunt, I trust that you will keep everything here in good order. No harm will come to anyone, or else I will come after you." Todd then picked up an almond and placed it between the nutcracker. He squeezed hard and watched as the shell exploded into pieces. "And if I find out you've been messing with any of my friends, I'll turn your little torture device here back on you. And I won't be using your fingers, if you catch my drift."

"That's very noble of you, looking to help even those you don't know."

"Yes, it's quite the character flaw," Todd said, sarcasm dripping like humidity.

"Awfully confident are you?"

"You can call my bluff if you like."

"No, I'd rather call something else. I'm calling in everyone's marker—not just Patrick's and Ms. Mills. If you're in such a magnanimous mood, you can also finally close the books on both Jack Cashman's and Marty Beam's accounts. Finally bringing an end to this sordid saga—at least from my perspective. So, Mr. Gleason, you're assignment, if you choose to accept it, is easy: find the money, pay off all outstanding debts, and if there's anything left over the rest can be yours. Sound fair?"

"If you're redefining fair, yes."

Langston harrumphed, his belly rolling beneath his suit. "Take or leave it. And I suggest you take it. Leaving it leaves me with few options in dealing with a boat full of murder suspects. You never know which one could take the fall—or be the next to fall victim to a faceless killer."

Todd hated when a scam had too many hills to climb, too many switchbacks to maneuver around. Like driving on a treacherous mountain road in the black of night. With no headlights to guide you. And the brakes failing… But what choice did he have? Agree now, figure everything out later. And hope for a soft landing when the car went over the cliff. "Fine. Just one other thing. I get to take two people with me—for help in digging up the money."

"Not a chance."

"One person then."

Langston grinned at Todd, his fleshy face expanding to Jabba-like proportions. The man was clearly enjoying this art of negotiation, this game. Todd had said two because he meant one and you are always supposed to request more than you're expecting in order to settle with just what you wanted.

"Who?"

"Lana."

"Not a chance," Langston repeated. "I fear she would be too much of a distraction."

"Patrick."

"You want to fail?"

"Patrick and I proved to be a great team, once upon a time."

"I think he's lost his edge since then."

"I'll take that risk."

"You'll have to," Langston said. A pregnant paused filled with hesitation hung between them before the bloated businessman said, "Fine, we have a deal. Oh, and you have twenty-four hours."

"Only a day to find money that no one's been able to find for seven years?"

"We can hardly drag this out any longer, Mr. Gleason."

Formal again, all business. If nothing else, Todd felt he'd just earned the man's respect. One crook to another, shaking hands, agreeing to terms with no legal bearing. The truth of the matter was, as much as Todd hated when people called him a crook, he realized that given this current predicament he'd have to become a major league criminal to pull off the little scheme his mind was busily plotting. This one was going to be bigger than his usual cons. What he was planning now, this was felony stuff.

HE WASN'T King of the World. He wasn't even Leonardo DiCaprio. Hell, he doubted he was the crazed Billy Zane character, racing through the ship's levels with a gun, desperate to win back the affections of a woman who never loved him and who held in her possession the jewel that could solve all their problems. He was one of the poor Irish in steerage, destined to drown.

He was, of course, Patrick Scanlon, and the idea of a deadly iceberg hitting them was not without its appeal.

Yet this was the Pacific Ocean, it was September, and the prospect of an icy diversion was about as realistic as…well, as him finding the lost fortune of Jack "Fast Cash" Cashman. Still, from his position at the stern of the boat, bending forward to watch the surging water as it playfully hit against the hull, he was not without his own sad Hollywood ending. No, we're not talking suicide, Patrick was far too vain (and weak) for such a venture (in fact, he kept patting down his hair in the wake of the wind), he just knew that not every movie that came out of the studio's factories had a fabricated, audience-pleasing finale. Sometimes the movies were like real life and you had to fight harder than ever to achieve your goal. One difference, reality did not come with a catchy, anthemic James Horner score. Just the symphonic crash of waves, and the thundering in your own mind that you were in over your head.

But a guy like Patrick Scanlon, who always had his head in the clouds and whose dreams remained inside his brain and never saw the light of the day, he already knew he couldn't fix this mess on his own. Langston Livingston had seen to that. That man was a pro, and Patrick had never moved beyond amateur status in his dealings with him. So, truth be told, isn't that why he'd gone to see Todd? To enlist the help of the one man who fell somewhere between amateur and professional, a man who knew how to work a situation to his advantage…and usually win.

So then what was wrong with Patrick right now? Why was he looking at the water and wishing he was a fish…or a frog, a living creature who never looked beyond the oceans, who craved only the next meal and to not be swallowed up by the next biggest creature. It wasn't Langston and his ability to outsmart him that really ate at him; rather, it was his own wife's lack of faith in him. That's what had him standing alone at ship's edge, thinking about Leo and Kate and how their love for each other could not be denied, even in the face of the ultimate sacrifice. Cindy had shown she would happily take the rescue boat, and she wouldn't even wave goodbye as he descended into the sea.

She'd hired someone to keep him away. That was the truth, the simple reality of the situation. Even last night, when he'd finally returned to her side after a week of running and captivity, when he'd had the rare guts to return to his Manhattan Beach bungalow and say to his wife that he was back to take responsibility for their current situation, his efforts had all been for naught. She'd already moved on, she'd already stopped believing in him. She too knew Todd was the better solution, and she'd even gone as far as to hire someone to keep him out of the way. From getting in the way.

What was his next move? Damned if he knew.

Luckily, someone else was taking charge, as he was about to find out.

"Patrick."

It was Cindy.

He didn't bother to turn around, he merely continued to stare out at sea; even when she approached him and put her soft hand upon his shoulder, he gave her the brush off.

"You have to talk to me sometime. We are married."

Her use of the word marriage made him finally pay attention. His eyes fell upon the stunning features of his wife, and for perhaps the first time since he'd met her he detected some flaws. A slight scar on her upturned lip, freckles upon her bare shoulders, but most importantly a weakening resolve hiding behind electric green pupils. He'd always admired the strength and fortitude she displayed each and every day, as though there was nothing she could not achieve. That confidence was what truly attracted him to her all those years ago, and it's what had seen them through times both good and bad. From early struggles in New York, through the difficult days after her mother's death, to their impulsive decision to move to Los Angeles. Cynthia O'Neil Scanlon had been his rock, his anchor (they were on a boat, after all), and only in the face of failure did he wonder if the woman he'd fallen in love with was the same as the woman he found himself married to now.

"Some marriage," he finally said. "You had no faith in me, Cindy."

"What I did—hiring Barney and Fred. I did it for your own good—for our own good. Look, Patrick, it's not that I didn't trust you or believe you couldn't outsmart Langston. It was Langston who was the wildcard, he's ruthless and unforgiving. He deliberately drew us into his web until we were also in his debt. He's a formidable man, and I didn't think the two of us alone could handle him. So when you went to find Todd, well, I guess it got me thinking. About the past, about our college days and early years in New York, you had these petty schemes that never came to fruition and eventually you gave up on them and we settled into a boring, working-for-a-living lifestyle. We lost our edge. Todd on the other hand, he honed his skills and he heightened his edge, and I thought...well, I guess I just thought he would have a clearer mind, a fresher approach, to helping us sort out our problems."

"And having me work alongside him would what? Slow him down?"

"I thought that if he had to constantly be looking over his shoulder to see if you were all right, it might distract him. You know Todd always works better when alone. So, I took matters into my own hands and made sure you couldn't interfere with whatever he was plotting."

"Pretty extreme, Cindy. Those thugs scared the crap out of me. If they had told me their kidnapping of me was really just for my own protection, well...maybe that would have sat better with me than thinking they worked for Langston and I was soon going to be swimming with the fishes. My God, we're already in debt up to our eyeballs and what do you do, hire a couple of bone-headed detectives?"

"I needed them both. One to keep an eye on you, the other to find Todd. Yes, Patrick, I was in New York, too. Right after you left. I found them, hired them. They tracked Todd down in Bermuda; without them we would never be in this position now. Besides, finding Fast Cash's fortune would more than pay for their services—and erase our financial obligations to Langston."

"Except that as far as we've been able to determine, that money doesn't exist."

"Oh, but it does."

That wasn't Cindy talking, and both Scanlons spun around to find themselves looking at Langston Livingston. Given his greedy girth, it was amazing they hadn't heard the creak of the floorboards as he'd approached. By his side was Todd, looking every much the sinister man's sidekick.

"And the resourceful Mr. Gleason here, he's going to find it once and for all."

Todd added a coda to his statement. "Except that I need help. So, are you ready to get to work?"

"Whatever you need," Cindy said.

"Sorry, Cin. Your track record on this thing isn't so great. So, Patrick?"

Patrick looked from a smiling Todd to a disheartened Cindy, and then, ever so briefly, he gazed back at the swaying sea. A grin hit his lips as he realized perhaps there was still one person left in this messed up world who had a bit of faith in him. Todd Gleason and Patrick Scanlon, together again, and ready to pull what Patrick had to assume was one major league con.

"Oh, man, it's good to be back," Patrick said.

CHAPTER EIGHTEEN

THE RENOWNED Silver Spoon diner on Santa Monica had been in its strip mall location forever, known for its simple fare and has-been celebrity sightings. Faded pictures of faded stars lined the faded walls of the diner, their signatures barely legible behind aging frames. Dalrymple and Benes were sitting in a back booth, the former pushing an omelet around his plate while the latter indulged in baby back ribs; between them was a plate of shoestring French Fries. Dalrymple tried to avoid watching his partner eat; this morning they stumbled upon a dead body and a skeleton, and this guy goes and orders ribs? And douses his fries with so much ketchup the waitress asked him if "you want some fries with your ketchup?" His plate looked like its own crime scene.

Speaking of, they were dining at this noon hour and not out questioning people because they were waiting for certain results to come back from the lab. Results that would lead them down the next path of their investigation. They had two murders on their hands in a week's time, and now a years-old case had suddenly come to light. They were both hot and cold, these cases, and at the moment neither detective felt warm and fuzzy toward them. Too many questions still, too many bodies.

They had spent the bulk of their morning at the Cashman estate, watching as CSU took photograph after photograph, as they sifted through the dirt of the basement, at the plasterboard mixed in with the filth, at the various holes they suspected were recent digs in the floor and wall. They also shot, tagged, and bagged the myriad currency that had been spread about the crime scene, and currently those bills were being tested for fingerprints and having their serial numbers traced. The skeleton had finally been removed, as an intrigued medical examiner had been quick to the case; Dalyrmple's old friend, the beautiful Dr. Marcus, who had done the autopsy on Beaufort, came in on her day off when she heard about the case. She liked the complex mystery the skeleton promised; so many secrets to decipher from reading its bones.

"Sure you don't want a rib?" Benes asked.

The ringing of his cell phone saved Dalrymple from having to answer. "What have you got for me? Answers would be appreciated." He listened, nodded, then he listened some more. "But nothing stuffed down the vic's throat? No suspect's name? Nothing convenient like that?" More listening, more nodding. "Interesting. Okay, thanks. Call me when you know more." Dalrymple then put the phone back into his suit jacket pocket.

"What'd Marcus have to say?" Benes said, chewing on a fry.

"Her associate is handling the widow's autopsy. Says the bullet wound is in a different location from Beaufort, though we knew that. He was shot execution style to the back of the head; the widow was shot clean through the heart. Which tells me the bullet locations may be different, but the shooter is very definitely the same. He shot his victims with intent, and chose his hits with deliberation."

"What makes you convinced it's the same killer?"

"My gut."

"Good enough. Anything else similar come to light?"

"No, and that's the curious part. If Beaufort's killer stuffed Patrick Scanlon's name down his victim's throat why didn't he do the same with…uh, you know, Cashman? And what's with all the bills strewn about the body and the skeleton? I wonder why didn't we find any such calling card surrounding Beaufort's body?"

"Remember, Ernie, Beaufort's body was moved. He might have been found along the freeway, but his clothes were soaked with chlorine. He'd taken a permanent bath in someone's pool before being dumped along the 405. Could be there were bills at that scene, too."

"Good point, Sandy, I'd nearly forgotten."

"I assume no word yet from ballistics, right?"

Dalrymple gave his partner a look. "Have we not been inseparable since we arrived at the scene of the crime? Has ballistics called us yet?"

"Geez, you're touchy this morning. Everything okay?"

"Sorry, I'll be fine. It's just…I really hate cases like this. No, change that: I hate this case."

"Why? I mean, other than trying to track down a killer, this one makes me think you've got a personal investment in its outcome."

"Sandy, how long have we been partners?"

"Six years."

"Right. Before we were teamed up, the Fast Cash case was

mine. It went unsolved, has irked me ever since."

"Yeah, I hear you," he said. "Hey, Ernie?

"Yeah, Sandy?"

"You're a damn good cop. You remember, you care."

"Sandy?"

"Yeah?"

"Shut up and eat your ketchup."

They ate in companionable silence, even while Dalrymple stewed over these recent developments. A key clue had evaded him. He could feel that clue on the tip of his tongue, and suddenly he stopped chewing, not wanting to swallow it alongside the remnants of his omelet.

"What is it?" Benes asked.

"Sandy, you're a genius."

"You know who offed the widow?"

"No, not that, but come on. Forgot those ribs, if what you said turns out to be the turn in the case we needed I'll buy you your own cow."

"Pig."

"Whatever," Dalrymple said. "Now let's go."

As they slapped money down on the table and headed out the door, Benes kept pestering his partner with requests and questions, what's going on, what did I say, where are we going. It wasn't until they were in their appointed seats in their unmarked and speeding down Santa Monica to La Cienga and eventually to the 405 Freeway did Dalrymple finally ease up on the pedal and look back at his partner.

"All along I've been focused on Beaufort and this Scanlon character, trying to somehow link them together. We know both this Gleason guy and his friend, the real Patrick Scanlon, were out of town when Beaufort's body was found, but there's one person we kept forgetting here. The Mrs."

"The hot redhead?"

"Yes, Sandy. Redheads, fiery personalities. Could be Beaufort was writing a column about the Scanlons, maybe they've got something to do with this whole Fast Cash mess and he was threatening to expose him. So she shot him."

"Pretty brutal way to shoot the guy, in the back of the head. Guy never saw it coming."

"Yeah. And maybe the force of the blow took his body off a patio and into a pool."

"I seem to remember the Scanlons having a pool."

"One more stop, and then that's where we're headed?"

"Why, we missing something?"

"A search warrant."

IT WAS thirty more minutes of start and stop traffic before they wound their way around the side streets of the coastal town of Manhattan Beach, and five more before their memories served them correctly and they were pulling into the Scanlon's driveway. Their first observation, no cars. Their second observation, and that came after they had knocked repeatedly on the front door, nobody was home.

"Where is everyone suddenly?" Dalrymple said. "This place was hopping with activity on a Sunday night last time we were here. And now, middle of the day and it's deserted?"

"What do we do?"

Dalrymple said, "We check out the pool."

"Let's hope we don't find anything unexpected," Benes said. "Jesus, the last thing we need is another body."

They walked across the front lawn and swung back around the driveway, where they opened the wooden gate that led them toward the Scanlon's backyard. Though they had no solid evidence that something bad might happen, the judge had granted them the search warrant nonetheless; probable cause was a slippery slope. They drew their guns and kept them carefully tucked against their bodies as they crept to the back patio. They saw no person, no activity of any kind; the entire setting was peaceful and serene, not even the leaves of the trees rustled. The early afternoon had an unnatural calm about it, as though the wind were taking a deserved siesta.

Dalrymple moved forward to the backyard furniture, where he noticed an empty wine bottle and two glasses discarded on the patio table. For the moment, he ignored them, they could be tagged and bagged later in case they needed fingerprints. He moved beyond the chairs and found himself standing on the edge of the pool. Here, too, the water was calm, motionless.

"Got a baggie?" Dalrymple asked.

"Yeah, grabbed one from the glove compartment."

"Good, let's get a sample of the water. We can have the lab run tests on the chlorine, see if we get a match with what was found down Beaufort's throat. Then we can at least establish a connection, and know with finality that this is where Beaufort was shot. Once we've got those answers, we come back and interrogate Mrs. Scanlon until we get the answers we want."

"Do we want to put an APB out on her?"

"Not yet. Let's get some answers first."

Benes leaned down with the sealable bag, opened it and

dipped it in the water, waited a few seconds for the pool water to rush inside before he lifted it out and locked the contents inside. "Gotcha," he said.

But then out of the corner of his eye he noticed something else entirely, something caught over by the filter.

"Hey, Ernie, check that out," he said, pointing to the other side of the pool.

Dalrymple maneuvered his way over to the filter, carefully putting his hand in the water to retrieve the object. Most would have assumed it was just a fallen leaf, caught by the currents and dragged to the filter's webbing. This was no leaf, Dalrymple noted.

"A twenty dollar bill," he said, lifting it with a nearby twig. "Sandy?"

"I'm on it, another bag."

As Benes went back to their car, Dalrymple examined the bill a bit more closely.

"Strange as it may seem, I believe Fast Cash's fortune is starting to turn up."

Just then his phone rang and with the bill still dangling from the twig in his one hand, he grabbed the phone with his other and flipped it open.

"What have you got? Uh-huh. Right. Okay, looks like I need a CSU unit," he said, and then gave them the address of Patrick and Cindy Scanlon.

He was putting his phone away when Benes returned.

"What happened?"

"That was ballistics. Beaufort and Lottie Cashman? Same gun killed them both."

"Is that good news or bad?"

"Good in that we know we're only dealing with one killer."
"The bad?"
"Said killer is still out there."
"What about this Scanlon guy, shall we attempt another follow-up?"
"Might be a good starting, place," Dalrymple said. "Although let's make sure this time we pick up the actual Patrick Scanlon."

"SO, CALIFORNIA Fidelity? Bank of America? Citi? Which bank should we hit? They're all corrupt, like it would matter."

"Rob a bank? Are you crazy?"

"Which is the one with that penny arcade that exchanges your change for real cash?"

"Um, Todd, we owe millions and you're talking about pennies?"

"I like that bank, nobody uses pennies anymore and they just pile up…not since candy was inflated from penny to a dollar can anyone use them. Whichever bank it is helps you get rid of them easily, they're off the list. I'd hate to rob them."

"Why do we have to rob a bank at all?"

"You got a better idea on how to get our hands on a quick, cool three million dollars?"

Patrick frowned. "Todd, I think it's time to involve the police."

"Yeah, that's a good plan, Patrick. Walk into police headquarters and ask for the two cops who are investigating the Beaufort murder—not to mention Lottie Cashman's fresh kill—and say you think Langston Livingston has kidnapped a bunch of people on a boat and somehow it's all related to the story of Fast Cash's robbery reign. Oh, don't forget to tell them who you are."

"Meaning what?"

"Patrick, the cops arrested me, thinking I was you."

"Yeah, you want to give me the lowdown on that one?"

Todd stole a moment to explain the events of the Open House, the map, the digging in the basement, the body they found before the police did, the culmination of all those sequences of events leading to Todd's unwanted night in jail. He made sure to make a point of the fact that both Dalrymple and Benes considered some guy named Patrick Scanlon as "a person of interest in this case."

Todd wisely added, "So, for now I suggest we keep the police out of this."

"Sure. That is, until we get caught robbing a bank. Are we armed, dangerous? Or just stupid? What makes you even think this is a good idea?"

Todd gave his fearful friend a withering look, wondered where the once-upon-a-time devil in him had gotten to. A scam or a scheme, the very notion used to widen Patrick's pupils and now his eyes were just darkened with nervous apprehension. He clearly wanted no part of any of this unfolding ploy, despite the fact it was all his doing. For a moment Todd considered whether his choice of including Patrick was the right one; perhaps he should have brought along a heavy, like Fred or Barney…or Cindy. Someone good in a fight.

"Look, Patrick, if robbing a bank was good enough for Fast Cash and Marty Beam, why not for the team of Todd Gleason and Patrick Scanlon? We at least know to trust each other." He paused. "Right?"

"Of course, geez, Todd, I flew all the way to New York because I knew you were the only person who *could* help me. But...becoming actual criminals? I could count on both hands and feet and still need more digits for counting the reasons why not to go ahead with this idea. But for starters, both Fast Cash and Marty Beam disappeared and at least one of them met up with foul play in that basement. Consider that bony skeleton the cops discovered alongside the body of Lottie Cashman— that's what becomes a bank robber. By the way, which one do you want to be, Fast Cash or Marty?"

"Depends," Todd said.

"On what?"

"Which of them turns out to be said skeleton."

"Geez, that inspires tons of confidence."

Three hours into Langston's twenty-four hour deadline, and the only true progress our intrepid con man and his insipid cohort had made so far was reaching land. From their successful, if not surprising, arrival back at Pier 44 in Marina Del Rey, to the exact slip they jetted off from, to their twenty-minute drive back to Manhattan Beach, neither of them had spoken about the adventure they had set off on. They were too wired from concentrating on their own survival, too exhausted from worrying about what they had left behind on board *The Nutcracker*. It wasn't until they finally arrived back at the Scanlon home that they began to tackle the situation at hand: how to find the money and save their friends.

In the kitchen, Patrick had gone to the fridge and pulled out a beer and slipped the cap off and taken a deep pull before offering one to Todd.

"I think I'll keep my wits about me, thanks."

"Have it your way," Patrick said, and then took another swig. "So, okay, you want us to rob a bank. How do you propose we go about that? It's already after three in the afternoon, so most are closed or are getting ready to close. What do you propose, we hide inside one overnight and gain access to the vault? Or should we wait until morning? If we do, we run the risk of going past our twenty-four hour deadline. Langston, as we've come to learn, is not the most patient of men. I just don't see robbing a bank as a viable option."

"Viable option? Patrick, you're making it sound like we have a choice." Todd paused. "We don't. Cindy and Lana are being held hostage and it's our job to free them."

"Yeah, about that. Lana—she's the one you met in Bermuda?"

Todd nodded.

"Kind of a coincidence, don't you think?"

"What I find more of a coincidence is that Lana is Marty Beam's daughter."

Patrick was in mid-drink when he paused over that piece of news. "Excuse me?"

"You heard me," Todd said. "Kinda funny when you consider Cindy is the daughter of Fast Cash. Both daughters wanting to know what happened to their father, both of them unaware the other exists. I wonder how long it will take them to discover this on their own."

"How about you, Todd?"

"How about me what?"

"They're both doing what you vowed never to do. Find their father."

Todd grabbed the half-consumed beer from Patrick's hand and finished what remained in one gulp. He set the bottle down on the counter. "Come on, enough with the family history lesson, it's time to get ready for whatever awaits us tonight."

With that, Todd exited the kitchen and made his way to the guest bedroom, where he went about changing his clothes. Black pants, black shirt, a trendy outfit in New York, a blight here in sunny California. But he wasn't dressing for success. Nope, his outfit would serve one purpose: having him blend into the dark night, a cat burglar looking for the ultimate meal.

When he emerged, he found Patrick still in his sea-worthy clothes.

"I suggest you change."

"Where are we going with you dressed like that?"

"I told you, we're robbing a bank."

"Which one did you decide on? Let me guess. Since you're so intent on reliving Fast Cash and Marty Beam's last heist, we're headed down to Hollywood and Vine, right? California Fidelity"

"Cute idea, Hollywood would love it, but wrong. Even if that branch still existed, that's too poetic. And I'm not in the mood for perfect symmetry. I'm more in the mood for settling debts. And then settling scores."

"You still haven't told me which bank."

"The Livingston Vault," Todd said.

Patrick blanched. "Say again?"

"You heard me."

"You're insane. You're definitely gonna get us both killed."

"You got any better ideas?" Todd said.

"We're going to steal from the man we owe?"

"Yup. And pay him back with his own money."

Patrick didn't change right away into his black clothes. He reached for another beer.

CSU MIGHT have left the Scanlon house hours ago, but that's because they had taken as much evidence as they could, taken it all back to the labs for study. Dalrymple and Benes, they weren't held to such scientific trappings, they could still rely on their instincts and time-honed street smarts.

"Bingo," Dalrymple said. "Looks like our leak about the murder is starting to pay out some dividends."

"You said we were taking a chance. Good plan."

"Sometimes, Sandy, if you can't beat them, join them."

Sitting in their unmarked as night began to fall on the city of angels, they had staked out the Scanlon house in hopes of any sign of activity. And when they saw the car pull into the driveway and two men—one of them that Gleason fellow—they knew something was afoot. They could have acted right then and there, knocked on the door, inquired of the two gentlemen just what was going down. Or they could sit here, patiently, seeing what happened next. They decided on the latter.

Let the answers come to them.

An hour later, the two men emerged from the house, dressed in clothing that matched the darkening sky. The unidentified man got into the passenger seat, smoothing down his hair as it bumped against the doorframe.

"A man wrapped up in himself, oblivious to his surroundings," Dalrymple said.

"Yeah. Not so Gleason."

In fact, from their vantage point, they could see Todd Gleason scoping out the area, taking his time. Did his eyes just zero in on the unmarked parked down the street? That was the problem with stake outs, sometimes they left you exposed, vulnerable. Then Gleason got into the car, pulled out, and quickly sped down the street.

As Dalrymple gunned the engine, Benes shook his head.

"Clean record, my ass."

CHAPTER NINETEEN

NIGHT-TIME. THE clock had struck nine, and a dark curtain had fallen on this side of the Orange Curtain, leaving Los Angeles a city lulled by the quiet of the canyons and the lure of its ever-present neon lights. Cars sped down multi-laned freeways, along the famous boulevards Sunset and Wilshire, Hollywood and Santa Monica, legendary streets in a town that likened achievement to fame, success to fortune.

A sizable fortune was being sought tonight, this one at the corner of Sunset and La Cienega. The Sunset Strip was vibrant and alive, comedy clubs and night clubs alike awash in lights and lines; people distracted by their own lives and their own ambitions, none of whom could be bothered by a car they wouldn't be caught DUI in as it pulled into the rear parking lot of the office tower that rose high at the crest of La Cienega.

Patrick knew it well, he'd first come to it with such high hopes, a new job in a new town. The money, the address…the power, it had all seduced him as only the city of angels could, and far too soon he'd sprouted his own wings and gotten caught up in a new world shown to him by his deceitful boss. Langston

Livingston knew just what he was doing, he knew just how to trap people inside his wealthy web. He also knew when to move in for the kill.

Well, it was time to turn the tables on him.

Todd shut off the engine, let the headlights fade to black against the neglected brush behind the edge of the building. He took a deep breath and then said, "Ready?"

Patrick wiped wet palms against his black pants. Which told you two things: he'd finally changed into clothing that befitted a crook, and that he was still a bundle of nerves. Either that or the alcohol he'd consumed was sweating right through him.

"You okay, Patrick?"

"Let's just get this over with."

Todd went for the door handle, but then stopped himself and gazed at his friend. "Patrick—I need you to focus. This is why you came looking for me in New York, to fix a mess only you could create. And trust me, this is the only way to go about it. Robbing an actual bank is just out of the question. First of all, a single take would never secure us the amount of money needed to appease Langston, and I don't know about you but I'm not up for pulling a string of robberies and becoming known as Todd Thumb or whatever dumb label the press would assign to me. I also don't want to spend the next some-odd years in jail. So we're doing what we need to do—rob from the rich to pay the rich. It just so happens that the same man fits both 'rich's.'"

"I know, I know. Believe me, I know this is the only way. It's just…"

"What?"

"I keep thinking about the map—Fast Cash's map. Wasn't

the money supposed to be buried there in the basement of the Cashman house?"

Todd shrugged. "From what I can gather, the map was only supposed to lead people to the body buried behind the basement wall. Why the body was there, who put it there, and why it took seven years for someone to find it, I don't know. But whoever sent that map—to you and to Lana, too—must have had an ulterior motive. That map was never about the money—it was all about bringing closure to the past, much like Lottie Cashman petitioning the courts to declare her husband dead. She got her wish, and less than a week later she's dead. And her body is found next to another body, this one long dead but only recently discovered. Time will tell whether it's Fast Cash or Marty Beam. And so we have to assume that whichever one it's not, it's the other operating behind the scenes. He's a bit of a Puppet master, and apparently he's willing to kill to keep his secret safe." Todd paused, looked at his friend. "But that's for another time. For now, we're just two guys sitting in a parked car in West Hollywood and the last thing we need is to attract any untoward attention. So I suggest we get a move on. The quicker we're in, the quicker we're out."

"Not the first time that line has been uttered in this neighborhood," Patrick said.

"Nice. Like I'm back with Barney."

They stepped out into the warm night, closing the door quickly to avoid the lingering glow of the dome light. As it dimmed to nothing and left them blackened against the dark backdrop, Todd gave way and instructed Patrick to take the lead. After all, he knew the way inside the building. Hadn't he done this very thing just last night when he'd gone to outline his scheme to get all the players aboard *The Nutcracker*? Now it was time to crack a different nut: a vault that existed somewhere within Langston's office, one Todd had assumed was overstuffed with cash. Langston Livingston, he was not unlike Jack Cashman, neither man had much faith in the system or in being FDIC insured. Like the great fortune made off by Fast Cash, all of it cold hard cash, Todd assumed oodles of bundled bills awaited them somewhere inside this office tower. He'd seen proof just last night when Langston pulled out a handy wad of dough and tossed it Garth's way. Langston surely hadn't just cleaned out an ATM, that's for sure.

Patrick pulled out his electronic card key and slapped it against the electronic pad at the back entrance. It worked again, and just like that the door clicked and they grabbed the knob and they were suddenly inside, safe from prying eyes but not necessarily prying cameras. Talk about a juxtaposition, no one to see them but Big Brother himself.

"You know they caught my every move last night."

Todd smiled for the hidden cameras. "Send me two prints, please," he said aloud.

"Langston's going to know we were here—he's going to know how we got the money."

Todd's smile faded and he let out a heavy sigh. "Patrick, do you have any faith in me?"

"Yes, that's why I went to you."

"Then let me worry about the cameras, you just lead the way to Langston's office."

Patrick started up the back stairs, then stopped to look at his one-time best friend. "You wanna tell me why we don't need to worry about the security cameras? You've got something up your sleeve, don't you? What is it, have you been planning this all along?"

"Patrick?"

"Yeah?"

"Does Todd Gleason ever work just one angle?"

"When you refer to yourself in third person, it's always a good sign."

"You know what else is a good sign?"

"What's that?"

"Being able to get out of here as quickly as possible, means a smooth operation. Langston might be out of commission right now on board *Ye Ole Nutcracker*, but that doesn't mean we can act like kids inside a locked candy store. Guards are on the premises. So, let's get a move on."

"Consider us moved."

Patrick led the way, Todd followed. As they rounded each turn of the staircase Patrick indicated where he thought the cameras were hidden behind drywall. Todd would look and then he'd just wave each time, smiling as he did so, his dimples seemingly lighting up the otherwise dimly-lit stairwell. At last they made their way to the upper most floor, emerging into an empty hallway. Todd noticed Patrick pause.

"What's the matter?"

"This is the point when Garth manhandled me and dragged me before the Almighty."

"A different night, a different set of plans."

"Right. Right, geez, how can you remain so calm in the face of this?"

"Patrick?"

"I know, I've gone from the almighty gospel of Langston

Livingston to the quippy retorts of the unflappable Todd Gleason. You always have to win, don't you?"

"Just be lucky I'm on your side."

"Are you?" Patrick suddenly tossed into the mix.

Oh, dissention among the ranks was not a way to win a battle.

"It's not like I came to L.A. to score a film deal. I came for you. So, can we just get a move on?"

"This isn't about Cindy?"

"Christ, Patrick, save it…okay. Later."

Discussion apparently over, they slipped out from the stairway and crept down the empty hallway until they came to the offices of Livingston Enterprises, it of the questionable business of exports, imports, and extorts. Langston had laundered so much money inside these offices he might well take stock in Tide. Todd just had to hope that there was a big pile of dirty laundry waiting to be tossed into the spin cycle.

Patrick, his hands covered with black gloves, turned the knob on the main office door. It only went about a quarter of an inch before stopping. He looked at Todd and Todd looked right back at him, worry meeting annoyance.

"Let me guess, it's locked, and you don't have a card key that accesses this door."

"Last night I didn't need one."

"That's because Garth manhandled you and brought you here himself."

"Uh, yeah."

"Can I have your card key?"

Patrick withdrew the credit card sized key from inside his pocket. He handed it over but said "don't bother, I already know it's not going to work." For his part, Todd shrugged off his friend's pessimism and slid the card between the two doors, trying to slide the lock back into its frame and thus release the door for entry. Classic burglary entrance. He waited to hear a click or any such noise, but wouldn't luck choose not to be on their side right now. Patrick's prediction overtook Todd's confidence. He hated when that happened.

"Okay, got any other bright ideas?" Todd asked.

"Break down the door."

"And alert the guards downstairs by tripping an alarm or just generally making a lot of noise, sure, that's a great plan. Maybe once we break into the vault we can just pay off their silence with a few of the big bucks we're bound to find."

"Look, Todd, we're going to have this same problem once we get inside. Langston's not Fast Cash, he didn't exactly print us a map of his office, with a handy X marking the spot of where he hides his vault. Much less what the combination to said vault is. So, not only do we have the current obstacle in front of us, we have an even bigger one once—and if—we gain entrance to his office."

"Patrick, what's with all this negative energy crap? You're so filled with no and can't, problems and obstacles, I barely recognize you. Where's that swagger you once used to squeeze a passing grade from a teacher who found your charm more to her liking than your term papers? That confidence that stole a certain woman out from under me and straight into your arms…"

"Thought you didn't want to talk about Cindy," Patrick suddenly said.

"Why—are you angry with her for what she did?"

"Kept me out of commission and instead turned to the one man who she knew could help her. The aforementioned and flap-less Todd Gleason."

Todd had to consider the situation carefully. Emotions were running high. Not only were they in this predicament of having to steal a fortune in cash to save their collective butts, but adding to the mix was the very heart of the dynamic between these two. With Patrick and Todd, it had always been Cindy between them. Three friends that had shared experiences and emotions, failings and frustrations, successes and suspicions, now brought together one more time to lay to rest undefeated demons. Is that what their lives had been building to, this moment where guilt overran loyalty and where responsibility to others took precedence over selfishness? Todd knew there were matters left unsaid that would need to be spoken of, but right at this moment he and Patrick had to put aside unresolved issues and pursue their common enemy.

"Later, Patrick," he said. "I promise."

"I know all about you two," was what Patrick said.

"Look, leave it alone, okay? For now?" Todd said, his temper rising. The last thing they needed was to be further distracted by foolish fables about the fabulous femme fatale who had failed them both at featured moments. In an effort to diffuse the moment, he angrily swiped the card through the slit in the doorway again, and low and behold if his quick motion and eager thrust didn't disable the lock and gain them entrance to the inner offices of Livingston Enterprises. The click of the lock caught them both by surprise, and with no other words coming between them they silently surged forward through the open door and closed themselves off from the rest of the floor.

Apparently Patrick was done wasting time with words and subtle accusations, he wordlessly pointed toward the double set of doors that separated the outer office from the inner sanctum. Without a moment's hesitation he went to them and turned the knob and threw open the doors, as though some inner demon had taken charge, channeling the man he always wanted to be but somehow never could find. Whether it was Todd he was angry at, or Langston or even Cindy—but maybe, just maybe—himself, Todd was impressed with this sudden newfound energy inside Patrick Scanlon. Taking charge and taking no prisoners. Something had clicked during their exchange, and Todd for one wasn't about to question it. He just followed his friend's lead.

Todd had to admit, Langston sure knew how to live the good life. The office was beautifully appointed, with dark woods and leather furniture and prints and animal heads that resembled a gentleman's club gone wild, and if he didn't despise Langston for the way he took advantage of people's weaknesses, he might just have admired him for his good taste.

"Nice digs," he couldn't help but saying.

"Guy like Langston, everything is paid for by the interest he collects."

"Good thing. That mean the real cash awaits us," Todd said. "And I suggest we move quickly to find it. He may have Garth at his side aboard *The Nutcracker*, but you never know who else a guy like Livingston has working for him, or looking out for him."

"Yeah, that used to be me," Patrick remarked.

"Oh, then this should be easy."

"Hey, Todd?"

"I know, cut the wise cracks," he said.

For the next fifteen minutes both Todd and Patrick scoured the office, looking behind paintings for a hidden wall safe, through desk drawers and file cabinets, beneath the chairs and sofas, anywhere and everywhere that would lead them to a clue or a hint or any indication that there was money to be found. All during the search Todd kept instilling confidence in himself that he'd read the rich thug correctly, that there was no way he would distance himself from his money.

But just like that, Todd stopped searching. The physical activity had won out over his brain activity, and so he just stood in the center of the room, hands on his hips, considering everything laid out before him. Patrick started to speak and Todd shushed him; nothing could interrupt his thoughts, he felt on the verge of a discovery. He was just waiting for that brain impulse to go shooting through his system until it came to rest on the tip of his tongue. Once there, he knew where the money was. He looked out the window at the gritty world of LA; but he also saw his own reflection. Turning around, he saw the world through Langston's eyes. His own image stared back from a gilt-edged mirror located just opposite Langston's desk. Not only did the view afford an opportunity to see his own reflection, Todd imagined it was Langston's way of keeping an eye on what was truly important.

"Bingo," he announced, as though some master of ceremonies had called out the magic number that completed his diagonal string of luck. Todd stepped toward the mirror, Patrick close behind him.

As the two of them stared at their images, Patrick took a

moment to fix his hair. The mirror also captured the rolling of Todd's eyes.

"Okay, vain boy, you looking good?" Todd asked.

"Uh, yeah, sorry," Patrick said.

"Good, cause that's the last look this mirror will ever see."

Without another moment of hesitation, Todd grabbed a heavy item from Langston's desk and suddenly he was hurtling it through the air, intent on scoring a direct hit on the sheer surface of the mirror. The sounded shattered the quiet in the office and he shielded his eyes as shards of glass littered the carpeted floor. But it wasn't the broken mirror which attracted him; it was the gleaming gun metal safe that was hidden behind it.

"You know, that's seven years back luck," Patrick said.

Todd and Patrick side-stepped the messy shards of glass, grabbed hold of the frame and carefully removed it from the wall. A few stray glass swords toppled to the floor and broke into smaller pieces.

"You sure this was a good idea? I mean, Langston's gonna know it was us. Besides, this entire search and seizure has probably been captured on video."

Todd turned to where he thought a camera might be hidden. Again, he showed off that annoying wave and smile. Like he was taunting whoever was recording the incident. "Maybe we'll get to watch it on YouTube."

"Yeah, from prison."

"Oh, Langston would never involve the police," Todd said. "But enough talk, let's get to work on opening up this baby."

This baby was a wall safe about two feet tall by one foot wide. Not huge, but big enough to house a fortune begging to be found. Todd took a closer look, noticed it was locked via an electronic keypad as opposed to a combination. The keypad looked just like what you would see on a cell phone. Todd's task was to figure out the magic code, figure out whether Langston was the kind of guy who preferred a sequence of numbers or a particular word. Could be either, and deciphering the code could take longer to crack than it would to earn back three million dollars making minimum wage. The possibilities were endless. But hey, they've gotten this far on sheer brazenness and guts, what's a little problem-solving but a mere hindrance?

Todd made a move toward a button.

Patrick grabbed his hand and pulled it back. "What are you doing? You don't know the combination, do you?"

"Uh, no. Langston and I bonded but we didn't get so close we exchanged secret codes."

"Then don't try and guess—you don't know how this safe is wired, it may shut down after a couple of attempts. You know, like it knows someone unauthorized is trying to break in."

"Well, short of pure guesswork you got any brilliant ideas? He was your boss for a couple years—technically I suppose he still is, as long as you remain in his debt. Clearly you've never seen this safe before, since you didn't even know it existed. How many times did you look into this mirror to fix your hair?"

"I don't fix my…" Patrick trailed off. "Never mind. You're so reckless tonight, I'm leaving it all up to you. Figure out the code yourself; me, I need to sit down."

Todd was happy to see his friend settled onto the sofa far across the office. He was clouding his judgment, fussing with his confidence, tossing off bad energy. Pretty much just pissing him off. Better to work solo. He gazed about the office, looking for clues to Langston's personality. Something he liked, or someone he liked. Money? Cash? These were possible options. He figured this kind of safe had either a four or six-character code, maybe eight, and of those first few options, only cash applied. So why not, he tried it.

C.A.S.H.

No click, no nothing.

"Okay," he said.

He typed again. S.C.A.N.L.O.N.

No click, still nothing.

"Worth a try," he said.

Then he tried C.A.S.H.M.A.N.

The third time was not the charm.

Impulsively, instinct over-riding common sense, he typed quickly.

F.A.S.T. C.A.S.H.

Zilch.

Crap, that was four attempts and he was no closer to the other side of the vault. The reality of the situation was that the next attempt could be his last. Five tries and then you're locked out, the system possibly shutting itself down. And then he'd have to look for another trick up his sleeve. He felt a bit of sweat form on his brow, so he took a breather from opening the safe and retreated to Langston's desk, grabbing a tissue to wipe the condensation away. Leaning against the desk, arms akimbo, his eyes traveled around the office, looking at pictures in frames, at wall hangings, at a mini-bar and glasses, at the basket of nuts Langston kept on his desk.

He thought of Langston and he thought about his interests. Cash wasn't the key, it's what cash could buy him that was important. So what he came up with was a yacht named *The Nutcracker*. The fat bastard had sure enjoyed showing off his prized possession, even if only to a boatload of hostages. Pride, he thought, doesn't it goeth before a fall? Just then Todd thought he was onto something; a shiny gleam had caught his eye. He quickly moved forward, crouched down to the broken shards and reached out to pick up the one thing he'd forgotten to look at. He'd just thrown it, busted a mirror with it. But he hadn't known what he'd thrown.

"A fucking nutcracker," he said.

And that's when he realized the nutcracker wasn't just for cracking hard shells, it was the device used to make people crack under the pressure of interrogation. Marty Beam had once lost a finger that way, and Cindy nearly had just the other night. It was Langston's favorite form of torture, enough so to name his boat after it.

Todd returned to the safe, and this time he hovered over the safe, ready to type. He held back one moment, his mind dancing between two words.

About to type, N.U.T.S., he changed his mind at the last second.

F.I.N.G.E.R. was what he came up with as an alternative.

The lock clicked, and the door to the safe sprung open.

Todd had to wonder if Langston himself wasn't a bit nuts.

But that diagnosis would have to wait for another day, another time. For now, he dug out a slim flashlight from his pocket and peered inside the safe. Much to his liking, and not at all to his surprise, he saw stacks and stacks of precious green paper, all of it ripe for the picking. This was more money than he'd ever seen, certainly more than he'd ever scored, even during his London case when the pound had outweighed the dollar. There might be more here than Fast Cash might have scored during his entire reign. Langston Livingston was a man who beat them all at their own game of amassing a hearty fortune.

He was also a man of violence, because sitting beside all those yummy bills was a silver revolver, and Todd had little doubt it was loaded. Not unlike a venomous snake, ready to strike at its prey at the slightest provocation.

By now Patrick had rejoined Todd, and the two of them stood side by side, staring at the mother lode, knowing they had just saved everyone's butts. Patrick grabbed the duffel bag he'd brought and Todd began unloading the safe of its precious contents. As he grabbed stack after stack, he checked the denominations and was suitably impressed with the twenties, fifties, hundreds that quickly added up to hundreds, thousands, millions. He left a few stacks behind, he didn't want to be too greedy and besides, he was confident that they had more than enough to cover their debts. But then just for good measure he took one more stack and that one he placed in his pants pocket. For safekeeping.

"Okay, we're set. Let's get the hell out of here," Todd said.

Patrick paused. "What about that?"

He was pointing at the gun.

"Are you sure we won't need something like that?"

Todd shook his head. "No way. One hundred percent certain, leave it just where we found it. What's that old adage, you bring a gun into the picture you know it's gotta go off at some point. In fact, let's make sure that doesn't happen."

And so Todd worked quickly to remove the bullets from the gun before sliding the deadly weapon back inside the confines of the safe. There, that's better. You never knew when impulse would take precedence over common sense, you may as well remove the danger factor and save someone's life.

"NOW WHAT are they up to? I mean, we lost them on the freeway and those cars are a dime a dozen in this town…but still? Check the license plate?

They did, and they confirmed it. The Scanlon's BMW.

"Sure pops up in convenient locations doesn't it?"

"First the Cashman estate, now the parking lot of the offices of Livingston Enterprises."

"What do you think they're up to?"

"One way to find out."

This was Dalrymple and Benes, inside their unmarked, parked in the same lot as Patrick's BMW. They were careful not to park right next to it, but fortunately it was evening and there were plenty of parking spaces. Dalrymple shut the engine off and the two contemplated their next move.

"You think Gleason has a meeting with Livingston?"

"I don't know, Sandy."

"I'm just asking," he said. "You know, speculating as to the connection between Scanlon and Gleason, Livingston and the murders of Cashman and Beaufort."

Dalrymple just tossed his partner a look. "Do you ever use first names?"

"Sure, Ernie."

Great, nicknames.

"So, how long do you think we should wait?"

Dalrymple checked his watch. Time was closing in on ten that night. He stole a look up at the office tower, gauging the number of lights that were visible from the windows. Not many. Wasn't exactly prime business hours, unless you conducted lots of transactions with the Pacific Rim, they were the only ones doing business at this hour. Well, legitimate business. Dalrymple said, "We sit tight till we think we're wasting our time. That's the risk of a stakeout, sometimes leads pan out and sometimes they don't and only your mind and your ass are any worse for wear."

Benes shifted in his seat.

The two partners remained in the dark, the only hint of light coming from the clubs and restaurants on the nearby Sunset Strip. Snazzy cars whizzed by and even an occasional pedestrian wandered by. No one paid any attention to them.

Just then Dalrymple's cell rang, the sound deafening in the night. Damn, he should have switched it over to vibrate. He multi-tasked, answered the phone while checking outside to see if anyone had looked askance their way. The coast looked clear, and so he spoke.

"Dalrymple."

"Office Meehan here, you had asked me to call when the lab report came in?"

"Yup. What have you got?"

"First of all, the bills found around Lottie Cashman's body, definitely an older issue from the Federal mint, we're still tracing where they might have been printed. But based on their serial numbers they are at least seven years old; none even carry a recent year on their face."

"That's pretty inconclusive."

"Still, sir, it's possible those bills are some of the ones stolen years ago by the widow's husband, that Fast Cash character. Perhaps the stash was hidden in that basement all along, maybe hidden behind the wall along with the body."

"Doubtful, the money was too clean. Still, it's a good theory that Fast Cash's fortune is finally starting to turn up; we should be sure to match the bills with the one we found floating in the Scanlon's pool. Until then, it's all speculation, but it does give credence to my theory that Fast Cash Cashman is no more dead than I am."

"Uh, Detective?"

"Yes?"

"I had said first of all. That means there's a second of all."

Christ. Just what he needed, a junior talking back to him. "Shoot, Meehan. What is it?"

"The body. The skeleton. We checked dental records. It's a match. The body…he's…"

"He's who? Out with it?"

"We've identified him as Jack Cashman. Fast Cash has been found, and he's been plenty dead longer than the week it's been since the courts said so."

"Well if that isn't an interesting turn of events, I don't know what is," Dalrymple said. "Look, we'll be back at the offices in a little while to check over those reports, we may have…no wait, shit, we'll definitely have some company. Benes, slide down. Dalrymple out."

Dalrymple had little chance to process this new information, because the rear entrance to the office building opened up and a lone figure emerged into the darkness. He was wearing all black, and even at this distance there was something vaguely familiar about this guy. Dalrymple tossed his partner a knowing look, asking for confirmation that he saw what he saw. Benes nodded.

Just then the two detectives burst forth from their unmarked, their moves choreographed as though they'd been in rehearsals for weeks and were now ready for their opening night. Klieg lights lit the air from a nearby club, but you had to admit, the Hollywood setting really worked. As for their performance, the first line wasn't all that original, but it was effective enough to jolt the audience.

"Freeze, police."

Both detectives had their guns drawn and moved rapidly toward their prey. The man in black just stood there, like his legs had failed him. His head turned around, looking this way and that, as though searching for something, perhaps someone. But nope, it was just him, he was all alone, but certainly not for long. Benes and Dalrymple approached their man.

"Officers, I didn't do anything..."

"Put your hands up, and we'll do the talking."

The man's hands, unencumbered, shot into the air faster than a speeding bullet.

Benes took out a flashlight and he shined it forward, illuminating the man's face. "Wait a minute, you're not Gleason. Shit, it's the other guy who was with him..."

"Gleason? Not sure who you're talking about...officers."

"It's Detectives. Dalrymple and Benes. And who might you be?"

"My name is Patrick Scanlon, and I believe you've been looking for me."

It didn't take a brain surgeon to assess what was going to happen next. And so for the second time since this case had begun, Detective Earnest Dalrymple got to issue the following statement: "Patrick Scanlon, you're under arrest for the murder of Carl Beaufort." And then he added for good measure, "Oh, and for the murder of Lottie Cashman."

As much as he enjoyed this crowning moment, Dalrymple still knew there were loose ends to be dealt with. Because even though he had his man for these baffling, senseless murders, one other killing remained unsolved. That of Jack "Fast Cash" Cashman.

"Cuff him."

Neither Dalrymple nor Benes thought it odd that Patrick did not protest his arrest.

It was almost as though he'd willingly walked into their trap, and that the last thing on his mind was trying to give the police the slip. Now, who would try and do a thing like that?

TODD, THAT'S who.

He watched the entire scenario play out from a safe distance inside the building, careful to keep not only himself but his shadow from discovery. Still, he counted on the fact that both Dalrymple and Benes would be satisfied in capturing their Most Wanted Man, the elusive Patrick Scanlon, that they wouldn't bother to search the rest of the area. For Patrick's part, he knew he had to resolve this portion of the case, to turn himself in and prove his alibi for Carl Beaufort's murder. As for Lottie Cashman, well, he was definitely in town for that one and his only alibi for that one was his wife, Cindy. A woman who wasn't looked upon too favorably by the cops either.

Still, it was a close call. Good thing Todd had heard the ringing cell phone coming from the parking lot, they might both now be in police custody, and good luck trying to explain a couple million in cold cash that was obviously hotter than the L.A. sun. Neither he nor Patrick had heard a word of the call, but the duration of the call had given them time to think.

"You have to trust me," Todd had said when he suggested Patrick give himself up.

"Like I trusted you years ago?"

"Patrick, we are not getting into the past, right now it's about solving the problems of the present. Look, I got us the needed cash, I'll deliver it to Langston. You're going to have to deal with the police eventually."

Eventually happened to turn out to be now. So, as Todd watched the two detectives place Patrick in the back of their car and speed off toward Downtown LA, he emerged into the parking lot with a duffel bag he could barely carry. But he would, its contents were far too valuable to leave behind. Too many lives hung in the balance and the money he had looted from Livingston's safe was the cost of survival.

He tossed the duffel into the back seat of Patrick's car, and then he got behind the wheel. Just then his cell phone vibrated. See, he knew that when on a surreptitious mission, you turn the ringer off. Geez, that's Con Man 101.

"This is Todd," he said.

"It better be."

"Mr. Livingston, I presume?"

"Still not funny."

Todd decided to chuckle.

"You better have what I want."

Todd said, "I have the money."

"How very very industrious of you, Mr. Gleason," he said. "I'll be most curious to hear how you managed to find Fast Cash's fortune after so many others have tried and failed."

"Oh, Mr. Livingston," Todd said, "it wasn't really that difficult, you just needed to know what to look into. So, are we ready for the exchange, money for hostages?"

"I look forward to our next meeting," spoke Langston Livingston.

Todd did too, and so he turned the engine, swung the car out of the parking lot and headed back down the stop and go traffic of La Cienega Boulevard. This town they called Los Angeles, its streets sure were straight and narrow for a place with so many angles.

CHAPTER TWENTY

"**WELCOME BACK** aboard, Mr. Gleason. You're alone, I see."

"You're observant, I see."

"This way, please, Mr. Livingston awaits your presence."

"Did he miss me?"

Garth chose not to answer that. Instead he pulled open the gate and indicated that Todd should take the lead. Todd did as requested, walking down the plank and back toward a docked *Nutcracker*. He kept stealing looks behind him, trying to assess Garth's movements. Did he have a gun hidden somewhere? Was he going to hogtie him? Nope, he was just making sure Todd wasn't going to pull any funny stuff.

It was early morning, just after six o'clock. Nearly twenty hours had passed since they had all gathered aboard the yacht. Todd had spent the night doing what a thief who'd scored the mother lode would do: he'd counted his spoils, divided it up into appropriate piles, and then he'd organized it neatly inside a suitcase he'd found inside the Scanlon's closet. Yes, he'd gone back there after Patrick had been picked up by the police, and as he'd counted bill after bill, watched as hour after hour slipped by, he thought of his friend and wondered just what kind of grilling he was getting downtown. But Patrick's plight would have to wait, and Todd knew that ultimately his friend had innocence on his side. So, better to take care of more pressing matters, which meant finally getting Langston Livingston off their backs.

Todd stepped onto the deck, grateful for the trek from car to cabin to soon be over. This suitcase was weighing down his arm, altering his walk. Just then Garth stepped around him, opened the door to the main cabin and escorted their guest inside.

No one was there except for Langston.

"Where is everybody?" he asked.

"All in good time, Mr. Gleason. Where is Patrick?"

Todd grinned. "All in good time."

"If I didn't dislike you so much, I think I would offer you a job."

"Flattery will get you nowhere."

Langston harrumphed. "I trust you have my money?"

"You called, I said yes, didn't I?"

"Indeed, but you are hard to trust. Which is why I felt it better that both you and I have our exchange in private. As you pay off each debt, I will then instruct Garth to release my guests one by one. And just so you know I won't be pulling a fast one on you—perish the thought—you'll be able to see them walk off the boat and onto the safety of the land. From there, what they do is their business—as long as they stay out of mine." Langston folded his hands against his sizable belly, then grinned his alligator smile. "Care to tell me where you found

Fast Cash's money? Frankly, I'm surprised that you not only found it so quickly, but that it exists at all. Part of me thinks you found it awhile ago and you've been holding out on all of us."

"Nope, just found it last night. It was easy, really, once you gave it some careful thought. Everyone thought it was in the basement."

"And?"

Todd hesitated. He'd thought about this question all night, how he would answer it. Whatever story he came up with, Langston would know soon enough it was a crock. So he went for a simple one. "The attic of the Cashman house. Under the floorboards."

Langston nodded. "Clever enough, I suppose. Do the opposite of what everyone suspects. Only a crook would think that way."

Todd wasn't sure whom he was referring to there. He decided to let that "crook" comment pass.

"So, how do you want to do this?"

"Let's dispense with the least personal cases first," Langston said. "Ms. Beverly Mills, for instance. I believe you promised that some of the money you found would go toward freeing up her debts and ensuring she gains full control of her real estate agency."

"That's fine," Todd said.

He sat down opposite Langston, set the suitcase at his side with a heavy thud. Langston looked suitably impressed, no doubt assuming the entire bag's contents were his for the taking. Todd reached over and pulled the zipper open and proceeded to dig inside. As he riffled through the bag, he noticed Garth watching him hawk-like.

"Must he be here?"

"Security measures are always in place."

Yeah, Todd thought, like having cameras at the workplace.

"Let's go, we don't have all day," Langston urged. "I've been away from my other business interests long enough."

"Yes, I'm sure there are many more people littered about Los Angeles whose fingers were spared with your being away. Trust me, I'm more than happy to see my friends finally free from your threats."

With that, Todd withdrew the first of the thick envelopes he'd created, this one marked "Beverly Mills." Langston caught the bag Todd tossed into the air, his greedy fingers flipping open the flap and foraging inside. He sniffed at the money and let out a satisfied breath.

"Very nice," he said, with a nod toward his help. "Garth, please release Ms. Mills. And toss in one of those horrible bodyguards. The little one called Fred."

Garth disappeared from the room, only to return moments later, Beverly and Fred in tow. Todd watched as the two of them stepped off the boat and back up the gangplank. He noticed a worried Fred looking back and for a moment Todd felt bad for the little guy. Both he and Barney had certainly gotten more than they'd bargained for with this case. Still, he was safe now, and he imagined Barney would soon be making an exit as well, and the two of them could return to New York.

Onto the next package. Todd removed a second, equally thick package. This one said, "Scanlon." He began to hand it to Langston, whose arms were already outstretched and whose tongue wagged at the very thought of such a huge payoff. Based on the amounts Langston had given him, Patrick had gotten into more financial trouble than even Cindy had let on; or perhaps the amount owed had something to do with the interest due on running away from a debt. Those weren't exactly fixed rates by a bank.

As Langston's fingers touched the edge of the envelope, Todd chose that moment to pull it back.

"What are you doing, Mr. Gleason?"

"Before I hand this over to you, I want to see Cindy Scanlon. And toss in Barney, too. I want them already on deck, ready to leave this piece of crap boat the moment I place this envelope in your grubby hands."

"You're in no position to bargain."

"Actually, Langston, I'm very much in control. You see, I have my cell phone in my pocket and the police are on speed dial—a couple of detectives by the names of Dalrymple and Benes. Patrick is with them, and he's ready to spill everything he knows about your business practices, about how you've held a boatload of people hostage. At this point, he's got nothing to lose. The police already want to charge him with murder. If he's going down, so are you. So, the situation is this: if Dalrymple doesn't get a call from me in the next thirty minutes, this pier is going to be surrounded by so many men in blue you'd think it was an academy graduation—or a funeral. So, your choice, get Cindy and Barney up on deck right now."

Langston, clearly not happy, nodded toward Garth. "What he says."

A hesitant Garth finally did as instructed, and moments later there stood Cindy Scanlon, and at her side the big behemoth named Barney, a pairing straight out of Beauty and the Beast. Seeing they were in good health and relatively good spirits,

Todd tossed the envelope of cash at his portly adversary. Again, the greedy glutton went through the same ritual: opening, sniffing, exhaling. He then nodded once more at Garth, and the next set of hostages was released.

"See how well this works when everyone cooperates?" Todd said.

Langston grunted, then said, "Just get on with the next payment, I want back the money Jack Cashman owed me. I certainly deserve that, considering all of his money was ill-deserved. It was all stolen, he never earned a penny of it."

"Hello pot, it's kettle, you're black," Todd said.

"Mr. Gleason, I'm not sure what I find more tiresome, your empty threats or your sense of humor."

"Most people go with the humor thing," he said.

"Can we get on with things?"

"Sure, why not," Todd said confidently. "You showed good faith, releasing Fast Cash's daughter, eh?"

"Cynthia doesn't reveal that to just anyone, Mr. Gleason. You must, indeed, be someone of importance to her. Wonder how Patrick would feel about such a thing."

Todd thought of Patrick and he thought of Cindy and the complicated relationship the three of them had. Then he swallowed guilt and decided this wasn't the place for it, no matter what Langston tried to dredge up.

So, another envelope, another exchange, and at long last the long-held debt of Jack Cashman to Langston Livingston was finally brought to a close. Langston savored this one, since it was Jack Cashman's debt that first started his whole string of robberies, his attempt to free himself of debt, of obligations. To Langston, to the daughter he never knew. Seven years was a long time to wait, and truthfully Langston didn't appear all that happy. Todd really couldn't care. One more person needed his help. Lana.

"Well, Mr. Gleason," Langston finally said, stuffing the envelope into a drawer along with the other two. "We've come to the moment of truth, haven't we?"

"Meaning?"

"Mr. Marty Beam."

"Indeed," Todd said, mimicking the man. He turned to Garth and said, "Bring Lana here. To the cabin. I want to see her, talk to her."

"Not a chance in hell..." Langston started.

Todd withdrew his cell phone, his thumb on the keypad. "Shall I press send?"

Shifting uncomfortably in his seat, Langston Livingston shot Todd an unexpected look of admiration. "You know, Todd, had we not been on opposite sides this entire time, I think we could have been a good team. We still could you know, I do find myself in the market for a new right-hand man. Patrick Scanlon just didn't have the guts, that killer instinct. You though..."

"So you said. However, I prefer working alone. Bring. Me. Lana." Then Todd smiled, dimples enlivening the room. "Now."

A few minutes later a tired-looking but still ravishingly beautiful Lana Davies was escorted into the main cabin, fear and uncertainty written across her lovely face. At her side was Garth, and in his hand was a gun.

"Todd, what's going on?" Lana said.

"It's okay, I've got everything under control," he said. But Todd was not amused at the sight of the gun, nor its position. He glared across the table at Langston. "There's no need for that."

"Oh, I think otherwise, my boy. See, I've let you play out this little scenario as you've scripted it, but only for as long as it served my purpose. I'm rewriting it. Your relationship with Ms. Davies clearly means a great deal to you and I seriously doubt you would jeopardize her well-being with any of your funny moves. So, let's just play nice now, hand over the money owed to me by Marty Beam and I'll release his daughter. It's that simple."

"Actually, it's not."

Lana's eyes opened wide. "Todd, what are you doing?"

"Yes, Todd, what are you doing? This is hardly the time for games."

He shrugged. "No games. It's just that there's no money left. I paid you well over two million dollars just now, and frankly, I think that's more than enough. It has to be, because that's all I found under the floorboards in the attic. Either Fast Cash managed to escape with or spend some of the money he stole, or perhaps the amount he stole was misquoted. No matter, there's no money left."

Todd lifted the suitcase and turned it upside down. Nothing fell out because there was nothing left inside it. No more money, no more marked envelopes, nothing but empty air.

"I am not amused by this display, Mr. Gleason."

"You can cry all the way to the bank for all I care, there's no more money."

"Then Ms. Davies stays in my company until we find more."

"Not happening."

"Todd!"

"It's okay, Lana, I've got everything under control. Mr. Livingston here knows he has no choice but to release you," he said. "Don't you, sir?"

"I want my money," Langston said.

"Then I suggest you get it from Marty Beam himself."

"Todd, what are you talking about?" Lana asked, trying to wrestle herself from Garth's grip.

Todd gazed once at each of the assembled parties, and then said, "While you've all been cruising the ocean, I've been staying a step ahead of the case. Seems the police have identified the skeleton found in the Cashman basement—it belongs to Jack, and it's clear he's been buried there all these years. And it's also clear that's why I didn't retrieve all the money Fast Cash stole from his bank robberies, because obviously Marty Beam made off with the rest of it. I'm sorry, Lana, we can't be sure exactly what happened but it's going to be obvious to the police that Marty Beam had something to do with his late friend's death. So the case of Fast Cash is going to be reopened, and his death is probably going to be ruled a homicide." Todd paused. "Which means the police are going to be interested in anyone who had the slightest connection to Marty Beam. Including his employer. So you see, Langston, the more you keep Ms. Davies a hostage here, the more the police are going to be focusing on your business interests. You're right in the middle of everything, threats, mutilations, kidnappings. It only a small leap to murder."

A stalemate had been reached. No one said a word.

Wait, actually, Todd did, after holding up his cell phone again. "Cops. Speed dial."

Todd and Langston silently faced off, expressions saying

nothing and everything. Finally, a voice could be heard in the otherwise silent cabin.

"Let them go."

"Mr. Livingston?"

"Garth, I said let them go."

Garth released Lana from his hold, and she went running into Todd's arms, where she hugged him fiercely. Todd willingly accepted her embrace, and he even managed a big smile that he aimed Langston's way. Then he realized it was probably high time they got out of there. But before they did, Todd turned back at his new nemesis, and said, "And remember, Langston. Any trouble comes Lana's way, it's going to mean major trouble for you. Your to-date Teflon existence is over, soon the only thing that will stick to you are criminal charges. Good day, it's been a pleasure."

Todd and Lana walked out of the cabin, up on deck, and across the gangplank, and once they hit solid ground Lana began to shower him with kisses. When they broke, Lana asked him the simplest of questions.

"You were brilliant…almost scary. Did you really have the police on speed dial?"

Todd smiled those dimples of his when he said, "Of course not, if there's one thing you should know about Todd Gleason, it's this. Cops and cons don't mix."

SO, THEY were finally alone, Todd Gleason and Lana Davies. Still standing in the parking lot of Pier 44, the early sun shimmered down on them. The crash of the waves against the shore, the jostling of the moored boats, all of it added to the romantic feel of the morning. You could almost hear the music swell as the separated lovers reunited and embraced, their lips touching, gently at first, growing with passion...

Wait, it's not yet time for the happy ending.

For Todd and Lana, there was something keeping them from their carnal indulgences. That something was another woman. Yup, while Beverly and Barney and Fred had all gone their separate ways, Cindy Scanlon had remained nearby, waiting to finish unfinished business. Todd, Lana still in his arms, watched as Cindy approached.

"So, you want to tell me where you found Fast Cash's money?" she asked.

"It's probably best neither of you know where we found it."

"Yes, speaking of we—where's my husband? I think I deserve to know that much."

"Cindy, you think you're entitled to know where Patrick has gone? Maybe he doesn't want you to know, did you ever think of that? You manipulate him into a job with Langston so you can learn more about your father, and when the money begins to flow, well, you just flow right along with it, don't you? The car, the jewelry, the good life you always dreamed you deserved. The life you thought only Patrick could provide for you. But how do you reward him? You ultimately put your trust in another man—and not just any man, but in me—and you go so far as to knock him out of commission. Hiring Barney to keep track of me while Fred keeps Patrick far from the action, you know what that says to me? You don't trust anyone—not me, and certainly not your husband. Has it been worth it, Cindy? Finding out the truth about your father, was it worth risking your marriage, your life? What did Jack Cashman ever do to deserve such loyalty from you?"

That word, "loyalty," he practically spat it at her. Todd knew he was being harsh, and perhaps he was transferring his own feelings about fathers and responsibility and trust to the current situation, but at the moment he couldn't care. He had been manipulated from the moment Cindy sashayed her way onto Bermuda and disrupted his life. He'd been threatened, arrested, interrogated, and ultimately he'd resorted to flat-out burglary, all in an effort to get friends old and new out of trouble all of them could have avoided had they some control over their ambitions.

Cindy was about to speak, perhaps in her defense, but it was Lana who got the next words out.

"What a minute, Jack Cashman is your father?" she said to Cindy.

Todd shot Lana a worried look, a similar one to Cindy. He noticed both women had taken a step back from the other, like they were returning to their respective corners after a brutal round. Suddenly Todd wasn't their common point of interest, new light was being shed on this situation and it threatened to blind them all.

"Yes, yes he is. Why should that matter to you, Lana?"

"Because of who my father is."

Cindy's expression wavered. "What are you talking about? Todd?"

"Her last name is not Davies," Todd said. "I mean, her maiden name, it's Beam."

"Marty Beam's daughter," Cindy said.

Lana nodded. "And I've been wondering for years what

happened to him after that day of the robbery. Wondered from afar. It's only when Lottie Cashman started her stupid campaign to get Fast Cash declared legally dead that I decided to finally find out the truth. And then when…in the mail…"

"…the map arrived," Cindy said.

"Exactly. The case suddenly seemed more alive than ever before. Someone wanted me…or perhaps us, to finally know the truth."

"And so here we are, both of us working two sides of the same case."

"Looks that way."

"With both of us turning to Todd for help."

Oh, good, Todd thought, he was back in the picture. Frankly, he was just glad neither of the women had turned this into a catfight and turned on each other, or worse, on him. Since he'd heard Cindy's story of her father and then learned Lana's tale of parental woe, he'd been wondering when to tell them about the other, figuring the exchange wouldn't go over well. And perhaps if they had learned it sooner that would have been the case. But after surviving a day at sea, since ridding Langston Livingston from their lives, they seemed to have bonded. The two women reached out and hugged, an embrace seven years in the making, the coming together of families affected by the same turn of events, a mystery born from greed, from desperation, now playing out in the most uncommon of ways. The men's true victims, not the people whose money had been stolen from their insured bank accounts, but the little girls who wanted nothing more than a hero they called Dad.

"Uh, ladies, as great as this tender reunion is, there's still a few mysteries to be solved," Todd said, and the sudden shift in his tone had the two of them breaking from their hug.

"You know something more?"

"Cindy, I don't know how to tell you this. But I overheard those detectives Dalrymple and Benes discussing the case. The skeleton found alongside Lottie Cashman's body? It's been positively indentified. I'm sorry, it's Jack Cashman."

Cindy took a deep breath before she spoke. "You want to tell me where you 'overheard' this information?"

"Uh, it was just before…well, just after Patrick and I found the money. The cops, they were lying in wait for us."

"Todd, what happened?"

"Dalrymple arrested Patrick—for the murders of Carl Beaufort and Lottie Cashman."

"But we all know he's not a killer…I've got to go to him. He needs my help."

With that, Cindy Scanlon started to dig into her purse for her keys and Todd did nothing to stop her. He knew this was the right thing to happen, for him to take a step back and let the wife go to the ultimate rescue of her husband, perhaps it was what they would need to begin the healing process.

As Cindy started off down the lot toward her car, Todd called after her. Cindy stopped, turned back. The sight of her, caught in a beam of light that highlighted her hair, her figure, her mysterious allure, he couldn't help but smile that of a wistful collegiate, one who knew that all he'd once wanted was finally gone, released from some pent up fantasy of what was possible, what was unachievable. Cynthia Scanlon, she'd entered his life so simply, sitting next to him in Literature class, and now, all these years later, all these miles they'd gone, both physically and emotionally, it all came down to this last moment.

Cindy came running back and hugged Todd, tightly, deeply. "You know I'll always love you, deep down."

For his part, Todd just let her words sink beneath his skin, settle somewhere inside him, in a place where he held the dearest of memories. As they parted, Todd gave her a kiss on the cheek.

"Look, I should tell you one last thing."

"What's that?"

"Patrick knows. What happened between us, the night of your mother's funeral. He all but said so. When you were so vulnerable, after you'd learned the truth about your father. The fact that you turned to me and not your husband, I just thought you should know he knows."

Cindy swallowed heavily, guilt settling inside her. "Thanks, Todd, you know, for telling me. Guess I've got a few things to make up for."

"Here, maybe this will help," Todd said, withdrawing from his front pocket a thick stack of bills. It was one of the big stacks from Langston's safe, nothing but hundred dollar bills.

"What's this?"

"Bail money? Second honeymoon money? Your choice," he said, tossing it Cindy's way. "You can't exactly begin to heal your marriage with Patrick locked behind bars."

And just like that, with the world suddenly gone quiet and with the sun temporarily hidden by a random passing cloud, Cynthia O'Neil Scanlon walked off into the blazing morning, a flick of her flame-colored hair the last image ingrained upon Todd's mind. There was no soundtrack, just the click of Cindy's heels against the ground, until those too faded into the morning's ocean mist.

"You okay?" Lana asked, taking hold of his hand.

"Yeah, I'm good."

"So, you slept with your best friend's wife the night of her mother's funeral? That's the big secret between you two?"

Todd shook his head. "Nope. It was a betrayal far worse than that."

"What's worse?"

"That night, Cindy told me that life with Patrick wasn't what she expected, and not what she wanted. She told me she still loved me. It's one thing to give yourself physically to another person, but what Cindy wanted to give me that night was something more than her body. Her heart." He paused. "Which I couldn't accept."

"Todd Gleason, you're a funny guy."

"Gee, thanks," he said, a crooked smile bringing his dimples to life.

"Come on, it's been a long day. Let's go home. You spoke of mysteries, I've got one of my own to solve. It's time you met Mother Beam properly."

A freeway ride later, they pulled into the now-familiar apartment complex where Lana lived with her mother. Walking up the stairs, Lana turned to him and placed a kiss upon his lips. Todd liked it, he liked Lana.

"What was that for?"

"Consider it a promise."

He liked the idea of a promise, too.

Then Lana unlocked the door and escorted Todd into the apartment. And unlike the last time when she'd been sneaking him in, there was no blaring noise from the television. In fact, there was not a sound to be heard anywhere inside.

"Mother?" Lana asked wearily.

Something felt wrong. Very wrong.

"Mother, where are you? I told you to be waiting for me. Momma? Momma?"

Todd was first into the small den, where a piece of paper taped to the screen caught his attention. "Perhaps she's more in the mood for *Jeopardy*."

"What does that mean?"

"What is: you tell me," Todd said.

"Now isn't the time for funny, Todd. I'm worried, Momma's done something stupid...."

"Maybe that will shed more light on what's going on," Todd said, pointing to the piece of notepaper taped to the television screen.

An overly concerned Lana ran over and went to rip the note off the screen, but Todd at the last minute prevented her. It could be evidence, he instructed, they shouldn't tamper with it.

"Evidence? Oh, Momma, where are you? What have you done?"

"At the moment, I suspect only your mother knows."

He learned forward to read what Momma Beam had written. What it said could only be interpreted as an admission. A simple two words: "I'm sorry."

"What does your mother have to be sorry about?"

Lana Davies had nothing to say right now.

"Lana?" Todd asked, taking hold of her arms, making her face him. "You want to tell me what you've done?"

She wrestled away from him and ran past the television, where she stopped before the answering machine on the small table. The light was blinking and filled with hope she depressed the button. A disembodied voice filled the room.

"Ms. Davies, Randy Carter from the lab? I have your results back—but I think it's not going to be what you were hoping for. The fingerprints came up with a match. I'm sorry, the man whose fingerprints were on that glass was not Marty Beam. Uh, it was a man named Jack Cashman. Call me back, we can discuss further."

Lana exhaled, then dropped to a nearby chair. "That can't be, Fast Cash is dead, you said the police said so," she said.

Disbelief covered her pale face. Todd was a bit confused too. But that could wait, right now Todd crouched down, took hold of her hands and waited for her to focus on him. "Lana, what's going on? Maybe it's time you told me everything you know. Those lab results? Your mother's disappearance? And hey, here's a thought. How about, finally, you tell me the real reason you went to Bermuda?"

WHATEVER STORM had been threatening the island paradise of Bermuda, the wind seemed to have caught it, changed its mind about sweeping across the land and altered its course to instead do battle with the ocean. Because sunshine bore down on the little island with a vengeance, almost as though summer had returned and with it would come the cruise ships and the tourists and the occasional brave soul who would wander into the dank-looking Buzz Factory looking for something off the beaten path.

Such was not the case at the moment. Happy hour was still an hour away, and so even his locals represented a small group of drunken loyalists. He'd poured a few beers, a couple Irish whiskeys, and the boys went about their business, playing darts, watching football from England, just going through the daily motions of island life.

Buzz supposed he was doing the same. Washing glasses, serving drinks, watching the rise and fall of the sun, day after day, doing as he pleased as the rest of the world plotted, schemed, lived. Some days he actually felt bored, knowing all that his Factory and his patrons and their not-so-surprising revelations were all that awaited him each and every day behind the long wood bar. Still, he could have had it worse.

He could have been born a frog.

"Hey, little guy, you awake in there?" Buzz asked, tapping on the glass tank.

Toad didn't move, but he did blink. Big eyes stared right back at Buzz, his temporary guardian.

"You want some food, that give you some energy?"

Buzz plinked a couple pellets into the water, watched as they dropped to the bottom of the tank amidst the gravel. Toad still didn't move.

"Yeah, I know, I miss him, too," Buzz said.

"Hey, Buzz, you done talking to that froggie thing? How about another round for the boys? It's about happy hour, ain't it?"

Buzz looked at his patron, a guy who spent more than a few nights and paychecks inside the Factory and then for good measure he looked up at the clock. Six minutes to four; happy hour was mere minutes away. When he first opened the Factory, Buzz had been a real stickler for his details, if someone wanted a drink even a minute before happy hour began he charged them full price. You don't make money being a nice guy. Buzz, he was a businessman and he said rules were rules. You want it cheaper, you wait a couple minutes.

"Sure, why not, let's kick start happy hour a few minutes early," he said, and then began the easy task of pouring six pints of Fuller's Pride. He placed them like soldiers on the bar, and his patron took them two by two by two until each of his friends had been served. He came back and tossed money down on the table. Buzz took it, along with the tip, and brought the arm down on his ancient cash register. The action produced waves in the fish tank, and Toad rode them as he went in search of his snack. As he gobbled up his food, Buzz found himself staring down at the open cash register, at the assorted bills, Bermudian, British, and American. That's what he did all this for, for the almighty dollar, pound, whatever, it gave him his freedom and his life, and the ability to do as he pleased.

He smiled at the cash, then back up at Toad. "Yup, I agree boy. Sometimes you just need that extra push to get you moving. Todd, he's clever to look to you for advice, you're good on your feet—webbed that they are. Trust your instincts, I think that's what Todd said before he left for his little adventure. Me, I think I'd forgotten that a bit. Thanks for the reminder." And with that he tossed Toad another treat, just because.

When Buzz closed his register and turned back to the bar he found himself face to face with another patron, a new, wrinkled face amongst a crowd of familiar ones. Dressed in bright blue, almost like a giant blueberry.

"What can I get you, ma'am?" he asked. "Rum swizzle? Nice and sweet."

"How about a divorce?" the woman replied.

Buzz blanched, but then realized he had no choice but to reply. "Now those are bitter."

CHAPTER TWENTY-ONE

NOBODY LIKES to lose, especially in a town like LA, where failures are someone else's successes, where a scandal that shakes your reputation drives ratings for those who revel in the telling. Whether its a hyped TV show being canceled, a bad opening weekend for your latest movie, a wildfire sweeping across your million-dollar home, or an assistant posting your home videos on YouTube, most seek the advice of press agents, managers and agents before deciding on their plan of attack, whether to attack like a viper or shrink like a violet.

Beverly Mills, who had come to town filled with a mix of regret and ambition, wasn't going to take this latest incident lying down. The humiliation Langston Livingston had wrought upon her by threatening to expose her debts, the sordid truth about the genesis of her agency, her actual birth name, what she had done, well that was more than she was going to stand for. She had vowed to seek revenge upon the big beast once she was free of his clutches and claims, and now, thanks to that charmer Todd Gleason she was primed and ready to take charge.

And she had brought with her reinforcements.

Entering the office tower at the corner of Sunset and La Cienega, Beverly walked right up to the security center and asked to be announced.

"No, I don't have an appointment. But he'll see me."

"Mr. Livingston has left explicit instructions," said the guard posted behind the security desk. "He's not to be disturbed. No visitors." He paused. "Of any kind."

His wary expression had everything to do with the fact that Beverly was not alone. Flanking her like uneven walking sentries were Barney Stone and Fred Halpern, who had recently been hired by Beverly to act as her bodyguards for this upcoming confrontation. They hadn't needed much persuading, they weren't exactly pleased to have been held against their will either. They both were still dressed in black leather, but their outfits were new; as a thank you for their services Beverly had taken them to this shop off Santa Monica in West Hollywood that had clothes and accoutrements that would appeal to them.

"Ms. Mills has traveled clear across town, she expects to be seen," said Barney.

"Which mean she will be seen," Fred added.

"Are we going to have a problem here, gentleman?" the guard asked.

"As long as you call up and announce Ms. Mills, and only Ms. Mills, I don't foresee any difficulty," Barney replied.

On cue, both men crossed their thick, corded arms.

The guard picked up a receiver and dialed the number. He spoke briefly to Garth, said it was Ms. Beverly Mills…

"…of Beverly Hills…" she interjected proudly.

"…to see Mr. Livingston. Yes, I explained the situation, no, she's not leaving. I thought I would leave the decision up to you." Conversation over, the guard hung up the phone and told them elevator three, it was Langston's exclusive lift.

"It only stops at his floor, and Garth will be waiting for you the moment you step off."

Beverly thanked the man for his good sense and then made her way to the elevator, her men in tow. They shot up the ten floors quickly, and just as the doors were getting ready to reopen, Barney and Fred pressed themselves far against the walls. The ping sounded, and Beverly steeled herself for what was to come.

The doors slid open, and as promised there was the ever-faithful Garth, still dressed in his black chauffeur's outfit and looking none too happy for her having disturbed them. He was about to be even more unhappy, as both Barney and Fred, their bulk notwithstanding, moved with surprising stealth to disable Langston's trusted heavy, taping his mouth, tying his feet with thick cord, handcuffing his hands.

"If you struggle, the knots will only tighten," Barney said. And then, to no one really, he added, "I was once a Boy Scout."

"Yeah, it's where we met, actually," Fred said.

"Remember our first overnight?"

"I'll never forget it…" Fred said, gazing up fondly at his big guy.

"Okay, Romeos," Beverly said. "Let's get a move on. You can reminiscence later."

Leaving Garth alone in the deserted hallway, the three of them made their way down to Langston's office, threw open the main door and then continued on to the inner sanctum. Without any warning, Beverly entered the office and was met by the most unusual of sights. Langston's office, usually so clean, so organized, so…pristine, was an absolute mess. Shattered glass, papers everywhere, picture frames crooked, stuffing sticking out of a torn leather sofa. A buck with a missing antler. And in the midst of it all, Langston Livingston, looking none too well, sitting disconsolately behind his desk.

"Where's Garth?" he asked Beverly.

"Oh, he's indisposed at the moment," she said, a smile gracing her ruby lips.

In fact, she'd taken a page from Cindy Scanlon, and had dolled herself up but good. A flattering dress—even for a woman with a figure as full as hers—expertly-done make-up and nails, her hair perfectly styled. That's what it meant to be a true Beverly Hills sophisticate, always knowing how to dress for any situation, and Beverly Mills, she was willing to play the game no matter the cost. Hell, just as long as she won in the long run.

"Beverly, don't be ridiculous, what could you possibly have done to Garth?"

"Oh, not me. Them."

Another thing to know about this city: always know how to make an entrance. Barney and Fred did so just then, ideally timed to knock that supercilious grin of Langston's to the valley, and instead instill a sudden look of…well, newfound fear was the only description that applied. In the presence of an angry Big Hulk and Little Hulk, who were muscles upon muscles, Langston's fleshy self was reduced to a shivering pile of jellied mush.

Except for one thing. In his hand was a gun, and he aimed it squarely at Beverly.

"Make a move against me, any of you, I'll shoot."

"So what. There's three of us, you get one and two get you. Pick your odds."

The steel-plated pistol wavered slightly, perhaps a reflection of Langston's withering, waning confidence. "Beverly…Esther, what is this nonsense about? Your debts have all been cleared, we have nothing further to say to each other."

"Oh, I disagree, Langston. Boys?"

Both Barney and Fred started toward Langston, who quickly aimed the gun at the two moving figures and depressed the trigger. Both men hesitated, listened as the gun went "click" not "boom" and then they grinned with easy satisfaction. Langston pulled the trigger again, and again, and still the only sound the gun made was a harmless little click.

"That Gleason kid, he sure got me good," Langston said, tossing the gun to the floor. He started to get up from his chair, but his body weight impeded his progress. Barney and Fred made their way around Langston's desk and once again worked their magic, Barney pushing the struggling Langston back down while Fred attended to the wire constraints. A minute later Langston was immobile, his legs secured to his chair, his hands locked behind his neck. For a man whose body gave little room for flexibility, he was stretched to the breaking point. He claimed to not being able to breath.

"Do I look concerned, Langston? Consider this moment your comeuppance."

"You're too late for that," he said.

"What's the supposed to mean?" Beverly asked.

Langston indicated with a finger to look behind Beverly. "That Gleason, scam artist if ever there was one, he never found Fast Cash's supposed fortune. He and Patrick just brazenly came here and cleaned me out. Robbed Peter to pay Peter. Ballsy, I'll give him that, smug too. And how he figured out how to open my safe, not even the security video shows that. But he sure was all smiles on film, knowing I could never use them with the police. Left me nothing but my gun, and funny that, he seems to have emptied it of its bullets before he left. I've been done in by a two-bit con."

"Actually, you're not done in yet. But you will be. Boys?"

Barney swung back around the desk, and lifted from the bowl of nuts the handy metal nutcracker that had somehow been returned to it. He rejoined his partner, who had just unsecured one of the man's hands. Lifted high in the air, Langston tried valiantly to keep them from outstretching his fingers, but to no avail. The jagged claws of the nutcracker closed around the thick middle finger. There was lots of room between flesh and bone, so they would have to squeeze extra hard.

"Beverly, please, tell me what you want. I'll give you anything."

"Of course you will. Because it's not just about paying off my debts, it's forgetting anything you know about me. I want never to see your horrid body bearing down on me, hear your voice, your ugly threats…But we'll get to all that later. First… we crush," she said, and then quickly added, "but wait, let me get settled in for the show. Langston, dear, you still do keep a bottle of champers on ice, don't you? I just hate watching any form of entertainment without the requisite refreshment."

She found the fridge, she found the cold bubbly, and as she popped the cork and poured the liquid, another noise began to fill the room, overtaking the fizzy sound of carbonation. It was a whimper, but soon, real soon, it would be a scream.

"Oh wait, I forgot something," she said, and with that she removed from her purse a small tape recorder. "I always record our little business transactions, why should this one be any different?"

Langston's eyes widened as he realized just how powerless he was.

Then he screamed again as the pressure was applied, again, to the tip of his finger.

"THE TIP of his middle finger was missing," she said. "I noticed it the moment I walked into the bar; he was polishing a glass and I could see that one of his fingers was noticeably shorter than the others. I couldn't help but stare right at him, at it. You remember, surely, you were leaning against the bar right in front of him. You were staring right at me."

"Gee, and I thought you were looking at me."

"I was. Just…not immediately," Lana said. "I'm sorry, Todd. When I saw that you were chummy with him, well, I knew I had to get close to you, to learn all I could. In the end, I couldn't confront him, I needed to know more. I needed confirmation."

"And now you have it," Todd said. "But wait, let's get this straight. The entire time we were together in Bermuda I thought it was my charm and good looks that drew you to me. Instead, I find out you were pumping me for information."

"That's quite an image, Todd."

He smiled at that one. "You know, Lana, you've got a real future in pulling cons. There I thought you wanted me, and all along I was being used. Imagine, while everyone was focused on me that last afternoon—face slapped, drink thrown—you were busy stuffing a bar glass into your purse, because that's ultimately what you'd come to Bermuda for. Something with Buzz's fingerprints on it. Nice distraction, by the way, that slap. Nobody had a clue you were there to get the goods on a man I know as Buzz Smith. A man you thought could be your father, Marty Beam."

"Chip off the old block, aren't I," Lana said. "Or should I say, blocks. It's not just my father who was able to pull the wool over everyone's eyes, looks like Mother Beam had some hidden talents as well. My God, Todd, how is it this has become my life? I think I've finally found the father who disappeared all these years ago, and now my mother goes and disappears. You seem to think that they're together. Do you think they planned it this way?"

"We won't know anything till we get there."

There was, of course, Bermuda. Where were they now? En route.

"So, the two women you were supposedly traveling with. Why ask them to act as your friends?"

"Easy. A woman traveling alone attracts attention. Three gals not so."

"I'm liking the way you operate more and more," Todd said.

"I find it curious that you think devious is a good quality," Lana said. "Though of course you do, we can call your attraction to Cindy Scanlon Exhibit A."

Todd was saved from answering that one when the airplane hit an air pocket and they swayed a bit in the air. Lana let out a little shriek and grabbed Todd's arm. She had confessed little prop planes scared her, but if they were going to get to Bermuda as fast as possible, this had been their only choice. That's what he told her back in Los Angeles, and she knew there was no choice, especially after Todd had phoned the Buzz Factory, only to have it ring and ring and ring. He thought of Toad swimming around near where Buzz kept the phone, would have liked to leave a shout out to his trusted pet but alas, no machine picked up. They quickly packed and grabbed a flight from LAX to Charlotte, North Carolina, where Todd had arranged for a private plane to take them on their final leg of the journey, the short flight to the island he'd come to call home.

The grizzled pilot spoke over the intercom. "Sorry folks, we had some strong winds over the Atlantic the last few days, must have some remnants still sweeping over. Shouldn't be much of a problem. We'll have you safely on the ground in about fifteen minutes. Almost there."

Almost there. Yeah, and then what? Hop a cab to Hamilton, enter the Buzz Factory, ask for a drink, look around for a wayward near recluse from Los Angeles, who just might be angry enough to…what? Kill? Neither Todd nor Lana had given voice to such suspicions, and there was still much to be discovered, but the idea was certainly not without merit. Hence, the rush to intervene and stop any further blood from being shed.

"One thing I still don't get, Lana."

"What's that?"

"What led you to suspect your father might be in Bermuda to begin with? There must have been a clue that made you think Buzz might be your missing father?"

"Lottie Cashman, she inadvertently provided the clue."

"Care to elaborate? We do still have a few minutes before landing. It might be good to know everything before we intrude upon the unknown."

"It was easy, really. One day up at the Cashman estate while taking a meeting with her I confiscated her phone bill," Lana said. "It was after the first of Carl Beaufort's new wave of columns appeared about Lottie planning to have Jack declared legally dead. Everything started with that moment. Like I told you before, I had planned to testify against her, to prevent her from being able to find some kind of closure to her marriage, when all the while my mother and I were still left with the mystery of what really happened to Marty. Lottie was perfectly happy, it seemed, to put it all behind her. But then I got the idea to befriend her, to convince her to let me act as her real estate agent; she was very easily persuaded, what better way to send a message to the courts than to show them you were emotionally ready to move on. Selling Jack's house was the first step. And well, during that session with Lottie…"

"You snooped around her house."

"I was curious about what she would do after the court case was resolved. She kept saying she wasn't sure if she would remain in Los Angeles, and that got me thinking about who else she might know in the world, and where she might end up if she did leave L.A. I was able to secure a year's worth of phone bills from her desk drawer, and it wasn't until the last couple of months that a certain number began to appear with any regularity. So I called it. And do you know what the person on the other end said?"

"The Buzz Factory, may I help you?" Todd said.

Lana nodded.

"And some people think I don't pay attention. So, okay, your snooping around brought about newfound suspicions, and you felt it best to look into the matter first hand. Next stop:

paradise. So you arrive in Bermuda, head directly to the Buzz Factory. I get all that. What doesn't add up is this: if Buzz is Marty, wouldn't you have recognized him? It's only been seven years, surely he can't have changed that much."

"That's the weird thing. I couldn't place him, except for the finger. I don't know, maybe he could have had plastic surgery."

"So then why not have his finger repaired? The one identifiable trait."

Lana shook her head. "That's something only Buzz can answer."

"Well, I think we'll soon have our chance."

The plane banked to the left and had begun its descent through the low-hanging clouds and suddenly the lush, near-tropical greenery of Bermuda appeared before them. Watching out the window as the island grew ever closer, there was a certain intimacy to the moment that both Todd and Lana recognized. They might have met under duplicitous circumstances, but that did not diminish the feelings that had grown out of their experiences.

Just then Lana leaned over, pressed her lips against Todd's, and she ran her hand across his scruffy cheek. For Todd, he felt a familiar stirring and had to admit to wishing they had another half-hour or so before their scheduled landing. As it was, they were still lip-locked when the wheels screeched onto the tarmac and the tiny plane rumbled to the halt at the far end of the runway.

"Thank you for coming with me," Lana suddenly said. "I don't know that I could have done this alone."

"In for a dollar, in for a million," he said. "Besides, it's no fun doing anything alone."

"You have no idea how much I want to be with you."

Todd gulped, said something akin to "uh-huh. "Let's first take care of the matter at hand. The future lies just outside these doors."

And as if by magic, the cabin door opened with a hiss, and the steps presented themselves to the waiting duo. The next step of their crazy adventure awaited them, and so they grabbed their overnight bags and deplaned with a mix of trepidation and excitement. A quick passage through customs had them curbside in mere minutes from arrival, and from there they hopped into a waiting cab.

"Honeymooners?" the cabbie asked, a slight British accent to his voice. "Where we headed, some secluded cottage near the beach?"

"The Buzz Factory, downtown Hamilton," Lana said.

The cabbie, clearly a longtime local, looked impressed. He turned back to Todd and said, "She's a keeper."

"You got that right."

During the thirty-minute ride along narrow roads, where buses halted their progress and near misses with motor scooters threatened to end their trip altogether, they finally hit the city limits of the revered harbor town. All the while, Todd was mostly silent, once again breathing in the crisp sea air, realizing just how much he missed the laid-back atmosphere. From the moment Cindy had come back into his life, Bermuda had taken a back seat to everything, to New York and to Los Angeles, to the stress-free life he'd crafted and the languid pace he'd come to appreciate. Like a real-life Brigadoon, here it was again, emerging out of the mist and at his side was a woman of radiant loveliness, and if that wasn't enough to get the orchestra started, well, then romance may as well have left the building... er, island.

As it was, it wasn't immediate romance that enticed them back to the place where it all started, but an all-too real threat. Nope, on this island it was danger that lurked, and the two of them had come to prevent it. If they weren't too late already.

"Okay, folks, here we are," the cabbie announced. "Place you want is just a couple blocks away. You sure you want the Buzz Factory, it's not exactly known for its tourist trade, you hear?"

"That's okay. You can pull over at the next corner. We'll take it from there," Todd said.

"You're the boss, governor."

Moments later Todd and Lana stood on the corner outside a store that sold T-shirts and other trinkets; it was closed. They checked their watches and adjusted for the time difference, and realized it was late afternoon. The sun still shone brightly, but given the fact that it wasn't exactly the high season for tourists, much of Hamilton had closed up shop early. Todd knew for a fact that the Buzz Factory survived off the locals, so he had faith that the old stand-by would be open for business.

Which meant of course it wasn't.

A hand-written sign posted across the glass window of the front door greeted them.

CLOSED UNTIL FURTHER NOTICE.

"I don't like the look of this," Todd said. "Buzz would never close, not even for a hurricane."

"What do we do?"

"Well, we could knock. Or we could break the door down."

"Got any other options?"

Todd peered at the lovely woman at this side, smiled. She'd

been full of surprises since they'd met, had probably out-conned even him, and so he needed to show her that he wasn't all talk. He knew his way around a problem, too. So Todd crouched down near the doorframe, flipped over a broken piece of the cement pavement, dug down. At last he withdrew a rusted metal key, and he held it high, proud.

"How did you know?"

"Opened the bar a few times for Buzz. Remember, for six months I was one of his regular patrons, and I guess we established some form of trust between us. He cares for Toad, I look out for him. Not bad coming from a con man and a bank robber, people used to relying only on themselves."

"So, what are you waiting for? Open the damn door."

"Ooh, Lana, such forcefulness. That cabbie was right, you are a keeper."

"Do you want to give me the key?"

He grinned, but he also slipped the key in the lock and turned it. The deadbolt gave way, and soon the door opened to an unusual quiet. There were no lights on anywhere, not from beer signs in the window or from the tiny sconces that adorned the walls of the rickety old place. A familiar scent hit them—the fragrant smell of stale beer and sawdust. They stepped inside, and then shut and locked the door behind them. A few seconds passed before their eyes adjusted to the darkness. Todd whispered into her ear to remain just where she was, let him explore a bit.

"I want to come with you."

"I know the layout of the place, I won't bump into anything."

"I don't like this, Todd. Something's very wrong."

"Yeah, I agree."

Still, that didn't stop Todd from moving forward. He made his way across the floor until he'd reached the bar. Using the long bar as a guide, he walked further into the darkened pub. From there he looked up at the cash register, where above it he could make out the outline of the fish tank, home to Toad. He silently waved a hello at his pet. All was silent inside the tank; that was one thing about Toad, he knew that lights out meant beddy-bye. Good froggie.

Except Todd had to wonder just how long the lights had been off, and how long Buzz had not been behind the bar. He moved to the far edge, lifted the false shelf and let himself back behind the long wood and brass bar. From there he reached down to the sink, dipped his hand in the water Buzz used to wash used glasses. It was cold and lacked any remnant of soap. Checking a few glasses on the dish mat, those were bone dry. A sniff of the tap indicated that they hadn't been poured for awhile. What—hours, days? Longer? Couldn't be, Mother Beam hadn't been gone that long.

It occurred to Todd, perhaps his imagination was working overtime. The Factory might be closed because Buzz had an emergency, or the power was out due to the high winds inflicted upon the island the last few days. And if the reason for this closure was as innocent as all that, why then was he skulking around? He moved back to the edge of the bar, where he knew to find a light switch. Flipping first one switch, then a second, he watched as overhead lights and tiny lamps illuminated the dim room. He heard a nearby splash, and so he made his way toward the fish tank and got his first look at Toad in over a week.

"Hey, guy, you look good. Buzz been feeding you well?

Though with this place closed up as it is, maybe you missed a meal or two. Here, let me…"

Todd had gone to search for Toad's pellets but noticed instead a collection of broken glass splattered about the floor, along with a few dark splotches that could only be blood. "Uh, Lana, I think we've found our first clue that not everything is honky dory."

Lana came running over from the entrance and leaned over the bar to see what Todd was pointing to. She tossed Todd a worried look that appeared to ask more questions than he was prepared to answer. But perhaps someone else might be able to shed some light on what had happened—and that someone just then emerged from the darkness of the back room, and in her hand was none other than a hefty-looking revolver.

Todd turned, his mouth widening in surprise. "But wait… you're dead…aren't you?"

The corpse just smiled. "And now it's your turn."

THE ALL-TOO-FAMILIAR woman wasted no opportunity on niceties. The gun blasted and a bullet went wild and wide, hitting the ancient cash register just to Todd's left. It dinged off the metal and the drawer actually opened to reveal a temptingly generous stack of bills. Someone hadn't made a deposit lately. Given other circumstances, he might want her company at the arcade games, she seemed to be a lucky shot.

"Whoa," Todd said.

"Surprised?"

Todd looked back at Lana, then at his assailant. "Doubly."

The woman with the gun stepped out of the shadows, and that's when Lana shook her head with what could only be called utter, total surprise. It was clear to Todd that she had not expected this, not this woman, and not one that was homicidally hungry. This woman, she'd given no indication she was the shoot first and ask questions later kind of lady.

"Lottie?" Lana asked, "It's okay, it doesn't have to go this far. Remember me, from the real estate office? I helped you…I wanted to help you…"

Todd watched as the gun-clad woman's attention went from him to Lana, and that's when he saw a faltering in the woman's cockiness. "I know, dear, and you were a very big help to me, got me on my feet and realized that I'd been waiting in the shadows too long. Everyone affected by Jack's stupid actions had either already paid the price or had just gone on with their lives. Not me, I just sat and waited…and waited more. Foolish of me."

Todd realized he needed to step in, figure out what the hell was going on. Try and disable the gun from Lottie's hand.

"The police reported a body in the Cashman basement," he said. "They reported it as you."

Lottie smiled. "Those two detectives, no doubt, I figured they'd be the first to be called. Which is why I dressed her up to look like me, my bright yellow outfit making the great sacrifice."

"Who?" Lana asked, stepping forward, fear written across her face.

"Oh, she was the easiest of all people to dispose of, poor thing. Called her up, said I had info about Jack and Marty. She came right away."

"Who?" Lana said, a creeping suspicion winding its way up

her spine. She wasn't sure she wanted to hear the answer to her own question.

"Dumb Marty's wife, that gray-haired hag..."

Lana covered her mouth with disbelief and shock; an uncontrollable tear escaped out of the corner of her eye. Todd tried to offer comfort, but Lottie's heart was empty of compassion. She just waved the gun at him. "I shot this off once, missed. I can shoot again, maybe I won't be such a bad shot the second time. Listen to me, Lana, you're better off putting this entire mess behind you. Just another of Jack—and Marty's—casualties."

Lottie Cashman turned to Todd. "Don't mess with me, kid. Trust me, I'm not amused by you. Certainly not your 'involvement' in this case. Who the heck invited you anyway? I can kill you, just like the others."

"Lottie, you're talking crazy."

"Lana, dear, there's nothing you can do anymore. How did you even know I was here?"

"Todd figured it out—well, he thought he had. Since the police reported you dead, and I came home and found my mother missing, I just thought she'd come here to find out about...Daddy, Marty, that she came here because of what he did to us." Lana paused, wiping further tears from her eyes, her cheeks. "Lottie, you started all this with the court case, can't we finally bring it all to an end? Closure, for all of us?"

"How's this for closure?" Lottie let off another gunshot and again the bullet went wild. A bottle of top shelf vodka shattered, glass and liquid dripping onto bottles of lesser spirit.

"Lottie, stop shooting! Put down that gun."

"No can do, can't take the risk my prisoner will escape."

"Your prisoner?"

"Would you like a look at my prized possession?" Lottie Cashman flipped on a nearby switch that gave light to the back room of the Buzz Factory, revealing a pool table, a dart board with its darts firmly positioned as direct hits, and oh, the proprietor of the aforementioned bar. He was rather tied up at the moment, literally. "Say hello to Jack, aka Fast Cash. Jack, say hello to Marty's daughter."

Lana looked at Lottie, shock more evident. "You knew?"

"Jack told me, before we started this…to check to see where all the players were. Right, Jack, dear? "

Buzz tried to speak but it sounded like "mmph." Probably had something to do with the thick tape covering his mouth.

"You okay, Buzz?" Todd asked.

He nodded and he shrugged. Todd took that as sort of a mixed message.

"Hey, no talking to my prisoner, you deal with us and us alone," Lottie said, and by that she meant her and her metal friend. She turned a deadly eye toward Todd. "I told you, I'll deal with you later. What's your gain in all this, just busy corrupting this woman?"

"Corruption is a strange word considering you're the one with the gun," Todd remarked.

"A wise ass, huh? You know what I do with them?"

Todd ducked quickly and with good reason, the gun blew its load again. It missed him by miles as Lana screamed into the echoing silence of the bar.

"Lottie, what are you doing? Please stop shooting."

"Why? There's nothing left for me, dear. Jack and your father ruined my life long ago, and it's about time I get to exact my revenge. No one could just leave us alone, especially not that nosy reporter. He had to die, kept putting the Fast Cash case in the headlines. I decided the only way to move forward was to do away with anyone associated with the case. Your mother included. As for Jack, I just haven't decided what I want to do with him. Couldn't kill him, not just yet. Our reunion had just begun." She turned back toward him. "Lying bastard, thought he could run from me, leave me in the lurch…and then call on me when the money started to run out. Sell the house, have me declared legally dead—all the money will come to you, at last, that's what he said, that's what he promised."

"There's only one slight problem with this situation, Lottie."

"I told you, no talking."

"I thought that applied only to Buzz."

She waved the gun at him. "Spit it out, what's this slight problem?"

"Buzz. He's not your husband. He's Marty Beam."

"Don't be ridiculous, of course he's Jack," she said.

"The finger," Todd said. "That was Marty's trademark, not Jack's."

"No, no, that can't be," Lottie Cashman said, her brow suddenly furrowed, her mind becoming a jumbled mess. She stole a look back at Buzz, then to Todd. Ladies and gentlemen, doubt had entered the building.

"It's true, Lottie, it's just as Todd is saying," Lana suddenly said, trying to inch her way further into the bar. Trying to make some kind of contact with Lottie, whether physical or something deeper, a chance at exploiting the bond she thought they'd begun to develop during the business of the Open House. "The police back in Los Angeles found Jack's body. He was buried in your own basement all these years, you know, you saw it too. It's right where you shot…my…"

Lana couldn't talk, she couldn't find those last words.

"You're wrong," Lottie said.

"No, I can prove this man sitting here is my father, Marty Beam," Lana said, recovering, needing to, knowing she could grieve later. Once this mess was all over, once this situation had been diffused. "Your phone bills, Lottie, I stole them from your home, they led me here to the Buzz Factory. I stole a glass with Buzz's fingerprints, had them tested back in L.A.. They came back the other day: the man now known as Buzz is really Marty, that's why I came back…"

As Lana tried to talk sense into the homicidal Lottie, Todd kept a watchful eye on the situation. Lottie had gradually inched closer inside the bar, which meant she'd moved further away from her captive. Todd crept forward, cautiously making his way to Buzz's side. Lottie and Lana continued to talk…

"…to confront him, finally, to get him to admit to what happened that fateful day seven years ago at California Fidelity. To at last learn the truth…"

Buzz's eyes went wide when Todd began to loosen the tape and rope, he even struggled a bit. Perhaps it was easier to be a sitting prisoner than be a moving target, but Todd knew that if he didn't act now they might all end up like all others who'd run afoul of Lottie Cashman.

Buzz, now free of his constraints, muffled something to Todd. For his part, Todd had no clue what the guy was saying. So he moved to pull the tape from the old guy's mouth. He let out a small screech of pain; tape against beard and skin was not a good combination. That's when a scream filled the room.

"Leave him alone!" Lottie shouted.

She made her move just as Todd finished removing the tape from Buzz's mouth. The once widow, presumed dead, and now very much alive Lottie Cashman flung herself at both men and for a second it was just a pile of legs and arms and one gun. Todd felt a fist connect with his face and he was momentarily knocked silly from the impact. He slid away from the muddle in an attempt to get free and then put a stop to this potentially life-threatening scenario. Still, there was no rationalizing what was happening near him, as two people connected by an unsettled past finally brought to an end whatever pent up frustrations and anxieties existed between them.

All the while Lana stood on the sidelines, words uselessly falling on ears deafened by years of living with pent-up anger. "Lottie, stop fighting him, we'll figure everything out, please… nothing good can come of this."

Well, those words proved horribly prophetic. Because the struggle continued until the inevitable—the gun went off, and then it went off a second time, both blasts a cacophony of violence that brought a sad, sudden silence to the situation. Buzz crumbled to the ground, and so did Lottie, and blood intermingled between them, seeping deep into the floorboards of the old bar.

Todd watched as Lana rushed to Lottie's side. Whatever had transpired between the two the last several weeks, whatever Lottie had allegedly done to her mother, they were both victims of a bigger case, and as such, they had a bond. Todd rushed to his friend, busy holding his side. He feared Buzz was who had been shot. But Lottie's gentle sobbing indicated some all together other scenario.

"Buzz, your first aid kit, where is it? Can you get up, get it?"

"Yeah, kid, I'm fine, bullet just grazed me. I'll be right back."

As Buzz struggled to his feet and went dashing behind the bar, Todd joined Lana, who was cradling the weakening woman. Blood stained Lana's hand, and tears streamed down her cheeks. The moment was unreal, or perhaps surreal, a fuzzy picture laid out before them of a woman desperate to cling to the past and another who wished nothing more than to bury it. One of them would get their wish. Todd had to figure that first aid kit wasn't going to be of much help.

"Lottie, talk to me, please?" Lana managed to say through her tears, her hands caressing the woman's puffy cheek.

"I've suddenly grown tired of talking, Lana dear. Just know that the truth can't be contained, it always comes out in the end. Sometimes you just have to force the issue, see what results come your way. I have no regrets about what I've done and now it's time to find out if my maker has other plans for me."

"Lottie, don't talk that way. Help is on the way…look, Buzz…he's getting some help."

Todd watched as Lottie Cashman looked down the long length of the bar, her eyes focused on the man behind it.

"Jack?" she asked. "Marty? I don't know anymore. Oh, I'm so confused…"

And she never would, as Lottie spoke her last and fittingly appropriate word. Lottie Cashman let out one last final breath, her chest rising for the last time before settling down. As though the giant blueberry outfit had suffered a fatal leak.

Todd held Lana, who held Lottie, who might just be cradling her in an attempt to reach out to the mother she would never see again, never talk to again. Strange that her killer would be the person to offer her any level of comfort at this point, but that's the thing about human emotions, they were unpredictable, rampant, complex.

Together the three of them sat in silence on the floor of the Buzz Factory at a time that should have been called "Happy Hour" and where people should have filled the bar with life and liquid and lively conversation. Death had intruded upon them instead, and for now all they could do was hold each other, think about the precious thing called living.

Too many minutes passed, and still Lana would not budge from Lottie's body. Todd decided to give them a moment's peace, and so he picked himself up from the floor and made his way back toward the bar. Perhaps they all needed a shot of whiskey to help with the shock that ripped through their systems.

"Buzz, how about a shot of…Buzz? Buzz, where are you… oh shit."

Todd looked around the bar but found it empty. No Buzz, no first aid kit either.

"You old dog," Todd said, staring at the door, noticing it wasn't completely closed. Buzz was gone, and with him were still too many answers about the past and about his real identity. Because the truth of the matter was, there was conflicting evidence about just who Buzz really was. Was he Marty, or was he Jack? But all that would have to wait, Todd still thought Lana needed a hit of liquor. So he went behind the bar, where he heard a drip, drip, drip. He looked up and that's when he noticed where that second stray bullet had gone.

Toad's fish tank had a neat whole in it, and the tank was steadily losing its contents.

And Toad, he was just floating, as lifeless as Lottie Cashman.

CHAPTER TWENTY-TWO

DON'T WORRY, Toad's okay. No animals were harmed in the execution of this scheme.

"You scared the crap out of me."

You see, Toad was ever the preservationist. Todd had to figure his learned pet had opted to stop swimming because his motions only increased the speed at which the tank lost its water. And with the puncture wound near the bottom of the tank, after some time he would have lost nearly all of his lifeblood.

Todd busily sought out the thick tape Lottie Cashman had used to tie up Buzz, figuring if it was strong enough to restrain a grown man, it could easily stem the flow of water from Toad's tank. He found the roll at the end of the bar, and quickly ripped off a long swath. Returning to the tank, he placed the tape against the hole and admired his handiwork. Except his handiwork wasn't good enough. Water still seeped from the crack in the tank.

He pulled the tank down from its wooden shelf above the old cash register, placed it upon the bar and in the better light of the bar checked for other leaks. As he removed the tank, the cash register nearly came out of the wall, too, and Todd precariously dangled the tank in one arm while he pushed the register back into place. Once secure, he examined the tank again, figured one more piece of tape would do the trick. He tore off another strip and this time he placed the tape inside the tank, pressing it against the interior wall. Sealing the wound from both inside and out. There, that seemed to do the trick. He wondered where the bullet had gone.

A quick examination didn't reveal much. Perhaps the bullet had hit the bottom of the tank and bounced off? There was no exit wound, and seemingly no harmful piece of metal at the bottom of the tank. Todd had to wonder: maybe the tank hadn't been hit by a bullet, maybe it had been…sabotage.

Todd turned back toward the door. Buzz had been gone a good ten minutes, he could be anywhere, and Todd had to assume that before he left he'd punctured the tank in an effort to slow down any attempt to go after him. What kind of guy would jeopardize his pet's life for a slim chance at hunting down a criminal everyone thought was dead.

A terrible revelation washed over Todd. "Oh shit," he said, and with that he resumed his examination of the fish tank. The black casing at the base of the tank looked untouched, just the usual nicks from time and age, right? Wrong. See, there's a trick about this particular tank, it's got a false bottom, and Todd at this moment moved his hand to the left side of the tank and with a gentle push against it waited for the hinge to spring free.

The drawer opened.

"Oh shit oh shit shit" Todd said again.

Because of course it was empty.

"You sneaky bastard, Buzz, Jack, Marty—whoever the hell you really are."

That drawer was usually as well disguised as it was important. Todd kept certain important documents hidden inside that secret compartment. Documents that might probably be used against him, especially if they fell into the wrong hands. In this case, though, since moving the tank to the Buzz Factory he'd emptied its contents and replaced them with a single key. That's what was now missing: the key.

What to do about this situation would have to wait. There was the matter of Lana and Lottie and the fact that they would inevitably have to deal with the local authorities, who would no doubt put in a call to the LAPD, namely to a curious pair known as Detectives Dalrymple and Benes. Yet all that would have to wait, because that's when the cash register went crashing against the back counter, dropping noisily to the floor after leaving a damaging scrape against the back counter. The cash drawer, already opened from Lottie's early shooting spree, spilled out a series of coins and bills onto the sawdust-covered floor. But it wasn't this money which attracted Todd, his nose had managed to sniff out something far more richer.

It was like he'd struck gold.

Well, sort of. He'd just struck something far more usable: cash.

There was a hidden hole in the wall behind where the cash register had been, and now that it had been exposed so were its contents. Bundles and more bundles and even more bundles of cold, hard, good old fashioned American greenbacks. Can anyone say, "Jackpot."?

Todd knew exactly what he'd just unearthed. The long-rumored, now confirmed, stash of cash stolen by one Jack "Fast Cash" Cashman.

"So Patrick was right all along, it does exist," Todd said aloud.

And then a gambler's smiled crossed his face. Looks like Buzz didn't hold all of the aces anymore; Todd had found his bargaining chip. Cash for a key, sounded fair, didn't it?

At this point in the action Toad had happily resumed swimming around his repaired home. For him, life had returned to normal because his owner had returned just as promised. Trouble was, Todd couldn't luxuriate like his pet, he was getting ready to execute one more con.

THE DEVIL'S mistress arrived at the PAB in Downtown Los Angeles, the sunshine beaming down on her as stunningly hot as the lady herself. Cynthia Scanlon had found herself again, she knew what she wanted and she knew she had to play the performance to the hilt if she was to get all she desired. Her hair bouncy and loose and fiery red, her body lithe and supple, her dress flaming red and deliciously, temptingly revealing, she strode up the cement walkway, bypassing swaying palm trees and the prying eyes of a number of cops and pedestrians alike. It was almost as though they were waiting to see the camera following behind her, a true Hollywood scene unfolding before their eyes.

Except this was no movie, and this was no actress.

This was a real life, starring a woman determined to win back her man.

A police officer held the door for her, and as she slipped inside the cool air conditioned building she graced him with an easy smile and a "Thanks very much." He left with a spring in his own step, and again Cindy beamed with the pride of the beautiful. She knew her power, and now it was time to put it to good use.

"Mrs. Scanlon."

Cindy gazed forward and found herself staring directly into the face of a familiar-looking plain clothes detective. Which one he was, she couldn't recall. One of two she'd encountered at the Cashman estate, that much she knew. She had expected to have to call for him at the main desk, but of course he would be waiting for her, he'd met her before. And anyone who had met Cynthia Scanlon before, well, there was little they could do to withstand her allure.

"Detective…"

"Benes."

"Of course, nice to see you again," Cindy said, extending her hand.

Benes graciously accepted the proffered, manicured hand. "Is it? Most people don't say that kind of thing to an officer of the law."

"Perhaps you haven't realized it, Detective Benes, but I'm hardly 'most people.'"

Cindy realized their hands were still connected.

"Uh, shall we go upstairs? My partner is waiting for us. Uh, for you."

"Lead on, McDuff."

"It's Benes," he said, and then realized his gaff.

He was still red-faced when the elevator pinged open and

they emerged onto the fourth floor of police headquarters. Cindy, a rueful smile still painted on her face, was escorted down a long corridor and into a waiting room. Four walls, a big mirrored-window on the far end of the room, she knew where she was: this room wasn't for waiting but rather for interrogations. She looked forward to their questions. After all, she was completely guiltless in this entire escapade, and for that matter so too was Patrick.

"My partner, Detective Dalrymple will be right with us. Uh, you."

Again, Benes blushed as he closed the door on his guest.

Alone, Cindy took a moment to check her appearance. Staring directly into the mirror, she slid a finger against her lips in an effort to smooth down an imaginary clump of lipstick. She adjusted her blouse, which needed no adjusting. The revealing cleavage had already done its job, so no problems there. One last thing, she turned and gazed down at her legs, bare and sleek, tan and toned, then she drew a hand across her gams. A final glance in the mirror showed she was more than pleased with the end result. Truth to tell, her appearance hadn't changed from when she'd arrived at the PAB. It was all, of course, posturing for effect.

After learning from Todd the fact that Patrick was in police custody, Cindy had gone back home to their bungalow in Manhattan Beach to prepare for her full-frontal assault. Phoning downtown, she was finally connected to Detective Earnest Dalrymple, who said he would be happy to meet with her about her husband's arrest, but it would have to wait until the next day. He's being held overnight as a person of interest in the murder of Carl Beaufort.

"My husband was not in town when that crime was committed," Cindy said.

"Still, he knows much more than he's been previously willing to reveal. We'll see you tomorrow, Mrs. Scanlon."

A long sleepless night of tossing and turning had finally moved on to a different time zone, and the most picture-perfect L.A. kind of day rose from the horizon. The kind of day that could make you appreciate life's great possibilities. Yet here Cindy was, willingly walking into the lair of the cops who had arrested her husband for murder. She'd gone into the lion's den, but the thing about spending a night without sleep, it gave you a chance to sharpen your claws.

Just then the door to the interrogation room opened, and in stepped both Dalrymple and Benes. Dalrymple took the lead.

"Mrs. Scanlon, thank you for coming down. May we get you something, water, coffee?"

"How about my husband?"

"All in good time," he said.

Cindy wondered what that meant, and Dalrymple's eyes revealed no additional clues. In fact, his eyes held very little energy and she had to figure he'd gotten about as much sleep as she had.

"Do you mind if we ask you a few questions?"

"Fine."

"You don't wish to have an attorney present?"

"Am I being charged with anything?"

"Not at all."

"Good. Because I've done nothing wrong."

Dalrymple gave her a wearying look.

"Correction, I've done nothing illegal," Cindy offered. "And by the way, officers, neither has Patrick."

"Detectives."

"Of course. Look, Detective Dalrymple, first you arrest my friend Todd for murder, now you think my husband did the same dirty deed. Perhaps next we'll move on to the other men in my life?"

"We'd actually like to talk to you about that. See, we've done our research since we first encountered you outside the Cashman estate, and some rather revealing information came our way. Namely, the fact that Jack Cashman—who the world, or at least all of Los Angeles, knows as Fast Cash—is, was, or continues to be…your father. Do you wish to confirm that?"

"One's parentage hardly constitutes a crime, detective."

"Well said. Very carefully worded."

"All I did was speak the truth."

"We admit to jumping the gun on the arrest of your friend, Mr. Gleason. But given the circumstances—including your own admission at the time of the Open House that he was your husband—we had little choice but to suspect him, not to mention arrest him. His name was written on a piece of paper, stuffed down the throat of the first victim, Mr. Beaufort."

"Yes, I'm aware of that. A cruel joke played by…a friend."

"Mr. Langston Livingston, according to your husband."

"Patrick told you that?"

"Mrs. Scanlon, you claim not to have done anything wrong, much less illegal. What do you call tampering with evidence, removing a body from a crime scene, and interfering with an ongoing police investigation?"

Cindy decided not to reply to this statement.

Benes spoke up at this point. "We're not looking to charge you—even though we could and we should. Instead, in the last few hours certain pieces of a much larger case have presented themselves to us and with your help we can bring about a final, fitting conclusion to a number of open cases. Beaufort and a woman by the name of Loretta Beam. But there is also the matter of Langston Livingston—"

"I'm sorry…Loretta Beam? Who is that?"

"Marty Beam's wife, widow…whatever you want to call it. She's the woman who was found in the basement of the Cashman estate. Not Lottie Cashman."

"Ohhh," Cindy said. "Must have been quite an embarrassment to the police, mis-identifying a murder victim."

"Hardly. We put the story out there, intentionally."

"Whatever. I'm sure that this has nothing to do with me. I know nothing of it, since I was aboard a private yacht the other day, along with…"

"Yes, Mrs. Scanlon, we've heard about the little adventure on Mr. Livingston's yacht. Your husband told us all about it, it's no wonder we couldn't locate anyone that morning. Look, we appreciate your coming down here—again, talking with us and telling us the truth. Answer us this: when you discovered Mr. Beaufort floating in your pool, were there bills surrounding the body?"

Cindy was tired of this case, tired of secrets. She just wanted Patrick. "Immunity?" she asked.

Dalrymple shot Benes a withering look. "Should rename the city that," he said, before looking back at Cindy. "I thought you said you didn't do anything wrong, Mrs. Scanlon?"

Cindy said nothing.

"Fine. Immunity," Dalrymple said. "We're only after the big fish."

Cindy kind of resented that remark, but she let it slide. She knew they could make real trouble for her, for Patrick, make this move to L.A. a complete bust.

"Yes, there were bills floating beside the body."

"And where are those bills now?"

"With Langston. He moved the body, took the bills as…a down payment for services rendered."

Neither of the detectives responded; they just looked at each other and nodded. Communicating without words, and knowing what each was thinking. Cindy had to think it was rehearsed. Then finally the lead guy, Dalrymple, spoke, and what he said surprised her.

"Mrs. Scanlon, while you've providing us with such helpful information, your husband's release was being processed. We would imagine he's waiting for you in the lobby now. He's free to go, cleared of all charges. The same applies to you: you are free to go. Sound good?"

Cindy politely nodded, got up to leave.

Dalrymple paused. "On one condition."

"Yes, anything."

"The homicides of Loretta Beam and Carl Beaufort, as well as the man whose skeleton was discovered in the Cashman basement, they've all been solved, cases closed. We know what happened to them all, and we know why. That's enough to satisfy the two of us, the entire LAPD. And if you wish to know more you may want to get in touch with your non-husband, Mr. Gleason. Slippery fellow that one, but he's done less to interest us than your husband has. That doesn't mean he hasn't been in the thick of this thing, he's just better at hiding whatever true motives he held. Seasoned detectives that we are, we feel a bit cheated that situations have occurred that keep us from making more arrests, so we've decided to take this case one step further."

"You've lost me, Detective Dalrymple. Are you going after Todd?"

"Oh, on the contrary. We're referring to Langston Livingston, who has skirted the edges of the law for far too many years. With the full force of the LAPD we've decided to go after him—and of course that requires the able, knowledgeable assistance of both you and your husband. Consider yourselves material witnesses for when we finally bring Mr. Livingston in on charges too numerous to name now. So, I would suggest that the Scanlon's get used to life in Los Angeles, we're going to need you for the long haul."

"We'd hate to find other evidence of criminal misconduct," he added.

Cindy got the picture. "We'll cooperate in any way we can. Thank you, both."

They all shook hands over the new arrangement, both detectives lingering over the lovely touch provided by Cindy's soft, supple hands. She smiled devilishly at them again, realizing that even though they held all the aces and kings, enough cards remained for her to play a better hand. For now, as she walked out, it was enough to leave them flush.

"Oh, one last thing, detectives."

"Yes, Mrs. Scanlon?"

"The body in the basement? Who was it?"

"It's been positively identified as Marty Beam," Dalrymple said. "From dental records to the missing fingertip, all evidence says it's the Beam character, not the slippery Fast Cash. We are awaiting final DNA testing, but it's pretty much a given."

"Was he murdered, too?" Cindy asked.

Dalrymple shook his head. "Those tests are inconclusive. But we don't think so. We've checked the old files, reports that day indicated that Marty Beam may have lost a lot of blood from the gunshot he took. We have to figure he just didn't get proper treatment, seeing as though he was on the run from the authorities."

"So, Jack Cashman was no killer?"

"Doesn't look that way, Mrs. Scanlon," Dalrymple said.

"Yup, just your common everyday thief," Benes said. "You know, a con man."

"Yes, I'm familiar with the concept," Cindy said.

"**SO, HE'S** no killer?"

Todd shook his head. "That's what the detectives had to say. I spoke with them at length last night, while you dealt with the local gendarmes."

"So everything Lottie did…"

He held Lana close to him. "Ssshh, don't think about that now. There's plenty of time to figure everything out later, let's just sit here and stare out at the aqua blue water and watch as the waves crash against the shore."

"You're being so poetic for a crook."

"You know I hate that word."

"How else do you explain it—taking all that money you found behind the register?"

"Payment for services rendered."

"You know, Todd, after all this time, I'm not so sure I can trust you."

"Back at ya, Lana, back at ya."

Still on Bermuda. Still together. Still recovering. They had spent a long night at police headquarters in Hamilton, and then a quiet morning in Todd's cottage, sleeping off the effects of the day just passed. Lana had asked Todd to make love to her and gentleman that he is he'd resisted. Didn't want to take advantage of her vulnerable state, that's what he claimed, but after she'd teased him with her kisses, tempted him with her touch, drawn him in with her tongue, he had relented, and together the two of them had explored a deeper, personal, revelatory moment (or two) of passion. Afterwards, they had dressed and gone for a walk along the beach, which of course had taken them to the one place destiny had mapped out as their own. The stretch of white sandy beach where they had said their initial goodbyes all that time ago.

"Tell me about your mother. I only got to meet her that one time…as I was running away."

"You know, Todd, it's not until you lose a parent that you realize exactly what they mean to you, and all they do for you. Marty Beam got into a lot of trouble, financial at first, and then with the law, but I think he was a victim in all of this, too. My Dad wasn't the most aggressive of sorts, and I think people had a way of taking advantage of him. First Langston Livingston, then his so-called friend Jack Cashman. But everything he did, he did for me and for Momma." Lana paused as the wind swept passed them, rifling her hair, goose bumps peppering her skin. Summer was long gone, and the storm season was in full swing. The weather here could change on a dime. Heck, so could life, so could men and women and relationships.

Lana resumed her tale. "Momma was always stronger than Marty, but tended to have this negative streak about her. She always told me I could do whatever I wanted, to not rely on other people because they were bound to disappoint me, and all the while she instilled in me this positive message she failed to listen to it herself. As though she'd resigned herself to a life of mediocrity. When Marty disappeared, well, that was the final straw. She gave up on life at that point, and when we were forced to move to our small apartment in Glendale I think that was the end of the road for her. She'd given up on life. She knew she would die there."

Tears sprang from Lana's eyes, and they trickled down her cheeks. Todd held her closer, wishing to never let her go but knowing, inevitably, that he would have to.

Lana leaned in, kissed him. "What happened between you and Cindy? She doesn't exactly know how to take no for an answer, and you…you always do what you want to do. That's a gift, Todd, knowing yourself, knowing who you are and what you want, and the fact that you work all angles until you've achieved your goal. Take this case for instance. I know it started with you helping out a friend—Patrick. And I suppose Cindy, too. But in the end, wasn't it the allure of the almighty dollar that really attracted you? Three million dollars gone missing and everyone searching for it. You always knew you'd find it, didn't you?"

"Wasn't exactly three million dollars."

"It's enough for one person to live on for several comfortable years," Lana said.

"One person. I couldn't help but notice your use of that phrase," Todd said. "Is that your way of saying goodbye?"

"See what I mean? Just like you knew Fast Cash's fortune would end up in your pocket, you have this uncanny ability to predict what's going to happen. Don't get me wrong Todd, I can't imagine having gone through this entire experience without you, even when I was slapping you and thinking you were anything but honorable. Which, whether you want to hear it or not, you've always been with me. I can't say the same thing about myself."

Todd pressed his lips against hers, and the kiss lingered and lasted and the lust and even the love that fueled it left them each with an overwhelming feeling of warmth, closeness, tenderness. Because they both knew it was the end.

"My flight is in two hours," Lana suddenly announced, rising from her place on the beach. "I'm going to back to Los Angeles, and once the police release the bodies…Momma and Marty's, too, I'm going to hold a private double burial. No service, no memorial, no friends, just one last family reunion."

"I won't even ask if you want company."

"Thank you, Todd, I appreciate that you aren't pressuring me."

"Our relationship, it won't always hold good memories for you," he said.

"Oh, but that's where you're wrong, Todd Gleason," she said, and this time she leaned in for one last, perfect kiss. And it was, tender and soulful, sweet and wonderful. When at last they parted, she smiled at him and he smiled back at her and she touched his scruffy cheek and he drew a hand through her silky auburn hair. "Thing of it is, when you live in Los Angeles, you think in terms of the movies, and so it's appropriate that I leave you with a quote. But you know, I'd like to put my own personal touch upon it."

Todd said nothing, wanting to forever remember the sound of her voice against the crash of the waves. He waited for her parting words.

"We'll always have Bermuda. Toddly."

TODD GLEASON returned to his cottage, alone.

But he found he wasn't alone once he got inside.

"Hello, Todd."

"Buzz."

"You don't seem surprised to see me."

"Well, we each have something the other wants," Todd said, "so no, your being here at my cottage doesn't come as a shock."

"I don't see a hand imprinted across your cheek, am I to assume things ended better this time with the fair Lana Davies?"

"Some wounds don't always reveal themselves," Todd said, bypassing his one-time friend and heading instead to his tiny refrigerator. He withdrew a bottle of beer and twisted the cap and took a deep pull on it. He didn't bother to offer one to Buzz. He was a bartender, he wanted a drink he could go and fetch one himself.

"Is Todd Gleason suffering from a broken heart?"

"Why don't we cut through the niceties, huh, Jack?"

"You use my real name, I'll use yours."

"Fair enough, Buzz," Todd said. "So, when did you discover the hidden compartment in Toad's tank?"

"After I helped secure your friend's release."

"Patrick."

"A phone call from Cindy to release him, make it seem like Patrick escaped. She'd make it up to Fred later. Strange woman, always plotting something. Wonder where she gets it."

"Good of you to look after Patrick. But you know, family is family."

"Patrick Scanlon is no family of mine."

"He's your daughter's husband."

"Don't try and play that card with me. I never knew about a daughter, and I still don't."

"Easier that way, isn't it, Buzz? Not admitting to family keeps you from having to live up to your responsibilities. Just take your unearned cash and live life the way you want it."

"You're one to talk, Todd Gleason."

"We may share a love of cash, but I would never shirk responsibility to family. If you've learned nothing about me, Buzz, I'm a pretty loyal guy. Why else would I go all the way to Los Angeles to help a friend in need, risk my life to get him out of a near-impossible jam? Don't get me wrong, I'm mercenary when I need to be. When I see something I can work to my advantage, yeah, I'm right there. But not at the risk of those I care about."

"So where does that leave us, Todd?"

"I suppose we make an exchange," he said. "I mean, that's why you came, right? To get your money back? The money I found behind your register? I gotta hand it to you, Buzz, even after all this time you still have a distrust of banks, you've got to keep your money close."

"Even closer than my enemies."

"Oh, I'm not your enemy, and I never was."

"But those banking facilities, Todd? Unlike me, people do have to have trust in them, even when they nearly bankrupt the entire country. Your little key led me to your cottage, which led me to a small safe, which in turn led me to some curious documents. Like info about a little offshore account, right? You really think it's safe to leave such valuable information lying about? I kept wondering all these months, what is it with this Gleason guy and his pet frog? What's his story? What's he running from? So after Patrick left, and after that little muscle-guy Fred went after him, I focused on the one creature I was left with. Toad, the pet frog."

"So, are you prepared to return my documents to me?"

"Are you prepared to return my money to me?"

Todd considered the approaching stalemate between a pair of con men. He thought about how best to handle the situation. At last, he said, "I want to know one thing."

"What's that?"

"Are you really Fast Cash?"

"God, I hated that name. Stupid press, always assigning catchy names to criminals. Like it makes them bigger than life, like we've got more guts than everyone else. We just do what others wish they could do. Yeah, if it satisfies your curiosity, I'm the man Carl Beaufort first dubbed 'Fast Cash.' Happy?"

Todd nodded. "Are you?"

"What kind of question is that?"

"I'm just wondering, it's been seven plus years since you pulled these robberies, was it all worth it? Have you led the life you thought you'd be living?"

"Listen to me, Todd Gleason or whatever you want to call yourself, and listen good. This life, it comes with no guarantees. Not for the rich, certainly not for the poor. Whether you're as honest as the day is long, or as crooked as the San Andreas fault, you still gotta wake up in the morning and look at yourself in the mirror. No matter what you do, if you can't face yourself, you're doing something wrong. It's not about rules and it's not about the law, it's all about survival."

Todd got up from his chair, drained his beer. From there he went to a wooden cabinet inside the tiny cottage. He opened up a small safe and stared down at…nothing.

"I already took the money," Buzz said. "Remember, I have the key."

Todd turned back toward the old crook, smiling widely. "That's why I left it there, I fully expected to run into you again. Because I know you, Buzz. You operate on your own terms, and in that regard you're not unlike me. But one thing separates us: I knew in the long run this money wasn't mine, and so you're welcome to it. And know that, once you leave here with your precious money in tow and the secret of your identity safe with me, our relationship ends. Whether you choose to stay in Bermuda, whether I do, there's no need to ever bring this incident up again." Todd paused. "So, I'm doing the honorable thing. Can you say the same thing?"

Buzz said nothing. Minutes slipped by without either man saying anything. Finally, Buzz withdrew from his inside jacket pocket a thick manila envelope. He tossed it on the table that sat between them. Before Todd had a chance to check its contents, Buzz rose from his chair and made his way toward the door.

"You know, I'm not returning those documents to you

because I care what happens to you," Buzz said.

"Fair enough. So why then?"

"The truth? That damned frog. You left him in my care and I kind of got attached to him. I'd hate to see what happens to him if the authorities took a strong liking to you. You're not exactly an innocent in all this. Take care of yourself, Todd Gleason. And keep in mind what I said, money can't buy you happiness, it just enables you to stand on your own two feet and not take shit from anyone else. You can only control so much, life, fate, whatever you want to call it, shows up in the end and reminds you how vulnerable you are, how subject to the whims of the world you truly are. I made my share of mistakes, and in the end it was Lottie who paid the ultimate price for those mistakes. I thought she and I could be happy again, that's why I got back in touch with her. That's why I sent her some money, sent the map. I wanted to bring it all to an end, share my life with someone. In the end, what's it all cost me? Remember, that's what I'm left living with. Like, I said, no guarantees. You wake up, you live. Anything else, you're just not trying."

With that, the wily bartender known simply as Buzz Smith extended a hand to his friend, and Todd had no choice but to shake it. That missing finger felt weird, their handshake incomplete.

"The finger," Todd said.

"What about it?"

"Langston do that to you, just like Marty?"

Buzz smiled. "Nah. Part of my disguise, keep my identity murky. I could always claim to be Marty, same stunt you pulled with Lottie."

Todd nodded. "Quite a sacrifice."

"Made a lot of those. This one only cost me the use of one finger. Got nine more."

"Same as lives?"

"Think I'm down to six of those," Buzz said, laughing.

"Best of luck to you, Jack," Todd said.

"To you, too, son. Here's to your next big score…"

Okay, score wasn't really the last word Buzz said to Todd.

He used a completely different name.

To Todd, that name sounded as foreign to him as the name Jack did to Buzz. But that's the thing about fashioning lies out of truth, after awhile you tend to forget what's real, what's not, what sounds natural and what sounds like something you'd rather keep buried, whether behind a false wall in a basement, behind a cash register in a dank old pub, in the guts of a fish tank, or maybe just in some corner of the world you like to call your own.

EPILOGUE

COULD THAT really be the end of the story? Aren't there still some loose ends to be addressed? Is Fast Cash ever going to be caught? Will Langston Livingston get what's coming to him? Will Cindy and Patrick find their way back to each other? What crime did Beverly Mills commit? And what about our intrepid Todd Gleason? Was this really the end between him and Lana Davis? How is the fair Lana going to move on with her life without anybody at her side, father, mother, Todd. Just what happened next to our friends and our foes and those who fit a description that fell somewhere in between?

IN LOS ANGELES....

Beverly Mills opened more than a few bottles of champers with her staff to celebrate becoming the sole owner and proprietor of her real estate agency, Beverly Mills of Beverly Hills, and ended the party by hanging the deed to her near-Rodeo Drive office in a gilt-edged frame on her office wall. For a woman born Esther Grajkowski in some tiny town in some square state in the middle of the country, well, dreams didn't come more real than this one.

Turning states evidence against Langston Livingston had indeed provided her with immunity, and good thing. Seems she'd run out on serious debt back home, left behind three ex-husbands—one of whom had an assault charge against her for hitting him in the head with an empty bottle of…what else, "champers", a bankrupt real estate business, and a pile of animosity. Bored with small-town life, she'd picked up and re-invented herself, and by doing so had run afoul of the loan shark who enjoyed being owed more than he enjoyed being paid.

Now, Beverly Mills of Beverly Hills felt as though she had truly arrived, and in fact, when at last she settled into her office chair with a glass of her beloved bubbly she buzzed her secretary and said, "Lana, no wait…Vera…please book me a table at the Beverly Hilton for tonight, tell Bart to have the limo ready by seven." She was reminded that her new secretary's name was Tara and that her new driver's name was Garth, but Beverly just shook off the confusion, then drank down more of the Dom. Damn, but it was good to come out on top.

Someone not destined to come out on top was Langston Livingston. The police had come down hard on him, and in a flurry of press that required lots of column inches and just a few columns by some up and coming reporter for the *Daily News*, Langston could barely show his face in Los Angeles without someone snapping his photograph. But Langston was one of those types who'd always favored the night, when he could skulk about without anyone being the wiser, and now he was thrust into the Paparazzo's glare, flashbulbs and cameras seemingly catching his every crooked move. He had an upcoming court case and all the local channels were planning on covering it. Barely a day passed without Logan and Logan commenting on it. Los Angeles, they liked their celebrities to have a bit of dirt, and this guy was a virtual mudslide of copy. In effect, the city had created a celebrity out of a criminal, and the last time they'd done something like that…well, a not guilty verdict didn't exactly make everyone happy.

Detectives Ernest Dalrymple and Sandy Benes were not the lead investigators on the Livingston matter. They were homicide detectives, and as such the newly notorious Langston may have been charged with a whole bunch of crimes but murder was not among them. Perhaps it was the truest thing he'd ever said, but Langston had never killed anyone. And with the case of Jack Cashman seemingly neatly wrapped up—including the murders of Carl Beaufort and Mother Beam—there was nothing else for them to do. Actually, that was wishful thinking. This was Los Angeles after all, and the people who made this place their home had a tendency to keep their local police busy. It was over a plate of ketchup-dosed French fries that found Dalrymple and Benes responding to their next call.

But not before they cheered their efforts on the Fast Cash case. Duplicity had won out over detective work, and the fake-out over the woman's body in the basement of the Cashman estate went down in department lore—flushing out a killer the only way they could. Announcing to the world the wrong name of the victim. And heck, it had worked with Lottie and Mother Beam, so why not do it again when it came to the original tag team of thieves, Fast Cash himself and his little-remembered sidekick, Marty Beam.

As for Patrick and Cindy Scanlon, once the press got a hold of their names as the primary witnesses to testify against Langston, they started camping out in front of their tiny bungalow in Manhattan Beach, eager for a shot of the camera-friendly couple. Cindy was a natural, flashing a smile that held a gleam all its own, even when no flashbulbs had gone off. Patrick was often pictured in the background, his hands tending to his hair. Soon, though, the press had a tough time locating them, because it seemed that the Scanlons had suddenly up and moved. They had, in fact, moved into the old Cashman estate. As the sole surviving relative of Jack Cashman and legal heir, Cindy had inherited everything. The eager press had dubbed her Pretty Cash, and once that happened Patrick decided they needed some protection. He suggested bodyguards.

Cindy Scanlon was ready for her close-up.

Their first booking?

Logan & Logan.

SOMEWHERE BETWEEN New York and Los Angeles…

Barney Stone and Fred Halpern put their New York apartment and office up for sale, packed their belongings, which included lots of leather clothing and the various accoutrements that went along with such nighttime attire, and then they stuffed a car almost to the breaking point. Frankly, they had had enough of Manhattan, with its dank, dark clubs like the Raven and its crazy customers; they had fallen in love with the laid back lifestyle that Los Angeles represented. They also realized that the private investigation business had its drawbacks and its limitations, and in the glorious sunshine of the Golden State they knew there was so much more opportunity. They changed the name of their company from The Two Dicks Detective Agency to WeHo's Security, and it was their plan to set up shop along Santa Monica Boulevard and La Cienega, right in the heart of West Hollywood. In the former offices of Livingston Enterprises, in fact. They even had their first clients: Patrick and Cindy Scanlon. But before their arrival in their new land, they took an admittedly long detour. But hey, at the time, Vermont was the nearest place that was performing marriages for couples like them.

Such a thing was still a controversial proposition in California.

IN BERMUDA...

The Buzz Factory remained closed for several weeks, and when it reopened it had a new name and a new owner, same décor. The proprietor was a beautiful young woman, her hair as red as a burned sunset and a lovely smile to match, and for a time the locals were wary and the tourists were thrilled. Who was this newcomer with the mysterious background and a wily, feminine touch? But gradually the locals came back, the pool table and dartboard once again saw steady action, and the taps got quite the work out.

One day a guy was hanging out near the bar, started up a conversation with the new lady of the island. She hadn't made many friends till now, liked to keep her distance.

"So, where you from?"

"Los Angeles," she said.

"How could anyone live there, nothing but crooks and thieves."

"Oh, I think Bermuda has had its share in its history," the woman said with an alluring smile. And then she extended her hand. "Name's Lana. Welcome to Momma's."

IN NEW YORK...

As for Todd Gleason, he'd returned home to his tiny apartment. He tossed a pellet of food into Toad's new tank, and watched as the little guy hungrily ate it up. Yup, that frog, he always knew how to pick up Todd when a mood struck him. See, here was this creature, abiding by his instincts, eating with zest, swimming with passion, and that's what Todd needed too. His fingers itched to get going again, and he supposed that's what the L.A. scheme had taught him. He was only at his best when he was doing what he loved.

But his next scam, his next adventure could wait for tomorrow. For now, he had stacks of money situated on his coffee table, the remaining money he'd scammed from Langston, the money that would have cleared Fast Cash's debt to the old crook. He would be making a very nice deposit to his offshore account real soon. He'd already transferred his London take to a newer account, so Buzz or Jack or whoever he was calling himself these days couldn't readily access it—if he had the inclination. But Todd held secrets of his own, and if needed the dried up trail for Fast Cash could be made public at any given moment. Not that anyone would really care, to the world and to the courts, Jack Cashman was long dead. Todd was different, he operated somewhere else, between the lines. Such was the life of a con man, genial until the moment came when you needed to exercise your hard-learned talents.

He sat down, turned on the television for a distraction while he prepared to count his cash. Todd, though, wasn't alone.

"I can't believe you invited me over for a drink."

"I can't believe you stuffed your number inside the pocket of my jeans that night. But glad you did, I owed you big time. Without your help I never would have found Patrick. You more than proved your loyalty."

Night had fallen on Manhattan, and all around the city lights were going on inside its various apartments, people were home from a long day's work, just wanting to forget their troubles with a little mindless trifle put out by the Hollywood dream factories. Todd and his guest took their beers and situated themselves on the sofa.

Todd grabbed the remote and turned on the television.

"Channel Seven," his guest said.

"Why?"

"Trust me. It's just starting…"

It certainly was. An awards show had just begun, the red carpet littered with glitter and glamour. It was time for Hollywood to appreciate itself once again, and you know what? They could applaud themselves all they wanted, Todd Gleason didn't need the accolades, just the reward. The music swelled as a disembodied announcer stated, "Live from Los Angeles, it's the 69th annual…"

Todd flipped off the television.

"Hey."

"Sorry. I think I've had enough of Hollywood for awhile."

His guest decided to move closer, reaching out to touch Todd's knee. Todd shot him a dismissive look, then reluctantly turned the television back on. Yeah, they needed something between them, like an hours-long awards show.

"Enjoy."

His guest looked slightly disappointed, but he'd at least won the first battle.

"What's the matter, don't you like Hollywood?"

"Sure I do, movies and TV, what's not to like…except…it's just…well, the endings always bother me. They're always so neat and tidy, never leave any loose ends. The bad guys finally get what was coming to them and the good guys win their hard-earned victory. Where's reality? Where's the ending for those who straddle the fence somewhere between good and bad? Where's the resolution for them, Scooter?"

"See, that's the thing, Todd. That's why we like movies so much, there is a resolution, a satisfying ending. Real life doesn't work that way. It just continues."

Todd smiled, his dimples lighting the room as he drank from his beer. Then he said, "There's surprising wisdom in your words, kid."

"Don't call me…oh hell, you can call me anything. Toddly."

"Hey…Scooter, never call me that."

Just then the program went to commercial. Someone's gotta pay for all this.

Cut and print.

CPSIA information can be obtained at www.ICGtesting.com
Printed in the USA
BVOW022226150412

287616BV00001BA/1/P